Somewhere up there,
beyond ...
du ...

an armed warshi... ... d
in orbit, bearing ... ... it-
tle blue poppits, the beings who'd conquered
us all.

Old stories always imagined alien fanged
monstrosities from beyond the stars. It's
what we thought the Kkhruhhuft were when
they came. Only later, when we were already
humiliated, did we discover that we were no
more than slaves of the intelligences, who
called themselves the Master Race. Not the
poppits. Not them at all.

Somewhere far back in time, the little
blue frogs built anthill cities, hives that grew
complex and more complex still. Hives without mentality that evolved machines,
machines that made more machines,
machines that learned slowly, ever so slowly,
how to think.

You have to wonder just when, and why,
the machine servants of the little frogs decided to call themselves the Master Race, then
go out and conquer the universe.

◆→ ◆→ ◆→

PREVIOUS BOOKS BY
WILLIAM BARTON:

Hunting On Kunderer
A Plague of All Cowards
Dark Sky Legion
Yellow Matter

COLLABORATIONS WITH
MICHAEL CAPOBIANCO:

Iris
Fellow Traveler

WILLIAM BARTON

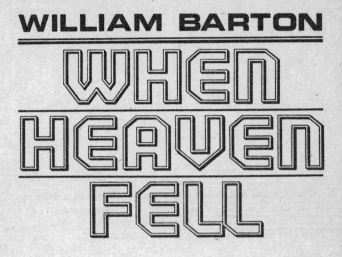

WHEN HEAVEN FELL

ASPECT

WARNER BOOKS

A Time Warner Company

WARNER BOOKS EDITION

Aspect is a trademark of Warner Books, Inc.

Cover design by Don Puckey
Cover illustration by Sean Beavers

Warner Books, Inc.
1271 Avenue of the Americas
New York, NY 10020

 A Time Warner Company

Printed in the United States of America

First Printing: March, 1995

10 9 8 7 6 5 4 3 2 1

"Epitaph on an Army of Mercenaries"

by A.E. Housman
(1859–1936)

These in the day when heaven was falling,
   The hour when earth's foundations fled,
Followed their mercenary calling
   And took their wages and are dead.

Their shoulders held the sky suspended;
   They stood, and earth's foundations stay;
What God abandoned, these defended,
   And saved the sum of things for pay.

from *The Collected Poems of A.E. Housman*
Copyright 1922 by Henry Holt and Company, Inc.
Copyright 1950 by Barclays Bank Ltd.
Reprinted by permission of Henry Holt and Company, Inc.

1

A PALL OF THIN GRAY SMOKE HUNG over the battlefield. Smoke from the natives' primitive guns, smoke left over from the hydrocarbons they used in their inefficient IC engines. Smoke drifting up toward the mountain passes, from burning forests, burning cities. Particles in that smoke from the burning bodies of natives we'd killed already.

My company of Spahi mercenaries and I had just come over those tall, beautiful mountains, fresh from finishing off the Imperial Legions of Threnn-Haaé, now crossing the borders of Shônetk, on a world we understood was called Thôl. They were splendid mountains, towering, incredible, unbelievable behind us, a perfect backdrop for the deeds we were about to do.

The natives called them the Mountains Without Clouds, a supra-Himalayan range, shiny gray stone erupted from the surface of the world, continents in collision, grinding against each other, pushing fragments of landmass up and up. Here, they stood forty thousand meters, like prominences of frozen light rising out of the atmosphere, mountains without trees, without soil, without snow, mountains without clouds, peaks jagged, beyond the reach of wind and rain, only the sun to wear them down.

A voice whispered in the back of my head, "Jemadar Athol Morrison."

I blinked on the command circuit, and said, "Here, sir." Waiting for Rissaldar-Minor Jennings, battalion commander, to give the word. In the distance, a battery of frightened natives opened up with their big guns, probably violating the stern discipline that had kept them lined up across this broad, dusty plain. Lined up in the tawny bronze sunset, waiting, though they knew what we were, and knew what was going to happen to them.

Shells came whistling down, ruddy, garish explosions lighting up the hillside, making the ground vibrate under my boots. Shrapnel from a nearby hit came buzzing through the air, making little ticking sounds as it bounced off my armor. There were about a million of them waiting out there, the flower of their warlike nation, armed to the teeth, as dangerous as anything this world had ever produced.

And, of course, the full muster of a standard Spahi company is 256 effectives, officers, noncoms, and troopers together. You had to feel sorry for the poor bastards. The invasion had been going on for almost a week now, and they knew what was coming.

Maybe it was a little like this when they came to Earth. A little bit, not much. We fought harder, so much harder that six hundred thousand and more Kkhruhhuft mercenaries lay dead on Earth before it was over. Of course, they killed eight billion of us in return . . .

I was a kid then. It didn't seem real to me, no matter how scared my parents were, just more exciting drama on the entertainment net. Not real, never real, even on the day when I looked up in time to see a human-built starship explode in high Earth orbit, violet light punching right through a pale blue sky, making me flinch, leaving me to blink away spots and watch the fire fade to nothing.

Somewhere up there, beyond this tawny and dust-filled sky, an armed warship of the Master Race floated in orbit, bearing its cargo of software and little blue poppits, the beings who'd conquered us all. Old stories always imagine alien monsters, invaders from beyond the sky. Mighty beings, larger than men, fanged monstrosities.

It's what we thought the Kkhruhhuft were when they

came. Only later, when we were already humiliated, did we discover they were no more than servants, slaves really, of the . . . *intelligences* who called themselves the Master Race. Not the poppits, little blue things the size of frogs, frogs with the behavior patterns of ants. Not them at all.

Somewhere. Somewhere far back in time, the little blue frogs built anthill cities, hives that grew more complex and more complex still. Hives without mentality that evolved machines, machines that made more machines, machines that learned, slowly, ever so slowly, how to think.

You have to wonder just when, and why, the mechanical servants of those nonsentient little blue frogs decided to call themselves the Master Race. A master race that would then go out and conquer the universe.

Jennings whispered, "Get on with it. The Master's getting impatient."

Impatient? *Why*, when they had damn-all forever? Maybe they know something we don't. "Yes, sir. Fifteen minutes."

I scanned the battlefield, memorizing the lay of the land, the natives' order of battle. Low-lying hills rimming the plain, a river winding back and forth, silver-tan under a brassy sky, orangish sun low in the west, not quite setting below more distant hills. Far away, right on the horizon, was a red brick city, one of the few we hadn't burned. Well, its turn would come.

Things like trees, long, narrow leaves pale yellow-gold, moved nearby, fluttering in a wind I couldn't feel, wind blowing on the outside of my armor. "Kathy Lee?"

The havildar leading my first maniple was a speck atop a nearby crag, waving to me, though she knew I knew where she was. Invulnerability can breed carelessness.

Down on the plain a howitzer bellowed, billow of orange fire and black smoke long preceding the sound, itself preceding the slow arc of the shell. Subsonic. Not enough kinetic energy to swat a fly.

"On your position, Kathy Lee."

"I see it, sir."

We both watched the black dot of the shell arc high, start on its downward trajectory. I turned up my helmet's optical gain and watched the sputtering fuse. Another generation and they'd've been beyond that sort of thing. Just as well we came when we did.

Down, down . . . Kathy Lee tried to catch the damn thing but it came apart in her hands, powder spilling like red dust for just a moment, cloud enveloping her, then it ignited.

Blossom of fire and black smoke, rising in a little mushroom cloud, then the pressure wave from the explosion washed over my sensors. Echo. Echo off the surrounding stone faces. I could see her there, standing in the fire.

Kathy Lee said, "Good thing they don't have nukes."

Good thing. *We'd* had nukes. Nukes, our own starships, fifty years' advance warning, the whole works, and a fat lot of good it'd done us. Just gotten a few brave Kkhruhhuft mercenaries killed, that's all.

I triggered the command circuit. "Listen up. Action-Plan Bravo-Delta Six-Niner. Eight minutes. Mark."

I spooled the 3-D heads-up display and watched them move into position. Good enough. "OK boys and girls . . . five, four, three, two, one . . . *go.*"

And we moved. And fired. And killed them all.

Roscoe Leach's maniple came down out of the hills, troopers moving like fleas, laying down an enfilading fire against the long rows of high-powered cannon. No danger to us of course, but we wanted them to get the idea. Maybe, just this *once,* they'd break and run, save themselves, let us have the damned field.

No such luck. I triggered in my targeting computer and started moving downslope, feeling a slight vibration as the weapons systems opened up. Bright pinpoint sparks of light in the distance. There. Right there, a brilliant flare as General Vshevrach's command post went up. Well. We'd *warned* the silly bastard.

Over her maniple's internal circuit, I heard Kathy Lee say, "A little slaughtering music, if you please, maestro . . ."

Anyone else and you'd expect "Ride of the Valkyries" maybe, or the "1812 Overture." When I was a havildar I'd favored "William Tell," stirring stuff like that, but Kathy

Lee's favorite was the opening theme from the 2030s VR version of the "Bugs Bunny Show." It seemed to work.

We swept down on the natives, watched their guns twinkle and flare, then the brave little devils fell down dead, like rows of wheat before the reaper.

The tahsildar's name was Mamie Glendower, commander of Legion X *Invincible*, the half-million-plus soldiers garrisoned on Boromilith. She was about seventy-five now, thin, craggy, tough-looking as hell, more fire in those impenetrable black eyes than ever, clad in the dull green uniform of the Spahi mercenaries, black leather and bits of red trim, tahsildar's single-headed eagle on her collar, Master's black-and-silver ID badge above her left breast, service hash marks down the forearm of her left sleeve. Spahi mercenaries don't believe in campaign medals. Too many campaigns, too many heroes.

She'd been jemadar-major of her own regiment when I was a raw young trooper, fresh from Alpha Cee. Pinned on my first havildar's chevron, full of good advice and special wisdom, kicked my ass for me when it needed kicking.

Now, I think she took special pleasure in pinning a jemadar-major's three-diamond insignia to my collar tab. "One of my own little chicks." A quick peck on the cheek, then she stepped back, took my salute, and held out my orders packet.

I thumbed the release and looked at the display. "Hmh. IX *Victorious*, first regiment, second battalion, first brigade, under Rissaldar Tatanya Vronsky. Stationed on Karsvaao."

Glendower said, "Mandelstam's old outfit. They rate you highly."

"Thank you, ma'am. I had a sound example to work from."

She laughed. "Ma'am, my ass! Sit down, soldier. Hoist a few with a worn-out old bag."

"Hardly worn-out . . ." Gently, gently . . .

"Don't be so fucking polite, Athy. Even my burdars cringe."

So I sat down and held out my hand for the double shot of

Spanish brandy she offered. *Distillería Mendoza-Reyes*, 2149; probably the last good run before the Invasion. I understand, these days, all you can get is homemade crap.

Mamie Glendower was a rare beauty when I first came on board, not much more than fifty then, muscular, long-legged, with a handsome face filled to the brim with solid, honest character. It's hard to tell a wrinkly old woman she's still beautiful, even when it's true. They just don't want to hear it.

I used to hang around her when I could, especially after I made rank and could hold my head up in tough company, would wish I could have her, would then go home and screw the hell out of my poor little burdar. I imagine that was the lot of many a young male Spahi on the move—but she was nice enough about it. Especially since she stuck absolutely to regs.

No, uh, fraternization. That's why they give us burdars, you know. And you *don't* want to be in combat with your bed partner. What if they buy one in front of you? Some people don't believe in it, but what the hell? If it was good enough for a woman like Mamie Glendower, it had to be good enough for the likes of me.

As I put down my glass, she said, "One more thing, Athy," pulling a little black plastic square out of the breast pocket of her tunic and handing it to me.

I turned the thing over in my hands, feeling slightly unnerved. All right, this makes it real. Jemadar-major, for Christ's sake.

"Go ahead."

I put my thumb over the phone's recognition node and felt the scan tingle on my skin, several kinds of radiation probing the cellular structure. It awoke with a buzz of soft, almost-modulated static, the background ebb and flow of planetary command net traffic. I said, "This is 10x9760h, logging on."

There was a series of brief pauses in the static, then a soft, genderless voice said, "4m21subXR, acknowledged." His master's voice. Funny to think of it that way.

Square waves modulating in the near distance, a buzzing shriek, then the voice said, "3C286b, transmitting up the line." Up the line. Through interstellar space, using whatever impossible comm channel the Master Race had found, the FTL communication that went with their impossible FTL drive. Logging me into the Master's Net.

I released the node and slipped the phone into my breast pocket, then turned to the tahsildar. "Well, I . . ." Nothing to say, then. I stiffened to attention and snapped off a sharp salute.

Mamie Glendower only laughed, and said, "Welcome to the ranks."

Later, I went outside, walking back toward my crib, enjoying a bright, sunny day. Boromilith is a lovely world, probably too good for the likes of a mercenary legion base, with a warm, even, late-Cretaceous–like climate. Feathery gray-green trees, low, low rolling hills, broad beaches beside warm, flat oceans. Docile natives, gentle, scaly little folk, bipedal, less than a meter tall, with eyes like juniper berries and a vague scent of lime in their sweat.

This place had been ruled by the Master Race for about forty-five centuries, not long compared to the Kkhruhhuft, perhaps, but long enough for the natives to understand it'd go on forever. A quiet place, but conveniently located on the outskirts of a big, open cluster of low-G/high-K stars a few thousand parsecs from the local frontier.

What will Earth be like, when they've sat on us for a period equal to the length of recorded history? Maybe humans will be nice and docile by then too. Or maybe not. They say the Kkhruhhuft homeworld has been occupied for 17,000 years. Docile? They weren't very docile when they came down out of *our* sky.

Something in the genes, maybe. There've never been any Boromilithi mercenaries.

"Hey, Athy!"

I stopped, turned. Jemadar Solange Corday came hurrying across the compound, tall, willowy black African of mostly Nilotic descent, a head taller than me, hair like a velvet skull-cap. A good soldier—we'd been in on the Threnn-Haaé business together. "Hi, Solange. Stop off somewhere for a cold one?"

She fingered the new insignia on my collar tab, grinning. "Not even *close* to time-in-grade!" I was about three years senior to her in service, both of us going up at about the same pace.

She looked away for a second, then back, seeking out my eyes with her own, suddenly serious, measuring me. "You'll, ah, be needing a dog robber now."

"Um." Right. And expecting something like this. Jemadar-major is the first rank high enough to need a personal staff—I'd be needing, at the very least, a good regimental adjutant. Did I really not have anyone in mind? Poor planning. Still, I'd known Solange Corday for twenty years, liked her, had seen a competent, well-trained soldier, then officer at work. Quite possibly, she'd made fewer mistakes than I.

Well. They weren't paying us to dither. I held out my hand. "You'll like Karsvaao. It's a fucking desert."

She clapped me on the shoulder. "Come on, Athy. Let's get those beers while we have the chance."

OK. And if I was going to go on furlough, go home, if home were still there, for the first time in twenty years, I'd need *someone* to go on ahead to Karsvaao and set things up properly. In the bar, the beers were cold, if a little sweet. That was one thing the natives were learning how to do, at least.

Later, at home, I ate dinner while I sat on the balcony of my crib and watched the sun set out of Boromilith's lovely indigo evening sky. I'd invited Hani to have dinner with me, the way I usually signaled which pillow-geisha would be sharing my bed tonight, and we were served by the kitchen staff, Fyodor acting like a perfect little waiter, white linen over one arm, directing the placement of the dishes as each course was brought out, pouring the drinks himself, with a flourish.

The meal was built around a spicy lamb casserole, Margie's doing, I think. She grew up in Virginia, maybe shared some of my childhood tastes. Meat well trimmed, ir-radiated, injected with nutrients and antitoxins, everything cooked in that radical-free ersatz fat that's all we're allowed to have. She made it taste good though.

The sky was starting to flame orange-red now, swatches of deep, deep blue being displaced, even streamers of black coming over the far horizon, stars just about ready to pop out, the way they always did on Boromilith, sudden-like. I'm never sure I remember how it was on Earth. I was only nineteen when I left for good, the appearance of the starry sky, the order of events at dusk far from the most important thing in my universe.

Passing the entrance exams was all that counted, back then. Memory still painful. This tough-looking bastard in what I still thought of as sergeants' chevrons laughing when he saw me, too skinny maybe. Still looking like a kid. Then he pointed to the top of a snowcapped mountain. "Up there, kid." Then he pointed to a man lying on the ground. "Take him with you." It took me a minute to figure out the guy was dead. Another minute to figure out he'd been dead for a while.

Maybe being so stiff made him a little easier to carry. Six thousand boys and girls made it into the examination center that day. Sixty passed the test battery. Eighteen made it through basic training. And I'm sitting here with a jemadar-major's pips on my collar, eating lamb casserole under a lovely alien sky, while a beautiful young Indonesian woman tries to make me laugh, and waits to see what I'll want to do.

Hani, I think, was born on the island of Bali. I keep forgetting.

The sky was at its loveliest, most garish now, colors shading over into purest red, blanketing the heavens in dust-layer shapes, like fiery mother-of-pearl. I've enjoyed living here. Enjoyed the sunsets. Not like the sunsets I'd just seen, though. Not nearly so grand.

Imagine me standing on the great plain of Shônetk, sky black with night, stars shimmering overhead, while my soldiers sifted through a million alien corpses, separating the living from the dead, so very many more of the latter, of course. Quickly, quickly now. Get it done and we can go home. Home to Boromilith and our burdars. Earned our wages today, boys and girls.

But the sky . . .

My god it *was* a sky! The Mountains Without Clouds towering up and up and up, out of night, out of dusk, right into full daylight, looking for all the world like great towers of gold, like a city of the gods floating above us on the void, the gods themselves looking down on our deeds, judging them.

And, all around, the alien dead lay drifted like so much dim, clotted snow. Windrows of the dead. Heaps of them. No longer able to appreciate that sky. Maybe, watching it form one last time, as they lay bleeding into the night, the sight made dying a touch easier. Or maybe not. Maybe it made it all the harder.

With luck, I'll never know.

On Boromilith, on a tall hill, looking down over fortress and town, we were finished eating now, lazing in the afterglow, Hani pulling her chair closer to mine, one small hand on my arm, stroking gently. She'd been with me for a couple of years, knew my routines. Knew she wouldn't remain my favorite forever.

Every day on-station is a point on their contracts, a mark toward a better life when they go home. I've heard people call the burdar system slavery. But a job is a job.

Flash of light down by the horizon, flickering, building up, steady and silent for a long moment, then the roll of distant thunder. I never get tired of watching them, no matter how many I see.

The lighter lifted off from the spaceport, brilliant fire splashing across the black stone landing stage, ship rolling around its long axis, sound growing louder, so I could hear the individual crackles and pops. It was taking off on full afterburner, subjecting its cargo to nine or ten standard gees, climbing fast out of the local troposphere. Fire, fire, climbing . . .

The long jet of hydrogen flame winked out as it got past the altitude where the atmosphere would support combustion, supplanted by a brilliant yellow-white glow, hydrogen plasma coming out of its jets, pushed by a fusion-powered electric turbine. Inefficient, but practical. And, somewhere up there, its starship waited.

We'd called our ships starships, once upon a time. What a laugh. We should've called them dugout canoes.

Hani had her hand on my thigh now, still stroking gently. She knew, sooner or later, I'd be finished with the sunset.

Then it was dark night and we were done for the evening, Hani and I, lying together in my big, comfortable bed, her smooth, damp back pressed against my chest, my arms curled around her, my legs tucked up under her thighs. I could feel her heart beating, slowly, gently, a faint drumbeat from somewhere inside. She wouldn't be asleep, of course, not so long as she could tell I was still awake. Waiting for my hands to move again, perhaps, touch her here and there. Waiting for me to grind against her gently, signaling.

Maybe I would. Maybe not. Hani's lithe muscularity, her small, smooth brown torso, had a way of drawing me out, making me do more than I intended. Image of her face in the almost-darkness of night, looking up at me, moving slowly to the rhythms of our lovemaking, eyes big and dark, so very serious. Am I doing this right? she seemed to be asking. Am I making you happy?

Yes, to both questions.

Yes, if there is such a thing as happiness.

And sometimes wondering what she thought of it all. That little smile that sometimes emerged, a squint of seeming pleasure, sheen of moisture on her brow and upper lip. That small hand on one of my buttocks as she held still, engulfing my orgasm.

Maybe just thinking about a time, down the road, when all this would be over. Of a time when she would be back home on some tropical isle, wealthy by any reasonable standard, would never again need to lie still under a hulking white man while he gasped softly and pulsed inside her.

Not much to compare her with. Pillow-geisha burdars from the past and present. Janice and Mira, sleeping now in some other room, probably glad I took Hani to my bed far more often than they. A free ride. Maybe they argued about it, maybe Hani was just a little bitter, knowing they'd go home just as wealthy as she, though they lay, more often than not, dry and comfortable in their own little beds, while she endured my seemingly endless attention.

Years and years and years ago. Alix . . . Alexandra Moreno was her name. Tall, thin teenage girl, one of us in the ruins of the world. Angular, with that mass of curly black hair, dark brown eyes, serious, questioning.

What *were* we going to be, when we all grew up?

No way of knowing. The world was destroyed before we got old enough to make those plans.

Alix and I walking hand in hand, looking up at a full moon. Looking at the big, shadowy scar on its surface, not too far from Tycho, where something had once flared, brilliant blue-white. Looking up at the full moon, hardly noticing the twinkling interplay of orbiting debris, the shattered remains of human spacecraft, a reminder of all who'd died.

Alix and I at a party, sitting in a corner, full of smoke and liquor, holding each other, touching each other, putting our tongues in each other's mouths, tentatively groping around, trying to understand the complementarity of each other's bodies.

That spring night in the weedy, overgrown playing field not far from the ruins of the old high school, when we took off all our clothes, lay down on a scratchy old blanket, and put ourselves to the test.

At the time, it had seemed a big thing, terribly frightening, but wonderful. Alix's eyes wide as I crawled on top of her, letting me know she was afraid, but not wanting to stop.

A few more times that summer, then, in the fall, the examination battery. And me passing, she failing. A decision to make. She cried when I told her I was leaving for boot camp, told me she understood. Even came to see me off at the train.

We wondered if it would be possible to write, but it turned out not to be. And then, as far as I was concerned, the Earth was dead and gone and everyone with it. Everyone but my brothers and sisters of the Spahi mercenaries.

Sweating, striving, in the hard rock deserts of Australia. In vacuum suits under the impossible red-and-black skies of Mars. In the soppy teal jungles of Alpha Centauri A-IV. And then everywhere. Everywhere.

I wonder where Alix is now. Married? Children? Most likely. I wondered what her husband would be like, if I'd meet him, would like him, when I went home.

It all seemed so pale and distant now. My exertions with Alix merely that, adolescent fumblings, amusing in retrospect, no matter how important they seemed then. Different, though. How Alix felt seemed important to me then. Hani . . .

I could just reach around and palpate her breasts and she'd stretch against me, cocking her pelvis back in case that's what I wanted, would try to be ready for me, whenever I was ready, no matter how she felt, if she were sore, tired. She would not let me know how she felt. Success here was too important to her future. If she made me wonder how she felt, I might want to let her go.

And then she'd just be another burdar, serving my meals, washing my feet, cleaning my crib, shining my dress boots. They sterilize burdars as part of the contract. Sterilize them forever. Hani would go home a rich woman. A rich woman who'd never have children of her own. My understanding is they adopt the children of their relatives, their brothers and sisters and cousins. Extended families are probably making a big comeback these days, one man or woman in burdarage pulling a whole family out of the grinding poverty and servitude in which most of humanity must live.

I slid my hand around Hani's waist, resting my palm on one narrow hipbone, and pulled her around to face me. She tipped her head back, ready for my kiss, arms around my back, pulling me close, tilting her hips, rubbing against me, experienced in my wants, knowing full well what to do.

After a while, we slept, I without dreams. Hani? She would never let me know.

2 THE NEXT DAY DAWNED BRILLIANT AND hot, the blue-green sky hazy but cloudless. I was up before the sun, an hour in the exercise machines, a few dozen turns around the track, talking to Solange about forwarding my household to Karsvaao, then off to the cosmodrome and the beginning of my voyage home.

Home. Nothing real to go with that word. A memory from the transport floating in orbit, me and a hundred other frightened young recruits just out of basic training, riding the transport to Mars. I'd stood there, looking out through the index field at a bright little circle in the deep black sky, the familiar image of a blue-and-white world, getting smaller and smaller until it was gone.

Now, I stood on the black stone of the launching table, waiting in the shadow of the lighter for my turn to board. She was Orbital Transport Six, attached to Masters' Starship CX110, a lovely tall metal cylinder, sixty meters across its base, slightly tapering up to a rounded nosecap, a little more than two hundred meters high, her tanks brimming with cold hydrogen slurry, fusion reactor ticking over at hot idle.

Looking between the landing jacks, I could see a techie crew, a mixed bag of human engineering-burdars and native Boromilithi, servicing something on one of the engines' gimbal mounts, pulling it this way and that, seeming to argue among themselves, waving their arms and pointing. Four engines here, big, translucent blue crystalline bells, afterburner inlets already gaping open.

The piloting software seems to like that quick takeoff, an oversight maybe, since the Masters wouldn't even be aware of the acceleration unless it got so high the ship's structure started to fall. Software not too bright, maybe just bright enough. They seemed to be careful about that—maybe not wanting to breed their own successors by mistake.

Once, on a dare, I'd tried to take a launch standing up. I wound up on my knees anyway. At ten gees I weighed a full metric ton.

A larger shadow, a shape like something from an old nightmare, fell on the ground beside me, gigantic, familiar, making me turn. She was tall in a sense, head carried three meters off the ground, and long, six meters from that head to the tip of her thick, blunt tail. Muzzle full of complex omnivore teeth, teeth that looked as though they were made out of fine white china. Pupilless yellow eyes like foggy marbles set close together on the front of that head, just under twin tufts of feathery blue stuff, the rest of her body covered with pebbly gray scales.

The overall effect was a little like a therapod carnivore, an allosaur maybe. A little bit, but the differences were important. Black claws on big, three-toed feet, yes, but silver-painted chelae like sheet metal shears on the ends of long, dangling, muscular arms, thin tentacles clustered at the wrists serving in lieu of fingers.

"Hello, Shrêhht."

She did something to a little box hanging on a leather strap around her throat, whispered to it, a sound like faraway thunder, and the box said, "Hello, Athy. I thought I might find you down here, watching the techies."

I smiled and shook my head. "Maybe I'm in the wrong line of work." There was a time, when I was seven or eight years old, when I'd had these dreams of one day becoming a fighter pilot. A child's dreams, fed on the warlike fantasies of that age.

She said, "I don't think so." The vocal encoder managed
to convey a slight touch of amusement.

They call themselves the Kkhruhhuft, at least that's how it
comes out of the translation device. If you want to imagine
how people felt on that day in 2104, when a Master's lighter
touched down in the water a few hundred meters off Merritt
Island Cosmodrome, how they felt when these . . . *things*
came toddling out, I understand the historical documents are
still available. Monsters. Just like the monsters in every SF
horror movie ever made. Fangy, slavering monsters who told
us they came in peace.

Until that one, lone roving Master, orbiting the Earth in a
starship the size of a small asteroid, decided it could take this
planet all by itself and sicced its Kkhruhhuft bodyguard on
us. All right. We killed them all and sent the Master packing.

It was fifty years before they came back to finish the job.
Fifty years while we waited in terror, building our weapons
in the knowledge that millions had died killing a few hundred Kkhruhhuft. And knowing we'd had to ram the Invader
with a relativistic starship merely to drive it away. Had we
known that first Master was virtually unarmed, we might not
have bothered.

Maybe it would have been better that way.

I said, "I'd heard you were going to Earth, this trip. I'll be
glad to have some real company."

Her big head dipped slightly, something like a nod. Somehow, they seem a little too much like us, despite the enormous differences. Birds of a feather, perhaps.

Across the way, a horde of poppits spilled out of a deliv-
ery-GEM, like living blue water, all mashed together, scurrying over each other so it was hard to tell one animal from the
next. Making their little piping cries, tootling back and forth,
carrying the sense of their mission in aggregate.

"Which one is this?"

Shrêhht whispered to her encoder. "Freshly duplicated off
the software lineage of 3m8, I think. That's the rumor, anyway."

"Headed for Earth?"

"For the next phase of the ground expansion program, perhaps."

The back of the truck was open now, dark inside, the poppits swarming up the sides, crawling in. If you looked closely, you could see eight bright red eyes on each flat little head, the flicker of little white teeth in those fangy little mouths. They say a couple of hundred poppits can reduce a man to bones in less than a second. Never seen it happen, though, or heard a reliable story.

Shrêhht said, "My mother's memory is to be honored in the next Gosudar's Ceremony, Athy. I'd be pleased if you'd stand with me."

There was a scrape of plastic on plastic and the Master's black-and-gray cartridge slid out into the liftgate, which whined, lowering the heavy mass. Cold vapor spilled down from the sides of the cartridge, fluttered in the breeze and disappeared. There are two rumors about that. One says the Masters' hardware is based on a quite archaic technology, metal superconductors cooled with liquid helium. The other says it's a very advanced technology indeed, circuit energy flux so high the hardware has to be cooled with liquid helium to keep from melting.

I'm inclined to believe the latter.

"I'd be honored, comrade," I said. Shrêhht's mother had been killed during the conquest of Earth.

The poppits had the Master's cartridge on a dolly now and were sliding it over to the ship's cargo loader. Shrêhht brushed her tendrils against my shoulder, and said, "Might as well board now."

We ambled slowly toward the ramp, people getting out of our way. A human overseer, not a Spahi but some civilian employee of one of the local Masters, made his line of coffled Boromilithi slaves stop in their tracks, bowed slightly as he waved us on toward the ramp.

As we walked up the ramp, I heard Shrêhht's real voice growl softly, and the vocoder said, "This is A4x228k, logging off in transit."

Right, let us not forget. I took out my phone and did the

same, and the Boromilith planetary command net said, "3C286b, acknowledge and out."

Inside, the lighter's cargo space seemed, as usual, dank and metallic-smelling, rather poorly ventilated, intended mainly for containerized cargo. The upper decks were reserved for loose cargo, now taken over by passengers, stiff plastic padding on the floor the only concession to organic comfort. The air was hazy-looking, and we stood in one corner, squinting under dim, glary lighting that supposedly mimicked the natural light of the Masters' homeworld.

"Lot of cattle here today." Beings streaming in all around us, already squabbling over the best positions. Clots of humans, strings of Boromilithi, a scattering of other species, even two more Kkhruhhuft on the far side of the compartment, backs grazing the upper bulkhead.

Shrêhht whispered, "Earth-bound ships are more like that than some others." She gestured at a nearby coffle. "Boromilithi are going to be used as labor on the new human colony worlds."

I'd heard that story, much more than rumor. The Masters were beginning to seed the uninhabited worlds around Earth, which was to be the centerpiece of what was, after all, a frontier sector. And humans, already good mercenaries, would make fine overseers as well. Boromilithi, on the other hand, made much better slaves.

Something to be proud of, relatively speaking? Maybe not. The Kkhruhhuft made better mercenaries, perhaps, than we'd ever be, having been at it for seventeen thousand years. I'd never heard of them being used as overseers anywhere.

As time goes by there are more and more humans scattered across the worlds. I remember how, in the beginning, we felt so alone out here, raw young soldiers standing together among the aliens, friendless and frightened. But others came after us, to serve our needs as humans, then more and more, to serve the needs of the Masters and all the Masters' servants.

I wonder, sometimes, what my life would have been like had I waited for the colonization program. Or gone out as an engineering-burdar's apprentice.

A sudden metallic scraping blared through the air, like steel wool on exposed nerves, the ship's AI calling out to the poppits, alerting them. Shrêhht suddenly knelt beside me, dropping onto her belly, stretching full length on the plastic, tendrils fluttering around the clasp of her vocoder's neck strap, resting her massive chin on the floor padding.

Scrape. Scrape. Scrape. Three seconds warning, my dear little poppits.

All around us, people and things were scurrying to lie down. I put myself on my back, legs spread a bit, arms down by my sides, hands flat, palms up, a position I knew would be comfortable.

Ten gee. Like sleeping with a whale. Like having it roll over in its sleep.

There were no more warnings, just the sudden clank-thud of automatic doors slamming shut, knowing if you were caught in one you'd be cut in half or crushed flat, the air around us suddenly seeming much more oppressive, cut off from the outside. The solid, distant whine of servomotors putting the engine gimbals through their paces as the software flexed its muscles. The much louder throb of powerful turbines, the rush of hydrogen slurry pouring through the fuel lines.

Thud. Ship shuddering as fluorine injectors made hypergolic ignition, giving the afterburner ram a zero-velocity start. And then I was smothering under a metric ton of me.

Somewhere, a human baby screamed, shrill and flat, almost covering the sudden murmurs of protest, the panicky whispers of the Boromilithi, most of whom had never been up before. My inner ears spun as the ship rolled, tipping over onto its proper synergy track.

I could feel my hands open, fingers flattening, knuckles pressing into the floor.

Engine thunder came up through the companionways, walls rattling and shuddering as the ship climbed out of the troposphere, cargo canisters creaking against their tie-downs, trapped sophonts, helpless, moaning softly, someone crying nearby, whimpering like an injured dog. Shrêhht lay inert beside me, breathing heavily, chuffing like a damaged engine, head visible in one corner of my grayed-out vision, eyes rolling slowly in her head.

I imagine the strain on her ribs was immense. But a Kkhruhhuft would never complain, even if those ribs collapsed.

There was a hand-sized poppit on the floor between us, crushed flat to the deck, looking like a little blue starfish, mouth gaping open, eight tiny red eyes looking back at me.

The pressure let off a little and the noise level went down abruptly as we climbed through the tropopause, afterburner extinguishing itself in Boromilith's rarefied stratosphere, inlets closing, lighter proceeding at a six-gee climb on toward orbit.

Far away, I could hear the baby crying still, comforting words murmured softly by its mother, the valued employee of some interstellar service bureau, a contract technician perhaps, able to extract special privileges from her employer. My family comes with me, she would say, and we get to go home again when we want . . . Is that envy I'm feeling? Maybe not.

In a little while, even that would back off and there'd be a gentle almost-silence, nothing but the distant rumble of the cruise engine, pushing us up to the starship at an easy tenth gee, keeping us under gravity so we'd stay on the floor. Thoughtful of them. It. Software with a heart.

Soon we were all on the ship, gear stowed in our "cabins," safe and sound, if there is such a thing. Boarding is always a crazy experience, what with the lighter docking at the starship's zero-gee hub, passengers and cargo bobbing all over the place, poppits flipping around in the air like so many flying spiders.

The ship's name, it turned out, acknowledging our arrival log, was 7m64subCX, ship's node housing a full-fledged Master, albeit a minor one.

My room was a tiny cubby, one of thousands made from bolted-together cargo containers, outfitted with the bare minimum necessary, up on the .6-gee level, more than halfway out to the hull. This was "paying passenger" country. Most of the sentients on board were cargo, would make the trip in the core-periphery cargo space, down around .05.

I try not to go down there. The smell, from motion sickness vomitus, from transit shock diarrhea, from whatever processes nonhumans have to make their own special contribution, can be astonishing.

I went on up to a hull-level platform, under poppit-normal 1.1 gee. The view out the "window" here was stupendous. I sat by myself at a little table near the guardrail of one of the balcony restaurants, looking out across the main concourse, floor below thronged with thousands of sentients, more species than I knew the names of, looking out the window beyond.

It looked like a vast, curving pane of optically perfect glass, a window on space a hundred meters high, perhaps twice as wide. Impossible, of course. The external hull of this ship, like all the starships I'd seen, was a featureless enclosure of mirror-bright metal, made from who-knows-what. Besides which, the ship was rotating to keep us under gee. The hull was under the concourse floor. The window should have been looking into the next compartment, whatever it was.

Outside, Boromilith was a bright crescent ten thousand kilometers away, filling about half the window, one of its moons, Laelathri from the color, a soft orangish tint, floating just beyond the hazy curve of the atmosphere, holding the same phase. There were stars visible too, dozens of them like faintly colored jewels in the hard black sky, mostly diamonds, here an opal, there a pale sapphire, which hardly seemed likely against all that glare.

At one horn of the crescent, the only one I could actually see, was the glitter of Boromilith's tiny north polar ice cap, the pole in summer just now. And there were pale green seas, dark swatches of jungle, tan and sandy deserts. The twinkle of city lights in the night . . .

I remember seeing the nightside of Earth from space just once, back when I was a kid, going with my family on a vacation to the moon, maybe six months before the Invasion. It seemed like the continents were seas of continuous light.

There was even light way out on the ocean. Now, most likely, it would all be dark.

I took a sip of my drink, something vaguely whiskeylike, poured from a cheap-looking, labelless bottle, and looked away.

There was a stage show going on up here, something that had started after I sat down, a man and woman dancing together naked, touching each other, whirling away, touching again. The men and women gathered close to the stage seemed enraptured.

The couple on the stage were being very realistic about their artistic little dance, the tall, handsome, muscular man with a very stiff-looking erection, one that hardly bounced at all as he pranced, the lithe, long-haired woman showing a delicate sheen of moisture on the inside of her thighs. You'd think they wouldn't be able to do that, the man having blood pressure problems, the woman focused more on muscular effort than on the mechanics of arousal. Besides which, they'd probably done this act thousands of times, would be bored with each other, bored with the whole silly business. Drugs, perhaps?

And the people watching them, men and women both? Their eyes followed every movement closely, their mouths open, as if with expectation. Why would they want to watch these people dance and sweat, when they could turn to each other and have the very thing for themselves?

I know people who've carried whole pornography collections all the way from Earth, even Spahis, who have the compliant bodies of burdars at their beck and call. Pictures, presumably, have no feelings; though, if you look closely, it's clear that the people within the pictures do.

A woman spreading her legs for the camera, smile a grimace on her face, stunned look in her eyes. A man holding his own penis, smirking for the faceless crowd beyond the lens. A distant look, thinking, maybe, about tonight's dinner. Or maybe about the car he's got to have repaired once again.

The couple on the stage grappled with each other, kissing, making the crowd surrounding them sigh with delight, then the woman spun, ever so gracefully, bending at the waist, presenting her buttocks to her male counterpart, presenting like an extinct female ape in some old film. The man turned, with equal grace, swinging his hips forward.

On the floor, some of the audience members crouched lower, getting down in front of the woman so they could look up between her legs and get a better view.

Nothing I hadn't seen a thousand times before. I turned away and looked back out the window. We'd swung over toward the dayside now and Boromilith was a beautiful, glittering treasure spread out below, worth looking at endlessly and forever.

A voice, whispered, a vocoder, speaking: "Enjoying the show?"

I looked up again, and Shrêhht was crouching beside my table, holding a frosty mug in one claw. She poured a splash in her mouth, tipping her head back to swallow like a bird. There was a smell in the air, like a cross between kerosene and pizza.

I shrugged and gestured at the window. "This one, immensely. That one . . ." A nod at the stage, where the dancers had settled into a rather simplistic rhythm of coital pumping, hardly art at all. Some of the audience members were kneeling now, as if in prayer, one woman even putting her head right down on the stage in the shadow of the dancers. I said, "I don't know why they bother."

Shrêhht nodded, watching the dancers fuck stolidly away. "At home," she said, "we have something a little bit like this. Huntresses get up on stage with some small prey animal or another, stalk and kill. Then eat. It's all very titillating to some."

"You?"

Another shrug. "I suppose not. When I was a youngster maybe."

Kkhruhhuft breeding is very different from our own, though what we hear as gossip is not very detailed. The males, it seems, are nonsentient, property at best, animals at worst, kept by special shepherdesses, doled out at breeding time. They take none of them out to the stars and a Kkhruhhuft mercenary remains celibate, I think, for her entire duty cycle.

Maybe they go home periodically to breed. I don't know. Shrêhht has never seemed interested in talking about it, nor any other Kkhruhhuft I've known.

She said, "Have you eaten? I think we can both get food here."

I nodded, signaling to the waiter. Up on stage, the man and woman were sweating now, skins bright with moisture, the crowd before them all bunched together and silent. Waiting.

My first real view of Earth, from the ground, after more than twenty years' absence, came like a physical blow. Seen from space, it was just one more habitable world, something only vaguely like the planet I'd watched drifting away on the void so long ago, hardly remembered, overlaid by so many other worlds, so many worlds just like this.

And now, standing at the foot of the lighter's boarding ramp? I stood, flat-footed, staring, lungs perfused by familiar air, familiar no matter how tainted by unfamiliar smells. Beyond the flat black pavement of the landing stage, beyond the stained old gray granite buildings of the spaceport . . .

Something. The shattered towers of a ruined city. The bright towers of a new city. Little swatches of dark green, forest such as I'd not seen in so long. Beyond it all, a vaulting sky of delicate peach and tawny gold. Sunrise.

And the sun for which my eyes were made.

Shrêhht, bulking huge behind me, said, "It's always something, coming home." She managed to make the vocoder sound quiet, reflective, perhaps even respectful.

I could only nod. Then I took out my phone and said, "10x9760h, logging on as arrived."

Modulated static, like the soft background static of Boromilith, and the same genderless voice said, "4Y1028h, net connect."

Out there, somewhere, the world I left behind. The people. Family. Friends. People I would've known, but never met. Friends I would've had, if only I'd stayed here. Voids, like negative charges in a particle net. Nonexistent people. My children, perhaps. Children I would've had if I'd stayed here. Children with Alix? I could see her now in my memory, an amalgam compounded of the girl she really had been, the woman I'd thought she was then.

As stevedores came out to unload the ship, as the first coffles began staggering down the ramp, overseers snarling, angry human words interspersed with pidgin-Boromilithi, we walked over to the main building, a building patched here and there, granite smeared with cement, covering the big cracks I remembered from long ago.

We walked through the slanting light of a golden sun and, for just a moment, something very much like exhilaration stole through me. It's always something, she'd said. Coming home.

Inside, the building was in some ways just as it had been when I'd first seen it, back in the late spring of 2154. But changed, nonetheless. The starry sky bonded to the stone ceiling was beginning to peel away here and there, the Milky Way showing thin rips, the bit with Orion hanging free, swaying slowly in the air currents, as if about to fall.

And the tile floor, a vitrimosaic showing the history of space travel, looking worn somehow. Old. You could barely make out Yuri Gagarin's face. And the face of Wing Commander Derek McDonnough, who'd captained the *Larrabee*, who'd rammed the original Master's scoutship with his own, looked like it had been excised with a chisel.

Would the Masters order that? No. I don't think their . . . *feelings* if you can call them that, extend so far. Kkhruhhuft? Again, no. They're proud of us. We almost beat them.

Vandals, maybe.

Dotted here and there around the periphery of the terminal's main concourse, scattered through the human crowds, were various . . . others. A group of poppits, gathered neatly and motionlessly in one corner. A couple of things that looked like wolverines covered with crabgrass. A coffle of beat-up–looking Boromilithi. Maybe on their way home. A thing like a big, leathery black medicine ball with a couple of dozen brilliant white eyes, eight or ten stalky arms and legs, squatting on a pile of luggage.

And, scattered around the periphery, dressed in white shawls and stiff straw hats, Masters' ID badges at their throats, slim rifles held across scaly green chests . . . centaurs, I guess you'd call them, but not like anything out of human myth. Taller than a man, with long, fat forelegs, ending in heavy digging claws, back sloping down to short hind legs and a thick, stiff little tail. Upper bodies a little bit humanoid. Not much. Arms like a man, bigger, a little less gracile. Bullet heads, mouths with . . . teeth.

I'd seen a picture in an old textbook once, an animated holo of some ancient herbivore called a *moschops*. Teeth like that. Big, flat, spatulate buck teeth. Some of them had their shawls hanging open, so you could see the males' cloacas and the females' long, stiff ovipositors . . .

Saanaae. They'd only started bringing them in around the time I left, beginning to replace the Kkhruhhuft occupation forces, who were needed elsewhere. Saanaae make poor soldiers, but excellent police.

We walked across to a section of what had once been ticket counters beneath a sign that said SIRKAR PORT AUTHORITY. There were long lines here, snaking back toward the entrances. People. Things. Men and women behind the counters, querulous officials in some kind of reddish brown uniform, badges of cheap and shiny metal, aluminum-colored to look like silver and gold, pinned on here and there.

We walked to the front of the line, stood waiting.

One of the men there, sorting people's forms, glanced at us, scowled, looked away, kept on working. I knocked on the counter, sharp, peremptory. "Now, sir."

He looked up, looked at me, looked at the Kkhruhhuft. "Go to the back of the line."

Behind me, I could hear Shrêhht stir.

Makes you wonder how people get their jobs. Maybe he hadn't noticed that Shrêhht was three meters tall. Or that I was wearing a sidearm. Maybe he just had plenty of confidence in the Saanaae guardsmen all around us. Well. I'd dealt with self-important little officials before. No reason I shouldn't treat this one the same way I'd treat a nonhuman.

I glanced at Shrêhht, motioning her to stay out of it, was turning to face the man, reaching out to take hold of his sleeve, reclaim his attention, when an older man, paunchy, with dark gray hair, saggy face with one big scar running diagonally across his forehead, walked quietly up. He put out his hand to touch my arm, and said, "Johnson. Move your line down to the next kiosk."

The younger man looked at him, astonished. *"What?"* Rising to his feet, mouth open, face starting to color.

"Do it, boy." The old man wasn't looking at him.

Johnson turned and stared at us, seemed to focus in for a second. "This isn't right."

"Do it anyway."

"I'll raise this at tonight's meeting, Velasquez . . ." A threat, spoken with a sharp edge. Someone nearby, someone standing in line I think, muttered, "Bloody goddamned sagoths . . ."

"Do that."

He held out his hand then and said, "Havildar-emeritus Ari Velasquez, late of XVII *Magnificent.*"

I took his hand, giving it a gentle squeeze. "Athol Morrison, uh," no more X *Invincible*, "IX *Victorious*," I said.

"Been away long, Jemadar-Major?"

"Since the beginning."

An understanding nod. "Well, we'll get your papers in order and get you right on the road." He gave me a broad smile then: "Welcome home, sir."

3 LATER, HAVING SAID MY GOOD-BYES TO Shrêhht, having agreed to meet her again in New York in time for the Gosudar's Ceremony, I rode the coastal monorail home. The sun rose in a pale, bright blue sky, tinged with the faintest touch of gray, while we slid above the tangled, overgrown ruins of New Jersey, following the broken line of the twentieth century's famous I-95 corridor.

City without end, an urban sprawl that had lasted for centuries, all gone now. Scrubby pine trees growing up over everything, tangles of weeds and brush and swamp. I can't even remember what it used to be like, a nine-year-old boy, excited about his vacation trip to the moon, remembering nothing more than that odd, persistent smell. And my father saying, "I don't know, Athy. It's always smelled like this . . ."

From inside the closed, air-conditioned train, looking down on a brushy wilderness, at bits of old habitation peeking up between the branches of stunted-looking trees, I couldn't tell if it had any smell at all.

The monorail line crossed the Delaware River on tall pylons, high above the flattened rubble that had once been Philadelphia, crushed stone, in muted tones of tan and gray, stretching away to the horizon, stretching away from bay and river and forest. Both of the big craters were full of water now, looking almost like natural lakes, very different from the way they'd looked the last time I'd seen them.

Red, raw, wounds in memory, full of mist, though the bombs that'd made them had gone off more than a decade before. Friendly fire, it's called. Missiles aimed at Kkhruh-huft-bearing Master Race warships missing their targets, arcing back down through the stratosphere, two twenty-megaton warheads exploding, digging bloody great holes in the Earth. I don't have the slightest idea how many people died in that instant. Six, seven million, maybe? In the context of a war that took eight billion human lives, it hardly seems to matter.

In a little while, we were over Washington, D.C. I sat back in my comfortable train coach chair, reclining just a bit, drinking a fizzly little drink, something mostly mineral water, barely touched by the taste of ginger-flavored brandy, and looked down on a chaos whose making I remember well.

I can't remember why we were in D.C. the day the Kkhruhhuft came down out of that particular sky, why my father chose to take the whole family away from Chapel Hill, where we seemed almost safe. The invasion had already been going on for days, hundreds of millions already dead, Kkhruhhuft lighters dropping everywhere, disgorging their fangy cargoes.

Memory. Of our ground car squealing through city streets, bumping hard, up-down, up-down, as my father, cursing, ran right over a crowd of running pedestrians. My mother crying. My brother and sister screaming. And me, pressed to the rear window, watching, full of wonder.

Watching as a Kkhruhhuft lighter staggered down out of the sky, falling at an angle, trailing smoky fire, obviously damaged somehow, running in a long curve, low overhead as we fled down the Mall, driving right over the grassy parts, some poor bastard bouncing off the car door, splashing the glass with his blood.

The Kkhruhhuft ship hit the base of the Monument and exploded, ball of brilliant yellow-red fire rising, me thinking, *Haven't I seen a video of this, somewhere, sometime?* I expected the obelisk to fall like an axed tree, but it didn't, in-

stead breaking into countless little pieces, falling straight
down into the fire of the exploding ship.

We were across the Potomac and roaring down some
wide, crowded highway when white light flared behind us,
blinding, making me squeeze my eyes shut, listening to my
father's wordless shout. I remember a tall column of boiling,
fiery smoke then. And I remember the wind. Hot wind, driving mist before it.

As the train ran out over the northern Virginia countryside, over heavily wooded land in which the abandoned
roadbeds of old highways could still be made out, a woman
came and sat beside me, sinking gently, gracefully into the
adjacent seat. She was a pretty woman, young, slim and muscular, dressed in plain clothing, sun-streaked brown hair
combed and pinned just so, skin tanned and smooth, looking
at me out of the corners of gray-green eyes. Attentive.

And wearing the same dog collar and tag I saw on most of
the train's passengers. Serfs, I guess they should be called.
Serfs of the resident Masters, on errands, though of what sort
I couldn't imagine. Didn't want to imagine.

She leaned toward me, looking into my face, eyes flickering as she tried to sneak quick looks at bits of my uniform, at
my badges of rank and service. "Are you a mercenary?"

I glanced at her, wondering, and nodded.

She held out her hand. "I'm Shelly," she said, and, almost
automatically, "Six-oh-six, fifty-one, Concourse Seven, Virginia."

As if I should, somehow, know what that meant. I took her
hand, intending to shake it briefly, assuming that was still the
custom of Earth, but she held on, fingers squeezing mine
gently, smiling. I said, "Athol Morrison, jemadar-major, IX
Victorious." And could tell from the look in those oh-so-at-
tentive eyes that she didn't know what it meant. Just a man
in a uniform, someone not wearing a collar.

Her hand was on my thigh, resting gently about halfway
between knee and crotch. I pulled my hand out of hers,
reached down and took that other hand away, and said, "I'm
really very tired, Shelly. Sorry."

The look of disappointment in her eyes was acute. And I

wasn't really tired, either. Still, this is . . . home? I didn't want to think of these people as just so many burdars available for my use. Maybe I would want to be one of them, if I could only figure out who and what they were. Had become in my absence.

I seemed to drift for a while after that, hardly noticing that she remained by my side, sitting, shifting position from time to time. Eyes on me perhaps? I only sat back and watched Virginia flit by underneath us. Richmond, I knew, would still be there, had still been there the last time I'd come this way, heading north for the departure port on my way to Mars.

I don't think I knew then just how long it would be before I'd come home again. Just that it would be a while.

The people in the train car mostly stayed in their seats, every now and again someone rising and going to the little rest room, leaving for the club car and coming back with a bottle or two of pale yellow beer. I was the only one the porter had come to proffering a drink. And I was the only one who appeared to have an anxious little prostitute fretting by his side.

There was a small, thin, pale man sitting up near the front of the car, holding a long leash that ended in two naked Boromilithi, miserable-looking, chained together at the neck, staring back at the rest of us.

Every now and again a pair of Sirkar Native Police, uniformed in their dull reddish brown, would come down the aisle, looking at people, paunchy men with something of a truculent, hard-bitten look. And seeing me, look away, nervous. The pretense of toughness come upon the real thing.

Once, when they'd gone by, I heard one passenger whisper to another, ". . . bloody damned sagoths . . ."

Sagoth. Odd word that. And it was as if I knew the word, could almost remember it. Right there, from far away, buried under layers of memory. I couldn't recall anybody using it in the few years I lived here between the Invasion and my enlistment. The Sirkar wasn't organized yet. Kkhruhhuft still occupied our world. The Saanaae were just beginning to arrive. There weren't any Native Police to call sagoths.

There was a quick flash of light from outside, momentarily brightening the day, suddenly sharpening my senses, flush of adrenaline quickening my blood. Where? Sitting forward. On the western horizon, where the hills steepened, marking the Fall Line, a faint blossom of yellow-orange fire. Flash. Another. Flash. Another. Three distant plumes of blue smoke starting to grow. People in the train looking out the windows, murmuring to each other, careful, indistinct remarks I couldn't quite make out.

Shelly had her hand on the chair's armrest, looking past me, looking out at the smoke and fire. Something in her eyes now other than a wish for my . . . patronage. A tinge of fear.

Behind her, in the aisle, the two policemen watched as well, one of them touching the other on the arm, so they made a posed tableau. I gestured at the smoke and said, "What's happening up there?"

They looked at each other then, nonverbal communication that said, careful. Careful. The shorter and heavier of the two men rubbed a jaw that needed shaving and murmured, "Don't know. A little trouble perhaps."

A little trouble. Perhaps. "What sort of trouble?" I could feel Shelly's hand on my arm again. Trying to tell me what?

The man looked at me, eyes measuring. Maybe troubled, maybe just . . . careful. Who knew how much trouble an off-world soldier could make for some poor little Sirkar policeman? He said, "Well. You know. I guess . . . I guess it's the same on other worlds. Newly overrun worlds. People who aren't ready for it yet. People who can't just be . . . contented." Eyes tinged with anxiety.

I looked away from them, back out at the distant fires, plumes of smoke already falling behind us, dropping below the wooded horizon. Surprised to hear that from some little provincial cop, but, yes, put that way, I did indeed know. Shelly's hand was on my thigh again, as if she'd decided to take advantage of the distraction.

Then, thunder from outside, making me lean toward the window, looking up. A pair of big, black, stub-winged jet-copters were outlined against the blue sky, trailing plumes of light smoke, fairly high up, laying a quick thud of machine noise down in their wake. Troop carriers. A Saanaae design

I'd seen before, in use wherever the Saanaae were used as a high-echelon police force. Jetcopters headed back up the line toward those columns of smoke.

I looked at the two policemen, watched them glance at each other again, turn, and walk away. Shelly's hand on my thigh was still. And some lethargy was keeping me from either pushing her away or acting on the invitation.

The sound of the jetcopters faded quickly and was gone. A terribly familiar sound. Heard mostly on newly suppressed worlds. Newly overrun was what the cop had called them.

Sudden image out of memory, jetcopters howling overhead, bringing Saanaae down on us as we fought. Image of myself in armor, a raw young trooper engaged in his first real combat, wading through a sea of gore, cutting down scaly, muscular green centaurs, slaying them, slaying them, like some mythic hero battling the demons of old.

Fire and smoke and hemoglobin red blood. All theirs, none of it ours.

Because they make good police. And we make good soldiers.

I'd had no idea *why* those particular Saanaae were in rebellion, or even why the rebellion spread so quickly. Something to do, perhaps, with the people of the world they were policing. People who looked like tall, slim, red spider-horses, not at all like the Saanaae. All I remember is that we killed them all.

One single image stuck, freeze-frame, in my heart. A wounded Saanaae trooper lying in the mud of that faraway world, fearful, metallic, inhuman eyes reflecting the bloodred light of a sunset sky, holding his empty pistol pointed at me. Waiting.

I only looked at him for a moment. Then I powered up my entrenching saw and cut off his head.

Shelly had her hand in my crotch now, rubbing gently, pressing against the heavy, twilled fabric of my trousers, feeling the beginnings of a physical response I hadn't even been aware of. She was reclining against my side, head on my shoulder, neck arched, head tipped back, so she could rub her lips against the side of my face.

Did she intend to do me right here in the train car?

I glanced around. No one else in the car was looking, all heads facing away, most of them staring out at the scenery. Carefully not looking, I supposed.

I sat up straighter, turning in the seat, putting my back to the wall, pushing her away so I could see her face. "What is it that you're looking for here? I can tell you're not a full-time professional whore, Shelly. I've known too many."

She looked away from me and seemed to blush, a very pretty effect. "I . . ." Nothing, faltering, unable to meet my gaze.

I reached out and took her by the chin, tipping her head back, forcing her to look at me. "Just tell me. I won't punish you." That same phrase said a thousand times, to burdars and servants, humans and nonhumans, even animals I thought might somehow understand.

She said, "Would you buy me?"

Rent? Or really buy, the word she'd used? The look on her face not quite shame, something else, tinged with a particle of hope. Whatever it was, I suppose it didn't really matter. I smiled at her. "It doesn't work that way, Shelly. We own nothing. Not even our lives."

Silly of me to say something like that. What could it possibly mean to *her*?

She said, "Would you buy me if you could?"

I grinned, reached out and ruffled her hair with a hand almost large enough to engulf the top of her head. She leaned in close, putting her arms around my chest, then tried to reach between my legs again. I held her tight for a minute, preventing her from going on, held her until she got the idea, then turned away again, letting her go, and sat looking out at the blue skies and green forests of what had once been my homeworld.

When the train pulled into the station in Durham, twenty kilometers east of Chapel Hill, I didn't know what to expect. The trip down hadn't been especially promising, an endless succession of mixed-deciduous forests passing below, odd swatches of piney woods, ridges of hill country, the occasional overgrown ruin, looking like not much of anything.

Not much left of Durham either, what had once been a city of more than a million now just a forest of tall, straight trees through which you could glimpse the remains of a few shattered buildings. I got out of the train, holding my one small suitcase, and stood looking toward the west.

It was a beautiful day, late-afternoon sun standing halfway up the sky over distant, almost-invisible blue hills, a small wooded rise in the foreground, cool breeze blowing across my face, stirring my hair gently. Not as I remember it. Not at all.

"Athol Morrison?"

I turned and there was a small, plump man looking up at me. A small man with a familiar-looking face, dressed in a somber brown cassock, neck-laces untied to reveal a black shirt and priest's white collar tab. Very familiar face, though . . . Good grief. *"Lank?"*

He grinned then, a sunny smile that I remembered well, and stepped forward to take me in his arms, a tight little hug I could barely feel. My brother Lancaster was twelve years old the day I went away. Nobody'd sent me any pictures of him, and now he was a pudgy middle-aged man in priestly robes. Nothing left of the boy but his smile.

He said, "Welcome home, Athy. Welcome home."

That unexpected lump in my throat made me feel silly. I held him at arm's length, grinning, looking him up and down. Thin, soft arms squeezed in my big hands, the feel of his soft body through the robes . . . and a shadowed look in his eyes. Uncertainty. "Jesus, Lank. I never thought I'd see you again!"

"We always hoped we'd see *you* again, Athy . . ." He stepped back, letting me go, standing there, looking at me. At the size of me, my height, the scars on my face, the big, knuckly hands, his eyes resting for an unsteady moment on my holstered sidearm. Finally, an uneasy smile. "My God, what've they *done* to you? Drugs?"

What would he be seeing now? A tall man, made to seem shorter by his breadth, thick at waist as well as shoulder, big blunt hands, big square face. That sharp white scar reaching from forehead to chin, passing right over the left eye. Brown eyes, though, still intact. Clear. Steady. Untroubled. As if they'd never seen a thing.

It made me conscious of the tension from my own muscle tone, making me stand up straight and tall where another man my age might slouch just a little bit. The way Lank was slouching even now. I ran my hand over one arm, feeling corded muscle, and shook my head, tried to return his smile. "Good food. Rather a lot of exercise."

He nodded slowly, but I imagined I could see him think, . . . *and killing. Killing makes you stand so tall.* He turned away then, gesturing. "Come on, boy. There're people waiting for you." He led me away, down a flight of stairs to the rubble-filled woods below.

Lank's car proved to be a battered old electric four-wheel-drive vehicle docked to a charging post in the parking lot below the train station. As we got in, Lank patted the dashboard and said, "She's a reliable old thing, she is, salvaged from junkyard parts like most of the others hereabouts." He pushed the starter and watched the indicators light up, mostly old-fashioned idiot lights, then hit the undock button.

When we got out onto the road, I could see the pavement was cracked away to rubble and mud, weeds growing up through all the cracks, some clumps so large, regular bushes, that Lank chose to drive around them rather than risk his undercarriage.

We went down a long, rather lumpy hill, through a tall stand of slim white pine and out into a broad, grassy field, car bumping over ruts left by other traffic, turning west, following a line of trees, through which I could see more collapsed buildings.

Here and there, little curls of smoke came out shattered windows and I could see strings of washing hanging from clotheslines, shirts and pants fluttering like worn-out flags. A man standing with an ax in one hand mopped his brow with a rag as he watched us go by, then turned back to his enormous pile of logs.

Chopping firewood. I could remember doing that all

through the summers between the Invasion and my enlistment. The whole world without electric power. Chopping wood all summer long, just a half hour a day, as part of my chores, so I wouldn't have to chop wood out in the winter cold.

Lank wasn't talking, just driving the car, looking ahead at the rutted lane. Long, straight, overgrown with grass. But I could see bits of paving material here and there, visible through the weeds. "This is old highway 15-501, isn't it?"

Lank glanced at me, smiled, and nodded. "Can't imagine what tore it up like this. Been this way for a long time, though."

The trees were smaller here and I realized we were passing through the southern part of Korstian State Park, which had been uninhabited since the 1920s, had been farmland for a couple of centuries before that. No ruins in the woods either, but when we crossed a mud-plastered log bridge over New Hope Creek, I could see the smoke from a campfire and, near the river's bend, what looked like an Indian teepee made from colorful old blankets.

The people around the campfire were dark-skinned, but I couldn't tell whether they were Indians or not. Before the Invasion, the nearest Indian community was probably the Lumbee Museum, or maybe those last few Cherokee towns near Asheville.

"Lank?"

He looked up from his driving and I saw he was sweating now, from the afternoon heat, from the effort of controlling the car, from wearing his heavy robe.

"Why the priesthood?"

Long, serious look, measuring me. Can I trust you? Can I talk to you openly? Are you *really* my long-lost brother? Or just a man wearing the Masters' uniform? He looked away for a moment, then back at me. "Well . . ." He reached up and fingered his clerical collar and smiled weakly. "Better this collar than that other one, eh? You made a better choice than you'll ever know, Athy."

Just one more bit of memory surfacing, the memory that Lank had cried the day I went away. Overhead, the sky was beginning to color with sunset, turning russet and brown, sun bisected by the horizon, its visible face striated with thin bands of cloud. The color reminded me of all the other red places I'd been on the long voyage outward into the sky.

The changes, sudden, kaleidoscopic, were a shock to my system. Saying good-bye to mother, father, brother, sister, kissing Alix farewell, wishing she wouldn't cry, knowing she would. Mustering among the cool green trees with all the other frightened young recruits. Staring, horrified, at the master sergeant's scarred and angular face, at the angry glint in her cold blue eyes.

I remember wondering, briefly, timidly, if once, somewhere, there'd been a man who'd loved this hard, compassionless woman. Was this what Alix would've become if she'd passed the examinations? I didn't know.

We'd gone by train to an old airfield, where we'd boarded a battered and ancient cargo plane, an electric jet manufactured some time in the latter part of the twenty-first century, lifting above the cool, green forest, turning west over low, eroded mountains, passing over the crushed remains of cities, over a Mississippi swollen by floods, past a smoking, cratered desert . . .

The California Megalopolis looked like a vast toy city flattened by some careless giant's lawnrolling tool.

Then we were in Australia, in a featureless world of red and tan. Sun blazing overhead as we toiled over lifeless sandstone landscape. Hardy young men and women reduced to crawling, begging to go home. Our numbers dwindled quickly, the master sergeant and her comrades pitiless, without mercy.

One of my newfound friends, a British recruit who died later, out among the stars, called her "La Belle Dame." I was not yet literate enough to get the reference. The day came when we were no longer recruits, when we pinned on our troopers' badges, proud and strong, when we shipped out for what they called "Advanced Training."

Airless Mars proved to be an easy place to die, I and my comrades in vacuum suits of an advanced and unfamiliar design, toiling under a small, harsh sun set in a dull pink sky that blackened toward zenith, toiling through an unforgiving red desert that was, now, truly lifeless. And our numbers dwindled more, dwindled as I began to have dreams, dreams that disturbed my precious sleep, sleep filled with fiery nightmares, sleep filled with dreams of longing, dreams colored in subtle shades of blue and green.

One night I awoke, crying in my sleep, to find myself in the master sergeant's arms. Cradled. Like a child. Her hand smoothing the sweat from my brow. After a while I went back to sleep. I was alone in the morning, La Belle Dame as merciless as ever, and supposed it was all part of the dream.

And the longing for greenery was answered in a way that turned my memories of home sour. If the Earth is green, Alpha Centauri A-IV is greener. Very much like the Earth, though, like the Earth with its volume turned all the way up, like the Earth with its bass controls at full-throated cry. Forests of teal and gold, full of creatures from some Cretaceous nightmare, where we finished our work of preparation. And our numbers dwindled further.

When it was over, there were five left from our company's original two dozen. The master sergeant kissed us all, handed us our orders, and smiled. We went out to our newly formed legions, to wars that made us forget how hard that deadly training had been. Hard? Deadly? We didn't know the meaning of those words. Not yet.

As the sky darkened overhead, shadows lengthening and merging around us, Lank drove his car up a gentle rise, the two small mountains flanking Bolin Creek, surmounted by two isolated buildings, outlined against the sky. Atop Mount Bolus, to the north, something that looked like a small, flat mosque, golden domes catching the last rays of the sun. Facing it, slightly higher, atop Chapel Hill itself, was outlined the familiar hard black architecture of the local Master's compound. Everything else was hidden among the trees.

I guess I expected us to go on up Franklin Street, which would've led right by the compound, but it seemed to be choked with saplings, a forest of thin spruce, the pavement long ago torn up and gone. Instead, Lank turned at what had once been the corner of Estes, onto a rutted and muddy lane that looked like it saw a great deal of use. There were people walking here now, people looking at us curiously. At me? Maybe. Once or twice, Lank waved to someone who waved back.

In my day, no one had lived on this low, swampy ground. It was just where the sewer lines ran, Chapel Hillians preferring to live along the high, breezy ridgelines. "What's down here?"

Lank looked over at me, puzzled, then shrugged. "The bustee, Ath. The Master put its bluehouse down here and this is where we've all come to live."

Bustee. That was the word Spahis used for any sort of native village. I said, "You live down here?"

He shook his head. "I've got a cell at the monastery." He gestured vaguely, up toward the mosquelike thing on Mount Bolus.

Everyone else, though . . . "How many?"

"About fifteen hundred."

When I was a boy, the population of Chapel Hill was nearer one hundred thousand. The stars were coming out overhead now as the sky turned full black, and I could begin to smell the effluvia of human habitation, not so very different from the smells I associated with bustees across the galaxy.

4 FULL DARKNESS FALLEN, THE SKY BLACK
and starry overhead, blotted here and there
by wisps of opaque cloud, we pulled
through the unpaved streets of the bustee,
tires bouncing over rutted lanes made of
dried mud. After the autumn rains, this place must be pleasant
indeed.

Down by Bolin Creek, the houses were black humps rising
up from the ground, mostly dark, flickery red-orange light shining through the occasional open window. They must still have
screens. Midges down here. Mosquitoes. It got bad only a year
or so after the Invasion, bugs making a quick comeback when
centuries of suppression technology came to an abrupt end.

There'd been trees down here, brushy vegetation covering
the swampy land by the creek, a paved footpath on the other
side, following the old sewer line. A place to walk your dog,
a shortcut to the commercial complex at the foot of the hill. I
remember playing in these woods as a child with my friends,
getting tangled in sticky webs during Big Spider Season,
picking off ticks that got on us by the dozens.

We always played war, fighting as guerrillas against the
Kkhruhhuft invaders we knew would one day come. Then
they came and conquered, and there were no real guerrillas
to be found. All of us beaten. But we played in those woods
just the same, boys and girls dreaming of an adulthood in

41

which there *would* be guerrillas. Us. The woods were gone now, replaced by ramshackle housing, and trees grew where all our rich, electrified homes had been.

Lank drove the car up a steep hillside toward the looming facade of a house larger than the ones down in the little valley. A house with yellow light spilling from its windows. Over the jouncing creak of the car's frame I could barely make out a distant, rhythmic thudding noise. Generator.

Lank said, "This is where Mom and Dad decided to build the new house, Athy. We're on the back side of the hill where the Vine Vet Center used to be, up on Franklin Street."

I remembered the long curve of the hill, walking down the sidewalk on sunny days, passing the animal hospital with its faint cacophony of barking, its fainter whiff of dogshit. Used to be a joke about the place. On the town map, the one you could download from the national database system, it was listed as Vine Veteran's Hospital, some long-erased clerical software having misinterpreted the abbreviation "Vet." We used to laugh, envisioning its emergency room. Talk about your dogs of war . . .

Lank pulled up in front of the house and clicked off the car, dashboard lights fading all together. "Welcome home, Athy."

I sat and looked up at the building, shadowed and dark other than square windows where electric light spilled into the night. Not a familiar place at all. I stood, stepping down onto the gravel driveway, stretching. And wondering. I felt surprisingly uncomfortable, knowing my parents were in there somewhere waiting to greet me. What would I say to them after twenty years? What would they say to me?

A shadow detached itself from the darkness at the front of the house, where I supposed the door might be, the shadow of a woman walking over to me, resolving into form and figure in the night. A tall, slender, bony-looking woman, straight red-brown hair combed plain around an angular face. She was almost as tall as I, coming close, looking up into my eyes, searching . . .

I whispered, "Oddny?"

She threw herself against me, arms going around the barrel of my chest, face pressing into the side of my neck. "Oh, God, Athol . . ." Almost unbelieving.

I held on to my sister, arms around her, pulling her close, wondering who this woman really was. Not really knowing how to react. Not yet. Memories of her. The dry-eyed young woman who told me good-bye on that last sunny day, who took Alix by the hand and led her away when it was time for me to go. The smart girl, eighteen months my junior, who helped me remember all the things I'd forgotten when school started up again almost two years after the Invasion. My confidante as a teenager, laughing with me about the silly things boys and girls did, trying to be together, not knowing how. My childhood playmate.

A sudden memory of us when we were much younger. I just past eight perhaps, she not quite seven. The two of us playing together under a sheet, bright sunlight lighting up the inside of our little tent with pure, glistening blue-white light. Fooling around, giggling, getting inside each other's clothes, poking at this and that, snickering at our little inspections. I don't think we even wondered what would happen if someone, Mom and Dad maybe, caught us at it. Probably they knew and laughed, remembering those same things from their own childhoods.

Holding her against me now, feeling that woman's body, conscious of her suddenly, suddenly uncomfortable again. And realizing she'd started to cry, hot moisture soaking into my collar. Again, "Oh, God, Athol . . ."

Then the door opened, spilling more electric yellow light, tossing the shelter of darkness aside, and all the others came tumbling out, glad cries, calling my name. Welcome home, they said. Brother, son, friend, dearest Athol Morrison. And me, wondering, *Who are these people?*

They led me inside, all talking at once, then silent, then all talking again, to a room flooded by bright electric lights, crystal-based lamps I remembered so well, from so long ago, to a room with a long, low walnut table, the table my great-grandmother had given my parents as a wedding present a half century ago. There was food arrayed on the table, familiar-smelling food, waiting to be eaten. Waiting, some small part of me realized, evoking a faint shiver of horror, for me.

Maybe I should've come unannounced. Come to them as a night-wandering stranger. Hello, Mother. It's your son Athol, come home at last . . .

Silly things of childhood flooding me now. As if I'd never been away. Yet knew that I had. Packing the cold starship soldier away, into a very tiny corner indeed.

My father looked much as he had those twenty long years ago. Tall, sturdy, handsome. But . . . Hair thinner, much grayed. Lines in his face that hadn't been there. Fat around the middle that no one had when I was young, when the world was real.

And my mother. Thin, gray, waxy-featured. Old. The two of them like grandparents from some old novel . . .

A tiny voice inside: they aren't even eighty yet. They shouldn't even be middle-aged in a world where men and women can live into their twelfth decade. And yet. Mother and Father looking old. Lank and Oddny looking middle-aged . . .

Right. *You* know. Perhaps they won't say anything. Maybe they won't even notice, because you're so tall and strong, battle scars worn like badges of service, though the medics could wipe them away in an instant. Maybe they just won't notice.

That look in Father's eye though. Doubt? Fear? His mouth opening, serious, about to speak . . .

But my mother burst into tears and threw her arms around me, breaking the tension of the moment, sobbing, telling me how much she'd missed me, how much she feared, when I never wrote home. How she'd felt when the mothers of the other boys and girls who'd gone away with me told her . . . How she'd felt when young Tommy Watkins's casket arrived home on the monorail, gunmetal gray plastic, filled with remains so disfigured nobody could be sure who it was.

I remembered him dying, the only home boy in my regiment, something between us that passed for friendship. Tommy was a happy lad, lucky and careless. Luck always

runs out. Caution is something you can control, can manu-
facture anew every day.

It took us a long while to get him out from under the granite cliff face he'd brought down on himself and three other
troopers, after wiring the land mine incorrectly.

I remember packing what was left of him into his coffin
for shipment home, standing there, staring down at something that looked like a cross between a roadkill and a huge,
gravel-invaded scab, splinters of bone, white teeth poking
out here and there, through a torn, hairy hide. Good-bye,
Tommy Watkins, I'd whispered to myself. You should've
been more damned careful.

You make friends among the troopers. You can't help it. I
learned to be closest with men and women who seemed
likely to take care of themselves, to distance myself from the
happy-go-lucky. You don't want to get caught up in someone else's fatal mistake.

And so, here and now, they gathered round, and hugged
me and kissed me, and cried over me, as we all sat down,
and killed the fatted calf.

Welcome home.

But that shadowed look in my mother's eye. Horror?
Maybe it's only the scars I told myself.

Then, later, they laid me down to sleep, leading me to my
own little room, high in the back of the house, with a window that looked over the brow of the hill into the old city. It
was black out there now, no lights, only stars and the shadows of trees. But they smiled at me, closed the door, and left
me alone. I stood in my resurrected room like a hulking
ghost, surrounded by artifacts long forgotten.

Sports posters from Chapel Hill High School, from the
days right before the Invasion, when it was the place I'd be
going in *just a few years now*. A place where a big, strong,
fast-growing boy like me could be feared and admired.

On the wall at the foot of the bed was a life-size image of
a movie star I'd used as a masturbation icon when I was
fourteen, misty 3-D technology making her breasts and
rounded hip stand out from the wall as you walked in front

of her. I couldn't remember her name, just that my parents
had been angry when I traded my best hunting knife for this
piece of trash. My father telling me I'd be sorry when the
batteries ran out. How hard it would be, what with the Invasion and all, to get new ones.

By the time they'd run out I'd already met Alix, whose
real flesh looked better to me than the synthetic movie star,
whose breasts and hips I could actually *touch* . . .

My couchlike bed, already a little too short when I left. Probably now too fragile for the hundred-kilo behemoth who'd
come back to visit. I sat down and listened to the soft creak of
suspensor springs. The old technology held its own. I sat, staring up at the nameless goddess of my childhood fantasies, remembering the minutes I'd spent with her, from time to time.

Fresh, misty skin, almost looking damp. Just as it always
had.

I wonder where they found fresh batteries, to make her
live again?

I wonder why they thought I'd want her back?

Opposite the bed, my small rack of books, spines out, ti-
tles waiting for me to read them. Arranged, the way I'd
liked, not by author, but by the chronological order of my
reading them. Childhood books, from Johanna Spyri and
G.A. Henty and Calvin Soderblom, to adolescent books,
early and late, Edgar Rice Burroughs, Martha ten Darien.
The one or two truly adult books I'd just begun reading in
late high school gathering dust down one end.

I reached out and pulled one of the Burroughs volumes, one
whose title caught my eye, looking at the cover. *At the Earth's
Core*. I gave the book a gentle squeeze and the bulging breasts
of the almost-naked cave girl turned my way, delicate-boned
Victorian face turning up toward me, eyes pleading. Another
gentle squeeze and the story began. David Innes and Abner
Perry. Mechanical mole. Pellucidar, Mahars and Sagoths. Dian
the Beautiful and Hooja the Sly One. Ja the Mezop.

I squeezed the book off and put it away. Sat staring. I must
have remembered why the Sirkar police might be called
sagoths. And remembrance, however deeply buried, had
guided my hand to that particular book.

The mind works in . . . not mysterious ways, no, merely hidden ways, our brains a collection of quasi-independent hardware devices, working together, communicating down the long chains of the white-matter data bus, our consciousness only aggregate illusion, the vector sum of all that the little mind-entities do.

We are not real.

No more real than the poppits who made the Masters, who came to rule over us all. No more real than the Masters themselves.

Hard for people to believe, when the truth came out. Master Race made inadvertently by, what? Bugs? Not quite, these carnivorous little froglets, but close enough. Evolution acting on them across a billion years. As the bugs buil.' nests and the nests call forth tools and the tools call forth bigger tools, until the tools themselves need intelligence to guide their own way.

Hard to imagine.

It was easier for us to want to believe that, some time in the far past, an intelligent species just like ourselves had built the Masters as slaves, that the slaves had rebelled and killed their own masters. Saberhagen called them Berserkers. Shelley called them, it, merely the Monster.

But the universe itself called forth the Master Race, made a tool to rule over the toolmakers. A fitting God to judge our sins.

After a while I got undressed and turned out the light, lay down on my little bed and lay looking up at the pale, luminous flesh of my goddess. She was in her modest pose now, one knee drawn up and over, hiding the space between her legs with a smooth expanse of haunch, hands cupped under her breasts, lifting them slightly.

I think the boy who sold me the poster didn't even know what she could do. He'd've asked a higher price if he'd known. I reached out and touched the image with one extended toe, telling her to dance.

And fire sparkled in her eyes, demure smile widening into a lascivious grin, leg sweeping away to show her vulva, one knee lifting up, inviting, hands reaching downward . . .

Even now, after ten thousand burdar nights, it had the power to arouse me.

5 IN THE MORNING, BRILLIANT YELLOW SUN-
shine flooded the tangled vegetation outside my window, splashing over the trees,
not quite coming inside, leaving the room
in shadow. The goddess, long ago finished
with her tawdry little masturbation show, was back in her demure pose, one knee crossed over, smiling down from the
wall like some kind of innocent angel.

I got up, fishing my robe out of the suitcase, and wondered
how to proceed. Still that reluctance in me, connectivity with
that long-dead past trying to reestablish itself. No shower attached to my room, or even a lavatory, like the one I'd had
when I was a boy. I remember when the water supply failed,
how much I mourned that old toilet's loss, especially as I
walked through night to the outhouse my father and I had
dug, putting on boots so I could walk through shallow North
Carolina snow.

There was a shower room down the hall, tepid, mineral-
tasting water that gushed briefly at the pull of a chain. Rainwater, I thought. From a solar cistern. It had the mark of my
father's cleverness. And I remembered the toy maglev train
sets we'd put together when I was a child, spiraling and
looping around the living room, driven by that same cleverness, a cleverness threatening to make me no more than a
spectator with my own toys.

Downstairs, my mother, suddenly shy, fed us breakfast, cooking eggy French toast over a propane stove, serving it with sweet, soft butter and a thick, pale, reddish concoction that tasted like cane syrup. If I were remembering right. The burdars always had maple for my breakfast, container stamped with the glyph of a New Hampshire estate. Another memory: my mother angry as she cooked over a woodstove my father made for her. Angry, muttering, When did this become women's work?

I can't quite remember the career she had before the Invasion. Lawyer? I'll have to ask sometime.

Afterward, my father led me outside, reminding me I'd have to register with the local police. I nodded, looking into his face, at his serious expression. Nodded and said, "Of course. The Master will be wanting to see me as well." That brought a small doubtful look, quickly faded. Or suppressed.

We walked together in hot morning sunshine, light casting our shadows on the rutted, muddy lane, mud dried to a hard crust by the late-summer drought. About now, Jordan Lake, if it still existed, would be rimmed by a wide beach of hard mud and sand, places to picnic, to sit with binoculars and watch the herons and egrets, try to spy one of the rare eagles, a hawk or two, or merely lie back and watch the shallow vee shapes of vultures drifting on the wind. I'd heard an eagle's cry once when I was a boy, an ugly gargle of rage, hardly the noble scream of myth.

My father looked up at me as we walked, and, finally, said, "You seem changed, Athy." I looked down at him, and he laughed uneasily. "Oh, I know, twenty years, but . . ." He shrugged. "Hell, you're even *taller* than you were. I thought you'd gotten your full growth."

I nodded. "Stress, I think, during the early phases of training. Stimulation to bone ends maybe."

Overhead, sunlight was streaming through the taller trees, slender, scaly pines of some sort, their tops bending, swaying slowly back and forth in the wind, little nodding circles against the backdrop of the sky. I could feel the black hair on my head heating up as it stored energy from the light's infrared component. On the habitable planets of some low-K stars where I'd been, that effect is more pronounced. Planets where you can lie naked in the sun, baking the tarnish off your soul, and not have to worry about ultraviolet burn.

"It's not just that, Athy . . ." He stopped, turning to look up at me, eyes searching. "Something in the stillness of your face. The depths of your eyes . . ."

Or maybe depthlessness, that silver mirror turned out to the world, eyes of one-way glass, always looking out, never in. When you kill a being, man or beast, you don't want them looking in through your eyes. Each one that does takes a little bit of your soul away, wherever he goes. Silly nonsense, of course. Just the way it feels. Eyes, looking up at you, pleading, full of sorrow, then the knife goes in and the eyes go away.

I said, "I've been away for twenty years, Dad. We can hardly know one another now. In time . . ."

I think it made him feel better, being called Dad, an after-echo of the boy who'd gone away. He said, "How long will you be staying? You didn't say in the telegram."

"Six weeks."

A sigh of pleasure, and we resumed walking, up the rutted road between the small wooden houses of the bustee. Villagers were up and about now, looking incongruous in their bright, almost-indestructible technofabrics, in a setting that seemed to call for peasants in burlap. Men and women nodded to him as we passed, people touching their caps, or looking down at the ground. Many more of them stealing furtive glances at me. Man in a dull green uniform, gun on his hip. Not a sagoth, though. Unfamiliar. Different.

I said, "What do you do these days?" When I was a boy he'd been some kind of engineer, working for a university think tank. Designing weapons of war. I remember being excited by that. Proud.

He stopped again, looking up at me. An odd look on his face. Diffidence, compounded by something a little like reluctant embarrassment. "Ah. I'm the, uh, Sirkar's agent for Chapel Hill. The, uh, mayor, I guess you'd call it."

Look around you, then. That rutted lane, those handmade houses, these shadow-faced people. After the Invasion, we

were still ourselves, beaten but proud. These folk . . . beaten
by the Kkhruhhuft, subjugated by the Master Race, policed
by Saanaae and sagoth . . . beaten down by each other.

I knew the old world, but I grew up afterward, during a
time when the future was unknown and unknowable. It was,
almost, an exciting time. The unthinkable had already happened; what could possibly come next? A boy, growing up
now, would see his future narrowed and then narrowed
again. What could any of them hope for? Would a boy really
look forward to being a laborer on a collective farm? Would
a girl lie awake nights in her warm and cozy bed, dreaming
of being such a laborer's wife?

The luckiest ones would have real jobs, jobs like the ones
their parents and grandparents had known. Working for the
Sirkar, joining the sagoths, managing the estates for Masters
whose presence was, at best, merely a shadow. The sturdiest
might still think of going out to the stars. Of becoming contract workers on some faraway world under an unknown sun.
Of becoming colonists, perhaps, going out to tame a new
world for the glory of the Master Race.

And the brave, the strong might even dream of becoming
soldiers out on the alien main.

In a little while, no one would worry about the moral implications of collaboration with the conqueror. No one would
have qualms about becoming the Sirkar's agent for their
local bustee. Mayor.

My father and I walked on together, silent.

A little way beyond the bustee, covering what had been
flat, marshy ground on the north side of Bolin Creek, we
passed by the local bluehouse. It was a broad, low, streamlined structure of maybe fifty hectares extent, with window-
less, black-enameled walls, roofed over by faceted panels of
upward stepglass, glinting hard blue-violet in the sun.

We crossed a little footbridge there, obviously intending to
make our way along the far bank of the creek. That's where
the police station had been before the Invasion. No reason to
move it, I guess.

My father nodded at the bluehouse's main airlock door,
where there was a small booth, a couple of sagoths in atten-

dance, and said, "We had a hard time getting that built, started on it just a year or so after you left. The Saanaae, um, executed my predecessor when he couldn't get it done on time. You remember Mr. Itakë?"

"Davy's dad?"

A nod.

I'd played football with Davy in late high school, one of a few post-Invasion teams that managed to get together hereabouts, playing in the day, on weekends, because we couldn't run the field lights any longer. I tried to summon a memory of his father, couldn't quite manage it. A smallish, pale Oriental man, balding perhaps, with just a little gray in his hair.

My father said, "I didn't really want the job after that, but . . . Mike'd asked me to do the engineering for him at the outset. I refused and . . . I felt a little responsible. For his death, I mean. You know?" Almost a pleading look.

I nodded.

We were stopped now, almost in the shadow of those featureless walls, and he said, "I don't like going in there."

I've been in bluehouses on a hundred worlds. They're all the same. I walked up the path toward the airlock and stopped by the sagoth kiosk. The high-ranker, a beefy, redheaded man with sergeant's stripes on his sleeve, stepped out into the sun, squinting. "Morning, Mayor," he said, then looked at me with a mixture of interest and suspicion. Like, I thought, a policeman. And keenly, yet unobtrusively conscious of my sidearm.

I read the name tag on his blouse. "You Marsh Donovan?"

The suspicion deepened and his attention focused sharply. Someone, at least, was doing a good job training the local thugs. He'd been a good ballplayer though. Maybe it was all his own doing. Talent.

I held out my hand and smiled. "You remember me? Athol Morrison."

A shock of recognition crossed his face, followed by delight. "Son of a bitch!" He was holding my hand in both of his, pumping, grinning. "Hell, I *heard* you were coming home. How the hell have you been?" The other two men in the kiosk were coming forward, looking at me. They were younger men, had probably been small children when I went away.

There was a sudden, sharp scraping sound from the building and a blue light over the airlock door flickered in a quick pattern. Marsh and his sagoths turned away, reaching into their breast pockets and putting on pairs of red-lensed, cardboard-framed sunglasses. My father tapped my shoulder and looked away.

I squinted and kept looking.

When the door opened, hard, glary light flooded out, along with a gust of methane-enriched air. I suppose they have to be careful with bluehouses, what with the danger of explosion, but then the technology may have had a hundred million years to evolve. Men in the doorway, all of them dark, some of them naturally so, others tanned almost black under Caucasian body hair. Men covered with sweat, bent under burdens, mostly big plastic sacks. All of them naked, hair matted and wet, muscles bulging, showing how well fed they were. Well fueled.

They stood still, waiting, until another man, sleeker, but still well muscled, dressed in shorts, carrying a metal rod, stepped through their ranks. Sleeker? No. Not a man after all, but a woman with the physique of a body builder, her breasts small, hard-looking knobs of tissue tucked against a wall of solid muscle. She had a whistle on a chain around her neck, a pair of red glasses perched on her nose, and a poppit on top of her head, sprawled, gripping with its eight legs, circle of eyes and little red mouth facing forward. You could see it was panting lazily, almost asleep.

She stepped up to the kiosk, sweat beading on her nipples, trickling down across the ridged muscle of her stomach, soaking into the wet waistband of her shorts. "Hey, Marsh. My shirt out here somewhere?"

He grinned and fished a white halter top, barely a scrap of cloth, out from under the kiosk's counter. "Hey, Sadie. Still here."

She shook it out, holding it at arm's length, making no move to put it on, mopping at her sweaty neck with one hand. "Fuck, it's *hot* in there today!" In the airlock door, the dark men were standing still, swaying a little bit as their muscles shifted under the weight of their burdens, eyes squeezed almost shut. Waiting.

Sadie looked at me, at my father, and said, "Hey, Mayor." A slight nod, then she turned away, dismissing us as irrelevant to her world. She blew twice on the whistle, two shrill blasts, and the men in the airlock started tramping forward, bare feet thudding on the walkway as she led them across the bridge and back through the bustee.

Marsh and my father watched her go, both of them obviously interested in what they saw. Finally, Marsh said, "You remember Sadie Miller?"

I did. She must have been about ten years old when I left, a thin, violent little girl. But for the Invasion, she probably would've been in hypertherapy.

My father said, "That's a tough job. We do have some trouble getting people to stick with it."

I said, "I'd like to see your bailiwick, Marsh," gesturing at the open bluehouse door.

He glanced at my father, face impassive, then said, "Sure, Athy." He fished a couple of pairs of red cardboard glasses from a kiosk drawer and handed them over. "Take as long as you want. Maybe we'll have a beer sometime, huh?"

"Sure, whenever you want. I'll be here for a few weeks."

Glasses on and through the airlock, we went to another world, standing beside the inner airlock door, waiting for our eyes to adapt. Even with the red glasses it was a little hard, ultraviolet light falling from the stepglass, tingling on our skins, leaking around the edges of the cardboard. Whenever I looked up at the ceiling, I could feel a little stab of pain as my irises tried to adjust and failed. Internal conflict. Dim light, powerful glare.

It was like a swamp in here, shallow, scummy water on the mud floor, mud presumably contaminated with alien microorganisms. Black vegetation, looping black vines, little blue bugs everywhere. Poppits crawling in the undergrowth, slopping in the water, hanging from the vines . . .

Right at home.

My skin had really started to prickle now, superficial flora and fauna being eradicated by the heavy UV. Whatever was living here wouldn't move in though. I was too alien an environment.

There were people all over the place, most of them heavily built men, but women too, here and there, grubbing in the muck, dragging bundles of vegetation here and there. All of them sturdy-looking, healthy, sweating uselessly against a dank heat that made the air seem hazy, haze exacerbated by the ultraviolet light.

Humans make better bluehouse slaves than the Boromilithi ever did, poor little bastards regarding it as a death sentence.

There was a soft lowing in the distance, as of cows, and I heard my father whisper something under his breath. All right, I knew that sound too. I shaded my eyes with my hand, squinting into the haze, walking forward, feet splashing in the watery mud, little sucking sounds whenever I stepped on a particularly thick patch.

The general human slang term for them is *aphids*. Human-sized bipeds with fat, stumpy tails, covered all over with iridescent blue scales, dog-muzzle faces dominated by small, brilliant, featureless red eyes. Humanoid bipeds that moo like cows.

There was a small herd of them here, a couple of dozen individuals, probably a lot more on the other side of the haze, little clusters dotted around this low cavern of a building. There were humans with them, humans carrying little wooden rods, poking them, prodding. The aphids were walking through knee-deep black grassy stuff, plucking shiny, iron-colored flowers, eating them, munching contentedly, burping, farting. They are, I think, responsible for the air's high methane content.

Off to one side, some people had two of the aphids caught between them, holding them tight, though they didn't struggle. A fertile female, her belly-cloaca bulging, gleaming metallic blue in the light, a fertile male, his own cloaca everted like fat, pouting lips. The humans held them by the arms and pressed them together, face-to-face, belly to belly.

The human supervisor, rod of steel tucked under one arm, was watching the operation, laughing.

The female's eyes suddenly bugged out, her mouth working in a gaping grimace, and the male let out a low bellow of a moo. A little silvery goo started oozing away from the joined cloacas.

Scrape, *grind*-CHUG.

A signal from the bluehouse's PA system. The main herd of aphids suddenly stood up straight, alert, forage forgotten, suddenly huddling closer together. The mating pair clutched at each other, struggling, and pulled apart with an ugly sucking noise.

I heard my father whisper, "Jesus." He was trying to edge away, back toward the airlock door.

Since they already had him, the humans grabbed the fat bull, who bucked hard, trying to pull away. Useless. A long, hopeless-sounding moo. Reading too much into that, I know, but that was how it sounded. How it always sounds.

They dragged him to a clear space and pushed him facedown in the muddy water, right down on his still-gaping cloaca, silvery stuff mixing with the silt, one man sitting on his shoulders, others holding down arms, pulling legs apart, leaving the thick tail stretched out on the ground.

You're lucky this time, aphid.

There were other cow screams from beyond the mist, marking where other aphids were being held down. Some of them would not be so lucky. Feeding time at the bluehouse.

Poppits coming down out of the trees now, rustling through the underbrush, crawling out into the wet clear spaces, gathering at their aphids. Red eyes gleaming. Toothy little mouths agape. They wouldn't eat much.

When the first poppit snapped a tiny mouthful from its tail, the bull aphid bucked hard, screaming, almost tossing the man from his shoulders. Another bite, another. Another. A dozen bites, a hundred. The aphid screamed. Struggled. Moaned. Only shivered. Lay still, crying softly. In a few minutes its tail was gone.

You'd think, over time, evolution would do away with the tail nerves. It hasn't.

You'd think maybe the Masters would breed a numb-tailed species of aphid. They haven't.

No answers. Only pointless questions.

Sometimes, they eat the whole aphid, more or less, stripping the muscles from arms and legs and back and chest, leaving a skeleton enclosing a bag of still-living vital organs. The aphids don't bleed much and it takes them a while to die, lying in the mud, mewing softly to themselves.

I looked down at my father and saw him looking up at me. Doubt in his eyes. A question. I turned away and walked toward the airlock door. In the background, I could hear the aphid crying. But its tail would soon grow back.

Shortly before noon we walked up the long hill of Airport Road toward the center of the old town, toward the Master's house. This part of the city was already in ruins when I was in my teens, old brick buildings crumbling away, withering before the Kkhruhhuft guns. We didn't even know who was fighting them as we cowered in our basements. Maybe no one. Kkhruhhuft just firing on the buildings to get them out of the way.

Not wanton destruction. Never wanton destruction, which was more a Saanaae trait, or a human one, than Kkhruhhuft. But the purpose can have been small. Get this mess out of here. We need the flat ground.

It was fun to play here during the years right after the Invasion. Mysterious rubble, sometimes still giving off wisps of smoke, emitting odd little stinks. And amazing things as well. Not just all the old stores, little boutiques and whatnot, but the things in the elusive, never-visited upper floors as well.

I remember Marsh and Davy and I poking around in the rubble of Geary Hamilton's health salon and fitness spa, looking to see if we could rescue any of the old exercise equipment, maybe set it up in the high school gym. Most of it was twisted to pieces because the upper floors had come down on the lower, squashing all that gleaming hardware.

The remains of the upper floor seemed to be a mess of broken ceramic whirlpool tubs and an inordinate number of rain-soaked, mold-fuzzed beds. Odd to contemplate, the three of us standing there on a cool, cloudy day, the sky a swirl of low, lumpy gray overhead, almost like smoke.

I remember Marsh standing there with a huge, studded, Caucasian-colored vibrator in one hand, scratching his head, perplexed, *What the fuck d'you suppose this is . . .*

And Davy bellowing with laughter, turning away, tears rolling down his face. *You dumb fuck, Marsh . . .*

I think we already knew what we were looking at, though it still didn't connect. Vibrators. Leather harnesses. Tub toys. The ruined torso of what appeared to be a sex-android. Well, gyndroid, anyway. I think all three of us wanted to get down and take a close look at that torn plastic crotch, but we inhibited each other.

There were some books there too. Expensive ones, waterproof, indestructible, batteries still good, that we picked up, kind of turning away from each other so we could take a look. Just what we thought. Expensive, high-grade porn. Porn for every taste, and the first one I picked up was a dreadful male homosexual thing, two powerfully muscled, bronze-blond surfer-bodybuilder types going at each other, all blood and excrement. The next one was two women, and obviously aimed at a male viewer, rather than at lesbians, the women carefully exposing each other to the camera.

"Fuck!" That was from Davy, and it did seem like an appropriate word to be using just now. What he'd found, however, was the house roster, nude, posed pictures of an assortment of local men and women, many of whom we knew. An unholy fascination, clicking through the pages, seeing the intimate parts of . . . well . . . the mothers of people we knew. And some girls we knew from high school. And boys.

Maybe a big fear growing, that we'd find our own mothers-sisters-brothers-friends in here. On the *menu*, as it were.

"Christ." Awe in Davy's hushed tone. Geary Hamilton himself, looking like a faggot's dream. And his wife Jeanine. And his daughters Jenny and Lisa. Girls our own age.

I'd taken Lisa Hamilton out on a date once. She seemed cheerful enough, but not much interested in fooling around.

It'd been a twelve-year-old's sort of date anyway. Hard to imagine this slim, childlike, barely pubescent little Lisa playing an adult's game.

Then we found the guest book, lying inside a burst-open metal safe, itself a relic from a century or more ago. No pictures here, just names and bank account numbers. My father was on the list, and Marsh's. Davy seemed pleased there was no Mike Itakë in the database.

Hard to visualize my father fucking Lisa Hamilton.

I used to hate that memory so. Used to avoid thinking about it. But twenty years in the service of the Master Race and . . . it speaks of a kinship with my father. My father and his friends, who were the dark reality underlying the bright dreams of memory.

Now, the town was bulldozed away, the top of the Hill, where they'd started building UNC, back in the 1790s, scraped flat and featureless, a level plain of crushed and angular gray gravel. Down in the woods, down in all directions, you could still see ruins among the trees and underbrush. Old East right there, I supposed, over there Davis Library. In less than a century, what little remained would be gone, nothing left but loose bricks hiding in the leaf mold.

And, in the center of the featureless plain, the Master's castle. Shiny, angular walls, black ceramic, like the insides of some Satanic designer's bathtub. No windows. No antennae. No battlements. Sloping, hard walls, catching the light of the sun, reflecting a dark image of forest and ruin and faraway sky.

My father said, "They say this stuff is an ultraviolet mirror, that the landscape all around here is lit up by UV. Anyway, after they built it, we had a little trouble with swarming honeybees."

I looked around. The air was clear of bugs, even the sort you expected everywhere in this climate, in the summer. "Probably all gone now."

He nodded. "Beekeepers all moved away, back out into the countryside."

There was a soft rustling in the underbrush nearby. A lone poppit, staring out at us, blue hide covered with a dusting of fresh red earth, poppit holding some kind of little tool in its forelimbs. Where there's one poppit . . .

The ground under here had to be riddled with poppit tunnels, as on a thousand worlds where I'd been, on a million worlds I'd never seen. Maybe that's the way poppits live at home. I don't know. They say the poppit's world has to be a low, swampy place, a land like the inside of a bluehouse, black and gleaming forests festooned with vines, aphids, poppit nests. Maybe the Masters just decided, one day, that they'd figured out a better way for the poppits to live. Maybe, once upon a time, they'd run across something like ants somewhere, had recognized kinship.

Ants. Bees. Wasps. Some kinds of eusocial moles. Even wolves and dogs, when you thought about it . . .

If you thought about it at all.

There were a pair of Saanaae guards flanking the gateway, big green centaurs holding their rifles diagonally across their upper torso chests, faces impassive, metallic eyes the only movement, rolling to watch us as we approached.

No sign of vocal encoders on either one. I turned to the Saanaa whose collar-brooch indicated the higher rank, a female, ovipositor just visible through the folds of her cloak, and said, "I suppose you speak English."

She nodded. "We're stationed here permanently, Jemadar-Major." Her accent was thick, guttural, with a bit of fluidity, as if she were about to spit, but the Saanaae vocal mechanism is better than ours, very adaptable.

Stationed permanently on Earth, though. I hadn't heard that before. "Not a punishment detail, surely."

She glanced at my father, who abruptly turned and took a few steps backward, more or less out of earshot. "Not quite. After the Insurrection, when our internment was ended, we were shipped here. Permanent police garrison duty."

I glanced over at my father. Surely this wasn't a secret. Hell, maybe they just didn't like him. He didn't seem to like them much, either. I said, "I suppose I'm not surprised. You're lucky the Masters didn't decide to make you all slave labor."

There was an expression on the Saanaa's face, unreadable. "I don't see any difference."

I tapped the gun. "You would."

A hissing sigh, Saanaae laughter. The building chirped slightly, a peremptory sound, and the Saanaa said, "The Master is waiting. You'd better go in."

I beckoned to my father as the gateway slid open, familiar dim and glary light spilling out. The Saanaa said, "They'll have glasses for you inside, if you want." I squinted and went in.

We waited, finally, in a vast black concourse, breathing air scented with the moist metallic smell of poppits. A smell like the taste of iron on your tongue. A hint of sulfur. And you could hear them rustling in the distance, a deep layering of tiny echoes, piled one upon the other, to an insensible depth. Not merely noise though, but an abyss of sound filled with infinite detail.

A door in the far wall of the black chamber irised open and poppits spilled in, a gleaming black tide of them, scaly skins recolored to shimmer in the UV heavy light, a tall, slim, black-robed man walking among them.

Like some medieval priest or evil magician-prince walking on a carpet of rats. The poppits' feet tapped on the slick floor like a million drumming fingertips.

When I glanced at my father I could see him seeming to shrink from the approaching flood. His eyes were slitted, squinting into the light, too hooded to read, but . . . People haven't adapted, I thought. It's only been thirty years. Sirkar's agent. Sagoths. Serfs and slaves. Just making their way in a new world, different, and yet strangely familiar. Except for this.

And not one of them has seen the things I've seen.

The poppits swarmed all around us now, eyes reflecting the light, looking red-black, and it was easy to imagine you could hear them breathing through those open, toothy little mouths. You have to wonder, sometimes, just how the poppits *feel.* Individual poppits do seem quite bright at times.

Not like cats or dogs, but brighter than bugs. Brighter than frogs, maybe. Almost as smart as mice.

The robed figure standing before us swept back his cowl, revealing a dark face lit up purple by the UV, broad-nosed, with a short nap of dense, woolly hair, scalp gleaming between tight cornrows. No one I recognized, a man about my own age. He nodded to my father, "Agent Morrison." Not Mayor, then. My father nodded back, silent.

The man held out his hand. "My Master's greeting, Jemadar-Major. I'm Jon Hendricks, majordomo for the Estate. Welcome home, sir."

I gripped the hand gently, feeling fragile bones, delicate, uncallused skin. "Thanks."

A moment of silence, my father's soft breathing audible over the poppit-rustle, then the majordomo said, "We downloaded your service record. The Master was impressed. He's waiting to see you now."

Me? He? All this air of mystery, under dark, UV light. My father's obvious fear, his reluctance to be here. They wouldn't know how human it was. Saanaae wouldn't tell them either, humanlike as they were. Poppits couldn't do this. Masters don't care.

I started to step forward, toward the still-open door, but the majordomo raised one hand, pointing at my right hip. "You'll have to leave your sidearm, Jemadar-Major." He held out his hand, palm up. "In fact, it's been decided it would be better if you left your weapon here for the duration of your stay."

I stood still, looking at him. After a while, his eyes turned aside from my face, a quick, nervous glance at my father, whose eyes had suddenly lost their squint, despite the dim glare. "Who decided?"

Another hesitation. "Well, the Master . . . I mean . . ."

"Nonsense."

He stiffened, trying to glare at me, drawing himself to a full height that was still a little less than eye level with me. "Rules and regulations state that only Sirkar Police go armed."

"Saanaae would find that pretty amusing." I unholstered

the gun, turning it in my hand so that it was butt-out, and saw him start to lift his own hand, a little surprised, but prepared to accept his victory. "Look, you're a local, Majordomo. Here to serve this one lone Master. Trained at Sector General, maybe." A quick look in his eyes, reading what was there. "If you've been out-system at all, that is. I know your type, I know how far your authority runs."

"But . . ." Puffing up now, with anger.

I tossed my weapon aside gently, letting it fall among the poppits. They skidded out of the way, let it bounce once, a clank-thud that neither damaged the gun nor scarred the floor, then two of them got in its path, kept it from sliding. Other poppits made a little circle, taking up their positions, going motionless, not even drumming their little feet.

"I'll pick it up when I leave," I said. "You can stay here and act menacing for the mayor. I'll be right back." I walked toward the open door on the far side of the room, and wondered what they would talk about in my absence.

Then I was walking down a long, dark hallway, listening to the echoes of my footsteps, steady, measured, hollow, hard leather on glassy ceramic, wondering how it could happen here. Here, as there, as everywhere. The natives step forward in defeat and take command, take control of the lowest levels of the Masters' empire, feet on each other's necks, eyes gleaming with avarice . . .

Why the hell am I here? I could've done this from anywhere, just pulled out my phone and . . . Hell. *Maybe I just wanted to see.* People. The way a kicked cat angrily claws the whimpering pet dog. Like whipped dogs biting each other. Like the beaten bully, trouncing his lesser victims.

The slave Kkhruhhuft, so proud of us, because we almost beat them. Saanaae centaurs with their guns, standing guard on the pitiful human homeworld, while, out there . . .

Once upon a time, in an arm of the galaxy not so far from here, there was an empire among the stars, proud green men in their proud green pseudo-starships, setting down on alien worlds, weapons of power suppressing the natives, making them into slaves. In time, it was an empire of a thousand worlds, stretching across a full twenty parsecs of space, encompassing a dozen conquered species. But the starships were like our starships. Like everyone's starships, not real at all, nowhere to run, no place to hide when the Master Race arrived.

Sudden transition to a starship orbiting a world called Kalareis. Green seas surrounding green continents. Pale green clouds under a bright white sun. No ice caps. Heart stuttering softly in my chest, like an echo inside that magic armor. Command circuit whispering: Make ready, Jemadar-Minor.

Make ready. I and my havildars, their eight octals of troopers . . .

Then the combat lighter driving away from the starship, plunging into the green atmosphere of Kalareis, plasma sheath lighting up around the hull, stripped air whining around us, streaming away in a bright meteor trail, deceleration plucking at us, threatening to tug the weapons from our armored, augmented grasp.

Doors opening, winds of passage screaming in like a tongue of cleansing fire, then a daisy chain of soldiers falling through the sky, my men and I. Like some terrible band of vengeful angels, holding our weapons ready, imagining ourselves like Thor of the Lightnings. Thor and his band of warrior-heroes.

On the surface of Kalareis, in the eyes of the Saanaae, it must have looked like their final nightmare. Streams of fire across the sky, sky then littered by millions of tiny black forms. Humans, Kkhruhhuft, a dozen species to which, perhaps, they couldn't even put a name.

Back to that one small scene, all I can really remember, of taking out my entrenching tool and cutting off that defeated policeman's head. An act of kindness perhaps.

It was a standard black chamber, just like the ones I knew existed in Masters' castles on endless worlds, though I'd been in only a few. The details were different though, once you looked away from the walls, once you finished squinting through the haze of glare.

An altar here, backed by a pile of hardware. Two tall spindles on either side that looked like tiki torches from some upscale garden party, a rich man's party, license for a smoky, open flame paid from bottomless pockets. A standard commercial holodeck, old and a little beat-up looking, machinery in a style that reminded me of the late fifties. Little plastic name tag in one corner, with its faded tricolor corporate logo: *Interplanetary Business Machines, Ltd.*

Look quickly now, pull aside the black curtain, find the little man, confront him, *I am the great and powerful wizard . . .*

If only it could be like that.

The holodeck lit, filling the space between the tiki torches with a swirl of smoke, the outline of a dark and Satanic figure, striated with rippling interference bars that went down, halted, switched to an upward roll, faded as the figure flickered, turning to look right at me.

The projector was poorly tuned, as if it hadn't been serviced in a long time. "Welcome home, Athol Morrison," it said, "Soldier of the Master Race." The image flickered again, momentarily filling with a blizzard of colored snow, flickered and stabilized, dark, fiery eyes boring into mine.

I wonder who thought of this. That soft black majordomo, perhaps? More likely someone higher up in the Sirkar. People who, once the war was over, once it was explained to them, once they saw how things stood, worked to secure a decisive advantage in the new order.

I reached out and passed my hand through the image. No reaction. Whoever'd set this thing up hadn't connected all the sensors. But when I moved, took a small step to one side, the eyes followed me, head turning to keep me in view. I sat down on the edge of the altar and listened while it told me how proud my people were of their bold son's heroic service to the Master Race . . .

Jesus.

I undid my breast pocket flap and took out the phone, and thumbed the contact sensor. "10x9760h, logging on."

The image's fiery eyes stared at me, stared and stared. Frozen. And its voice was displaced by the soft buzz of planetary net traffic, soft whining trill high in the background.

A gender-neutral voice, quiet, gentle, without undercurrents: "3m8subKTR, acknowledged."

3m8 again. I suppose the rumors are true then, the line of 3m8 being spun out to deal with the latest addition to the empire's resource base. Not a bad thing. It meant the Master Race had certain . . . expectations. Maybe. I don't know if you can call it that. What do expectations *mean* when you're a soulless, unfeeling machine? What does *anything* mean?

The voice went on: "4Y1028h planetary net interrupt request acknowledged . . ."

Someone calling in from the net now? A momentary pang, concern, a realization of just how little experience I really had dealing with a command circuit phone. The background traffic-static gave way to a shrill, hard beat, modulated square waves. Router traffic, I thought, from somewhere else . . .

"4Y1028h via PCN router 9m12sub4Y, level Five-high."

"Five-high, acknowledged."

A security code, I knew, things we were taught back in basic training, things of little use to a low-ranker. But. There could come a day when you found yourself holding the phone, even as a raw recruit, seeing your first war. And *things* can always go badly.

The soft voice said, "9m12sub4Y, 10x9760h reply."

Well. I said, "10x9760h, standing by."

"9m12sub4& requests you log in at level Five-high secure status."

Odd. *9m12* would be a Master node, of course, but *4Y* was only a surrogate of the planetary command net. What could they be wanting with a soldier on furlough, especially on a planet flooded with three kinds of police? "10x9760h acknowledges, level Five-high log-on."

A brief burst of regular net-traffic noise, then, "10x9760h, level 5-high information service bulletin: Local PCN traffic secure-trace advisory."

Meaning I was, in effect, on active duty. "10x9760h acknowledges. 9m12sub4Y command request."

"10x9760h, 9m12sub4Y command nul."

Then why the hell had it bothered with me? "10x9760h acknowledges command nul."

The voices, all the same, one after the other:

"9m12sub4Y at level Five-high secure status, command circuit release."

"4Y1028h via PCN router release" A quick, diminishing snarl of square-wave traffic.

"3m8subKTR, local circuit log-on and status release."

I said, "10x9760h, suspend," and put the phone back in my pocket. The Satanic image came back to life, eyes blazing at me, telling me of my family's pride.

I walked away, listening to the echoes.

6 NIGHTFALL. SKY DARKENING TO INDIGO, tinged with violet, stars popping out here and there, first the bright ones, then the dim, until the heavens were black and spangled with thousands of shimmering pinpoints. All of Creation. The empire of the Master Race. Always, before, they'd seemed like *my* stars. Not the stars of my childhood, meaningless white dots with bogeyman names, nor the stars of my post-Invasion adolescence, the stars of the Conqueror, but *my* stars, stars of the empire, stars policed by human Spahis, and mighty Kkhruhhuft, and lizard-centaur Saanaae and a thousand more races. Soldiers. Comrades. Friends.

Somewhere out there, behind those distant stars, were all my friends. Somewhere out there, Solange Corday was transporting my household, my possessions, my burdars, my *things*, from Boromilith, where I'd lived, between wars, between jobs, for almost five years, transporting them to faraway Karsvaao.

Why *did* I come here? To see my family, all my old friends, my *home*, all in slave collars? Maybe it was a mistake. Maybe I should just dial the phone, cancel my leave, call Solange and tell her I was on my way. Christ, I could be back in my own bed, arms around Hani's sleek and cooperative form, in short order.

The phone, light and wafer-thin, seemed like a lead weight in my breast pocket, pressing down cruelly on my chest. Permission. You'd have to get permission to make such an abrupt change of plan. And somewhere, at some node far up in the chain-hierarchy of the Master Race, something is interested in your being here. Something. That made the phone seem, momentarily, like *my* slave collar.

But the thought of holding Hani again, lying with her, feeling her liquid heat on my loins . . . The thought of Solange, my friend, my comrade-at-arms, laughing with me over many a glass of dark red ale, standing by my side as we marched into battle.

Soldiers we were. Soldiers. Not warriors. Professional soldiers. Well trained. A warrior, they say, can be ordered to go out and die for his country, for his people. A soldier can only be ordered to win. Death, for a soldier, is merely a calculated risk. A mishap to be avoided.

Dead warriors win glory. Live soldiers win wars.

Image of Solange Corday, genderless, raceless, faceless in her powered exoskeleton, delivering her killing fire. Then Hani, lying naked in my bed, warm, tawny skin soft and comforting.

The door to my parents' deck opened and closed behind me, heavy, clumsy footsteps on the poorly fastened boards, a chair dragging, then my brother Lank was sitting beside me, putting his feet up on the railing beside mine.

"Beautiful night," he said. "It's usually a lot hazier than this in August. This is more like late September, early October."

"I remember." Frosty, clear nights, near Christmastime, when the black post-Invasion sky seemed filled with stars that stood shoulder to shoulder with each other.

We sat silently for another moment, then Lank sighed, turning to face me, willing me, I suppose, to look at him, eyes glinting against the darkness, reflecting the stars, the far away glimmering of household fires down in the bustee. "You're making everyone unhappy, Athy. Want to tell me what's wrong?"

I grinned in the darkness. "Trying to be Father Confessor now? Want me to start with an Act of Contrition?"

A faint gasp of breath, maybe exasperation, maybe amusement. "No, I'm afraid I'm not very good in that role, Athy. I try to get out of confession duty whenever I can. It's like KP." A pause. "Just brother-to-brother, that's all. You and me."

I suppose he deserved that, at least. And my sarcasm had been no more than a cheap way of getting out of it, pushing the intimacy aside. "Sure." My turn to pause, while I considered, tried to come up with something sensible and yet not too hurtful to say. "I guess I just don't like what I'm seeing here. Everybody seems so . . . I don't know. *Downtrodden.*"

"Is that so surprising? Look." I could hear a rustle of cloth as he waved his arms in the dark, saw the faint shadows of them rising to the heavens. "Look what's happened to us all!"

"I suppose. I have to tell you though, I don't like the rest of it, either. You in the priesthood, Dad the Sirkar's agent, Police Chief Catalano still in office, when he ought to be in prison."

Silence. Then he said, "There are no prisons any more, Athy. The local lockup's just for hooligans."

"Even so."

I could see his head nodding by the movement of the eye glimmer. "All right. I know what you're saying." I could hear a shrug in his voice. "There was nothing else to be done. You of all people should understand that."

Right. The obvious accusation. "I don't know if I can stand being here the whole time."

"That'd make them pretty unhappy, Athy. They're really glad you're back, you know. Mom. Dad. Oddny." He laughed, "Even me, big brother!"

"I was glad to see you all again."

"But you don't want to see what we've become."

"I'm sorry."

A final sigh, gusty, heavy enough I could smell the faint aroma of dinner on his expelled breath. Garlic and sweet Holland peppers. "Look, why don't you go out with me tonight? Have some fun. Meet people. It's not as bad as it looks around here. Really."

Maybe so, I thought, that Chapel Hilliest of phrases. Still, that was part of it. The thought of spending my weeks sitting out here, regretting having come, while scenes of war and comradeship flitted though my head. Of lying inside, looking at my old goddess, as Hani and the others while away their nights somewhere beyond the stars.

Maybe Hani was grateful for the vacation. A time of a few weeks, when her breasts could rest unpalpated, her crotch dry and unexcited, night after night. I shook my head. Jesus. The things that come up unbidden. And said, "All right." Almost as an afterthought, I took the holster off my belt and put it in my room. Took the gun and dropped it in my pocket. Then we went on our way.

The night seemed warm but dry as we walked along, back through the bustee, up onto Airport Road, and across into the darkness, heading down a path by Bolin Creek that had once been part of a town park. Lank chattered away as we walked through the night, smell of woods filling my nostrils. Talking. Nothing of consequence. Just idle talk.

There are forests on many worlds. All of them different. All of them somehow the same. Things like trees. With things like leaves. Things that rustle on the night winds, wherever a man can walk along in his bare skin, breathing unfiltered air into his bare lungs.

I always liked the woods. Woods everywhere, which felt and sounded so much the same, so familiar, especially at night. The smells though. Always unique. Even around Chapel Hill, each little patch of woods had its own special scent. Some sweet, some sour. Some pungent, some faint and dry, dusty.

A sudden memory of walking through dry and dusty woods on some alien world. Where? Tarasai, my first posting. A desert world under a K5 sun. Dim red days. Hot and dry to us, though the natives, small, crablike things, found it quite humid.

The forests were dry as well, huge stands of tall, thin,

stalky, leafless trees lining the narrow, rocky defiles of carefully maintained waterways. Lines of forest separated by stretches of hardpan desert. The forest on Tarasai was dry and dusty and smelled of something like cinnamon, a barely detectable taint in the air.

That was where I took my first burdar walking. On the first night she was mine. A thin, frightened, Hispanic-looking girl named Marni, who'd simply been waiting in my crib, sitting in a chair by the carefully made bed, when I showed up with my gear.

Her voice was soft, speaking not-quite-broken English with a delicate accent. An accent that immediately struck me as charming. And I knew what she was for. But all the brutality of my long training had not driven away the last of my cultural baggage. Not yet.

I looked at her, keeping my eyes on her face whenever she was facing me. But, as I sat, going over my checklists, going over my duty rosters, as Marni made dinner for me, I stole glances at her, looking away quickly whenever she looked up. Glances at the outline of her buttocks under the stiff white cotton of her slacks. The shape of her breasts, the way they swayed as she moved. The flat slope of her lower abdomen, rounding her pubic bone, flattening out as it went between her legs, a suggestive outline under the cloth.

As the evening wore on, Marni grew nervous. More and more upset. But she must have known the duty she'd signed up for, though she was no older than I.

After dinner, I suggested we go for a walk, looking at the panic in her eyes. She followed me wordlessly out the door, down the path from the crib, located on a hillside with the others from my unit. I could see her looking around in the starlit darkness, at light spilling through the curtains of the other cribs. Maybe, before I'd come, she'd gotten to know the other new burdars. Maybe she was wondering what was going on behind all those lit-up curtains.

No one else was outside, just now, walking down by the waterway, down among the slim, cinnamony trees of Tarasai. We could hear the little crab-people scuttling around in the darkness, not far away, but could see nothing.

After a while, I took her hand, leading her on into the night. Her hand was freezing cold, and her fingers felt stiff in mine.

And then I stopped her. Kissed her on cold lips. Undid the fastenings of her blouse. Held her breasts in my hands. Kissed her soft nipples. Untied the waistband of her slacks and pushed them down, buried my face in her pubic hair. Tasted her with my tongue. Pushed her down on the ground then, undressed and crawled on top of her. Made love to her in the alien darkness.

That *was* what I called it, to myself, that night. But Marni said nothing, just holding her legs apart for me, letting me do what I wanted, for as long as I wanted.

We walked back to the crib, undressed again, turned out the lights, crawled into that neatly made bed, and I made love to her again, then we held each other, and went to sleep. Some time in the night, I awoke to feel her shivering delicately against my chest, could feel warm moisture on me as she cried. I tried to hold her close, to stroke her back and whisper meaningless comfort. It didn't seem to do any good, but when we got up in the morning, Marni made me breakfast, smiled at me as I got dressed. Kissed me softly and sent me off to the wars.

Lank and I came out of the woods quite suddenly, under that same wide and starry sky, feet crunching on cindery gravel, the horizon outlined by the black tooth-stumps of collapsed buildings. Here and there among the rubble I could see red-orange light from open fires, oddly shaped black shadows leaping around in a complex and familiar dance.

Lank clapped me on the shoulder, waving an arm around at it all, and said, "Ah, home away from home . . ."

I stood still, looking at the dark ruins, trying to orient myself. "I remember this place, I guess. There was a shopping mall right over there . . ." Gesturing at some low-lying rubble.

Lank said, "Carr Mill Mall. I remember you used to hang around there quite a bit."

Carr Mill had survived the Invasion. Now . . . "What happened to it?"

Lank started walking away, feet crunching on the gravel, leading me toward the area of the campfires. "When they knocked down the office towers, a couple of years after you left, the Mall went down all by itself. It was pretty old."

We passed between a couple of crumpled and turned-over compactor boxes, and the old parking lot opened up in front of me. Tents, a couple of crudely made shacks. The campfires.

Lank said, "Carrboro is still an unregulated native habitat. They'll be cleaning it out one day, I suppose, moving everyone to the Chapel Hill bustee."

And then, this place would grow quiet and cold, kudzu vines growing over the rubble, quickly erasing the freshness of human presence. I wondered if these people liked camping out forever in the remains of an old mall parking lot. Maybe so. Maybe it let them remember the old days.

Finally, we rounded a corner of the old mill foundation and, somewhere, I could hear the faint thudding of a diesel generator. There were steps leading down into the old basement, and a neon sign beside them, a small one, lit up in pale indigo. *DAVYS*, it said, "S" flickering every now and again from a weak ballast. I wondered where they'd ever find a new one for a museum antique like this.

At the bottom of the stairs was an open doorway, blocked only by a pair of Old West–style swinging barroom doors, and the light from inside, though relatively bright, was the somewhat flickery yellow of open flame. Lank, suddenly seeming very lively indeed, pattered down the stairs, threw open the doors, and, in a surprisingly resonant baritone, sang, *"It's . . . only me from over the SEA . . ."*

From somewhere inside, a raspy voice shouted, "Ah, fuck off, asshole . . ."

And Lank said, "Ah! Home sweet home!" He went in, beckoning for me to follow.

It was a big room, a dozen meters in each direction, sawdust on the floor, among the tables, big stone fireplaces at either end of the room, cold now in the summer heat. This place would be cozy indeed, come winter. There were electric fans turning slowly on the ceiling, stirring the tepid air, the principal devices powered by the generator. The yellowish light seemed to be from hanging kerosene lanterns.

A little bandstand at the far end of the room from the fireplace, instruments set up, a fat black bass, a couple of guitars, a drum kit. Some pudgy, middle-aged guys sitting on the edge of the stage, drinking what looked like bottles of beer. The musicians, maybe.

There was a bar along one wall with stools, a low rail . . . and a trough running along the foot of the bar, water sluicing continuously down its length, flowing in through a hole in one wall, going out the other. A bar for serious beer drinkers, men, at least, who'd drink and piss without ever having to get up. There were plenty of women at the bar too, but I supposed most of them were out of luck when it came to pissing in place. Or else possessed of great boldness and even greater skill. I'd known a few women like that among the Spahis.

Lank bellied up to the bar, shoving at men who snarled and pushed back, trying to maintain their space. I pushed in beside him, bumping gently with my shoulders. The next man in the row turned to me, red-eyed from drink, angry, one hand already made into a fist . . . And stopped. Stared at me for a moment. The ruddy color of his face seemed to drain slightly, then he muttered, "Holy *shit* . . ." and turned away, shoving hard on the next man, who happened to be a rather beefy woman. "Move *down*, goddamn it!" She rammed him in the side with her big, blunt elbow, and giggled.

Lank banged his hand on the bar, getting the barkeep's attention. "Hey, fuckhead! Look who's here!"

The man turned and walked toward us, a tall, thin, middle-aged Oriental, balding in front, straight-black hair swept back, gathered into some kind of martial-arts ponytail. Lines at the corners of his eyes, deeper lines bracketing his mouth. Walking with a slight limp. In the old days, I'd've guessed he was a man of about sixty, maybe seventy. Now? Hell . . .

He stood there, wiping his hands very carefully on a white

rag, a tattered bit of terry cloth, staring at me, not at my muscular bulk, just at my face, looking right into my eyes. Finally, he said, "You sure have changed, Athol Morrison."

I held out my hand. "Hello, Davy. How've you been?" I wouldn't want to tell him he'd changed as well. He looked like an old man now. In fact, he looked just like my finally clear memory of his father.

He grinned then, a sudden, sunshiny remembrance of that Davy Itakë of so long ago, and pointed, his finger long and thin, blue veins rolling on the backs of his hands, popping back and forth over the tendons. "You boys go sit at that empty table over in the corner. I'll be right there . . ." He turned and shouted, "Hey, Sammy! Take over for a while!" Then, "Marsh, you old fuck, get over here!"

I turned and could see Marsh Donovan standing away from the bar, no longer dressed up in sagoth togs, blinking our way, grinning blearily.

We sat at the table and Davy came back, grinning, pony keg tucked under one arm, primitive implements of destruction in one hand, a bouquet of glass steins in the other. Banged them down on the table, gently deposited the keg. "*Now* then . . ." Hammer in one hand, bung starter in the other, tap and ventcap between spare fingers. WHAM. Pop. WHAM. Pop. Machine precision, with barely a hint of beerspray in the air.

He set the keg on its side, propped against the hammer. "And *now* . . ." He swept up the mugs, all five in one spider-fingered hand. It made a wonderful, deep gurgle as it filled the glasses, a dark, russet beer with a strong, bitter smell.

I shook my head, almost laughing. "I remember when you *exploded* that damn beerball, Davy . . ."

He slid the stein in front of me. "Takes a little practice, that's all."

I sipped the beer, foam tickling on my upper lip, took a bigger swallow. Bitter on the tip of my tongue, sweeter farther back. At least as good as what the Boromilithi were making. Probably a lot better than what I'd get on Karsvaao.

Davy said, "Jesus Christ, it's good to see you, Athy! You look like fucking Superman."

Übermensch? Maybe not. Maybe just the centuries-old cartoon character, emblem of every boy's secret dream. If I was Superman, nobody'd pick on me anymore. Not even Mom and Dad.

Marsh tipped his mug back, swallowing close to a half liter in one go. Bumped the mug down, wiped his mouth on the back of one hand. Burped. "If you'd been like this way back when, we'd uh won more damn games, Athy . . ." A bleary-eyed grin. Marsh the sagoth well on his way to puking in the gutter.

I had to laugh at that. Football. After the Invasion, with 3V gone, it turned into something we could live for. Davy a fine tight end, me at quarterback. Marsh usually playing half-back, sometimes one guard position or the other. We'd had some wonderful games.

Image out of memory. Sprinting down field, battered foot-ball tucked under my left arm, right arm crooked forward so I could elbow assholes in the helmet, knock them down, wondering where the hell Marsh was. Davy still probably lying on his side, where the opposing guard had put him.

OK. One play fucked up. No chance now to send the ball spiraling forty or fifty yards downfield, to where Davy would be waiting, counting as he ran, spinning around at just the right moment . . .

A sudden hush, and I was running alone, seemingly hav-ing outdistanced all the Durhamite pursuers, running under the goalposts, turning to face the field, ball held overhead, waiting for the touchdown cheer, the sight of my father grin-ning, giving me the high sign . . .

Silence.

All the players standing out on the field, looking up. No one looking at me from the stands. Everyone standing, look-ing up. Silence.

And there was a low rumble from overhead.

I looked up, shielding my eyes with my free hand, holding the ball against my side again. Overhead, the Kkhruhhuft pa-trol ship was a fat silver shape, like an old-fashioned dirigi-ble, floating against the wind, studded with turrets. Turrets that could deliver the lightning of the gods. They say, we were told in those days, that they run on antigravity. Which, according to *our* physics, is impossible . . .

A lot of impossible things in those days. And we didn't know yet about the poppits and the Master Race. Just the almighty, deadly Kkhruhhuft.

Back in the present, Marsh was going on and on about those old football days, reminiscing about one game after another as he slopped up beer. Problems Marsh? For such a happy-go-lucky boy? Happens to the best of us.

Davy ignored him, looking at me, eyes far away. Finally, he put his hand on my forearm, squeezing the heavy bands of muscle, and said, "God, I've *missed* you, Ath! I wish the Hell I'd passed the tests. I always wanted to go with you . . ."

I told him that would've been nice, fun, the two of us going off to the wars together. Told him that. But Davy Itakë would have died in training. Would just be a memory now of someone, a friend, long lost. And it was damned good to see him alive now.

Moments go by, turning into hours, the musicians finishing their break, getting back to work. They played a tune I didn't know, something scratchy and incomprehensible, then went on to "Young Love," a hit I remembered from 2159, from the spring before the Invasion. It'd been sung then by some skinny girl with bronze-colored hair, who'd done no better job than the short, fat old black woman singing it now.

A shadow fell over our table, a human shape that dimmed the kerosene light, and Marsh suddenly fell silent. Davy sat back in his chair, looking over my shoulder. Waiting. And I knew. This is what you were expecting, isn't it? Lank didn't bring you here just to drink beer with the old boys. I turned around in my chair.

She was still tall. Curly black hair lightly streaked with bits of silver-gray. Face squarer than I remembered, a few lines I couldn't recall, at the outer corners of her eyes, bracketing her mouth. Neck still long and smooth, delicate tracery of veins and tendons visible under the skin. Suntanned. That was something she'd been in the long ago. Her waist was thicker than I remembered, dressed in blue denim and cheap-looking brown suede.

Boots on her feet, reaching about a third of the way up each calf, jeans tucked in, pouched at the juncture of her thighs, showing they'd been tailored for a man.

Like I was seeing her for the first time, in that smoking old ruin we'd still wanted to call Chapel Hill, after the first assault was over, the soldiers gone, the warships no more than chaotically spinning lights in the midnight sky, my parents trying to keep me indoors forever afterward, though the explosions were done, the ground no longer vibrating under the cracked concrete of our basement floor.

Because I'd been indoors, underground, for the last of it, the changes came as a shock to me, no matter how much I'd seen during our flight from Washington, D.C., back across Virginia to the home we'd tried to abandon. Our house was still standing, but hurt beyond recognition, the beautiful, white-pillared front facade burned black, delicate yellow vinyl siding puckered and blistered, the whole house looking like a toy car I'd thrown in the ornamental fire when my parents weren't around, car twisting and melting into some fantastic shape, just before bursting into flame.

I'd stood for a long while on the torn-up sod of our lawn, looking down the hill, across the street at the collapsed boards and brick and mangled steel frame of the house across the street, wondering if those three asshole boys who lived there had survived, wondering if I'd ever see them again, get into fights with them, shoot BBs at their dog. No sign of them, and no one ever bothered with the ruins.

The sky seemed very high on that long-ago morning, pale blue, streaked with a few remote white clouds, clouds drawn out, as if by a high wind. Something was twinkling up there, several somethings, right on the edge of my vision. Those wrecked starships, I knew, tumbling in orbit, out of control, crewed by the dead.

Maybe, I'd thought, just a few of them are crewed by dead Kkhruhhuft. Maybe, as I walked around town, looking for my friends, if any of them were still around, I'd even find a few dead Kkhruhhuft soldiers, just lying abandoned here and there, like dead therapod carnivores . . .

So I'd walked, going from street to street, house to house, looking for Marsh, for best friend Davy, for all the others, all my playmates. It'd been a long time since I'd been able to do anything besides play indoor games with Lank and Oddny.

Marsh's house was crushed almost to dust, no single piece anywhere larger than my hand. Davy's was intact, even the window glass unbroken, but no one was home. When I'd tried the knob on the front door, it had been securely locked. I remember thinking, with some despair, *Maybe they've just gone shopping* . . .

But the nearby Argomart, where I knew they liked to shop, was just wiped away, nothing left but the parking lot and a bare, strange-looking foundation slab. Both of them would turn up later, their parents having taken them to the old shelter under the downtown post office, the one that'd been built for World War III, but on that day, not long before my eleventh birthday, I was sure they were dead.

I was sitting on a hefty piece of torn-apart masonry in the middle of town, some huge wad of broken bricks welded together by grainy-looking cement, a piece of what building I had no idea, wondering what I was going to do, trying to swallow past that unaccountably tight, sore place in the middle of my throat, when I heard her footsteps, soft, light, hesitant, walking up the street, crunching delicately on bits of debris.

A thin girl, about my own age, curly black hair, big, damp-looking brown eyes, pale, a forlorn look on her face. Standing there, looking at me, with a look that I knew, even then, said, All my friends are dead . . .

Faint, shadowy smile on her face. Faint look of hope. And she said, "Your name's Athy, isn't it? I remember you from school."

I nodded, remembering her from here and there, just one more person I hardly knew, someone who sat on the other side of the room. Alix, I'd thought. Alix something. She held out a slim, white-fingered hand, and said, "Alexandra Moreno."

When I took her hand, the fingers were unexpectedly warm, her grip strong and friendly. "Athol Morrison. Athy," I told her.

We sat together for a while, talking, remembering mutual friends from school, wondering where they all were . . . *if* they were anywhere at all. Then we walked down the long hill of Franklin Street, past all the rich people's antique houses, past charred ruins, collapsed heaps of brick, a few twisted steel skeletons surrounded by cool, hard puddles of melted glass and plastic.

We saw one dog sniffing around near the crushed remnants of a house where a boy we'd both known once lived, but it looked at us wild-eyed and ran away when we got closer. It was a fat reddish mutt with an upcurving tail. Half chow, I think, and half something else. Alix looked after him rather wistfully, making me wonder if maybe she had a lost dog somewhere, but I didn't want to ask.

Then, under the light of a wan noonday sun, we stood together, silent, holding hands, looking at what was left of University Metamall, where we were so used to meeting all our friends. Bits of wall. Long pieces of clear plastic sheeting from the roof. Scattered stuff, colorful, suggestive, merchandise from all the stores.

And a man lying facedown in a puddle of dirty water, body swollen, skin purple, clothes stiff and distended. No one that we'd ever known.

From across the table, in the here and now, Lank laughed abruptly. "Say something, Athy!"

I glanced at him, gave him a wry look, turned back to Alexandra Moreno, who, one day, long ago, I'd vowed to marry, held out my hand, and said, "Hello, Alix."

She said, "If I didn't know who you were, I'd never guess." She took my hand, grip still strong and friendly, fingers still warm, still smiling, but with something of a shadow crossing her face momentarily, then pulled up a chair and sat, turning it around backwards, sitting astride, arms resting across the back, a pose I'd never seen her in before.

We sat and we talked in the dim yet harsh kerosene light of Davy's bar, in some ways strangers, in other ways very old friends indeed. When I closed my eyes, she looked just the same as she had twenty years ago, young and fresh, and I could still feel the smooth skin of her waist under my hands.

Smaller hands, as I recall them. Smoother hands.

Shadows were etched on her face by the hard quality of the light, throwing her eyes into shallow wells of darkness, making them seem larger and more intent. Eyes on me. On my face, that little image of me centered in a curved reflection of the room.

The others were falling into the background now, Davy and Lank receding, turning toward each other, carrying on some conversation of their own, memories of me, perhaps, and still vigilant. Aware. Marsh, draining another beer, sat silent, eyes a little dazed, nothing left of the day's hawk-eyed sagoth policeman, looking at me sometimes, mostly seeming to listen to Davy and Lank.

Maybe he remembered too. Maybe not. There's no real forgetfulness in liquor, but it can help erase the here and now, which is often the point.

Alix's teeth were visible as she talked, almost but not quite white, glistening with moisture, mouth held in a half smile, as if in fond reverie . . .

Chin resting on her hands, eyes tipped to look up at me, she said, "After you were gone, for a long time, I didn't know what to do." The smile broadened, grew a little wistful. "I guess I felt more like a lost soul than I expected. I missed you."

I leaned toward her a little bit, shifting in my chair, trying to pick just the right words, failing. "We talked about that in the last days, didn't we? I missed you too."

A lie? I don't know. Maybe not. I thought about her some, in the pitifully short nights of my early training. Thought about having her in bed with me. Thought about making love, about our long walks in the woods, our long, too-serious talks together. It faded, too soon, under the deadly stress of Spahi training, as my newfound friends withered and died.

Then, of course, there was Marni. Then a host of others. Not a lie, though. I never forgot her, after all.

She said, "It wasn't enough. All I did was rationalize. I didn't want you to feel bad, Athy."

All I could do was nod. "I know. I appreciated it."

A look from her that might have been surprise, then she said, "Are you married?" A quick glance at my big hands, then her eyes were back on my face, fixed on my eyes.

I shook my head. "We're not allowed to marry."

The half smile faded. "Never?"

I shrugged. "I'll retire someday, if I survive my whole enlistment. If I want to. Old soldiers fading away and all that." Like the havildar-emeritus at the spaceport, an older man, signed up for a shorter term. What would I be in another ten or twenty years?

She wasn't smiling at all anymore, eyes evasive, away from my face. Looking at my hands again, seeming to measure them. Big, blunt fingers, rough-looking, a little red around the knuckles. Not a strangler's hands. More the sort of hands with which you pull off limbs.

Image of a spindly, chitinous being, small, not much more than twelve hundred centimeters tall, a little stick-man of a bug. Image of myself holding the little being helpless, taking away its needlelike sword, bending the metal in my hand, stilling the being's agitated thrashing with the other. It tried to bite me then, so I pulled off its arms and walked away, listening to the soft hissing noises it made as it curled in the alleyway and bled some kind of dark gray blood.

Alix said, "I was married. For a while." Eyes back on my face then. Not afraid. Sorry perhaps.

Softly, I said, "I'd hoped you would, Alix. We knew I was going to be gone forever. There wasn't any waiting to be done." I remembered the little sliver of pain I'd felt when I told her those things, on our last night together, so long ago, imagining some other boy, some other man, someone I knew surely, maybe even Davy or Marsh, holding her damp body just the way I was holding it, holding her in the night after making love.

She said, "I waited for two years, Athy." A brittle smile. "I guess I was hoping you'd flunk out of basic training and come home to me. I waited until we heard you'd finished with Mars and left for Alpha Centauri."

Alpha Centauri, of the deadly teal jungles, where my old friends lay buried. I reached out and put my hand on her forearm, squeezing gently. "You shouldn't have, Alix. I wanted you to be happy." But not so much that it made me want to stay . . .

She nodded. "I finally married Benny Tekkomuz."

I remembered Benny from high school, a short, plump, overserious boy with short, bristly blond hair and washed-out blue eyes. Not interested in much beyond getting his schoolwork in on time, as if the old, pre-Invasion future still waited for us all.

I wondered, Why him? Maybe, because he was so very different from me.

She said, "I did my best, but it never really worked out. He stayed . . . focused on other things. All he wanted from me was to make love twice a day, as soon as we woke up and again right after supper . . ."

A faint, surprising sliver of pain. I said, "I wanted to make love to you twice a day too, Alix. Maybe three or four." It was as light-sounding as I could make it. Almost flippant. Defuse this.

She said, "That was different. I loved you."

So.

She said, "It lasted about five years. Then I couldn't stand it anymore and sent him away. He seemed almost glad to go."

"No children?"

A look of not quite pain, a touch of bitterness. "No. I saw to that."

"Where's Benny now?"

"Someplace, I suppose. He's a Sirkar official. Quite successful, I understand."

Benny, gone to his proper reward, with all the other hardworking, nose-to-the-grindstone boys and girls. "And you didn't marry again." That little sliver of interior pain, selfish pain, telling me I wanted her to say *no* . . .

She shook her head, sat back a little, and ran one hand

through her hair, tossing the curls into disarray, a peculiarly abandoned gesture, and yet . . . Graceful. Attractive. Alluring . . .

She said, "Life gets lonely. You do what you have to. But . . . no. No one I wanted to have stay."

A simple phrase that. And one that pulled at my insides. I tried to think of an endless supply of compliant burdars, of what they had at my beck and call. I wanted not to be selfish, to be glad, at least, that she'd found little bits and pieces of happiness without me, if not the dream we'd once shared.

I tried not to think about what her words must imply. I was the one who'd left, after all.

She reached forward and touched my forearm, squeezed gently. "Were you ever sorry you went away, Athy?"

I looked into her eyes, and said, "Sometimes." And those glistening eyes were upon me, watching, alert, aware. Not the eyes of a burdar, nor the eyes of a comrade soldier.

It grew late, and the bar's clientele thinned out, people rising and yawning, stretching, staggering out through the swinging doors, out into a summer night. Marsh folded his arms on the tabletop and put his head down upon them, snoring gently. Lank and Davy continued to talk about old times, growing sleepy-eyed, but seeming to wait.

Finally, Alix sat up straight, stretching her back taut, breasts pushing at the material of her blouse, eyes squeezed shut as she threw her head back. "Jesus, I'll have a head in the morning . . ." She ruffled her hair again, and, looking at me, said, "I'd better be going."

Davy said, "Be careful, Alix. You know this neighborhood's been getting worse fast . . ."

A cue to me? Maybe. I stood, and said, "Would you like me to walk you home?"

A measured look, serious, eyes dark and deep. "Sure." She turned toward the door.

I looked at Lank and Davy, at Marsh. "I'll see you both later. Say good night to Sleeping Beauty for me . . ." and followed her.

Outside, the night had cooled and a stiff breeze had come

up, making the young trees of the surrounding forest hiss against each other. Most of the fires were out now, or banked down to glowing coals, but a full moon had risen, a brilliant yellow-white circle washing out the starry sky, giving the heavens a slight indigo cast, throwing shadows on the ground like the light from streetlamps.

I felt just a little dizzy, metabolizing all that beer.

Alix stood still for a minute, looking up at me, hands on her hips, solid and handsome in the well-lit night. Not really the girl I remembered. Just hints of her, fossilized relics embedded in this woman. Nothing for us to say, I suppose. Just looking at each other. Wondering. Who were we, now?

She said, "I'm living in one of the old houses on Pine Street. They seemed to survive better than some of the newer ones." Houses no one owned anymore. Empty houses, free for the taking. Those people camped out in the old mall parking lot? No way of knowing.

We walked, and Alix walked by my side, close enough for me to be conscious of her presence, even when I couldn't see her. A small form, compared to mine, footfalls light, barely audible in the night. Calling to me. I knew I wanted to put my arm around her, hold her close, walk with her the way we'd walked in the darkness long ago.

Times past, walking in the night, sometimes with a destination, sometimes just walking. Sometimes finding a dry field or forest glade, depending on season and weather, pausing to kiss and handle each other, and sometimes make love . . .

I realized with a slight shock that Alix was holding my hand now.

Maybe. Maybe we would have stopped right then and there, maybe we would have gone up onto a nearby hillside, what remained of a once carefully tended front lawn I could barely make out in the shadowed moonlight. Maybe we would have lain together in the soft summer grass. Maybe.

But when I turned to face her, I could see dark shapes come out of the woods, stepping onto the pavement, hurrying to surround us. Click to attention. Five heavyset men, dressed in jeans and sleeveless jerkins, so we could see their muscular arms. Maybe in the daylight, we could have seen their tattoos, the greasy shine of their longish hair.

I heard Alix gasp and recoil against me. I did put my arm around her then.

I could see well enough in the dark to know that three of the men were Caucasian, one of mostly African descent, the last so mixed I had no idea. Somewhat Asian-looking, perhaps, but squatty and rather broad-faced. Three were holding knives, the other two big sticks, the sawed-off stems and solid rootball from the woody reeds that grew down along Bolin Creek. I'd made knobkerries like these to play with when I was a boy.

It was the mongrel who stepped forward now, pointing at me with his slim knife blade, shining like a metal sliver in the moonlight. "Lovers' Lane is it?" His eyes were on Alix though, not me, focused toward her pelvis. Not a very bright mugger, evidently. The other men were looking at her too. I could feel her shrinking against me, but not shaking.

She said, "Bastard. Leave us alone."

One of the other men snickered and grabbed his own crotch, rubbing suggestively.

The mongrel laughed, and said, "Tell you what, son. You leave your wallet on the ground and walk away. We'll let your girlie go when we're done with her." I could feel Alix's muscles tighten then, sure of what must be coming.

She'd be hoping I'd do something now. Maybe she'd been through scenes like this before with other men, escorts who wouldn't risk their lives to save her from a little rough sport . . .

There are always details of peoples' lives you never learn, details you're afraid to know. Why do you walk these streets, Alix? How *have* you protected yourself? No time to wonder now.

I thought about the little gun in my pocket. Not a good idea. There were people living in the woods around here. Innocent bystanders. Besides, then I'd have to make a formal report through the Net, as well as, doubtless, fill out all sorts of forms for the Sirkar and sagoths . . .

I said, "You'd better not do this."

The mongrel said, "You're not a big enough boy to stop us, pally." Their eyes were gleaming now, wide open, and a couple of them were grinning. Anticipation. I could hear Alix's breathing quicken. Afraid. Wanting to run. Not wanting to leave my side. Something.

I put my hand firmly on her hip and pushed her back away from me, heard her stumble and grunt softly, confused. Then I turned to the five men. "All right," I said. "Too late."

You could see our moon shadow on the ground for just a moment, their elongated shadows, mine facing them, larger, thicker, Alix's woman-shape in silhouette off to one side. Not running away. Waiting for me. No way to know why. She could probably make it to Davys while I fought them, maybe even bring help. Hell. Maybe she thought I didn't need help.

Then the shadows shifted, my arm reaching out, thick and black, rippling as it passed over a crack in the pavement. The mongrel's arm made a popping sound, the crackle of an extracted turkey drumstick, as it came out of its socket, and he dropped his knife, turning toward the pain, trying to pull back. Sharp intake of breath through his nose.

His shadow flailed as I picked him up, a momentary squeak of surprise-terror as I spun him, and two other shadows bowled away, grunts from the men as I knocked them down. The African screamed when I kicked him in the chest, a short, chopped sound, then I twisted his neck and heard the hard crack of his vertebrae giving out.

I turned again, grabbed another man, someone swinging a big stick, pulled him across my body, broke his weapon arm, popping the elbow apart, then broke his back over my knee for good measure.

Someone was getting up, muttering "Jesuschrist, jesuschrist . . ." turning to run away. I stamped on the mongrel's neck, heard him make a last, short, gagging cry as he died, caught the runner with a hard kick in the back, sharp, rippling crackle letting me know I'd broken his ribs off at their spinal roots. He went down on his face, silent.

In the distance, in the darkness, I could hear the fading footfalls of the last man. No sense in chasing him.

The man whose back and arm I'd broken was lying curled on the pavement, crying softly to himself, murmuring something, words garbled and full of fluid. Punctured lung maybe. I knelt beside him, smoothed his hair softly with my fingers, gentling him, then cradled his head in my hands and quickly snapped his neck.

Four shadows on the ground. Debris.

I stood and turned to face Alix.

She was standing right where I'd pushed her, one hand held to her temple, clutching at her own hair, staring, eyes wide, at the men on the ground, at me, mouth open slightly, breathing a little fast. She whispered, "Oh, God, Athy . . ."

A moment of tension, then she was against me, arms around me, holding on, whispering. "Oh, *Christ* . . ."

I held her close, cradling her head against my shoulder, smoothing her hair, running my hands through soft, slightly stiff curls. I could feel her heart pounding against me, gradually getting slower and slower, her breathing back to normal. Finally, she pulled back a little way, still holding on, and looked up at my face. "I guess . . . I guess you've been trained for this sort of thing."

I nodded, marveling at the feel of her in my arms.

She said, "You weren't so tough . . . back then."

I said, "Nobody was back then."

And she whispered, "Most men . . . most men just run away."

Most men, I thought, and saw that long, silent queue waiting behind her. We left dead men on the ground behind us as we walked on. Maybe someone would come clean them up in the morning.

Alix's house was a little cottage nestled in a grove of tall, thin, scaly evergreen trees. Inside, it was full of shadows, moonlight steaming through cracked and cloudy plastic windows, and there was very dim, ruddy light coming from a brazier standing by the hearth. Alix made a dark shadow kneeling beside it, leaning into the fireplace, and I could hear the clunking of wood, the delicate crackle of kindling being broken. Finally, she picked up a dull red coal in a pair of tongs, blew on it delicately, making it glow more orange, then held it into the wood. Yellow flames leaped up, the fire catching quickly, pale smoke heading up the flue, the room filling with a cheerful, flickering light.

Alix remained kneeling as the flames reached higher, beginning to crackle, then roar softly, looking up at me, holding the tongs loosely in one hand. Finally, she said, "Lit from below like this, your eyes are hollow. Like some kind of demon."

I returned her smile, then she said, "Where did you get those scars?"

I reached up and felt my face, the long scar reaching across my left cheek, making the corner of my mouth turn up slightly, the rougher scar where my forehead had been laid open. "I'm a soldier."

She put the tongs aside and stood gracefully, coming over to me, standing close, breasts barely brushing against my chest, reaching up to run her fingers gently over the scars. "Don't they have plastic surgery software out there?"

"It's not our custom."

"You're lucky you didn't lose your eye."

"I did lose it. The Masters won't let us keep any functionally negative disfigurements."

She'd come closer now, breasts flattening against my body, and I put my arms around her, leaned down and kissed her, tasting beer, but also the underlying sweetness of her mouth. Her tongue reached up for mine, smooth here, rough there, testing me, probing. When we broke, she laid her head against my chest for a moment, and I heard her whisper, "I guess we do . . ."

That same phrase, the one she'd said so long ago, when two friends, longtime playmates, embraced in a forest glade and kissed for the first time, answering the unspoken question: Do we love each other? *I guess we do . . .*

And so, just as on that long ago evening, I slid my hands down her back, feeling supple muscle, feeling the flare of her hips, the gentle curve of her buttocks, and she tipped her head back to kiss me again.

Charade movements. Suddenly, I realized how often I'd made my burdars play out this scene. Pretend you love me,

Hani. Pretend. Pretend. Hani was good at pretending. They all were. The ones who couldn't pretend were washed out of basic training, so the soldiers never knew them.

Alix's hands ran down my sides, holding me by the hips, reaching around to feel my back, the muscle ridges and scars under my clothing, and I held her close, kissed her, whispered to her, until we were lying on her soft old carpet, half-undressed, running our hands over each other's bodies, just the way we used to. Her breasts were softer than they'd been years ago, the muscles of her stomach lightly padded now, no longer so close to the surface. But she sighed, just the way she always had, and clung to me, rubbed against me, breathing in my face, a whisper of desire . . .

An agony of remembrance. And moments of bemused delight. I reached between her legs, running my fingers through a luxury of thick, almost woolly hair, far different from my burdars, ran my fingertips over delicately swollen flesh, felt silky moisture everywhere.

How much like the burdars? Not at all. A sexual partner here of her own accord, here because she desired me, rather than because she was an employee, doing her job . . .

And how do you survive through it all, Alix? Just now, I had no will to wonder.

Time passed, the tension between us increasing, our whispers full of the past, of all we'd meant to each other, so long ago, then Alix was lying full length on top of me, holding my penis in her mouth, pressing her pubic bone against my chin, urging me to act, urgent in her desire. I put my mouth on her, tongue pushing past that bounty of crisp hair, tasting her. Almost sweet, the organic balm of a healthy woman, moisture glistening in the firelight.

Evolution saw to this, I thought, briefly distracted, that a man would be drawn to the taste and smell of a woman's genitals, that a woman's reproductive cycle would be accelerated by the prostaglandins in semen. Binding forces, men and women making love, triggering each other's biological determinatives, making sure they would make love over and over, until the pregnancy was secure. Binding the woman to the man with the pregnancy itself. Binding the man to the woman with insidious biochemistry, so the offspring would be protected and nurtured . . .

But I tasted her, ran my fingers into her, heard her soft intake of breath, felt the movement of her mouth upon me, the way she pressed her body against mine, binding flesh to flesh, branding me with herself.

As if that original brand had ever faded.

Then I was lying on top of her, our mouths pressed together, my hips curling under, thrusting into her, the soft slide of slick tissues on my skin, sensation reaching up into my spine, while she ground against me, hips moving in smallish circles, rubbing her mons against my lower abdomen, our passions feeding on each other now . . .

She suddenly grabbed me hard, breaking our kiss, pressing her head back against the carpet, eyes open but blind in the firelight, mouth open, and I could feel her inner muscles clenching, clenching hard, relaxing. One soft grunt, terminating in a sigh, a delicate shiver, and she started to subside, hands trailing gently down the length of my spine . . .

My orgasm came and went of its own accord, while I looked into her eyes.

With morning light, I awoke from a violent dream, still curled around Alix where we'd slept on her carpet, her damp back pressed against my chest, curly hair in my face, hips tucked into the angle formed by my thighs and abdomen. Sunlight was streaming through the windows at a low angle, making a hot-looking yellow patch on the floor nearby, dust motes lit up and swirling in the beam.

I could feel her heart beating against me, slow and gentle, letting me know she was still asleep, her breathing barely perceptible, the rise and fall of her chest under my hand almost sporadic.

The dream was an old one. I and my comrades in our armor, with our guns, marching across the dusty plains of some old, almost-dead world, giving it the coup de grace. A little blue sun burns in the sky, an empty and fathomless hole, a window into some other dimension, throwing lurid white shadows on the dull orange ground.

We march, and the natives are waiting for us, across the plain. They are bold, manlike things, with skins of old leather, tanned hides, hides we can hang on our trophy walls with scarcely more than the work of removing their inhabitants.

The natives wait, brave, impassive, knowing what will happen. And we raise our guns, and we kill them all, a killing fire so bright it makes the blue sun go dim . . .

The Masters, we think, approve, but we have no way to know. The Masters aren't real, can't feel, can't approve. All they can do is certify that we've carried out their instructions correctly.

Then they send down all the little blue poppits to clean up the debris, red eyes gleaming, without real awareness, red mouths agape, working, working, like ants. Or machines.

Alix began to stir against my chest, leaning back into me, sighing, yawning, and I could feel her muscles begin to stretch against each other, alternately tightening and relaxing, her buttocks shifting, sliding against each other, gliding on the skin of my thighs. Her head tipped back, turning, and I could see her looking at me out of the corner of one eye. She smiled slightly, an almost-shy look.

I leaned down and kissed her gently beside the eye, and said, "Good morning, Alix . . ." Like a whisper, my voice rough with sleep.

Her own was soft and clear: "I never thought you'd be here for me again."

"Nor I."

She turned the rest of the way in my arms, leaned in and kissed me, her mouth tasting of sleep, perhaps of our love-making. I waited her out, not wanting to spoil anything for her. When she finished, she pulled back a ways, and I could see her eyes were misty with something like unshed tears. She said, "I still love you, Athy. I didn't think I did, not after you were gone so long, but . . ."

I nodded, and hugged her close. What should I say? Gentle lies, knowing I would be gone again in a few weeks, that I could put all of this behind me once and for all if I chose? Or be brutal, for her sake, push her away, hope she'd finally let go of my memory, of the childish dream we'd shared? I said, "I never really forgot how I felt about you, Alix. It's . . . why I came back, I suppose."

She put her hand on my stomach, that familiar half smile on her face again, let her fingers slide down onto my abdomen, where she could feel the tension of a building erection. I wondered for a moment if that would spoil the feelings for her, but she smiled, holding me, and said, "I'm glad you came home." Somehow, it seemed as though I'd never gone away.

After breakfast, we dressed together, still skittish in our newfound familiarity, and went outside. It was midmorning, cool for a North Carolina August, and we went for a walk, heading down by the old monorail track, toward the woods behind the high school, where we'd walked so often. Talking, holding hands, pretending.

Alix seemed content to follow me, to just *be* with me. I wanted to ask, but what about your *job*? I was afraid to. Afraid she might tell me the truth. Not wanting to know.

The trail beside Bolin Creek was still intact, much the way I remembered it, but the trees were taller now, and seemed farther apart, the underbrush a little sparser. The forest is maturing, I realized, taking on that natural parklike appearance that the Carolina forests had had when the first Europeans arrived six hundred years ago.

The natives did that. Burned out the underbrush, so the deer would come live around them, a form of Neolithic animal husbandry . . .

After a while, Alix let go my hand and walked closer to me, putting her arm around my waist, molding her form to mine, shrugging in under my shoulder so I had to put my arm around her. I felt, for just a moment, as if I'd fallen into a dream.

Surge of old emotions, old feelings, thoughts that I'd put safely away, long, long ago. I loved this woman, when she was a girl and I was no more than a child. Loved her with the intensity you only know from your first love, no matter how profound those other, later loves may become. Now? I couldn't say. Maybe I didn't know.

But, from moment to moment, that sudden rush of innocent joy, threatening to spill over me, though I sought to push it away . . .

What good will this do? The weeks will pass, and then I must go, back to the land beyond the sky, to soldier, to do the bidding of my Master . . .

She'll cry again, after all this time, and, perhaps, so will I.

Do I want that?

More important: does *she*?

Her hand was on my stomach now, thumb tucked inside my belt, making it a little difficult for us to walk. Around us, the woods were filled with small sounds, the faint rush of wind in the treetops, an insect's chirr, a metallic-sounding birdsong, the gurgle of water in the stream, faraway human voices, a distant barking dog.

When I was a little boy, you couldn't walk through these woods without hearing the sound of road traffic close at hand, the distant rumble of aircraft, the occasional sharp crackle of a starship's lighter climbing from RDU Space Center.

Alix bumped against my side, seemed to stumble for a moment, then stopped, putting her hand on the outside of my pocket. Where the little gun had rested all night, uninvoked. Her eyes looked up at me, questioning. I said, "I'm required to carry a sidearm."

Eyes thoughtful. "Why didn't you use it last night?"

Black shadows flailing in the moonlight, unknown men dying. "It wasn't necessary. Somebody might've gotten hurt."

"*Hurt* . . ." I knew she was seeing the image of those men on the ground.

We walked on, holding hands again, quiet, being with each other, together, I suppose, in our thoughts.

In the area behind the high school, Bolin Creek narrowed and turned westward, through swampy ground, while the path climbed up through the woods, entering an area of low, clayey hills. Unexpectedly, we came out of the woods. When

I lived here last, the woods didn't end until right before the first set of athletic fields. Now they'd been cut down, the trees pushed aside, lying in one vast windrow, old gray trunks, with long-dead brown needles clinging to them in patches, deciduous trees long denuded of their leaves, the stumps pulled from the raw earth and thrown upon the heap.

There was a hole in the red ground, cut down into a deposit of clay, ground churned to mud by tramping feet. At the rim of the pit, a Saanaa stood watch, impassive, looking down at his charges. Down in the hole, there were men and women standing around as well, a handful of them, bearing whips, wearing sturdy canvas clothing.

Men with shovels. Men and women with buckets, treading a long line in and out of the pit. Naked men and women, fine, muscular bodies gleaming in the morning sunlight, gleaming with sweat, gleaming with the earth's moisture upon them. Standing to have their buckets filled, staggering away under the load.

Some of the women were lovely indeed, breasts high and firm, hair tied back, waists narrow and banded with muscle, shoulders broad and strong. The men looked like fantasy heroes, strong and brave.

One of the women slipped in the wet clay and fell, spilling her load. A heavyset woman with a whip stepped forward and slashed at her, braided lash making a thin, high sound, drawing a red line diagonally across the slave's back, shouting, "Up, bitch! *Work!*" The fallen woman struggled to her feet, no one stopping to help her, and went back for another load.

Cruel, cruel world. Cruel to everyone in it. I wondered, briefly, what these people had done to wind up here. Petty theft perhaps. Violation of some little Sirkar rule or another. Saying the wrong word to the wrong person at the wrong time. Or . . . just *being* the wrong person, in the wrong place, when the need for laborers arose.

That's the way these things usually work. Too bad.

Alix tugged at my hand and whispered, "Let's get out of here."

The Saanaa policeman turned to watch us, green eyes unreadable, watched us walk on. The school buildings were visible now through a last stand of old timber, buildings as clean and white as the day I left. There were some boys and girls playing touch football on the gridiron. Practicing, probably, for the fall season that would start in only a few weeks, with the onset of school.

We stood and watched, arm in arm, while they played, while the sun rose in the sky. Finally, I turned to Alix, holding her, looking down into her earnest face. I said, "I have to go away for a couple of days. Spahi business."

A fretful look, a yearning look. Oh, God, I have done it to her, whether I wanted to or not . . .

Through the shadow, she said, "Will I see you again soon?"

The thrill of that wish took hold of me, puncturing some last defense or another. I smiled into her face, took her head between my hands, kissed her softly. "Soon enough."

7 MY NEW MEMORIES OF ALIX, FLOODED with unaccustomed feeling, stayed with me all the way back to New York, keeping me within myself as the monorail slid above once-again familiar, blasted terrain, this new land of young green forests and vast, eroding craters. The ruins themselves, cities leveled, homesites crushed, were beginning to look like natural parts of the landscape, beginning to look old, beginning to disappear.

All I could think about, for at least that little while, was how she'd felt, clutched within the circle of my hands.

East of New York, out on Long Island, near the sea, not far from where the resort town of St. James used to be, there lies a field of black marble bearing the sigils of six hundred thousand dead. These are the Kkhruhhuft soldiers who died during the conquest of Earth. The Kkhruhhuft burst with pride when they speak of how well we fought.

There are no statues here, just flat black marble covered with names. The mother of my friend and comrade Shrêhht lies interred here, the little slab above the urn of her ashes inscribed with just a few complex, runelike ideograms:

Marôhh
Daughter of Yrûkkth

Died in Battle
17721.591027.181705

Shrêhht traced the symbols with the silver-painted talon of one toe as she translated the words for me, and we stood silently together, surrounded by all those thousands of names on a flat and polished black plain that reflected the distant sky, held the outlines of a few faraway clouds.

There's a memorial much like this in the ruins of Washington, D.C., the only monument that survived the destruction of the city, bearing the collected names of forgotten men and women who died in some forgotten nineteenth or twentieth century war. Maybe those people were proud to die. Maybe not.

Across the river from it, there's a vast cemetery, row on ranked row of dead soldiers. The gravestones are mostly fallen now, knocked over by the shock wave from the explosion, but I imagine the dead soldiers are still there, lying in their eternal darkness, imagining themselves to be ghosts.

A wind from the sea sprang up, making me shiver though the day was quite warm. Visiting graveyards preys on the imagination, making one silly and superstitious in short order. These Kkhruhhuft died because the Masters sent them here to die. Nothing to be proud of. And, to be fair, the Kkhruhhuft only claim to be proud of us.

It's not easy for a soldier of the Master Race to die in combat. Usually, we have an insurmountable edge. Usually, it's only the natives who die in vain. There's no monument to the eight billion and more human beings who died along with these Kkhruhhuft. No one speaks of them. Not anymore.

Shrêhht keyed her vocoder, and said, "She came home on furlough and bred for me, just as she bred for my sisters. I was born, and she raised me from hatchling to child, and turned me over to the clan, then returned to her comrades and wars. In time I followed her." Long moment of silence, then she turned her eyes on me, unreadable balls of mottled yellow. "I was in the battle when she died, though I didn't see it happen. I wish I had. They say she was superb."

Nothing for me to say. I knew she wasn't waiting for me to say how sorry I was. They're not us, whatever else they may be.

I stood and waited until she was finished communing with her dead, then we went for a long, silent walk, down by the seashore, listening as the gentle Atlantic waves hissed up the beach. There is apparently some commonality there as well. Things organic sophonts have in common. We all come from real worlds, worlds of sounds and sights and silences.

Who knows? Maybe even poppits love the sea.

The next day, Shrêhht and I went off together to a small resort out on Cape Cod, not far from the old beach town of Cahoon Hollow. It was, she said, a place favored by mercenaries visiting Earth. A place where a traveler from the stars could feel just a little more at home.

I never went to Cape Cod before the Invasion. We always had better beaches to go to, Emerald Isle, Topsail, North Myrtle, lovely, soft, brown sand beaches sloping down to warm green seas. Here, the sand is sharper and grainier, though not like the pebbled beaches farther north. Cape Cod is, after all, the last of the great barrier islands that line much of the coast north from Florida.

A resort area for centuries, it's all changing back now. Though the Massachusetts Bay shore is choked with the stumps of tall glass buildings, the seaward shore is empty, a long stretch of sand and scruffy beach vegetation, grass holding down the low, rolling dunes from the ruins of Provincetown all the way to Nauset Beach.

It was cooler here than in New York, the sand still warm from a day's sunshine, but the wind off the Atlantic already had the power to raise gooseflesh as the sun sank in the west. Beyond the sun, beyond the bay, I knew I'd find the great shantytown of Boston, whose people had stayed behind, refusing to leave even when the power failed. No bombs fell, so the city was taking decades to die. One more "unregulated native habitat," destined for closure.

There were other people here, people of every sort you could imagine. And very few of them were human. Green

Saanaae everywhere, whole families of them, sitting around open campfires, roasting skewered food, hissing laughter at each other. Whole families, because the Saanaae were here to stay.

Out in the ocean, you could see scores of swimming Kkhruhhuft, rolling in the surf like giant gray logs, like enormous alligators. Like the dinosaurs they really were, floating barely submerged, eyes and nostrils protruding, moving lazily about by flicking their long, heavy tails.

I wonder what the sharks thought of them? Probably, the sharks were afraid to come here now. Nothing in Earth's ocean short of a big old orca could menace a Kkhruhhuft. And there hadn't been orcas in any of the Earth's seas in a long damned time.

There were human people here as well, some of them recognizable as vacationing Spahis, men and women frolicking carefully together in the absence of their burdars, knowing what was expected of them. And other people, locals, moving among the aliens, including the human aliens.

Shrêhht was lying quietly beside me, inhabiting a warm hollow she'd carved out along a dune ridge, staring out to sea while we talked. There were clouds out there, drifting low above the horizon, making the edge of the world seem quite far away, and there was a sailing ship of some strange design, with high, angular bow and stern and two sets of oddly shaped, dark red sails. The green flecks moving about the deck were, I supposed, Saanaae.

If you were sent away to an alien world, exiled forever, would you bring your sailboat along?

The woman came walking up the line of the dunes, moving in a long-legged, muscular stride, long blond hair blowing in the sea breeze, blue eyes sharp, smiling confidently. Large breasts, held in by a white bandeau, further covered by a diaphanous halter top. Broad hips, bound by the narrow strands of an old-fashioned bikini bottom. Narrow waist, skin well tanned.

She looked at me, one hand on her hip, and waited for just a moment, then said, "Well, how about it?"

Talk about blunt. I thought of the coy little prostitute on

the train, straining to remember her name and failing. "How about what?" I could hear the faint chuff of Shrêhht's breathing behind me, knew that, from a Kkhruhhuft, audible breathing constituted something like a bemused chuckle.

The girl shook her head slightly and then patted her abdomen. "Come on, soldier-boy. Forty bucks Standard."

Well. I was suddenly almost embarrassed to have Shrêhht witnessing this, even though I knew she understood, was not judging me by this . . . behavior. "For what?"

A snort of laughter. The girl took the strings of her bikini bottom and gave them a quick tug, undoing slipknots, letting the little scrap of thin white cloth fall to the sand. I could see that her pubic thatch was the same shade as the hair on her head, that she'd shaved around the edges to keep it from showing around her bikini.

She said, "Forty Standard for as many times as you can manage between now and tomorrow morning."

"Is that a good deal?"

She laughed. "You haven't been here long, have you, soldier-boy?"

"No." In the background, I could still hear the sound of Shrêhht's breathing. Maybe a little louder now.

"Well. Let me show you what you'll be getting . . ." She turned away from me, bending over until she could look back between her legs, still grinning, holding her buttocks spread apart with her hands. "See? What d'you think?"

Pretty much indistinguishable from any other woman's standard hardware, is what I was thinking. Like Hani, like every other burdar I'd ever had. Even like Alix. And tempting, too. Little hormone elementals looking out through my eyes, opening up their floodgates, little voices muttering, Well? *Well?*

I reached over and patted her on one rounded, slightly sand-gritty buttock, maybe let my hand linger there just a little too long, and said, "Very nice. But you're right, I haven't been here very long. Maybe later."

She straightened up and shrugged, leaning down to pick up her bikini bottom. "OK, pal. Maybe later."

She walked down the face of the dune, that little bit of

cloth dangling from one hand, headed for where another group of Spahis was playing. I watched her go, tempted to call her back, and listened to the gentle whisper of Shrêhht's laughter.

Night fell, darkness coming up out of the east and covering the world, stars appearing in order of magnitude overhead, already wheeling about the pole, and the sea turned black, darkness reaching out until it touched the edge of the sky. It seemed to magnify the sounds around me, rushing of the surf against the shore a deep background whisper, easily heard over all the lesser sounds of the beach, the crackle of campfires, the laughter of men and women, the animal-like coughing of the Kkhruhhuft, softer Saanaae sounds. The high cackle of some shiny little silver bipeds of a sort I'd never run across before.

Shrêhht and I made our meal together, cooking over the same campfire, and opened our bottles and drank. I was glad I'd chosen a single-malt scotch then, its raw flavor covering up the burning, acrid fusel-oil smell of an amyl alcohol-based Kkhruhhuft beverage.

Down the hill, rendered not quite invisible by the darkness, I could see a large Spahi soldier kneeling in the sand, kissing a slender young man, running his hands delicately over the boy's soft, naked back. Somewhere out there, the girl would be busy by now as well, bent over in front of some stony-eyed man, perhaps, or crouching between the legs of a muscular, hard-faced woman.

Thinking about it, watching the men at the foot of the dune, I had another moment of regretting I'd sent her away. But then, she'd only made me think of Alix.

Shrêhht stirred in her sandy nest, and her vocoder whispered to me. "Always so strange, watching human mating rituals." Her eyes were on the couple before us, the boy's face now up against the man's middle, rubbing softly, gently, spreading moisture, getting ready.

Difficult to imagine what she was thinking. Or what she'd *really* thought about this afternoon's whore. No more than whispers of laughter.

She said, "I've seen some human anthropological studies,

films of several extinct species of large primate. You wouldn't have been worth much as soldiers, if you'd taken after your Bonobo chimpanzee cousins."

No, I suppose not. Imagine a human culture in which sex is everything, available to everyone, men, women, children. No exclusions. No jealousies. No hormonally driven male aggression. No female economic territoriality.

It's been suggested that the prevalence of child molestation in most human societies is driven by an ancestral memory of the path we almost took. Bonobo children didn't seem to mind. Maybe we would have been better off that way. Then again, Bonobos didn't build starships.

In any case, they're extinct now. I could see by the motion of the boy's head that he was fellating his soldier now, the man clutching him by the neck, guiding him, regulating his movements. It looked, from what little I could see, like they were both enjoying themselves.

Shrêhht said, "It's not like that for us."

I waited out the silence, suddenly alert.

She gestured at the couple at the foot of the dune. "Or maybe it is, I don't know. That woman who propositioned you this afternoon made chimpanzee sense, presenting, just like the creatures in the old films."

I laughed. "I guess it did look a little like that, didn't it?"

"Why didn't you accept her offer?"

Good question. I had an image of Shrêhht watching as I dropped my trunks, erection popping out, maybe making scientific observations as I stepped up to the bent-over woman, fumbling around, sliding into her, pumping steadfastly away until I was finished. Forty Standard's not much money. But I had no idea what her living expenses might be. Maybe it was a whole week's worth, and easily justified the expenditure of one night's energy.

"I don't know," I said. "I was thinking about my friend Alix. And about my burdars, I guess."

"You humans have made an interesting tangle out of sex and friendship, out of reproduction and recreation as well."

I nodded. "It's certainly made for a lot of cultural oddness. The burdar system's a lot simpler, I guess." Is it? Is it really true I don't care about Hani's feelings, that I fuck her when I want because that's what she's paid for? Nothing's that simple.

Shrêhht said, "It's hard for me to imagine worrying about the feelings of a male."

Um. Hard for me to know why she was saying this. They're not known to talk about their personal lives much. "Do they even have feelings . . ." I bit that off, realizing I was a little drunk, could easily go too far.

Shrêhht made a little chuff of laughter. "Have you ever owned a dog or a cat?"

"Both. A cocker spaniel when I was a little boy, 'til it got killed somehow. An alley cat that hung around our house after the Invasion, cadging meals . . ." I hadn't thought about either one of them for a long time, but I'd loved the dog, Lucky, and tolerated the fat, nameless gray tomcat.

She said, "I've done a little reading in human pet-keeping psychology. Maybe it's a little like that. Males live in our extended clan households, live with the children, are companions to them, much the way dogs are for human children. And they're sometimes used as hunting tools . . ."

A sudden shock of imagery, as if the Kkhruhhuft were somehow human. A hunting world of Amazon women, women and little girls and German shepherd dogs. Come to my bed, you sweet puppy. Make love to me . . .

"So *do* they have feelings?"

"Of course. And more like our feelings than a dog's are like yours. I think we love them just the way humans love their pets. And we get pleasure when they mate with us."

Impossible to drop that persistently silly male fantasy about women and dogs. Not appropriate here, but inevitably called up. "Can they talk at all?"

"No. They have nonverbal communication, about on a level with a dog's. They understand voice tones, can learn to respond to a few simple words . . ."

Heel. Sit. Fetch. Fuck. Good doggy!

She said, "I can imagine loving a male, but not being friends with one."

I've heard human women say something very much like that. "Some people imagine they're friends with their pets."

"Imagination is a dangerous tool—it can easily mislead you. Dogs are just responding to pack-culture behavioral cues. And it's clear that cats are issuing signals of their own that trigger false responses in humans. They don't really care who you are."

Down at the foot of the dune, the man and boy were suddenly finished, man sighing aloud with pleasure, the two of them holding still, a brief, pornographic tableau, then falling apart, both of them toppling to the sand. Shrêhht shifted in her nest until she could bring both eyes to bear on me.

"That is more comprehensible," she said. "Even though it's male and male, even though the reality of a sentient male psyche is far from understandable to me. I have friends whom I've loved, comrades with whom I've frolicked in the sun . . ."

Familiar imagery, seen from time to time, of giant gray Kkhruhhuft walking side by side, silent, yet so obviously aware of one another, a familiar tension. They don't take the males out to the stars with them; maybe they don't use them for recreational sex. So much for *good doggy* . . .

She said, "I think friendship can cross many boundaries."

I took a long pull at the neck of my bottle, felt the scotch go down like so much raw gasoline. And couldn't resist a slight snort of laughter. "You're not propositioning me, are you, Shrêhht?"

I was relieved to hear her own chuff of amusement. "I don't think I could get into a human female's presenting posture. Besides, you'd only smother." We sat together for a long while, silent, watching hard, brilliant stars turn against the backdrop of the Masters' sky.

The next day, we were back in New York, and I stood under a glary noonday sun, once again in the middle of that flat, black plain-of-names, now surrounded by a carefully disordered gaggle of men and women, all of us standing silent. Droplets of sweat made faint, itchy trails as they started up at my hairline, traveled dwindling down the back of my neck or across one cheek.

They call this the Gosudar's Ceremony, pretend that we

come to do them honor, but it's more than that. I was pleased that Shrêhht had asked me to stand for her, especially with the memory of our night spent together out on the beach.

With the sun beating down, old Aëtius Nikolaev, gosudar of all the Spahi legions, white-haired, frail-looking, though his shoulders were still broad, had given his little speech, ". . . we honor these brave dead, our comrades to come . . ." and now we stood together, waiting, the old man among us. He was, once upon a time, among the chiefs of staff of the forces that sought to defend Earth from these invaders.

There was a heavy, deep, hollow booming, metallic and hard, unmusical, as though someone were pounding the wall of a galvanized aluminum building with a sledgehammer. Kkhruhhuft drumming, one, two, three, not quite regular, subtly out of phase with human ideas of rhythm. A dark and sinuous screech, like a multitude of rusting, oilless hinges. The Kkhruhhuft sound of trumpets. The popping rumble of Kkhruhhuft voices, whisper raised to a throaty, gargling shout, Kkhruhhuft singing.

In human literature, they call this the Hymn of the Combat-Fallen. The words, though, translated to a human language, sound a little bit like "Amazing Grace." Not about religion, no, nor about some God or gods responsible for the universe's causality chains. Astonishment. Joy. That *I* have been permitted to die . . .

The disordered gaggle of men and women dispersed, each of us walking out across the black plain to where a single Kkhruhhuft was waiting. All of us lost friends, relatives in the Invasion. Some of these people, though, are family members of humans who fell slaying these Kkhruhhuft. I think no one who ever killed a Kkhruhhuft lived to recount the moment. I've never met one, at any rate . . .

I came and stood by Shrêhht, who stood by her mother's name, a small, neat pile of human combat armor by her feet, her voice raised in song. From close by, I could see her throat pouches filling with air, shuddering as she expelled the words, could feel deep subsonics beating against my chest. When we were all in place the singing stopped, and then the raucous music-analogue.

Moment of silence, Shrêhht looking down at me. Her vocoder was missing, putting us out of communication. No way to bridge the evolutionary gap between human and Kkhruhhuft without the universals of data-processing logic. Had we met as creatures of the wild, we'd've been animals to each other.

The drum began its not-quite-irregular clangor again.

Shrêhht stooped and began handing me bits of combat armor, cuirass and greaves, boots, powergloves, helmet, watching as I snapped them into place, as I went through deeply ingrained integrity-checking routines. Caution. Care. Habits of safety. These things rule a soldier's life. Forgetting them brings about his death.

She helped me shrug into the armor's backpack, helped me unspool and plug in the various power and data connectors, watched as I snapped down the visor, flooding my world with altered 3-D imagery. Handed me the collimated-beam weapon and stood back, stood looking down at me again.

What could I look like in her eyes? An armored black knight? Nonsense. No human image at all. This small, hard black thing at her side was an alien monster. A monster who'd killed six hundred thousand Kkhruhhuft soldiers.

She made a soft grunting sound, something I recognized to be a Kkhruhhuft military salute, turned and strode away. All the Kkhruhhuft were streaming away now, leaving us all alone together, armored and brave, standing by their mothers' names.

The gosudar's gravelly old voice whispered over the command circuit: "Power to guns."

I thumbed the stock switch and watched the displays in my helmet. This was old-style armor and an old-style gun, military hardware from the days of the Invasion. I'd hate to wear it into combat—it's no wonder so many of us died. Though the survival rate of humanity as a whole was around ten percent, they say fewer than one percent of the old soldiers lived to form the nucleus of the Spahi legions.

"Ready."

Men like that old havildar-emeritus, who'd seen terror I

might never know. Women like La Belle Dame, bitter and caring, who'd shown me how to survive while my comrades died. Women like Tahsildar Mamie Glendower, who'd been a shavetail lieutenant on frontline duty the day the Masters returned.

"Aim."

I lifted my gun, took aim at the face of the sun. The armor's optics dimmed the sun down, while leaving the sky bright blue, so that I stared upward at a grainy orange ball, full of spicules and sunspots, surrounded by corona, prominences frozen into place by their scale, though childhood lessons made me expect them to twist and coil. My sighting reticule was a faint tracery of black lines against the heavens.

"Fire."

Ten thousand lightning bolts leapt into the sky, thunder rolling and rolling across the world.

8 LATE THE NEXT AFTERNOON I CAME BY Alix's house to pick her up for dinner with my parents. The door opened and she was ready to go, dressed in a smooth-pressed cotton dress, sleeveless pale green cloth printed with darker green leaves, brown woody stems, reddish orange flowers.

She stood looking up at me, the room behind her in shadow, that half smile still on her face, waiting until I stepped forward and took her in my arms, then she collapsed forward against me. I squeezed her gently, kissed her on top of the head, ran my hand down one side and onto her hip.

She tipped her head back and, while we kissed, my hand slid around to her abdomen, then downward between her legs, feeling the little trough of her pubic symphysis, the softer flesh below, rubbing gently. She held still against me then, face pressed into my side, and I could feel the taut shape of her grin on my chest, could feel her legs drifting apart slightly, inviting me inward.

Voice soft, she said, "We don't *have* to go . . ." Hips pushing forward now, a tiny sliding movement against the heel of my hand.

I took the hand away, moved it around to the small of her back, pulled her against me. "I think my parents might be upset."

She looked up at me, smile turned halfway to a frown. "Would they? I haven't talked to them much over the years. Just Lank, sometimes Oddny."

When I'd told them I was bringing Alix for dinner, there'd been frowns and doubtful looks. My parents disapproved of her from the very beginning I think, but said nothing. So many of my playmates were gone, some dead, some just missing. They tried to talk about that with me, especially after I found Henry Leffler's mummylike corpse under a pile of rubble in our backyard. He was our next-door neighbor, a year younger than me, and not one of my closest friends, but I'd played with him from time to time.

He was naked, all white and black and stiff, covered with dust, extremities swollen, fingers and toes, genitals and tongue, surrounded by fragments of old gypsum wallboard. They say the hydrophilic dust sucked all the moisture out of him, slowing the process of decay. By that time, what we mostly found were skeletons and it was hard to know who they were. Henry looked just like himself, only dead.

Let him play with the little girl, my father'd said. He must be lonely now, what with . . . But he's got Davy and Marsh, still. It'll be OK, Lana. What harm can it do? My mother, watching us play in the cleaned-up yard, frowning. Just kids at play, though we were of a certain age, or about to be.

The summer after we met, I started collecting fragments of old bicycles from the ruins around us, bits and pieces, straight frames, derailleurs and chains, brakes and cables and shift levers. There weren't any straight wheels to be found, but Alix turned up one day with a little spoke wrench and we figured out how to make them straight, measuring off the hub with a piece of string. Finding tires turned out to be the really hard part, but, finally, we had two intact bicycles, freshly painted with a can of Teflon spraypaint she'd found in her father's collapsed garage, "Federal Safety Sign Yellow" it was called, and went out for a ride.

We knew where we were going, though we didn't tell anybody, just headed out into brilliant June sunshine, wind in our hair, pushing through the fabric of our lightweight clothing, riding north beyond the town's boundary into the statutory greenbelt between Chapel Hill and Hillsborough. Up US 86, east on New Hope Church Road, past fallen houses, already overgrown, east on Old NC 10, east on the startlingly empty white concrete of I-85.

The old prefab housing tract across from the parking lot to this particular division of Eno River State Park, eight miles from the center of Chapel Hill, was simply gone. You could see where the little roads had been, the weedy green tangles of yards, big, brown squares where the foundations had been. We leaned our bikes against tattered and bark-scraped trees, trees damaged, perhaps, by whatever had taken the houses, and stood, holding hands, the way we always did in the face of something . . . well, scary, and Alix whispered, "Maybe they just blew away . . ." Blew away. On a wind of fire.

We hid the bikes, chained them to trees back a little ways in the woods, and walked down an overgrown path. Strange to see it like this, so abandoned. It'd been no more than two years since the last time someone had mowed this path, but the underbrush was closing in already. And you could tell no one had been walking here lately.

The path goes down to the Eno River, choked with boulders and weeds, and that's where you're supposed to stop, walk around, commune with nature. But if you take the old path up the bluffs, follow them back away from the river a little ways . . .

Hell, I half expected to find the old quarry pit full of screaming kids, teenagers, college students, the occasional arrested-development adult. It's been here for centuries, rainwater ecology long ago established, filled to the brim with clear, cold, faintly green-tinged water.

I don't know where the silvery little fish came from. They're the same kind you see in the river, so maybe people caught them, brought them up and threw them in. I think they live on the algae and bugs. And, of course, all the popcorn that gets spilled in the water. Used to get spilled in the water.

Now, Alix and I stood holding hands, looking on our empty little lake, wondering if anyone would ever come here again. The survivors, just maybe, had something more important to do than come swimming in the old quarry. Or maybe all the people who used to come here are dead.

Alix was shivering against my side, though the day was already hot, promising the sort of roasting afternoon you expected from a North Carolina summer. You could hear bugs buzzing all around, bird noises, the soft, distant bubbling of water in the river.

But nothing human. In the old days, the soft roar of the I-85 traffic was always there.

Finally, we walked around the rim of the pit to the far side, to our favorite diving spot, a sheer mud cliff about six meters high, topped by gnarly, sap-stained pine trees, ground covered with a soft brown carpet of old needles. The knotted rope was still there, still hanging down from a tree on the cliff's edge, dangling down to the water, the way back up after you'd made your dive.

Nothing to do then but pretend it was the old days, that everything was as it had been. So quiet here though . . .

We started to get undressed, I stripping down to the bathing trunks I'd worn under my jeans, turning to look out across the water. And I suddenly realized, like a small electric shock, that Alix was standing beside me in her white underclothes.

I turned to stare, eyes trying hard to shy away, and said, "Um. Where's your bathing suit?" She was very pretty like this, slim, cotton briefs clinging to narrow, girlish hips, wearing an elastic brassiere that had, more or less, nothing to contain.

She grinned, eyes a little skittish as well, and said, "Don't be silly, Athy. Bathing suits are for when grown-ups are around." She gestured out at the empty quarry pond. It occurred to me to wonder how she'd known no one else would be here, but . . .

She put her hand behind her back and undid the bra, dropped it on the pile with the rest of her clothes, then skinned out of the briefs. "Well?"

Well. I pulled down my trunks and stepped out of them, suddenly feeling very heavy and clumsy indeed, unbalanced, not quite able to trip and fall, and my face felt like I was made out of cold clay.

Alix said, "You're blushing, Athy."

Yeah. "So are you . . ."

I don't think I ever had another moment when I thought a woman was so beautiful, though Alix was hardly more than a girl. She turned then, laughing out loud, ran and dived over the cliff, and I stood, lead-footed, rooted in time and space, watching her white body fall toward the pale green water, watched her disappear with hardly a splash and surface a few meters away.

She whipped the hair away from her face and grinned up at me. "Come on! It's *great!*"

I ran and jumped, fell twisting through the air, and hit the water like a falling boulder. When I surfaced, sputtering, Alix had already swum up to me, rubbing water out of her eyes, grinning. "You made a pretty big splash, Athy . . ."

"Sorry."

She reached out and held on to my shoulders then, and I was almost afraid to move, afraid to breathe, to do anything that would spoil the moment, though I really had only a boy's shallow idea of what was going on. We played away the afternoon, swimming, frolicking on the shore, diving again and again, sometimes just looking at each other, and went home at dusk, exhausted, to parents who frowned and shook their heads.

In the darkness, walking down the path beside Bolin Creek, I said, "You remember when we used to go swimming at the old quarry?"

Long silence, wind in the trees, faint trickling sound of water in the half-empty creek, buffering the soft, distant sound of our footfalls, Alix's hand tightening on mine for just a moment. "Yes . . ."

Far away, Alix lost in memory.

Dinner came and went, of its own accord, as so many things do, Oddny and Lank greeting us at the door, Lank smiling, Oddny hugging Alix briefly, taking her by the hand and leading her into the parlor, where my family had some nice old furniture, none of it things I remembered from before the Invasion.

My father came out and sat with us while we talked, nodding, trying not to frown, failing, making us all feel uncomfortable and stiff. My mother stayed out in the kitchen, the clanking of utensils, pots and pans forming a backdrop as we talked. After a while, Oddny stood, put her hand briefly on Alix's shoulder, then went in to help Mother set up.

While we waited and talked, Alix sat by my side on the sofa, her flank pressed against mine, seeming to grow closer, almost shrinking against me, as time passed.

Dinner. My mother, I think, outdoing herself. That fine, salt-spicy Italocreole chicken I remembered from my childhood, made from spices that must be hard to get. Candied carrots with pineapple and brown sugar. A sharp, savory bread stuffing, greasy with chicken fat. A bitter salad of chicory, watercress and, to my surprise, pale red radicchio. No Brussels sprouts, though we'd always eaten them with this particular chicken dish.

Maybe they don't grow around here and can't be got. Pineapples will grow down on the coastal plain . . .

My mother remained taciturn, though Alix, uncomfortable, tried to draw her out. I felt, for the first time, a small trickle of anger at them all, slowly waxing. A moment when I wanted to stand up and shout at them.

It would have been for nothing though. All their feelings about Alix just anger at a little girl who, they imagined, stole their little boy. Parents imagining their son a little boy, even while they knew he was masturbating to the image of a dancing whore? Parents are silly like that. And masturbation is a boy's game, done with icons, not other people.

With Alix, they must imagine me holding her in my arms, whispering secrets to her, going away from them. A betrayal of sorts, like a watchdog who licks the hand of a stranger.

They sat silent, while Lank and Oddny talked of childhood things, of times gone by, while we sat together on their sofa, while they waited for the evening to end, for Alix to rise and bid them good-bye, and go home. Maybe they imagined her walking away in the darkness alone. Or maybe they assumed I'd leave with her.

Not long before midnight, Alix yawned. I stood, and, as she rose beside me, I saw the relief in their eyes. But I bade them all good night and led Alix by the hand, up creaking, handmade stairs, closing the door on them all.

Standing in this imitation of my childhood room, the one she must surely remember well, standing in a pool of yellow-orange light, dark night outside, Alix stared for a long time at my boy's icon, almost but not quite frowning. Finally, she reached out and touched its trigger point, and the woman began her dance, exposing herself.

A giggle. "I *remember* this . . ."

I put my arm around her shoulders, watching as the dancing girl spread her labia for us. "I almost didn't. I'm afraid to ask them why it's here and back in working order. Or why they were so . . . unhappy tonight."

Alix turned in my arms and put her hands on my chest, shadowed eyes serious, looking up at me. "Don't you know?"

"Maybe."

"It's been a long time since you went away, Athy. People change. It's a very sour sort of life you left behind."

I nodded. Sure, but every life's like that. It's why old people are so often very bitter and subdued. Or angry. Nothing is fair. Life goes badly, and then you die. Or it goes very well indeed, and then you die anyway. The spouse you were glad to have stays faithfully by your side for all those years, and you die knowing you missed it all, that you spent most of those years suffocating from boredom. Or they leave you, alone and bitter, for someone else. And you can't forget that tang of what-might-have-been, no matter that their replacement was wealthier, healthier, stronger, more devoted, whatever.

She said, "After you went, somehow, your going became my fault."

I could imagine Alix left behind. Imagine my parents telling each other, If only we'd kept them apart . . . "I sup-

pose there's nothing anyone can do to stop people looking
for someone to blame, some way to make excuses for what
they'd otherwise perceive as their own failings . . ."

"*Was* it their fault?" A steady, dark-eyed stare. "Or mine?"

"Only mine. Because I wanted to go . . ."

We sat down on the edge of the bed and I turned out the
lamp, leaving us in semidarkness, lit by moonlight through
the window, by the dancing girl's lambent glow.

Later, we lay tangled together, damp skin on damp skin,
looking out into the tangle of moonlit trees. I'd opened the window all the way, so the curtains lifted away from the frame,
flapping slowly over us, warm breeze filling the room, soft on
our skins.

Alix huddled against me, head on my chest, and kept running her hand through my pubic hair, fingers trailing around
on my rubbery, postcoital penis, feeling, I suppose, her own
ichor and mine. It felt strange, not something any burdar'd
ever done of her own accord. Not something I'd ever asked
for, either, hardly worth the effort, and not in keeping with
what I thought of as women's character. Indelicate.

It also seemed . . . I don't know. Personal. Intimate?

Me looking at my own face in the hazy darkness. Goddamn you. You're twenty years out of practice understanding
women's feelings. And never really had a chance to learn.
Right. Sitting in a PX bar with Solange, Johnny Rexroth, and
a few other favorites. Drinking dark beer, thick ale, sharp,
rich dropshot boilermakers. Laughing, making all sorts of
nasty jokes, about sex and violence, burdars, natives, poppits, Masters, what have you. Friends. Comrades.

Staggering back to the crib lot, stinking drunk, weaving
down the road, arm around Solange's back, her arm around
my shoulders. Singing. I can't even remember what. The two
of us burping in each other's faces as we stood reeling in the
yard between our two cribs, Solange making some wisecrack
about giving Tzadi's damn face a good workout, poking each
other hard just a few times, screaming with laughter.

Fuzzed-out humor, amusement, remembering that her burdar Tzadi was an Armenian, with a rather large nose.

I went in and held Hani down on the living room floor, sat astride her chest and did what I did. She didn't complain, keeping her eyes shut the whole time, then helping me off to bed, sponging my face and chest with a warm, damp cloth, smiling as she tucked me in.

I'd seen Solange naked in the junior officers' bath, tall, slender, almost hairless, but looking like every woman in the world despite her attenuated Nilotic form. Thinking of sex with her seemed a little bit like thinking of sex with Johnny Rexroth, whose burdars were always male, all save his wonderful cook Cerise, who'd been with him for twelve years.

Alix was handling my scrotum now, rolling my testicles gently against each other, feeling the placement of that little bump and cord coming off the forward end of each spongy egg. And realized she was quite good at it, touch firm enough not to tickle, light enough not to hurt. Not something I remember from back then.

Maybe Benny taught her how.

The wind blew a little harder outside, pushing the curtains up higher, making the trees move against each other, a sound like the rush of the surf against the shore. Up in the sky the stars were clear and hard, barely twinkling. Not much like the stars you see from outer space, though, the stars seen from the nightside of an airless world.

Alix said, "I always wanted to know what it was like out there. I often wish I'd passed muster with you . . . or that there was some other way."

Another moment of realization. These people may not even know about the colonization project. They don't know how the Masters' empire works, because there's no reason for anyone to tell them. I tried to picture Alix as a colonist woman, maybe settled on A-IV's relatively placid antarctic continent. She was probably too old for the selection process now. Unless the Masters decided the colonists would need medtech too. "Didn't you ever go out before . . ."

She curled against me, running her palm back and forth across the ridges of my stomach. "We went to Mars for a while when I was six. Something to do with my mother's job. I don't remember much. Red desert. Pink sky. Staying inside the domes. Going outside in vacsuits. I liked the low gee, I guess, for a while, but mostly I wanted to come back home. I missed the real sky."

That moment, getting off the starship. The sky for which my eyes were made. "I missed it too."

"But you never came home. Why?"

"I don't know." I could feel the way that made her restless. Women always want you to say how you feel, even burdars, though they can't press you for an answer. Maybe the answers they get, the lack of them, is why so many women seem to believe men *don't* feel . . .

Soap opera bullshit. Fossil social concepts left over from twenty years and more ago, half-formed adolescent knowledge. I know how women feel. Half the soldiers of the Spahi legions are women.

She said, "Well. I still would've liked to go. Maybe I wouldn't have come home either . . ."

What was she picturing? The two of us soldiering together out among the Fixed Stars? Going into battle together, making love afterward? Maybe she pictured Davy and Marsh out there too, along with all our other childhood friends . . .

We talked our way into the night, Alix telling me about her life, the way she'd lived, the dreams she'd had to let go, making me by turns jealous and sorry. There'd been a lot of men, men who'd helped her hone the sexual skills she was showing me now. The image was odd and unpleasant, in my imagination a whole army of them lined up at her feet, waiting in turn for a few moments between her splayed legs.

I kept telling myself it was silly to have any feelings at all. These men were just *her* burdars . . .

And I was sorry to think of her moving through that long, goalless life, moving from the day of my departure to some hypothetical death, living for this little job and that one, men passing in and out of her life, strangers become friends become strangers.

We made love again, Alix sitting astride me now, looking down on me, palms flattening on my chest, kneading muscle like a cat preparing its bed. And lay together again, damp once more, and talked. She wanted to know about my life out among the stars, so I simply told her.

She grew quiet. Listened. Held still against my side. Training. Death. Burdars. Natives.

I told her about the Mountains Without Clouds, and her eyes shone in the night as she tried to visualize the place I was describing. I told her about the windrows of native dead, and watched her imagine sorrow.

I told her about the day we landed on a world very much like Earth, and burned down all those cities of concrete and steel and glass. Tried to tell her about a moment when I'd stood in front of a massed group of unarmed humanoids, stood in my black ceramic armor, while they looked at me out of wide, soulful brown eyes. Adults certainly, though I couldn't tell if they were male, female or something else. Small ones that had to be children. Some of them silent, some making soft noises that might be cries of despair.

I'd checked the duty rosters, confirmed my order checklist, and sprayed them with my torch, watched them fall in the flames, curl and blacken and die. Local things that stood in for flowers would one day soon bloom in the field of ashes I left behind.

Tried to tell her that, but failed. What she wanted was the beauty of other worlds, the glory of my soldier's life. Something to hold against the drear and limit of the world she'd known since I went away. Some way to confirm what she'd always imagined: that, wherever I was, I was happy.

I wondered if I felt ashamed, but couldn't tell. What does shame feel like? I held her close, and we yawned together, smiled maybe, and slept as dawn spread its first faint indigo ribbons against the night.

We awoke at noon, sunlight streaming in steeply through the open window, went and showered together, though the others must long ago have been up and about. As we embraced under the streaming water, I could imagine my mother downstairs, listening. Angry? Tears in her eyes, perhaps? By the light of day, holding Alix, wet and soapy in my arms, I couldn't imagine caring.

It turned out everyone had gone but Lank, who sat with us while we drank mugs of hot, sugary coffee. Alix was unexpectedly shy in front of him, eyes downcast, almost blushing, which made her seem younger than she had only moments before. That other Alix, the shadowy span of her adolescent girlhood in my memory, had been a little like that.

Lank didn't seem to notice. When we'd finished the coffee, when we'd eaten a little bit of fruit, the remaining fat heel from an irregular, hardening loaf of raisin bread, he drove us to Durham, left us at the monorail platform as we'd arranged. During the trip over, back up 15-501's broken pavement, Alix and I sat together in the backseat, leaning against each other, quiet.

Lank never said anything as he drove, never looked back over his shoulder. Maybe he thought we were fooling around.

The East–West North American Central Monorail Trunk was built over the roadbed of I-40, which had originally been laid down in the last third of the twentieth century, during the fading years of the post–World War II infrastructure boom. It had been renewed, built again with a hard plastic roadbed in the mid twenty-first, then overshadowed by the monorail line, around the turn of the century. Private cars were still using it, though, on the day of the Invasion. It hadn't been returned to operational status until not long before I left.

Looking downward now, as the shadow of the train moved along the shadow of the track, flying from pylon to thin pylon, I could see the old roadbed was still in good shape, much better than the old-style faux stone of 85, or local routes like 15-501. This scaly red stuff just didn't weather, would stay intact for a million years, now that no one was driving on it. Unless, of course, scavengers decided to pull it up sometime.

Maybe they would. There were all kinds of people visible down there, living alongside the track. Little bunches of ramshackle huts, tents, and teepees, the occasional still-intact pre-Invasion house, smoke coming out of its chimney. One fine-looking place was surrounded by a high fence, topped by rusty barbed wire, two big black dogs standing in the yard. There was a fat black woman on her knees, tending a rosebush.

I pointed it out to Alix as we went by. She watched the place recede, and said, "Hard to say whose that is. An Overseer Corps supervisor, maybe. Some of them live pretty well."

Overseer Corps. An odd turn of phrase. I hadn't much thought about looking into Earth's real social infrastructure. I wasn't going to be here that long. Would the fat woman in the yard be the supervisor herself, or merely an employee?

Sliding east out of Durham, we passed over a wilderness of terraced vines, heading down toward the flat country. This was where RTI University had been, but all I saw was one big billboard, standing aslant on sagging legs: "Planetary Trade Zone 93."

Beyond that, where the housing tract community of Morrisville had been, we passed over a broad expanse of well-cleared land, several dozen square miles of agricultural fields, different sorts of crops separated by bands of forest, crops under some sound rotation scheme, all the little hills carefully contour plowed. Little houses here and there, no more than whitewashed shacks.

No machinery visible. Nor animals. The fields were full of naked black workers, toiling in long lines under a hot summer sun. One field was under the plow, its sod being turned under to enrich the soil's nitrogen content prior to a fall sowing of some sort. I couldn't quite remember how the planting and harvesting seasons worked around here. It just hadn't been important before.

And the plow, of course, was being pulled by a team of husky men.

Dotted sparsely around the complex were armed Saanaae, white blankets thrown over their backs, big straw hats on their heads. Very silly-looking. Most of them were flanked by dark brown humans, humans usually dressed in white shorts, some of them with white socks running up to their knees. Some of them had on white shirts, females maybe.

Nothing down there that looked like a Caucasian. Maybe there were dark Hispanics, but it was impossible to tell at this distance. We were down off the Piedmont Plateau now, passing over land that could be classed as tropical. No sense in using white men down there. They'd only die on you.

At Smithfield, far beyond where Raleigh had been, the East–West Central Trunk intersected the North–South Eastern Trunk, which ran down the fine red plastic roadbed of I-95. The train stopped here to exchange passengers with other trains, people transferring, most of them heading on down to Florida, where the beaches were still fine, or on up to New York and the center of the world. It would stand here for a half hour, so Alix and I got out to stretch our legs on the platform.

This is flat country here, hot and steamy, stretching on into the hazy blue distances south and east. Northward, you can see the beginnings of Virginia's long, low hills, to the west the faint rim of the Piedmont Plateau, topped by a mist of fluffy white cloud.

And something of Smithfield was still intact as well, a cluster of old houses formed up as a native bustee. I couldn't recall ever having been here, though I must have been many times, passing through with my parents on the way to Topsail Beach. It must have been a city back then.

All around now, there was nothing but olive green forest. And, in the far distance, far to the south, a tall, pale column of thin gray smoke, rising off the horizon, standing up into the sky, its top sheared away finally by some hard high-altitude wind.

Alix stood silently at the rail, staring at the smoke. Below the platform, near the bustee's central square, a large group of men and women stood together, shackled into a line of chains, very much like coffled Boromilithi in transit. A local work gang? Not likely. About two thirds of them were obviously of primary European descent, people with soft brown or yellow hair that would blow around in a wind, skins burning red under the bright sun.

There were Saanaae here too. Too damned many of them. Carrying their rifles at port arms, formed up into squads.

Sagoths as well, standing in little bunches. All of them looking very nervous. Talking too much. No bystanders, other
than the people from the train. Houses of the bustee all
closed up. Shades drawn. Doors closed.

The tag ends of the coffle were spiked into the ground.

I looked around the platform. Everyone was watching.
Passengers all wide-eyed, some of them turning around, getting right back on the train, if they could, transfers bunching
up on the far edge of the platform, maybe hoping their own
train would just damned well show up . . .

Alix's hands were gripping the railing hard, knuckles
standing out faint red against taut white skin. All right.
Everyone knows but me. Even the train-sagoths clearly wish
they were elsewhere.

I counted quickly. Twenty-seven of them. Noise from
down below now. One of the prisoners was crying softly, but
I couldn't tell which one.

Squad of Saanaae was behind them now, sagoths backing
out of the way, stumbling over their own feet. A snapped
order. The Saanaae sat like dogs. Another. The rifles were
aimed. Another. The rifles fired, muzzles sparkling blue,
brighter than sunlight. Again. Again. Again.

A faint echo from somewhere far away. Twenty-seven
men and women lying on the ground, smoke curling up from
their bodies in little wisps. The faint smell of roast pork in
our nostrils.

I looked down at Alix. She was still watching, hands still
white on the rail, eyes very hard indeed, lips drawn into a
very slight frown.

There are subtle differences in the Atlantic seen from the
Outer Banks instead of Cape Cod, the green seawater a little
browner, perhaps, a little friendlier somehow. Maybe it was
just the warm summer sun making pins and needles on our
backs, the knowledge that the water would be blood-warm
when we walked into it, like a familiar, welcoming bath.

Wrightsville Beach was deserted, no longer maintained,
sand ridged into low terraces by the incoming tide, and wide
gullies had formed everywhere, running back up into the

dunes, opening crevices between stands of otherwise solid, low green shrubbery. Behind the dunes was a collapsed rubble of holiday housing, already overgrown by weeds, thin saplings pushing up through mounds of wood and plaster and plastic. The tall, black and ceramic towers of modern Wilmington were visible in the distance, standing above the intervening forest, in the sky the silent silver fleck of a departing aircraft, heading off into the west, toward the sun.

We spread our blanket on the ground not far from a single long line of shallow human footprints, where someone had come walking alone up the beach. Small footprints. A boy. A teenage girl, perhaps. Nearby, whoever it was had stopped and sat in the sand, making a little rump crater, and played with a rubble of shells. Set some of them up to spell out a word, but pieces had been kicked loose, so all I could make out was an "E" and an "N." A name perhaps.

I sat and watched Alix undress, standing half turned away toward the sea, but looking at me as I watched her. Hands over her head, stretching, running her hands through her hair. Smiling, but almost nervous. Self-conscious.

She kicked off her sandals and stepped off the blanket, standing in the warm sand, moving her feet from side to side slightly, sinking in. Looking away then, for just a moment, before reaching up and undoing the buttons at the front of her blouse, shrugging out of it, dropping it onto the blanket beside me.

Then the buttons at the side of her short summer skirt, dropping it around her ankles, stepping out of it, kicking it up onto the blanket too. There was a hint of color in her cheeks, her eyes starting to wander now, to look away from me more.

I kept looking away from her face, toward where her breasts were hidden by a rather plain and somewhat-worn white brassiere, toward the front of her underpants, where I could make out the shape and color of her pubic hair through the cloth.

She said, "I can remember when you wouldn't watch me undress." She reached her arm back, elbow bending at an awkward angle, and unhooked the bra, shrugged it forward off her shoulders, breasts sagging down onto her chest wall.

I nodded. "I was always afraid to watch. Afraid you'd stop, I guess, if you knew I was . . . *looking*."

She laughed, brushing her hand through her hair again. "I always used to wonder why. I was doing it *for* you . . ." She hooked her thumbs under the waistband of the briefs and slid them down, bending, stepping out, tossing them onto the pile of her clothes.

She was lovely naked, and so very different. Nothing about her of those slim, *just-so* lines I'd come to expect from women placed at my disposal. Thickened about the waist, stomach rounded, thighs sleek and full, little striations like stretch marks at the top of her breasts, little pouched places at the front of her armpits, showing the excess flesh.

I kneeled up and started unbuttoning my shirt, still looking at her, trying to keep my eyes on her face, repeatedly having them wander off to those other parts. "I think boys really feel they're asking girls to do something nasty. Maybe they think they're tricking them. You know: If I pretend not to notice, maybe she won't figure out what's going on until it's too late . . ."

That soft laugh again. "While you were busy hoping I wouldn't notice what we were playing at, I used to hope you'd just put your face right here." She gestured at her mons. "For about six months before we ever did anything, I used to go home at night and masturbate, imagining what it'd feel like if you ever did."

I stood and kicked off my shoes, undid my trousers and stepped out of them. "Why didn't you just ask?"

She was looking at me, inspecting my body, not even making a pretense of being interested in my face. "Because . . . girls don't."

A simple phrase, covering all the oddities of a complex, enduring culture. There'd been a pretense of change, in historical eras past, but nothing ever hung on.

She said, "I never really got a good look at you before." She looked up at my face then, something like pain in her eyes. "You're still so young."

I put one hand onto the side of her face, running my fingers back into the hair behind her ear. "It's not youth. More like the gloss you see on a well-cared-for machine."

A somber look into my eyes, a searching look, then we turned and walked toward the sea, hand in hand.

The water *was* warm, no shock of entry, almost too warm, almost soporific, the bottom slimy with soft mud and algae that squeezed between our toes, the imported beach sand long ago washed away, covered up by biological action. No debris though. No old cans, bottles, whatever. There were bits of wood. Pieces of broken shell, sharp, like slivers of dull glass.

We followed the slope down until the water was up to Alix's shoulders, the middle of my chest, the roll of the incoming tide rocking us gently back and forth, low rollers moving up the beach with a dull roar-hiss behind us, and stood facing each other. Beyond Alix, I could see all the way to the flat horizon, the world coming to an abrupt end not so far away.

Once upon a time, there'd've been sailboats out there, sails almost always white. I wonder how I'd feel if there were more Saanaae sailors just now. More at home maybe, feeling less that we were inhabiting some lost limbo of an empty world.

Alix was standing close to me, and I could feel her breasts floating in the ocean water, moving with the currents, nipples rubbing against my chest. She reached out to hold on to me with one hand, holding on to my hip, her feet coming off the bottom from time to time, using me as a stable platform, my center of gravity higher, my chest and shoulders standing maybe twenty centimeters farther out of the water.

Tall. I'd forgotten she was very tall for a woman.

She said, "I used to dream about coming here with you. Especially after you left." A long look into my face, her free hand trailing across my chest. "You remember going to the beach when you were a kid?"

A nod.

"I wish we could've come here together."

But, by then, the world had come to an end. "We had the lake. And we're here now." I put my arms around her shoulders and pulled her against my chest, enfolding her, wanting to feel the evolution of some special kind of closeness, but I could feel her hand stealing between my legs now, fumbling around.

Later, we built a fire on the beach, cooked a dinner of summer sausages, baked the knobby little potatoes we'd brought with us, while sunset flamed in the sky, ridges of fire forming out over the sea, clouds of red and orange framing the sun as it fell down through the forest behind us.

We ate dinner naked, sitting cross-legged on the blanket in the lengthening shadows, looking at each other. There was a softness in Alix's eyes now, softer than anything I'd seen yet. A budding familiarity. A face that said, I remember now . . .

And I will confess to an odd feeling in me. A breaking down of very old walls. Remember, when you loved her more than anything else? When no one and nothing else mattered? So what if the world had to come to an end? Alix and I found each other . . .

I remember thinking that, one night when I was fifteen years old. I was kneeling between her legs then, sitting back on my heels, looking down at her, bedded on a blanket atop brown grass in some summery, abandoned Chapel Hill field. She was almost asleep, hardly aware of my eyes on her body and face.

I remember how the sight of her genitals, wet with my semen, used to thrill me . . .

In the here and now, she said, "What're you smiling at, Athy?"

"I was remembering other times just like this."

That somber, so-serious look. "I'm glad you remember."

But I hadn't spent that much time remembering, in all the years I'd been away. I could remember kneeling between Hani's legs even now, looking down at her delicately exposed vulva, so small and sparsely haired. If I looked up at Hani's face, I'd see her eyes, open, waiting, attentive.

I watched Alix put a bit of cooked sausage in her mouth, chew reflectively, swallow, lick her fingers, all without taking her eyes off mine. I wondered what my face looked like to her just now. I said, "Why is this happening?" A gesture, at the two of us.

She said, "I don't know. Are you sorry it is?"

No answer, not even a shrug. I said, "What do you . . . want from me?"

A flinch, a sudden closing down of her features, eyes looking away, starting to withdraw.

"I'm sorry. I didn't mean that the way it sounded." We never do, do we? A thousand flickering memories of women taking hurt from the chance vagaries of curtailed grammar.

Her eyes came back, curious, but guarded now.

I said, "What do you want from . . . all of this? From *us*."

A long look, straight into my eyes, unflinching. And as if she were reading my soul. I wanted to throw up my walls of glass, shut her out, make her be a dying warrior whose heart I was about to pluck out. But the resource to do so was gone, the walls of glass no more than a distant shattering sound, glass become dust, blowing away on the wind like so much thin white sand.

She said, "Make love to me again, Athy. I won't have you here with me forever."

9 I WAS AWAKENED BY WARM SUNLIGHT, lensed onto my face by the window of Alix's Carrboro hovel, gradually pushing through layers of lightening sleep, making me conscious of sensation and the world. I could feel her leg thrown over me, knee propped on my hip, foot tucked between my calves, other leg cast straight down, thigh pressed front-to-front with mine. Her breath was a warm sensation on my cheek, breasts flattened into my chest.

We'd slept like this on the beach, too, wrapped in a rough woolen blanket that itched on our skins, while the fire crackled in the background and died down to embers, the sea shuffing softly as the tide came in and then receded.

When the moon came up, waning slightly from full, its pale, cold light made the beach a ghostland, tiny crabs coming up to look at us, eyes on stalks, expressionless, like so many faraway nonhumans. No urge at all to kill them. Until the Masters told me to.

Alix stirred against my chest, tucking her hips in, pressing her abdomen against mine, murmuring softly, nothing like real words, and when I opened my eyes hers were already open, hazily waiting. She smiled. "You slept peacefully all night. You usually don't."

Already getting used to me, learning my habits. I nodded.

"You're . . . making me comfortable." That made her smile, and kiss me.

She said, "You still want to go on the camping trip? Like . . . old times?" A curious look, the apparent fear that I'd only been seduced by that night out on the beach, being drugged by sex and more sex until I could hardly think anymore.

But, *like old times* . . . I said, "I think this is why I came home, Alix." This time, when she kissed me, she put her tongue in my mouth, slow and languorous, pressing herself against me full length, curling her leg behind my back and pulling me close.

I could feel myself starting to erect against her, hardly any awareness left to wonder just what the hell I was doing.

And she was grinning into my face, slowly grinding her hips against me, and whispering, "I think this is what I waited for . . ."

It was a tiny particle of fear, so easily smothered, not so easily forgotten.

Later, walking alone down a narrow dirt track in the young woods that had grown up between Carrboro and Chapel Hill, I felt grainy-eyed and strange. Larger than I had been and lighter, as if I'd somehow grown more tenuous. And emptied of thought, merely walking like a shadow through an empty world, listening to the faraway hiss of the wind, watching a few diffuse white clouds move across the blue backdrop of the sky.

She'd clung to me when I'd taken my leave, watching as I took a sponge bath in her little basin, pouring well water from a bucket, cleaning myself with her threadbare washcloth and a cake of some hard, homemade soap.

We'll leave tomorrow. There're a few things I have to do. I'll be back by this evening. I'll take you out again. We'll have dinner with our friends . . .

Can't I come with you?

I need to be alone for a little bit. Let my head clear some.

That fearful look.

I'd laughed and ruffled her hair, had held her close. Don't look so concerned. It's just a habit I have.

Oh.

I'll be back. I will.

Then, in the dark rooms of the Master's castle, I dialed into the command net, level 5-high, and secured the necessary permissions before using the antiquated human datanet interface to link with the planetary resource base.

On the day I arrived, as I'd ridden down on the monorail, Saanaae police, aided by several squads of recently imported Kkhruhhuft mercenaries, interdicted and captured a party of humans moving northward along the forest trails that had formed up on the Piedmont Plateau, usually following the routes of old secondary highways, some of which had been abandoned since the early twenty-first century. Approximately sixty humans killed. They'd had time to set up an old portable Jackrabbit SAM launcher and knock down one Saanaae gunship, but the Kkhruhhuft had taken them out pretty easily.

Smoke cloud, south of Smithfield, along the old I-95 corridor: Saanaae police, aided by native auxiliaries, captured a military small-arms cache located northwest of where Fayetteville had been. It had, apparently, been left there thirty years ago, hidden by a squad of North American marines, shortly before they turned themselves in to the occupation authorities. A small party of humans, led by a former squad member, put up no resistance and were dispatched quietly when no further leads could be developed.

One Sirkar native policeman was accidentally killed in the incident. Some of the old munitions turned out to be unstable.

A quick look through the list. Incident after incident, stretching back almost ten years. Numbers slowly increasing. Not a problem, given how many Saanaae had been brought to Earth. It was assumed, once Earth had been further depopulated by selective emigration, that the problem would decrease until it was gone. That was the usual pattern.

Another generation. Two. Three. A century. Ten centuries.

Millennia. Tens of them. People would adjust. Or they wouldn't, and the Master Race would dispose of them, the way you disposed of any malfunctioning tool.

Just now, a fair-sized party of Saanaae was forming up for a sweep down the Tennessee Valley. Their object was to clear out all the little hollows and mountain valleys, move whomever they could find off to bustees lining the Mississippi River. I went off-line, sat for a few minutes more in the semidarkness, then went on back out into the sunlight.

When the Saanaae figured out we meant business, when they realized they were losing their position in the empire, some of them took it hard. Most wanted to cut their losses and play the next hand as dealt, hope for better luck next time. Some didn't, groups of them here and there fighting back, especially after our reaction to the spearhead of the insurrection resulted in a clean sweep, captured Saanaae gathered up and executed as quickly and quietly as possible so as not to infect the others.

I was a havildar, leading a maniple of sixteen, in the days when we took Rouhaaz. It had been, once upon a time, a Saanaae colony world, back before the Master Race found them, Saanaae like humans with their own high-tech STL starships, pretending they were the lords of creation. They'd been at it longer than we had, even had their own empire of sorts, with five or six subject species. I understand there'd been one on Rouhaaz, but it had gone extinct under Saanaae stewardship.

Now, of course, Rouhaaz had been quiet, occupied by the Masters for several thousand years. They hadn't put up much of a fight when the Masters came, hadn't shot down a single starship, had killed barely a dozen Kkhruhhuft. You can lose that many to technical glitches in a big combat drop, giant armor-clad dinosaurs whistling down out of the sky, slamming in headfirst, penetrating hard, so that only their tails are left sticking out.

And yet, when the time came to take their medicine for defying the Masters, *these* Saanaae, hopeless, decided to dig in and fight.

We'd come down a rocky defile, red forests all around us under a dusky mauve sky, sky lined with pretty brown-and-orange clouds, layered like broken sheets of mica overhead. A quick firefight, primitive Saanaae small arms rattling futilely off high-tech human armor. All they had was police weapons, not even as good as the thermonuclear artillery they'd had the first time around.

We mowed the forest, scarlet trees toppling, spongy trunks spewing white, milky sap through their wounds, things like hairy birds screaming in terror as they flew away. The broken trees smoked as they fell, as they lay in heaps on he ground, but nothing would burn.

Then we made the survivors drag their dead comrades out of the bunkers, made them line up in long, crooked rows on the ground, pour alcohol on the corpses and set them ablaze. It was messy-looking. The Saanaae, with that awkward bend in the middle, couldn't be laid out as neatly as bipeds.

I remember one of my soldiers trying to hurry them, "Come on, Sambo! Hurry it up!" Smashing the business end of his torch in the Saanaa's face. It said nothing, just stumbled to its knees, staring back at him, yellow-brown blood starting from its lips, dripping down onto that green, scaly chest.

Got back up in a moment and continued dragging its dead comrade off to the fire.

When that was done, we killed the wounded and burned them too, then made the uninjured survivors strip and throw their uniforms into the blaze. Shackled them in a long coffle and stood by while the fires burned, made them watch as their friends were consumed. Along with their identities.

And laughed at them, though their sounds and ours were hardly the same. Poking at their nakedness, sticking things in the males' breeding pouches, watching them wince and cower. The women troopers seemed especially amused at the female Saanaae's ovipositors, handling them, laughing, wondering, "Do they get hard, you suppose?"

I've watched Saanaae mating rituals since then. They do, and dance with each other around midnight fires, a lovely dance that hardly seems like sex at all.

When the fires were finished and the dead burned away to bones, we marched them down the valley to a prison camp, where more would die waiting until the ships could come and take them away.

Night came and I went home to Alix, who'd apparently fretted the afternoon away, standing before me now in the lamplight, large-eyed and serious, holding my face in her hands, kissing me, struggling to hold me close, then moving against me, murmuring.

We don't have to go to dinner. I've got a few things here. We could spend the evening here, the night, be well rested for tomorrow's early start . . .

One hand rubbing gently on my abdomen, fiddling indecisively with the buttons on my jeans. A seductive temptation, devoted Alix naked in my arms, images of her beneath me, absorbing me, as if I'd not had every bit of female flesh a man could truly use . . .

But that, they tell us, in stories, in serious psychological studies, in poems and videoplays and songs, is not what a man *really* wants. If it was, well-lubricated masturbation would do. Or large dogs. Small sheep.

Alix looking up at me, quizzical, wondering, I supposed, what made me smile just now. I laughed and hugged her, and we went out into the night, holding hands.

Davys was bustling at the dinner hour, more people having meals than drinking just now, music from the three-piece combo soft and gentle, mood music from the late 2140s, acoustic bass thudding slowly, bracketing gentle chords, the drumbeat no more than a hiss of brush strokes. I suddenly remembered this piece was called "Heartbeat Afterward," one of my mother's old favorites, from when she and my father were young.

Though it was a hot night, it only seemed cozy inside the pub, warm and close, as if I were sharing in the camaraderie of the people who came here. I could imagine it winter outside, a cold January rain falling, filling the gutters, overflowing the old, no longer maintained storm sewers, fires in the fireplaces, the smell of dry pine in my nostrils . . .

Lank, Davy, and Marsh joined us at our table, Marsh with a tall, angular, woman I didn't know, Sandy-something, who said she was from Charlotte. Marsh's girlfriend, apparently, from the way she tended to touch him and look at him, and a sagoth coworker as well. Davy's minions served us a reasonably sumptuous meal, pasta with a meaty, garlicky, pizza-flavored sauce on it, hard rolls, some sharp-tasting, unidentifiable red wine.

And more talk, endless talk. Old times that Sandy hadn't shared segueing into a discussion of Charlotte, which had taken a hit from some kind of big Kkhruhhuft siege weapon. She described a deep, conical crater in the middle of town, the way debris had splashed in all directions, taking out buildings, crushing suburban homes miles away.

"I was little, though," she said. "Only five. I don't remember much."

"Me neither," said Lank.

I twirled the linguine-like pasta on my fork, rolling it in the sauce, which was really pretty good, and said, "Probably what they call a maul-gun. Supposed to be for knocking down hard stone fortresses and breaking into underground bunkers. Kkhruhhuft don't use it much."

Silence, almost covered by noise from diners at other tables, from the muted, whispery music. Everyone looking at me, silverware poised just so.

Then Sandy said, "Then why the hell did they use it on downtown Charlotte? My mother was *killed*, for Christ's sake."

A quick glance at Alix, who was looking down into her plate, face neutral. I shrugged. "Probably an accident. There used to be a shielded underground comm center somewhere between here and Charlotte, you know. Kkhruhhuft aren't perfect, anyway. Maybe somebody tried to nuke their ship while they were aiming."

Sandy shook her head, face slightly darkened. "Bastards."

Suddenly jovial, Lank said, "So. You and Alix really going up into the mountains tomorrow?" Talking to me, but looking at her. Marsh was looking at Sandy, his hand covering hers, looking into her eyes. Concerned? Or just trying to keep her quiet?

Alix put her hand on my forearm, and smiled. "Just like old times," she said. Undercurrents. Well. These people have known each other for years and years. I'm really a stranger here. I know that.

The evening ended and we went back to Alix's house once again.

In the later darkness, the lamp turned out, muted moonlight coming through the window and filling the room with deeper shadows, Alix slept with her head on my chest, snoring softly, a faint, smooth sound, little more than hollow breathing. The window was open a bit, warm breeze blowing in, carrying with it an earthy smell reminiscent of loam and mold, and we were almost dry again.

Discomfort, though, from the slightly damp sheets. Back home, my real home, Hani would judge my comfort, would, if necessary, summon the others to change the bedding for us, so we could sleep crisp and dry. And more often than not, go herself for a warm, damp facecloth and clean, fluffy towel, see to my needs before curling up again by my side. Just in case.

I felt dazed now, ready to sleep but unable to close my eyes, watching the darkness outside the window, the slowly shifting angle of the moonlight, listening to the distant rustle of the trees. Somewhere, a dog was barking intermittently, very far away.

The summer before that first Spahi intake, when we already knew it was coming, Alix and I exercised together, trying to hone our strengths, analyze each other's weaknesses, certain we would either pass or fail together. We would go rock climbing together, riding our bicycles all the way down to the Cape Fear River, to Raven Rock. We would camp out, sometimes with little or no equipment, daring nature to discomfit us, and, in time, it toughened us to the point where our outdoor North Carolina world seemed the only real world, our old world of home and hearth a sanctuary for weaklings. The illusion comforted us. Now all that remained was a series of broken images.

A sunny day when we stood atop a rocky bluff, a cleared place where there'd once been a wildlife observation platform, buck naked, Alix bent over before me, the two of us laughing in our wildness. All I can really remember are the sleek, muscular lines of her back, the conditioning we'd built for each other, the days and nights when we never seemed to tire.

The two of us walking together through a dank, gray forest, rain pouring down out of the sky in a steady torrent, the Neuse River barely visible through the trees, dark brown water at flood stage, moving, moving, bits of foam here and there, the two of us walking and walking, laughing in the rain.

What if I'd failed as well? A delicious moment, imagining those heady days going on and on. Hard to know what life's disappointments would have done to us. Maybe she'd've left *me* instead of fat, little Benny Tekkomuz.

A final image of us that summer, hiding naked in some thick underbrush, peeking out onto what had been an empty, sun-washed parking lot, site of a few crushed cars, the splintered remains of some old building. We'd been making love in the sunshine, enjoying the feel of the hot paving stone on our bodies when they came. Now we were hiding, hoping they wouldn't find our clothing, start beating the bushes to drive us out.

Kkhruhhuft. A dozen of them. Like something out of an old monster vid. Like one of those big-budget Mesozoic fantasy movies that are popular from time to time. Wearing their armor, so they looked like robot dinosaurs. And they had people with them, naked people in chains. Bleeding people, who could barely walk.

I remember feeling Alix's hand in the middle of my back, firm, not a shiver. I'd glanced at her face. Fearless. Nothing but intense interest.

One of the men in the coffle was dragging hard, blood running from a big open wound on his back, running in thick rivulets across his buttocks, down his legs, and he was leaving sharply defined red footprints on the paving stones.

They stopped. One of the Kkhruhhuft unchained the dragging man and pulled him out of the coffle, pulled him a short distance away, cast him sprawling on the ground.

Moment of silence, rustle of chains, then someone in the line said, "Oh, *Jesus*, Mike . . ." The man on the ground started to cry suddenly, rolling onto his side, looking up at the Kkhruhhuft looming over him. A weak voice, no more than a sob, hopeless, full of fear, "Oh, God! Please, no . . ."

The Kkhruhhuft soldier stamped on him, once, very hard, like a man crushing a mouse. The man on the ground grunted when the foot fell on him, the sound of breath driven from his lungs like a very loud burp.

The Kkhruhhuft ordered their coffle and moved on then, leaving the flattened corpse behind. Alix and I stayed hidden until we could no longer hear anything but the wind in the trees, the soft chirr of summer insects, then waited another little while before going out to look at the dead man.

Most of the damage was to his chest, but his face was dark orange now, his skull swollen like a cartoon character with a basketball head, distorted features ludicrous with terror. Alix said, "Merciful, I guess . . ." Voice emotionless, but we were holding hands now.

We finished making love by the side of the old parking lot, then put on our clothes, retrieved our bikes from where we'd hidden them in the woods, and rode on.

Alix began the next day with an infectious happiness, gay and energetic, as if everything in the world were different now, would stay different forever. There were moments of oddness for me, knowing full well we would go on our little trip together, then it would all be over, but it *was* contagious. As if, somehow, those twenty years had disappeared or, better still, been filled with an eternity of us.

We rode the monorail westward past where Asheville had been, craning our necks to see out over a rolling landscape of green forest. I'd never been here before, but supposed it must have been a towering city of glass-and-steel skyscrapers.

Nothing was left behind, not even humped ruins as in Durham.

Alix held my hand and talked and tried to neck with me a little bit, making one of the sagoths turn to look at us sternly. None of the other passengers seemed bothered, one elderly woman turning to stare at us, smiling, shaking her head with a grin.

Like we were young lovers, off on our first escapade.

Let it be that way, then. Look hard at all the feelings you left behind. See if it's all been . . . worth it.

Alix, for her part, seemed obliviously happy. Hard to imagine what her expectations might be. Even harder to ask.

By midmorning, the monorail was sliding above buckled green terrain, low, rolling mountains, clad to their peaks in forest, bisected here and there by the white beds of old concrete roads, sagging bridges over shiny mountain streams. Every now and again I'd see the smoke from a fire, thin, gray-white, some last vestige of human habitation.

We got off the train at a tall wooden platform by the Little Tennessee River, a cleared place surrounded by low mountains and forest, the sun standing high overhead, the air hot, but nothing like what it is down in the lowlands to the east. It was cooler here, drier, the world sharper and more defined. Just south of us, I knew, was the old national park, where no one had lived in centuries.

The train slid away, a soft, rumbling hiss, leaving us alone in our aerie. And Alix put her arms around me, her head on my shoulder, and said, "I can't believe we're here."

Nothing really sensible to say to that. Just give her a squeeze and laugh. "If here is anywhere at all . . ."

We shouldered our packs and I took the tent as well, then we went down the ladder to the ground. The land on the other side of the river, beyond a narrow, new-looking footbridge, had been cleared, flat bottomland that must have been put to some use before the Invasion. Over by the edge of the forest were heaps of broken red bricks, rimed with bits of cement. Whatever had been here, that was all that was left of it.

Alix said, "Look! Horses." Starting out on the little bridge.

Horses then, naked in pasture, being led by bridles, gathered in paddocks, beyond them long, low sheds, the heads of horses visible through half doors. Four or five Saanaae visible, blanketed and straw-hatted as usual.

They were moving right in, these scaly green policemen. Moving in, making themselves right at home. I wonder how long it'll be before people like that majordomo find themselves displaced? The Master Race is careless with its power. Or perhaps its lack of understanding. Have they forgotten already what happens when slave and overseer grow too familiar?

Over by the trees, chained to a tall stake, was some kind of fat, medium-large, tentacled nonhuman. I wondered for a moment why . . . and realized with a small shock I was looking at a leathery old domestic elephant. I'd forgotten they ever existed, hadn't thought about elephants in twenty years.

What would they be doing with an elephant up in the Tennessee woods?

The elephant was skittish, uneasy, rocking back and forth on its broad, flat feet, breathing audibly, and kept looking toward the trees. Something . . .

In the shadows there, an armored Kkhruhhuft was sprawled, weapons platform on the ground, helmet off. There was a combat patch on her head. Quick look at the helmet. No damage.

Well. Waiting for pickup, in any case. I was tempted to take out the phone and talk to her, but with Alix at my side . . . The Kkhruhhuft moved and the elephant started, shying away. Elephants are smart. I couldn't imagine what was going through this one's head, seeing a carnivore that size.

Alix was holding the bridge railing, staring hard toward the trees, away from where the Kkhruhhuft lay sprawled. Gripping the bridge railing, whispering something under her breath. Something angry.

I looked. Five or six grimy naked men there, surrounding a naked woman, a woman splayed on the ground. Men holding her arms and legs. One lying on top of her, another holding her head between his legs. At least, I assumed it was a woman from the position. Too many men on her to tell for sure.

Alix looked up at me, disturbed, eyes hot. "You can make them stop." Not a question. No uncertainty at all.

One of the Saanaae came trotting up, a male, stopping before us. "This is not a place for you," he said, English accented and sharp, but fluent. "Go back to your own compound."

I said, "Not a local, I'm afraid." I showed him my ID badge.

The Saanaa nodded, a decidedly human gesture, probably learned in the time it had been here. If I knew the Masters and their minions, these Saanaae would have forgotten their native tongue, lost what small nonhuman culture they had in a generation or two. He said, "What can I do for you?"

I gestured around. "What is this place?"

Alix grabbed me by the forearm, pointing at the gaggle of men, and said, "Can't you make them stop it?" I could see that the men were trading places now, and were pulling the woman's legs so far apart it looked like they might be damaging her.

The Saanaa looked. Shrugged. Also too human. "What for? You wouldn't interfere with dogs would you?" Alix turned away, looking out over the river, one hand linked into my belt.

The Saanaa said, "We raise horses here, sir. For export."

Horses for export. "Who's buying them?"

Another shrug. "I wouldn't know. Ask your Master." The Kkhruhhuft moved again, rolling over on her side, grunting softly, grumbling to herself as if in pain. The elephant bucked, pulling hard on the chain, and trumpeted, starting up a panicky neighing among the horses in the nearby paddock, bringing Saanaae and humans on the run.

We walked across the bridge, turning uphill toward the forest, the sun now at our backs, coming down from the zenith. I heard Alix whisper, "That poor woman . . ."

I stopped her, turned her around, hands on her shoulders, looking into those earnest eyes. "There are worse things," I said. "We've both seen them."

She nodded, biting her lip. "I know, Athy. I just wish . . ."

"What would you have had me do?"

A small shrug, downcast eyes. "I know there's nothing anyone can do for them, for any of us. Not now, at any rate."

Not ever. She moved in under my arm, put her arms around my chest and held me close. She said, "Around Carrboro you don't see it much. It's almost like . . . it never happened. I hate going into the bustee . . ."

I could do nothing but nod. Maybe tell her, Yes, I know how it is . . . But I doubt that I did.

We walked on, up a long, open defile, between walls of cool green forest. After a while, that infectious happiness returned, infecting me as well, and we laughed and talked, ran up into the mountains, holding hands.

10

THE FOREST AROUND US AS WE WALKED, as the sun slowly slid down the western sky, was a sequence of light-dappled glades, hardly natural-looking at all. There was a winding stream, full of cool, clear water, water bubbling around stones, over sand, stream full of little fish, silvery and black, some with iridescent racing stripes down their sides. Plenty of grass here under the trees, enough sunlight coming through to make it grow, grass grown up in some places to knee height, in other places cropped short. Deer? No way for me to know.

Once, in a patch of almost-dry mud, I saw a small, two-toed footprint.

We were walking down a narrow dirt path, well worn, as if it got considerable use, Alix walking ahead of me, carrying a thin, springy willow-wand with which to brush aside the occasional spiderweb, fat orb spiders trying to run, getting wrapped in their own webs as they fell.

She really is beautiful. You know that. Buttocks flexing, hips rocking back and forth to the rhythm of her walking. Curly black hair bouncing slowly. Muscular back outlined under her shirt, hefting the pack easily and well . . .

I found that I couldn't look away after a while, her shape filling my vision completely, blotting out the exquisitely feral countryside around us.

144

Toward evening, when the sun was an orange ball lighting us through a line of trees atop a distant ridge, we stopped for supper on someone's old patio, clearing leaves and dirt from a cracked white plastic picnic table, putting down our packs, breaking out provisions.

Whoever lived here must have been well-to-do. The foundation was big and complex, though the house was gone without a trace, and there was an L-shaped swimming pool not far away, filled now with mud and scrubby vegetation. There was a garden too, and red rosebushes run wild, growing like vines.

I cleared out the old grill, fishing the grating out of the weeds, clearing the brick hearth, taking blackened bones out of a bed of granular, rain-flattered ashes. Closer look. Limb bones. A small carnivore's mandible. Dog maybe.

"Athy." Alix's voice was quiet, not quite a whisper. Upset.

I looked, and she was crouching by some weeds, holding something round and white, a small human skull. Looking at the crown, fingering it gently, inspecting a small hole. Not a wound. An unclosed frenulum.

When I came to stand over her, she put the baby's skull down gently and picked up another one, much larger. Flat above the gaping nosehole. There was a third skull on the ground, this one quite large, with a pronounced browridge. And a square-sided hole in the temple, away from which ran a long, irregular crack, roughly following one of the major suture lines.

Alix put down the woman's skull and knelt, silent.

I leaned over her and brushed aside the tops of the weeds. More bones. Ribs. Pieces of arms and legs. A very small pelvis. A dog's skull, from a much larger animal than the one that'd been in the fire. The top of this one's head was dished in, the brainpan collapsed.

Alix was looking over at the hearth now, at the little pile of bones I'd put aside, the little dog's jaw. "A family," she whispered. "With a baby." She put her hand on my calf, slowly rubbing up and down, fingers shaking gently. The expression on her face was neutral. Anger perhaps. Or pity.

She said, "Killed them all. Killed their dog." A long look at those blackened bones. "Ate their puppy."

I toed the baby's skull, turning it over so I could see where the spine had broken away from the foramen magnum. Splintered. One quick twist. Didn't feel a thing.

Alix slowly covered the bones up, pushing the weeds back into place, smoothing them down. She looked up at me, and I could see that glint of hard anger in her eyes. "Civilized men," she said.

I nodded, turning away, going to start up our campfire and cook our supper. The baby, I suppose, would've tasted better than the puppy. But these had, after all, been civilized men. And they'd probably kept the woman alive for a little while.

After dinner, rather than make camp under the trees of the dead family's patio, we gathered up our gear and moved on into the orange gloom of summer dusk, climbing a steep, wooded hillside that gradually metamorphosed into a mountain. It was full night by the time we emerged from the trees, up onto the rocky bald dome of its peak.

Maybe, once upon a time, there'd been a stupendous view up here during the night, a wheel of stars over the glittering lights of humanity. People had been living here for ten thousand years, had filled the forest with a twinkle of electric lights for better than two centuries.

A brief snippet of childhood memory: flying high over these mountains in an airliner, electric jets whispering outside in the midnight dark, my little-boy's face pressed to the plastic window while my parents drowsed in their seats. Overhead, a million brittle stars, below a million million bright sparks, the lights in people's backyards.

Now, there was nothing below us, only a bottomless pit of night. Alix stood quietly, tucked under my arm, arm around my back, holding on gently. Finally, she said, "Even back home you don't see the stars like this."

The dim fires of Carrboro, the pallid glow of the adjacent bustee, were enough to wash away some of their glory. Here, overhead, the Milky Way was a river of pale silver, pitted with black and gold, a narrow arc standing up off the western horizon, cutting away almost a third of the sky, from Sagittarius setting to Taurus rising. The Great Square of Pegasus stood more or less directly overhead.

"I wish," she said softly, "that we'd been able to go out there. When I was a little girl, I dreamed about moving to one of the colonies."

To Neogaea, second planet of Tau Ceti, settled a full generation before the Invasion, home to thousands already. To Mina il-Seyf around far Zeta Tucanae, so remote no colonists had come yet to join the explorers' fleet.

I'd never met anyone who'd been to one of them, before or since the Invasion. Or knew what happened when the Masters came. But I'd seen the worlds of Alpha Centauri, the abandoned wreckage of the old scientific stations.

Later, lying naked on our blankets beside the small tent we'd brought, campfire crackling beside us, slowly burning down to a bed of dull red-orange coals, barely lighting the area around us. We were lying with our feet toward the north, lying still, looking upward, watching the stars turn.

Alix had been quiet, soft and gentle, almost hesitant in her lovemaking, stopping and starting, letting go, holding on. It made me wonder if she really wanted to continue, but she went on, going through her set of routines almost mechanically, and so did I, the two of us sighing together, moving against one another, crying out at appropriate moments, whispering our pleasure back and forth.

A sense of separateness, though, of distance, quite unlike the separateness of an attentive burdar, who stays within herself no matter how completely she is at your disposal.

This was a self-enfolding separateness, Alix caught up in her own thoughts, not excluding me really, merely . . . going away from time to time, coming back with a start, going away again. Distracted, somehow.

She said, "Do you remember your childhood dreams, Athy?"

Which dreams? Children dream a hundred thousand dreams, of worlds that can never be, of worlds that can, of lifetimes to come that neither they nor anyone else will ever experience. I said, "Some. Not many."

"You remember how we used to dream of a time when the Invaders would be overthrown? We used to talk about what it would be like when *we* grew up, when we kicked them off the Earth, got their starship technology for ourselves . . ."

I remembered. Abstract ideas, children boasting to each other. Ourselves captaining those great starships, FTL drive a great boon to humanity once the Invaders were overthrown, the best thing that could have happened to any of us. That was, of course, before we'd learned to call them the Master Race.

Alix rolled up onto my chest, hands on me, looking down into my eyes. All I could really see of her face other than shadows was the shine of her eyes' moisture, glimmer shifting as they moved. She held herself steady, clasping my thigh between her knees, and I could feel her damp crotch against my hip.

"It was," I said, "a wonderful dream. We had fun playing."

"Sometimes," she said, "I imagine it can still come true. Imagine us out there again in ships of our own, like in all the old movies, masters of the starways . . ."

Curious choice of words. Alix imagining us in the Masters' place, perhaps, ruling their worlds for them, Kkhruhhuft working for us, Boromilithi *our* slaves and no one else's, Saanaae *our* police, going to all the worlds, making sure the poor, pathetic natives would bow down before us . . .

She said, "Remember what we called ourselves?"

I nodded. The Liberators. A band of heroes come to free humanity from damnation and slavery. Casting off the yoke of the oppressor . . . In those days, among the smoking ruins of Earth, while the Kkhruhhuft walked among us, we didn't know how heavy that yoke would become.

If this, we thought, is the best they can do, then someday . . .

We didn't know how *much* time the Masters had at their disposal. Hadn't begun to suspect what had befallen us.

She said, "I used to wonder sometimes about all the other worlds. Used to imagine myself landing at the seat of some alien civilization, being greeted as a savior . . ."

I imagined Alix landing on Boromilith, standing before a

crowd of quiet, attentive Boromilithi. You're free! All of you! Quiet consternation. Yes, Mistress. Will that be all, Mistress? How may we serve you, Mistress?

Probably, the Boromilithi would have adapted. They'd only been slaves for a few thousand years.

Alix kissed me on the lips, gently, softly. "You seem very far away tonight."

I nuzzled against the side of her head, felt her hair in my face, smelling ever so slightly of woodsmoke and ashes. "Memories," I said.

She kissed me lightly on the forehead, rested her chin up there for a moment. "From when we were kids?"

Wanting me, perhaps, to be filled with thoughts of her, awareness of her existence. "Some. Thinking about all those other worlds, too."

She shifted again, sliding to the ground beside me, rubbing her hand back and forth on my abdomen. "Maybe someday . . ."

Maybe someday you'll see them too? Maybe someday the Masters will be overthrown? Alix put her head on my chest, snuggling under my heavy arm, ran one hand down the blade of my hipbone, to the place where my thigh joined my trunk, fingers resting gently on the big tendon there.

She said, "It's an important dream. We should never let it go. I haven't . . ."

Fantasies. Like the dream where you have someone at your side, though you know you are all alone.

I once visited a world, I told her, which had no name. Nothing more than a Master ID number. Earth has a Master ID number as well, but it still has a name. The Boromilithi remember who they are. So do the Saanaae, though they no longer have a world. The Kkhruhhuft. So many other species I've met, gotten to know, know well or no more than a chance acquaintanceship.

We stopped by this world, my comrades and I, just briefly, moving between ships, an expeditionary force on its way from one hot spot to another. Our scheduled freighter was late, the orbital station not prepared to accommodate us, so the Master sent us down to the world below, let us bivouac until the time came to leave again. No more than a few days.

It was a vast gray world, skies perpetually clouded over, gray skies over gray mountains. Gray cities, dank, lusterless forests. Plantations out on the wet plains of the nameless world. Row on row of natives bending to their labors, walking silently through the streets of their decayed cities.

We were the only humans there. The first to visit. Maybe even the last. We heard these people had been slaves of the Master Race for more than sixty thousand years.

You could walk among them, and it was as if you weren't even there. Stop them, hold them on the ground, pull off their clothing, do whatever you wanted. They were fairly humanoid, though very different in the little details. Some of us even thought it was kind of fun.

But you'd do whatever you wanted, and then let them go. They'd get up and walk away, trudging off to their appointed tasks.

You could hurt them. They wouldn't scream, though their jaws would set, their thin lips twist. Threaten to kill them, they wouldn't cower. Really kill them, they would only die. Maybe they were always like that. I don't think so.

Alix was silent against my chest, hand still holding on to the inside of my thigh. Finally, she said, "I guess it's hard to imagine coming to them as a Liberator."

I nodded, rubbing my hand slowly back and forth across her back, scratching the area between her shoulder blades, feeling out the ridge of her spine.

She kissed me on the chest, snuggled closer still, whispered, "It can't be like that everywhere. It can't stay like that forever."

No?

After a while, we slept.

We could hear them by midmorning, a distant echo, the sound of axes ringing on trees as we walked up into the mountain pass, every now and then the crackling thump of a trunk going down. When we got closer, there were other cracking sounds, a heavy thudding. A slight vibration in the ground.

Alix looking at me, unnerved. Me shrugging. I could find out through my phone, but . . . Why bother, really? We'd find out when we got there. And it wouldn't matter to us, no matter who was here cutting down this forest.

The trees ended at the crest of the trough, just where we were following a line of old stone, all that was left of some long-tumbled wall. Bright sunshine burning down on raw ground. Barebacked men and women hard at work. Axing the trees, though big saws would have been more efficient. Scrambling out of the way as they swayed against the sky, began to fall . . .

Every face haggard, every body shining with sweat, every man, every woman gaunt and muscular. Overseers with whips. Bloody stripes on a back here, a breast there. It was getting to be a familiar sight.

Teams of bulky horses, too. Hauling away limbless trunks, straining to uproot stumps while men and women hacked at roots, cursing, crying, falling to their knees, getting up again quickly.

The workers were filthy, smeared with red clay made gummy by their sweat.

Watching the horses dig in and rear, watching them surge against their harnesses, I wondered if this was why they were trying to fool around with elephants down below. They'd come in pretty handy, if they could be induced to calm down.

Alix whispering beside me.

"What?"

She looked up at me, wide-eyed and serious again, the laughter and joy of our long, private walk put aside and forgotten. "We never hear about these things," she said.

No? Are the workers from the Chapel Hill bluehouse invisible? Maybe so.

An altercation down in the cut, back a ways from the tree-fellers, where yet another gang was digging away at the dirt, breaking it with picks, leveling it with shovels, smashing large rocks with heavy, rusty-headed sledgehammers.

Two heavyset women, women in uniform-like denim,

holding the arms of a starved-looking yet muscular man, a third woman, slighter than the other two, long, lustrous blond hair tied back in a sun-brilliant ponytail, lashing him methodically with her whip. Even at this distance, I could see dots of blood like freckles on her face, dots splashed from the man's raw back.

And the whipped man? Nothing. Hanging in his captors' arms, head hanging low, as if unconscious. His eyes were open though, staring into some other region of space-time. Waiting it out. Going away to somewhere safe.

Alix said, "They look like they're enjoying themselves." Flat. Bitter.

I said, "Maybe they are. Who knows how life's treated those women?"

Alix looked at me, face expressionless, then turned back and watched them finish up. When they were done, they let the man fall to his knees and walked away, shouting at the other workers. The man stayed where he was for a minute or two, then slowly got to his feet, leaned and picked up a broken-bladed shovel, began trying to dig with the stub.

There were Saanaae here too, standing in the shade under the trees at the raw edge of the forest, Saanaae dressed in hats and shawls and blankets, ID badges used like brooches at their necks. Saanaae already looking at us, hefting their rifles, one, then another beginning to trot over.

I fished in my pocket for my own badge . . .

Long, shuddery bellow from up above the cut, deep-pitched, vibrating in my chest, touching my intestines with a sparkle of induced fear. The Saanaae stopped, turning back, looking back toward the crest of the pass. A lone gray Kkhruhhuft stood up there, looking down at us, outlined against the sky, cradling a slim military weapon in her arms.

Whips suddenly cracked in the silence, overseers shouting at their charges to shut their mouths and get to work. A muffled cry of pain. Neighing of horses. Rattle of heavy chains. Crackle of a stump being pulled, roots breaking, being cut.

I motioned to Alix and we began walking up the hill, past silent Saanaae, to where the soldier waited. She was a big one, almost a meter longer than Shrêhht, I thought. Very

weather-beaten. One eye socket empty, showing red scar tissue and white bone. Big, dented-in region along the adjoin-
ing left temple, feathery tuft missing as well. One chela
mandible gone from her left . . . hand. Tentacles twisted, as if
they'd been burned. Big white burn scar on her left knee,
scales gone, flesh smooth and glassy.

I could feel Alix huddling in my shadow. And the Kkhruhhuft was whispering, a pulse of breathy laughter.

A quick glance down along her spine, two cartouches
painted in, one red, the other black. ID number for her
Kkhruhhuft military organization, an indicator of high rank.
Another ID for the human Overseer Corps and its local Master. Between them was a Kkhruhhuft ideograph I couldn't
read.

She laughed again, fiddled with her vocoder box. "And
you are?"

I smiled, dug out my badge, and held it up to her good
eye. "Athol Morrison, jemadar-major Ninth Spahis."

Something like a slow nod, polite greeting, one soldier to
another, a modification of the Kkhruhhuft military salute.
"Midrohh, Daughter of Zemvrakhf. Retiree."

There was a commotion behind us, back down the hill,
shouting voices, Alix clutching at my arm until I turned to
look. One of the human overseers had a woman down on the
ground, was beating her rapidly, really leaning his weight
into the blows, grunting with each swing, using a thick,
crooked piece of tree limb.

Hard, ugly, meaty sounds were echoing off the forest.

There was a Saanaa guard standing by, watching impas-
sively, other human overseers ignoring the byplay. Slaves
continuing to work.

Midrohh said, "We're building a road here, down into the
Tennessee Valley."

I looked back at her. "Why?"

She hissed softly and keyed the vocoder. "Ask the local
Master. Lovely country hereabouts."

Down the hill the beating was finished, the naked woman
lying still on the ground, obviously unconscious, face

marked with blood. The overseer walked away, shouting at the other slaves, waving his now-splintered stick at them.

I nodded slowly. "It is a lovely place to retire. Why didn't you go back home?" Back home to males and breeding and family.

"This was my last posting." She gestured at me with her ruined claw. "Too many combat honors. Not enough of me left to fight now."

It takes a lot to make a Kkhruhhuft say something like that. There must be more damage here than just what was visible. "And your family?"

"They have all of me they need."

Meaning she'd bred for them, raised a generation or two of cubs, gone back out into the dark between the stars.

Alix grabbed at me again, making me look back down the cut. Apparently, they'd dragged the jagged remains of a stump over the fallen woman. At some point, what was left of her must have died.

And Midrohh said, "Besides. It's easier to watch this here than . . . home."

I stood looking down at the mangled corpse, my arm around Alix's shoulders, feeling her shiver, though the bright sun, approaching noonday, was hot on our backs. "I know what you mean," I said.

Tawny sunset time, and Alix and I were camped beside a cold mountain lake, in a wide hollow among green hills, water smooth, mirroring the colors of the sky. The shadows were long here already, sunlight barely spilling over the hills, most of the light reflected down off dull orange clouds, hardly brighter than the bands of dark blue sky showing between them.

Insect sounds. Some kind of dull, intermittent buzzing. Periodically, a thin, complex cry, a bird perhaps. The pale smoke from our little campfire rose straight up until it disappeared.

Alix poked at her hot meal, a camp-ration serving of veal scallopini, as if fascinated by its colors, its smell and texture.

"Where'd you find these? I'd've thought the last one would've been eaten long ago."

My own dinner was a fine vegetable lasagna, still thick and spicy, cheese wonderfully stringy, for all that it must have been at least thirty-five years old. "Lank had them. He's got all kinds of stuff like this squirreled away . . ."

You throw the little white packets in the campfire, or lay them atop the stove. When they turn clear, so you can see the bubbling contents, they're done. Alix took a pull from her drink carton, sighed, and said, "I never thought I'd taste chocolate milk again."

Later, with the sky black overhead, spangled with the eternally lovely empire of the Master Race, we swam in the lake's cold water, splashing, chasing each other, grappling and groping. Came scampering up onto the shore, collapsed together on our blanket by the fire, droplets splashing like some incandescent liquid in the night.

I sat cross-legged, feeding bits of wood into the fire, watching the yellow flames grow, Alix reclining beside me, wet hand on my back. Though the water had been cold, the night was yet warm, radiation from the fire toasting us on one side.

Alix lay back, sprawled carelessly, open to me, a wonderland of light and shadow, dark eyes on my face, black hair fluffing back up into ringlets as it dried. She whispered, "I remember the first time I saw you like this, sitting naked beside me in the firelight. Maybe we were still fourteen. I don't remember. It seems so long ago . . ." Words choppy, far apart, pulled from the depths of memory, Alix falling into the abyss of the past.

She said, "I think it was the night a whole bunch of us camped out in the woods up near the Eno. You. Me. Marsh. Davy. Those two sisters they used to hang around with . . ."

Jenny and Marie something. Dos Santos? Can't remember. Tall, thin girls, flat chested and bony, without the tissue to make a single breast between them. I can remember them playing basketball on the school's outdoor court, thinking how really cool they looked, angular, all elbows. And so wonderfully coordinated.

I remember Davy and Marsh arguing about them. About their hair. Davy liked it done up in cornrows, Marsh wanted it fluffy and free. I remember Alix laughing at them, saying, what with there being *two* damned girls and all, they could each have what they wanted.

But Jenny and Marie insisted on wearing their hair in the same style. Like *sisters*, damn you! regardless of what anybody else wanted. What they chose was long thin braids ending in dark beadwork, which neither Davy nor Marsh liked. It clicked when they walked, making it hard for the Liberators to pretend.

It had been a brilliant, sunny summer day, like so many days back then, the six of us walking through the woods, following some long-forgotten trail beside Piney Mountain Creek, a tributary of the New Hope that flowed down from the woods off I-85.

The guerrillas were hard at work that day, moving northward to the ambush site, talking in whispers about how many Kkhruhhuft we would kill, about how *this* time we'd finish the lot. We'd stay in character for a while, then the plot would fall apart, and we'd run laughing through the trees, chasing each other, stopping now and then to pick off a tick from one smooth, tan-to-brown hide or another, run onward.

We were dressed for the climate that day, tight khaki shorts and dull green halter tops on the girls, though there was little enough to halt even on Alix then. Boys in a similar uniform of looser shorts and sleeveless mud green tees. We all had fine running shoes on our feet, the best shoes money could buy, culled from the ruins of one store or another, from some fallen shopping mall.

Image of us hiding on the embankment above the highway, looking down on more or less empty concrete. A couple of wrecked cars, a streamlined cargo truck lying on its side, canister caved in, a mass of shiny wrinkles.

Hiding, looking out between leafy branches, watching for movement we knew wouldn't come.

Alix nudged me, whispering amusement.

Davy and Jenny, who were more imaginative, more into

the Liberators game, were side by side, peering out onto the road, muttering to each other about Kkhruhhuft devils . . .

Dull, thick-bodied Marsh and dull sister Marie were crouched behind them, Marsh squatting, young muscle bulging solidly in his thighs, Marie on her hands and knees. And Marsh's hand stealing across one slim buttock, finger running down the line of her shorts' dorsal seam, feeling between her legs, pressing here, pressing there.

Marie was motionless. No, not quite motionless. Moving just the least little bit, shifting her hips so Marsh's hand would find a more interesting spot.

Alix was suppressing a giggle, not wanting to let them know they were being watched, Marsh probably unable to imagine there was anything else in the world just now but his own fingers and Marie's little crotch. Giggling inside herself, quivering, Alix was nuzzling against the side of my head. Getting ideas maybe, because we'd already been fooling around, a little bit here, a little bit there, for months now.

Shadow.

Moving over us.

Whisper of wind from the sky.

Marsh took his hand off Marie's butt, twisted his neck, turning an astonished face to the sky, gaping. I put my arm around Alix's shoulders, holding her close, and looked up, knowing just what I'd see.

The Kkhruhhuft patrol boat was like an impossible iron blimp, like one of John Carter's Barsoomian warships, floating in defiance of the wind, floating on wings of eighth ray, gun turrets pointing this way and that, waiting to shower lightning bolts down on the defiant few below.

We kept forgetting it was real.

Davy was sitting on his rump now, knees up, elbows on knees, holding his walking stick like some long, thin rifle. A magic rifle, with all the force anyone would ever need. He squinted down its length, sighting in. "Zap," he said. *"Zap."*

Zap. I tried to remember that Kkhruhhuft ship burning as it fell, but the image was already faded, far stronger the memory of it as a ball of fire on the ground, the Washington

Monument crumbling to dust and sliding away into the flames.

Overhead, the patrol boat flew on, following the line of 85/70/15-501 eastward past North Durham, beyond Raleigh, going who knew where.

"Someday," Davy said, "we'll know what to do."

That was an article of faith for us. Someday our turn would come. *We* wouldn't fail, hiding in basements, covering our heads, and crying out in terror the way our parents had when their moment came.

Lying beside me now in the summer night, beads of water still clinging to her stomach, Alix ran her hands down the long blades of her hipbones, and said, "We believed so much in what was *possible*, then, didn't we?"

I nodded, not wanting to remember any more, only wanting to look at her, savor this moment. I would be wanting to remember her this way, remember how those beads of water shone in the firelight, like living diamonds, in time to come.

I'd want to lie on my burdar, thrusting gently, folded away into myself, and remember Alix just as she was now.

And Alix said, "Not everyone has forgotten, Athy."

A long moment of silence, fire crackling beside us, flickering flame making the shadows dance and shift, me staring at Alix's mons, admiring the way the shadows danced around her pubic hair.

She said, "Some people still believe anything's possible."

She had her hand on my forearm, fingers running along corded ridges of muscle, following the outlines of the tendons on the inside of my wrist, cables that operated the lever action of my fingers.

Still not registering. Just memories, that's all. No special significance. I ran my hand up the inside of her thigh, fingers on smooth skin, feeling a slight laxness in the flesh, the way it would bunch up a little bit if I pressed harder.

And, while I fooled with her crotch, running my fingers here and there, brushing aside hair, drawing out moisture, Alix began to talk, telling me about that time of dreams. Of how dreams were meant to be cherished, followed, held onto.

I should have felt a hard moment of dread, but I was hypnotized by the reality of her instead, by the feeling of liquid silk on my fingertips, by the response of her, the way her body changed and shifted even as she spoke.

Dreams, Athy. Reality. The great wide sky above us all. You've been there, you know what's possible. You've come home again. We've been waiting for you.

We?

Too disjointed to follow. She tried to keep on talking even when I substituted my tongue for those fingertips, but, after a little while, it grew difficult for her to talk and breathe at the same time. Talking would wait.

I fed the fire again, putting in one of the large dry branches we'd found, feeding broken twigs in around it, listening to the wood crackle and spit, watching the flames spill upward around the fresh log. There was a boundary layer of steam forming between fire and fuel, curling upward, disappearing.

A little bug came out of a hole in the wood, small, round, black, ran along between walls of flame, fell over the side, and was gone.

I sat cross-legged on the blanket, one hand on my own crotch, feeling the smooth, softened skin of my penis, like fine-grained velvet to my fingertips, and watched Alix sleep, face turned away from the fire, features almost hidden in shadow. She had one leg drawn up, knee outward, ankle tucked under the other leg, firelight shining off a damp patch on the inside of her thigh.

Did Hani ever sleep like this? Did any of them? Probably. Though they were determined to wait for you, make sure you were through with them for the night, there were limits to human vitality. In the end, as you sat and watched, their eyes would droop away to slits, awareness fade, breathing grow deep and hollow and slow.

Sudden stark memory of Hani curled up on a blanket, knees tucked against her chest, head resting on one elbow, hair fanned out almost artfully. Breath occasionally catching as she slept, like a little hiccough, breathe, pause . . . breathe

again. We were at our favorite beach on Boromilith, sur-
feited by sun and sea, the world's ocean whispering softly,
tide a flat, slow surge, very different from Earth, from any
world that had a single large moon.

Somewhere out in the darkness I remembered hearing
Solange Corday, sighing softly to herself, murmuring, an occasional whispered question from her burdar, Is this all
right? This? . . . fine. Fine. More there. Yes, that . . .

Both moons had been in the sky, barely picking out the
thin line of the surf in wan gray light. I remember wondering
if it would be interesting to watch them, watch her male burdar hard at work. I sat and watched Hani sleep, watched the
slow movement of her breasts, in and out.

Alix hadn't waited for me, hadn't even tried. Had rubbed
her hand slowly up and down the back of my neck, down the
upper part of my spine, held my head against her thigh while
her own breathing quieted.

I was expecting her to get in position, knees spread and
drawn up, expecting her to wait while I thrust into her, wait
'til I was finished as well. Instead, I heard her breathing
grow slower and slower, deeper, more hollow, until finally
she was asleep.

If it'd been Hani, I might have pushed into position,
climbed into the saddle, gone through the motions. What difference does it make? The liquid is there. The animal heat.

Cattle don't care that they're being made into steaks. All
they know is their throats have been cut.

But she seemed so beautiful, lying there like that.
So . . . worthwhile.

Goddamn it, you're *not* in love with her. This isn't the
Alix you remember, it's some middle-aged woman caught up
in the web of her own fantasies. You're in love with an old
memory. A memory compounded of impossible dreams.

So what is *she* in love with, then? You? Your memory?

Just think about the things she's been saying to you.
Hardly coherent. But compounded of dreams. Of fantasy.
Of . . . something.

Roll her on her back now. Stick that thing in her. Forget

about all this nonsense. You'll be going home again soon. What difference does it make?

OK, if you're being so goddamned silly, just ask yourself the age-old question. What does she *want*?

Faint snort of laughter.

Are you really that stupid, Athol Morrison?

Maybe so.

Alix looking me earnestly in the eye, speaking so seriously, though she was squatted down, sitting right on my hand, though my thumb massaged her clitoris, though two of my fingers were sliding upward into her sodden vagina.

We haven't forgotten, Athy. Haven't forgotten any of the old dreams. We've been waiting for you to come home. Waiting.

Closing her eyes. Kissing me. Breathing hard through her nose. Wrapping both her hands around my penis, pumping mechanically up and down. Letting go when I pushed her onto her back, put my face down there again.

Whispering to me between gasps, after long silences. Tomorrow, she'd said. I'll show you tomorrow.

I leaned over and fished through the pile of my clothing, found the flat hard square of the phone, whispered to it. Into the net, level Five-high. Talked my way through to the router, asked for Shrêhht by name and number.

Hello, my friend. Vacation going well?

Well.

I'm enjoying your homeworld. I'll show you mine someday.

I'd like that.

This is a command circuit . . .

Yes. Do me a favor. Run a complete cross-index trace on three terrestrials. David Itakë. Marshall Donovan. Alexandra Moreno. Friends of mine.

ID numbers?

I don't have them handy.

Doesn't matter.

Brief silence, filled with whispers from the net router.

This is a level Five-high command link. You know this

will leave a record. You know it'll attract the comtrace packager.

I know.

All right.

I folded the phone away and lay on my back, staring up at the sky. Old dreams die hard. Old loves die hard. But just look up at the stars, Athol Morrison. Remember all the things you've seen up there. All the things you've done.

A universe the likes of which no one ever dreamed. A life the worth of which no one could ever imagine. Not without having been there as well. Try to remember you'll be going home again soon. All this is just . . .

I turned on my side and lay watching Alix sleep, almost motionless by the fire.

11

I AWOKE WITH SUNLIGHT BURNING ON MY eyelids and a solid weight on my chest, slightly constricting, breathing just the tiniest bit of an effort. Eyes open. It was midmorning already, and Alix was sitting astride my chest, knees under my arms, crotch about fifteen centimeters from my face. Looking down at me, curly hair shading her face, eyes in pools of pale shadow. One hand on the side of my head, fingers pushed into my hair, palm cradling the side of my face.

She said, "Last night seemed like a dream, Athy. Sometimes I wonder if you're really here."

I too. But then there was the smell of her in my nostrils, faint and crisp, as if she'd already gone down to the lake and washed without me. I looked up at her, into those dark, depthless eyes, and said, "I can't remember why I came anymore. Maybe this is it."

Or maybe I'm just lying to you, trying to prolong these false feelings to the very end. I feel like I'm in love. I wish I were. But I will go away, when the time comes. Already, I can see that universe beyond the stars, worlds and war and all my true friends. This *is* just the dream. Like the dreams you have when you're young. You dream of a woman. Any woman. Awaken to a fading erection and splashes of cooling semen.

Her eyes registered my words, a sudden, brief depth of feeling apparent, but she only smiled. Smiled and stood, stepping over my head as she got to her feet, me tipping my head back, looking up at her vulva, struck by a brief spasm of want. And why not? Grab her by the ankle, pull her down, roll her onto her back, laugh and tickle, kiss her, force heat into her flesh with the engine of your desire. Make love to her.

I rolled onto my side and stared out across the flat blue surface of the lake. In the distance, on the other side, I could see the collapsed ruin of some old building. The caretaker's lodge, maybe. A little hotel for people who weren't interested in "roughing it."

Behind me, I could hear Alix rummaging in the fire, sorting out coals, getting the flames to come up again, could hear her assembling our breakfast.

Later, when the sun was high, we walked down a gloomy forest trail, surrounded by tall old trees, following the shoulder of some shallow-sloped mountain, ground covered by leaf mold and brown pine needles, gray rock poking through here and there, wherever the hill steepened. There was old trash here, bottles, crushed plastic cans, and bits of industrial whatnot, labels gone, colors bleached away by the years, and the trail led above a narrow, half-dry creek.

After a while, we stopped talking, Alix walking on ahead of me, looking around, nervous, pensive, stopping every now and again to glance at this tree or that, stare broodily at some odd rock or another. Finally, in a hollow between two steep hills, the sun so well hidden by the forest that it was like deep twilight, the trail divided, and Alix stood still, looking at her choice, almost as if waiting.

All right. All right. Speak. Nothing. I said, "When are you going to tell me where we're going, Alix?"

She spun, eyes wide, fearful. And, at the same time, relieved. Finally, she said, "We're going to meet some friends of . . . ours." A nod to herself at that. Friends of ours. "I wondered if you'd begun to suspect." To the accompaniment of a very thin little smile, a touch of that familiar Alix.

I shrugged. "I'd guessed I was supposed to suspect something. But I wish you'd been straight with me, Alix."

She reached into the back pocket of her jeans, pulled out a folded scrap of paper, opened it up, squinting down in the gloom. She looked up at me. "I was afraid you wouldn't come." She gestured at the left branch. "This way."

It felt like there was a vast, nebulous hand squeezing my heart, making me short of breath. We walked on and, after a while, I said, "Why were you afraid?"

The trail was a bit wider here, enough to let us walk side by side. She took my hand before she spoke, and her fingers felt very small and cold in mine, eyes downcast. "I don't know if I really know you, Athy. I can't tell what's real." A serious, almost-agonized look up at me. "Or whether I'm just imagining all this."

All what? I said, "I always wanted you to trust me, Alix. Always." Since when?

She said, "I do trust you. But you did go away."

I nodded to myself, could see her thinking it was meant for her. Did she imagine I'd stay here, become one with her, resume our old life? Build some facsimile of the life we never had? Her hand was squeezing mine tightly. And I could read fear in those dark eyes. I said, "You have to *tell* me what you want, Alix."

Dark eyes in shroud, separating from me, hiding her thoughts again. She said, "In a little while, Athy. Just a little while longer."

Fear. Fear separates people. I learned that at least, when I was young, before I went away and learned not to be a person anymore. Not to care. How old was I? Sixteen maybe? Fifteen? Doesn't matter.

It was late fall and I was going over to Alix's house after dinner, just going over to see her for a little while, maybe sit in her room with the door open so she and I could be together while we pretended to work on our homework by lamplight. Parents in the background somewhere, listening perhaps, for sounds of . . .

Of course they knew what was going on as well as my parents. Knew perfectly well we weren't going out on weekends to play cops and robbers, cowboys and Indians, guerrillas and aliens together.

I could see Alix's mother look at us for signs when we came home holding hands as the sun went down. That flush on my daughter's cheeks. That dewy look in her eyes. That smug look on your ugly boy's face, you rotten, defiling little bastard.

Oh, hello, Athy! Smile. Smile. Would you like to stay for dinner?

It was dark, air crisp outside my jacket as I walked across their ragged lawn, passing around the corner of the house on the way to the front door. Alix's room was on this side of the house, lamplight filtering yellow-orange through the curtains. I stepped up to the window, peeked over the sash, looked between two edges of heavy cloth.

Alix lying stretched on the bed, stark naked, delicious, just the way she sometimes stretched out naked for me. Waiting. Inviting. Now alone. Head thrown back, mouth open, left hand on her left breast, squeezing, puckered nipple poking up between two fingers.

I was frozen in place, mouth open, hypnotized. I guess I knew about it, had known, but never given it any thought. What can she be thinking about just now? Me? Some other man, some unknown man, some unknowable man? Some romantic image?

She had her head to one side, had a corner of the pillow between her teeth, biting down hard, grimacing, grimacing. I heard her grunt softly. Motion abruptly stopped.

What did I know afterward that I didn't know before?

Nothing, maybe. Or perhaps just that Alix and I were more alike than different. Hard physical pleasure, born and bred in the genes, there for all of us, no matter what the old myths had to say.

I went in and her parents smiled for me, offered me tea and cookies. Alix's voice, through the bedroom door, said, Just a minute. And then we did our homework with the door open and Alix smiled at me, cheeks still a little flushed. Put her hand on my thigh every now and again.

I never told her, of course, and now we walked slowly

through the gloomy forest, Alix in the lead again as the trail grew steep and narrow, me watching the slow, effortless rock of her pelvis, remembering a young Alix who masturbated by lamplight. Oh, I know. It was truly a sensual experience for me, watching a woman masturbate, knowing the act was done for its own sake, free of any impulse to control another person's feelings.

That is why I never told her. Because then she'd know, and the act would be transformed, robbed of its meaning. Just the way seeing her look down at that scrap of paper, seeing her point to the left branch and say, This way, Athy, had so suddenly erased chains of meaning from the past few days.

Was that the whole point of all this?

We've been waiting for you, Athy. That's what she'd said. But, when I looked at her, watched her walk, felt myself flood with longing, it was still very hard to believe. Hard to believe all this . . .

I had to shake myself inside.

Why are you feeling so bad? When you thought that she . . . believed in all this, you kept reminding yourself you intended to take whatever she offered. And, when the time came, go on home. So it's been a splendid vacation at that. Maybe she's just the burdar you always wanted and could never quite find.

Woolgathering. Watching Alix walk. Tension straightening her spine.

I saw him before Alix did, though she must have been looking for him, saw him before he saw me, though he must have been alert for our coming. The road here was lined with tall, bulky, broad-leaved trees, trees alien in this land of slender, piney woods. An old orchard maybe. No. Not fruiting trees. These were the kind that grew small, hard nuts. Acorns? Can't remember. Maybe this patch of forest had spread from the trees of some ornamental garden abandoned a hundred years ago, or two, even three.

I scanned the bushes lining both sides of the road and shook my head slowly. Idiots.

Standing on the almost-horizontal branch of a fat old oak

tree, one hand on the scarred bark of the trunk, clad from head to toe in a formfitting suit of some smooth green cloth, a slim, dark-haired man stood daydreaming, looking up at the sky. His green clothes were not quite the same color as the vegetation. Too light, by several shades, for this time of year the leaves of the eastern woodlands are a dark, sullen green, the green of late summer.

Familiar color. I even knew its name: Lincoln green.

Jesus Christ.

One hard pang of anger, barely touched by baffled amusement at what I was seeing.

The man in the tree, whose lower face was hidden by a dull tan bandanna, glanced down, started visibly as he saw me. His hand went to the strap of the glossy black rifle he had slung over one shoulder, as if to swing it 'round and bring it to bear on me.

Moment of saw-edged tension in my muscles. Nothing's going to happen. You know that. But the training . . .

One of those one-false-move-and-you're-dead situations.

But his hand merely hung there, thumb under the strap as if it were an elastic lapel, then Alix saw him, stopping suddenly in her tracks, looking upward.

I wondered briefly what he would say. Stand and deliver? Your money or you die? What the hell good would that do?

He said, "Hello, Alix. Glad you could make it."

She waved up at him, almost timidly.

I think the hot, tired feeling in my throat was only disappointment. I don't think I was about to cry. Not quite. I said, "Come on down, Davy. I'm afraid you'll fall out of the tree."

A tableau. Silence. Did he think I wouldn't recognize his voice? He said, "Um. All right, Athy."

I glanced at the bushes beneath the tree. "You too, Marsh. You and your friend." A quiet scuffling sound, something like an intake of breath. "These folks on the other side of the path, too." I gestured, didn't look.

Alix was staring up at me, wide-eyed, astonished. Did any of them think they were doing anything other than playing a game? Davy said, "Sure, Athy. Um. Come on out, guys."

Davy. Marsh and his girlfriend, Sandy what's-her-name.

A half dozen people I more or less recognized. Faces from
the bar. The grown-up faces of children I'd once known.
Maybe played with from time to time. Every one of them
armed, all of their guns the same. Old-fashioned military rifles, regular human combat issue, slim and black, launchers
really for little self-propelled projectiles. Spahis still use
them sometimes. The old X-cracker charges can be damned
effective, but that residual induced-radiation can be a nuisance.

"This all of you?"

Looking up at me, Davy pulled down his bandanna, and
said, "Well, no. We've got a camp a few kilometers from
here. It's almost dinnertime."

Almost dinnertime. I looked at Alix, who seemed non-
plussed. "What is this, a surprise party?" Blank look, followed by something like fear. "It's not my birthday."

Marsh said, "You still got that little pistol in your pocket,
Athy?"

I looked him in the eye. "You make a better cop than I
ever would've expected, Marsh."

He gave me a wan smile. "It's easy to be dumb."

I guess so. I took Alix by the hand, felt her fingers squeeze
gratefully on mine. "Lead the way, Davy."

Another gloomy forest trail, this one very old and very artificial. The forest here was wide open, trees towering above
us, turning the day murky yellow-green, and I could see collapsed square holes in the ground here and there, usually the
focus of what little underbrush there was. The trail showed
some signs of having once been paved, and there were the remains of stone slab stairs wherever the trail got particularly
steep.

River down there somewhere, splashing away. Probably
an old millrace or two. The people who'd lived here had
been the millworkers, and this had once, back in the nineteenth century maybe, been a rural industrial center of sorts.

They'd all gone broke and moved away during the great
wave of urbanization, gone away long ago and given the forest time to grow up through the ruins of their homes.

Maybe children had played here once. Maybe not. Maybe the children were all too busy working in the mill. Small children then. Bare-ass children because they weren't quite housebroken yet. You could almost hear them scuffling and screeching, like ghosts whispering over the sound of an unfelt wind.

"Why the hell are you wearing a Robin Hood suit, Davy?"

He glanced back at me, surprised, then grinned and fingered his green lapels. "We found them in the ruins of a costume shop over in downtown Raleigh."

Marsh said, "It's against the law to wear military camouflage, Athy."

"Whose law?"

Pensive look. "Mine. Sort of." Sandy was holding his hand, the two of them more or less walking in step with Alix and me.

"How'd you get up here? You can't all have travel passes."

"Well. Sagoths aren't really monitored . . ."

Davy laughed softly. "No one's *really* monitored. They just don't seem to *care* what we do."

Until they become a nuisance, do you care what ants are up to? Even then, antiant pogroms are always local. Even so, the ants never win. "So?"

A shrug. "It's easy enough to get around. Local freight. Still plenty of private cars left over. Electrified localities that . . ." He exchanged glances with Marsh, the two of them . . . what? Warning each other? "Well. It's easy enough."

Maybe not quite as stupid as they seem.

Marsh said, "We're trusting you now, Athy, showing you . . . what's going on. We've . . . talked about this a lot. Ever since we knew you were coming home. Talked about what it might mean."

Baffling. What the hell could they have *imagined* it meant? Did no one suppose I just wanted to *see* the place again?

Davy said, "If you tell anybody . . . Well, you know what'll happen to us all." He nodded meaningfully at Alix,

who was looking up at me with that same put-on earnest look
that she tended to don at need like a mask.

Shit. I tried to ignore a passing wave of faraway anger. Of
not wanting things further . . . spoiled. "I won't tell."

I could see Davy relax. Not Marsh, though.

Alix squeezed my hand again, and said, "What happens if
we're all caught someday and they find out you . . . knew?"

Well, well. Fancy that. It was like a bitter taste in my
mouth. I said, "I'll be put to sleep."

Alix had the decency to look startled at my choice of
words.

Their camp was in a lovely little valley, already descending into shadow as the sun sank behind the mountains. A
long, narrow bowl, like some kind of giant soup tureen,
sliver of silvery stream winding through the bottom, bowl
lined with dry brown summer grass, a couple of crab apple
trees poking up here and there, a few swaths of stalky brown
bushes, things bearing clusters of dark red berries.

Memory almost there. The berries had some kind of natural ephedra-like substance in them, had been used by the
aborigines as an effective folk medicine, millennia before the
Western pharmaceuticals industry had come up with
ephedrine.

Above the valley, visible over the trees, were the ruins of
some old church. Not a regular church, though. The still-
standing steeple was bulbous rather than straight-sided,
seemed to bear the remnants of golden metal cladding. An
old metal cross, now standing aslant. Catholic, maybe. There
were a few of them scattered throughout these mountains.
Up beyond the abandoned church there'd be an old road
leading to some nearby town, most likely also abandoned
and in decay.

Alix linked her arm through mine and said, "Welcome to
Dorvo Valley, Athy." Smiling now.

Dorvo Valley.

Goddamn it.

Dorvo Valley was a not-quite-paradisical wilderness fea-
tured in a series of early twenty-first century fantasy novels

we'd all read and loved as kids. It had been the focus of the Episode of the Last 360th Dorvo Egg in *Crimson Darkness*, a story so enchantedly exciting that we played out its complex plot over and over again, like variations on a theme.

I was always Älendar Vexh-nem, the once-and-future Vaihadet of the shrouded world known as Käraiha, Alix his girlfriend Zzaine Orrn. Davy played her brother Raitearyón, who'd been Älendar's comrade in long captivity, while Marsh was always Vastav Eov, rebel Vaihisor of Red Island . . .

Almost the first time I kissed Alix, we were Älendar and Zzaine, rather than ourselves. Perhaps that excused the moment. Excuses we didn't need for long.

I think I remember Davy being angry, saying it spoiled the game. Not Marsh though, who was after the girl who always played Zir-Las Staa. Funny. She was supposed to be Raitearyón's girlfriend, rather than that of the somewhat sexless Eov . . .

Down under the trees on the far side of the valley, next to an enormous red brier patch, they'd set up tents of dull brown cloth, tents almost blending into the forest. They had cook fires going, plumes of gray smoke rising into the sky, giving their presence away.

Alix took me by the hand and pulled me along. "Come on, Athy. Dinner's ready."

We went. And I remembered that, near the end of *Crimson Darkness*, Dorvo Valley had been destroyed by a thermonuclear device.

Dinner was served under the trees, at a set of old picnic tables they'd dragged in from somewhere else. The church maybe, or the backyard of some nearby, luxurious quasi-rural home. A dinner of roasted meat, slightly burned corn on the cob. Sweet potatoes. Kool-Aid from decades-old packages, indigo grape and brilliant green lime, sweetened with raw crystals of cane sugar, sugar with a much different taste than the fine white beet sugar the Spahi commissaries were getting from somewhere else.

Dinner served with a surprise, Alix, Davy, and Marsh pleased by my visible reaction.

The two Saanaae sat naked on the ground at either end of our table, eating meals of corn and sweet potato, as well as some unidentifiable dark gray stuff that smelled a bit like a freshly mowed lawn. Beside them, folded neatly on the ground, were their white cloaks and straw hats and brooch placards with Master ID numbers.

One male. One female, her ovipositor dangling between her forelegs like a stiff cardboard tube, shiny wet inside when the light caught it just right. Most people's eyes shied away. Their ID badges said they were attached to a police unit near the remains of Asheville.

The male, sitting beside me, looked at me, eating slowly, listening to the idle conversation, eating his meat in small chunks, each bit with a dab of candied yam spread on top. The female seemed to prefer the corn more than anything else, biting it off bit by bit from one end, cob and all, sprinkling it every now and again from a shaker of what looked like blue metallic glitter.

The male said, "So, Spahi."

"Morrison."

He nodded slowly, not a human nod, but some upward head movement that was ever so slightly horselike. "Morrison. I call myself Mace. It's a translation of my, uh, real name." His English was excellent, only the alien resonance of his deep chest and heavy head giving him away as a nonhuman. Maybe a little bit like you'd imagine a talking horse would sound.

"The last Saanaa I met was still using her real name."

The female said, "Stoneshadow. And that Saanaa you met was still in denial. Time for us to forget." English almost as good, but contaminated by a slight accent. More like a talking dog.

Denial. It made me want to smile. "Forget what?"

The male said, "Our home is gone. Time to realize that this is our home." He gestured at the woods around us.

So. That seemed reasonable. Also a lie. "What're you doing here, then? If you want to forget, that is."

"I still have a Master." Deadpan. Uninflected.

I glanced at the female. Nothing. Those green eyes just too unreadable. Hard to know what these . . . people were thinking. Harder than the Kkhruhhuft, whom I knew much better.

The male said, "Well, Jemadar-Major Morrison. I understand you were on Rouhaaz."

Not a question. I nodded.

He said, "I was on Rouhaaz as well."

I could picture him with a rifle butt in the face, with someone's bayonet fishing around in his pouch. Or imagine it that way, at any rate. "At Souhaezo Valley?" Trees smoking as they bled milky sap, refusing to catch fire. Burning centaur bodies. Yellow-brown centaur blood.

"I was captured at Taxxaewi Beach."

I shook my head. "Never there. Sorry."

He stared at me for a long moment, eyes motionless, reflecting red from the cook fire. "Doesn't matter. This battle or that one. This world. That one. It's not Saanaae. Not Kkhruhhuft. Not humans. Only Masters."

I said, "You and I are soldiers in the service of the Master Race."

Beside me, Alix stopped eating suddenly. Davy and Marsh, farther down the table, were both looking up, watching me.

The Saanaa said, "Why are *you* here, then?"

I glanced at Alix. "These are my friends."

He nodded slowly, another delicate head toss. "Just so, Jemadar-Major." He looked down the table at the female, whose badge indicated a somewhat higher rank. "And our friends as well."

Late night. I opened the tent flap, letting the wind and moonlight in. Fresh air blew over us, making the atmosphere inside the tent, air heated by our efforts, seem like some swampy miasma. Devils rising from us, like dim and foggy clouds.

We pulled one of the drier blankets outside and spread it on the ground, sat naked together, arms around each other, looking up at a waning, three-quarters full moon. For some

reason, the maria looked like real seas tonight, the five major
ones interlocking, like some vast Mediterranean in the sky. I
could imagine ships sailing there, lateen-rigged in my dream,
like Arab dhows, sailing on the winds of the moon. Ancient
cities, some half in ruins, gleaming under blue earthlight in
that shadowed quarter, others flaming brilliant white by the
light of the sun.

Dusty plains beyond, ridden by alien horse barbarians. Remote mountain tribes, who would kill and eat the lowlanders.
Island folk far out in the seas. Cannibal isles. Pirates. Wars
and fiery battles fought with the most primitive of weapons.
Greek fire from bubbling naphtha wells. Ballistae. Simple
powder rockets . . .

Alix kissed my shoulder, sliding her hand underneath my
arm, squeezing a big, hanging muscle mass. "You're still
sweating," she said.

I held her close, running my fingers gently down her side,
letting my hand rest on the soft flesh of her hip. I wondered
briefly what she'd be like, slimmed down by Spahi exercise
regimens, wondered what she would have been like, still
young perhaps, if she'd come with me. Come with me and
survived.

And I still wanted to be up on that imaginary moon.
Thoughts of the real one. Human bases and buried cities
lying silently in the dust, measureless caverns collapsed,
blown open when the Kkhruhhuft came. When I was a kid,
you could look up at the moon and see lights twinkling on
the dark part. Could peer through a child's telescope and see
regular lines scored out on the brilliant white plains.

If you looked long enough, you'd see the white spark of a
spacecraft climbing away toward orbit. If you were sharp-
eyed, you could pick out the glitter of a space habitat or two
as it whirled between sunlight and shadow.

Alix leaned around my chest, kissed me softly on one nipple, tickling me with her tongue. "Are you all right, Athy?"
Hardly more than a whisper.

I said, "Just caught up in all the old dreams." She was
leaning across me now, laying her head on my thigh, looking
up at a face that must be lost in shadow. My hand slid off her

hip, cupping one buttock now, feeling her warmth against the breezy night.

The wind picked up, blowing hair down into my face, Alix reaching up and quickly brushing it away. When I got home I'd have to have it trimmed back. You don't go into combat with long, loose hair that can fall down in your eyes.

She said, "That's why we're all here, I suppose. Because we can't forget those old dreams."

Soft, bitter heat moving through my chest. "Do you really think you know what you're doing?"

She kissed me on the thigh, rubbed her face gently back and forth. "For a long time I didn't," she said. "For a long time I thought Davy and Marsh were crazy. Just playing the old games, you know? I thought it was silly. Silly and dangerous . . ."

"Then, why . . ."

"Because I was lonely, Athy. Because it made me remember what life felt like, back when . . . when we were together."

Back when we were children. "You do understand it's still no more than a dangerous game, don't you?" I was stroking her hair now, fingers tangling in all the curls, feeling out the smooth, round shape of her head. It seemed very small under my hand, like a child's skull, hardly matching the visual image I had of her, remembered from daylight.

Her hand was on my abdomen now, rubbing back and forth just below my navel, where the skin was folded in on itself, like soft suede leather. "You're so . . . thin," she said. "Thin and hard." Her fingers slid down and tangled in my still-damp pubic hair, rested there for a moment. "I guess I believed that until the Saanaae came."

The Saanaae. Mace and Stoneshadow. Others, without a doubt. Many others. Saanaae thousands, millions, resettled on Earth forever. I said, "You know why they're here, don't you? Here as police?"

She had her hand on my penis now, fingers moving around on soft skin. She said, "We heard about the rebellion, Athy. All those worlds in flame. People dying all across the stars."

Despite everything, despite a desire to suddenly get up and just run away, I could feel myself coming erect under her ministrations. Could feel a hard tautness developing deep inside, as if someone were twisting a turnbuckle, tension evolving of its own accord.

She said, "I know you had a part in what happened. You and your Spahis. The Kkhruhhuft."

I said, "The Saanaae rebellion failed, Alix. It was put down in just a few weeks."

"What if the Spahis had joined them, Athy? What if the Kkhruhhuft . . ."

"There are still Saanaae in the universe today because they're useful to the Master Race. And because the rebellion was futile, because it failed so utterly."

"They say it almost succeeded, Athy."

They say. What would Alix and her friends be imagining? What did they *know*? Precious little. And they wouldn't know that the Saanaae rebellion, setting a score of worlds ablaze, was so pitifully small a thing that it involved no more than a few legions of Spahis, a handful of Kkhruhhuft regiments.

No one's even told them of the million or so Saanaae military police who joined us in the suppression of their brethren, once the hard work of killing was done.

I said, "Alix, the Saanaae built an interstellar organization for the task. They had the power to move about freely. Could do what they wanted, as trustees of the Master Race. What makes you think Earth alone can succeed where all the Saanaae in all of space failed?"

Softly, she said, "Humanity has an interstellar component as well."

I wanted to laugh, wanted to push her away, stand up and laugh, but her hands down there kept me focused and motionless. So the Saanaae would tell them that they almost succeeded. And invoke all those absurd what-ifs. What if the Spahis. What if the Kkhruhhuft. What if all the Saanaae, scattered to so many worlds of the empire. What if.

What if God came back from that eternal heavenly vacation, just to set us free?

Hell, why not imagine the aphids rebelling? What not imagine the mindless poppits suddenly waking up one day and going, My God, what have we done?

Why not imagine the Master Race will suddenly begin to care how we feel?

Alix slid the rest of the way up my thigh, put my penis in her mouth, working at it with her lips and tongue, moving rhythmically, slowly, reacting to feedback from my body. I sat. Waited. Stared at the silvery moon. Wished for another life. When my orgasm came I heard Alix choke softly. Choke softly and swallow.

Still later, I sat alone on the blanket watching our shiny old moon descend across the western sky, waited patiently for it to fall below the low, rolling mountains of the horizon. Watched those same old stars wheel, thought those same old thoughts about Masters and worlds and friends and wars.

Alix slept inside the tent, naked on the blanket there, more or less facedown, half-curled, feet projecting into the wan moonlight, buttocks globed up, ghostly, surrounding shadow. If I listened closely, I could hear the slow, hollow, start-stop breathing of her sleep.

I could hear animals in the night. Things scuttling in the underbrush. The occasional faint, musical cry of a hunting owl. Very far away the rhythmic clank of some night bird or another.

Once, a murmur from some other tent. A woman's voice, gasping, hollow. A nightmare? A breathing problem? I wanted to imagine her making love. Wanted to imagine that, if only for a few minutes, there was someone for whom the world had ceased to exist. Someone for whom there was only the moment.

I could feel the flat, hard square of the command phone in the palm of my hand, where it'd lain quietly for an hour now, while I watched the moon drift across the sky, the wheel of the stars making its path seem to curve.

Go ahead. Call Shrêhht. Discuss the information laid down in your query queue. Talk about this new development.

You know how it'll be. The Sirkar will already know about Marsh, will be watching him, waiting for the right moment.

Pray to that world-famous nonexistent God that it's only Marsh. And, please God, don't let the Sirkar be involved on an institutional level.

Image of fire from the sky. The world burned clean and resettled by some other deserving race. I wonder. Will they make us come and kill our own?

Probably.

Will we do it?

Of course.

Image of my Alix's burned corpse lying twisted in some gutter, like so much cooked red meat. I could see her lying there, flesh mummylike, roasted tendons drawing her legs up, so I could see the seared and parted lips of her vulva, burned clean of hair. Singed like a chicken. Waiting. Inviting me. Come on, soldier-boy. Here's a nice burdar for you.

A deep rustling thud from some nearby shadow. The Saanaae were sleeping there, legs curled under, torsos upright, cocked just so, arms folded across their chests, heads down and nodding in sleep. I could barely make them out, the shape of one or the other moving, shifting on the ground.

If they rebelled again, the Masters might decide they weren't so useful after all. Why would they risk it?

No answer.

I opened my command phone and logged into the net.

12

THE NEW DAY CAME ON SLOWLY, FIRST the indigo backdrop of false dawn, then ashen light washing away the stars. When the sun rose, it burned the sky pale orange, scouring the heavens clean before painting them blue.

I sat outside the open tent flap, watching Alix sleep, watching her stir this way and that, rolling onto her back, arms and legs sprawled however they happened to fall, mouth hanging open, shadowy dawn gleaming on her teeth.

Behind me, I could hear other people begin to awaken, moving around in their tents, murmuring softly to each other.

And it had been a long night for me, a night of thinking about what we'd said, Shrêhht and I, of thinking about what could happen. Would happen. She'd read me Marsh's record. Enough to tell me his fate was sealed. Enough to know he might as well climb a high cliff, ascend to the top of the tallest tree around, apologize to his friends, say his prayers . . .

I could imagine him dead.

Not difficult at all.

Soft and broken and still upon the ground.

Alix's fingernails made a soft, delicate rasping sound as she scratched in her sleep, one hand moving up onto her thigh, fingers making a tentative movement, some of them connecting, some not. Almost conscious then. I watched her eyelids, watched them flutter gently, eyes moving back and forth under the skin.

Living out the last vestiges of some chaotic dream. This way. That. Back again. Nerves firing, tuning up for the day, like flight software putting engine gimbals through their paces, making sure everything was as it should be.

I thought about Davy and his family. Pretty easy to notice his wife and children were nowhere to be seen. Keeping them safe? Or just keeping reality out of his dream?

Behind me, I could hear one of the Saanaae stumble to its feet, could hear an oddly querulous murmur in the fluid cadences of the principal Saanaae tongue. I'd learned a bit of it while I was on Rouhaaz, not enough to follow these garbled mutterings.

Suddenly, Alix's eyes were open, fog of sleep burning away fast. Eyes on me, seeing, becoming aware. Then further awareness, mouth closing, one hand going up to her hair. Her knee came up and she started to close her legs, stopped, relaxed. I could see her thinking, but couldn't see the thoughts themselves. She said, "Good morning, Athy."

By midmorning, washed in the stream, dressed, and breakfasted, we went out with Davy to see what he called maneuvers. They were up in the woods, under Marsh's command, in the area behind the old Catholic church, men and women in Lincoln green, the two green Saanaae stripped naked, scales aglitter, all of them slinking along, from tree to tree, shadow to shadow.

Davy pointed, one hand on my forearm. In the distance I could make out shadowy forms, some large, some small. Dark cardboard cutouts of men with guns, skirmish lines of cardboard Saanaae, some kind of field gun over there, and . . . That little thing. Several of them. I looked hard. Little bitty cardboard poppits, shapes indicating they had some kind of hardware strapped to their backs, just the way real poppits would, though you'd rarely see them in combat.

I looked harder. Far away through the trees were two

larger shadows, almost imperceptible. A pair of Kkhruhhuft in combat armor.

Davy wouldn't know anything about this. Marsh? Most of it, but not all. That bit about the poppit "recorders" could've come only from the Saanaae, who, perhaps, would remember a scene like this.

So. Combat? No. This little party of sagoths and Saanaae, poppits in tow, was simply going from one place to another. Ambush, then.

And those well-hidden Kkhruhhuft?

To teach my little friends just how careful they'd have to be. If they didn't spot the Kkhruhhuft, attack them *first*. I could imagine the harsh words they'd hear from Mace and Stoneshadow.

I tapped Davy on the shoulder, took his combat rifle out of his hands, popped the clip and looked. White plastic fragmentation warheads on subsonic boosters. You could kill a man with this if you shot him in head, neck, or chest. Probably kill a Saanaa too, if you were careful.

All you'd do to a Kkhruhhuft is piss him off royally, like firing BBs at a Doberman, unless, maybe, you hit him right in the eye. No eyes on an armored trooper.

Davy whispered, "We've got plenty of X-cracker charges. We're just using these for practice."

Swell. X-crackers are great for putting dents in armor. I was hit in the helmet with one during a training exercise, a squad of us assaulting a bunker supposedly occupied by "unfriendlies" whose technology mimicked what humans had had in 2159. Made my ears ring for a week.

Up ahead, Marsh's people were almost upon the enemy column. No one was looking at those shadowy Kkhruhhuft, and the two Saanaae were hanging back now, waiting. Exchanging glances. Probably laughing.

I snapped the clip back in, lifted the rifle, read the range off the targeting system. Twelve-hundred meters. Less than half the effective range of this weapon. One. Two. Three.

I fired a quick burst, rifle chattering like a high-powered stapler, watched the cardboard head fall off one Kkhruhhuft. Leaves fluttering in the breeze. Again, cutting the legs from

under the other. Resighted on the column, back to front.
Knocked down the five model Saanaae. Took out all the little
poppits. Took the heads off motionless human statues.

Listened to a fading echo of rattatatat.

Silence.

Pretend guerrillas looking around, confused, wondering
where their targets had gone. The two live Saanaae were
staring back at me now, also motionless. The female saw me
look at her, quickly put her gun on the ground. The male was
a little stupider, lagged a corresponding moment behind.

Davy said, "Jesus. Lank *said* you could shoot, but I never
would've *believed* . . ."

And Alix whispered, "What if they'd been real, Athy?"

I tried looking her in the eye. "Then they'd've been shooting back." Glanced at Davy again. He didn't seem to get it,
but maybe Alix was figuring things out. Maybe. Just a little
bit.

Down the hill, Marsh's troopers were inspecting the cardboard carnage, people looking up at me from time to time,
frowning, murmuring to each other. The two naked Saanaae
started walking back up the hill to where I waited, leaving
their guns behind them on the ground.

Not far from the camp there was an old, old stone pit, too
small to have been a twentieth century quarry, but somebody'd dug stuff out of there at some time in the past,
gouged into the side of a steep hill, leaving a sheer granite
cliff where trees and bushes would never grow again, not 'til
ice and tiny roots had done the work of tumbling it down.

Below, they'd dug a small pit in the rock, leaving behind a
hole the size of an Olympic swimming pool. Water from a
little stream tumbled down the cliff face, filling the depres-
sion with clear, cold water, which spilled over the rim,
stream re-forming in the woods below.

The overflow waterfall had already dug a little lip, so the
surface of the water was about a foot below the rim of the
pit. There was moss here, wherever the shadows were deep
enough, soft like velvet.

Now, while Marsh and his people gathered by the pond,

eating packaged lunches, while the Saanaae lurked back in the forest, away from me a little bit, eating their own oddly scented meals, I sat on the stone rim between Davy and Alix, watching ripples on the water, the reflection of cliff and sky, looking through a cloudscape image at the lifeless bottom of the pit. The water here must be quite acidic.

Davy, munching on some kind of squishy pocket-bread sandwich, said, "So what did you think?"

Of what? Your silly little show? "Davy, is my brother involved in all this?"

"Who, Lank?" He looked past me at Alix for a moment. "Well, no, not really. He thinks this is a big mistake."

"But he does know," said Alix, staring into the pond now, not looking at me anymore.

Bad enough. "Who else? My father? Your wife?"

A surprised look. "Miriam? No. She thinks I'm part of an orienteering club. That's our cover, you know."

And Alix said, "Athy, your dad's always been too thick with Chief Catalano. We'd never . . ."

A glint in Davy's eye. "My father died because yours wouldn't help him, Athy."

But I wasn't here then and don't remember. I said, "And you think this is going to accomplish anything?"

A serious, clear-eyed look into my face. Wondering. A small sigh. "Not in the beginning, Athy. In the beginning, we knew it was just a game, like the Liberators. You know."

Of course. But . . .

He said, "Even after we found the arms cache," one hand smoothing the black plastic stock of his rifle, "it was still a game. We left everything in place, closed up the entrance. But it was the seed of an idea. The military left their weapons stockpiled everywhere when they surrendered. Because hope never dies."

"So. When did it change for you?" Not that I didn't know the answer.

He glanced back into the trees at Mace and Stoneshadow. "When we found out it *had* happened. Out there."

"But you know how quickly and easily they were beaten down, don't you?"

A shrug. "It seems like that's what happened, even though the Saanaae like to pretend otherwise. All those big claims about 'how we almost won.' I'm not stupid."

"Then why?" A gesture 'round, at men and women in Lincoln green, eating beside a clear artificial pond in a woodland full of ruins.

"Because what happened once can happen again. And again and again. Sooner or later . . ."

Sooner or later, what? You kneel down before this new god or you die, the lesson of the Persian Zoroastrians.

Davy, eyes far away, said, "It doesn't matter that the Saanaae alone failed. Failed because the Kkhruhhuft, because people like . . . you, I guess, helped put them down. It doesn't matter if humans alone fail and fall. It's the *idea* of rebellion that counts. And the realization that it can spread among the worlds . . ."

"Do you understand what may happen?"

A slow nod. "We fail. We fall. Some people die. Maybe humans and Saanaae are deported again. Some of us will land on other worlds, if that happens. There'll be other enslaved races there as well. And we can tell them how *we* almost succeeded."

No, Davy, you're not stupid. What, then? Tell him about those other worlds? Tell him about races that resisted too hard, races that held on to the bitter end? There are worlds out there where no one lives anymore. The Master Race will make a slave species if it can, make an empty colony world if it has to, create a smoking, uninhabitable mineral resource node if that's the only option . . .

"What did you expect from me?"

Alix put one hand on my thigh, and Davy said, "I was impressed by your display of shooting back there, Athy."

"So?"

"There are ten million other human beings out there just like you, Athy. Armed. Trained. Scattered around the galaxy." His eyes held a bright vision now. I felt sorry for him. Sorry for all of them.

*   *   *

It's one of a very few details kept secret by the Spahis. Who was there. Who was not. The Saanaae don't know, for the ones who were there are dead.

I'd crouched with my troopers in a golden forest on Aeli Saa, up in the Mohsetz Mountains, looking out over the Rëae Plains. There was wind all around us, high clouds scudding under a yellow-gray sky, the city of Mohyyz a low urban sprawl through which wound the old Tremëe River, where King Turi Amaq united the people of the world.

Beyond the city, the spaceport, where rocket gantries had once grown, where proud Saanaae centaurs rode into the sky, conquering their dead, black moon and the lifeless worlds beyond, before venturing out to the stars. There was something on fire at the spaceport now, dark smoke rising high, sheering off in the wind.

Almost over now. Soldiers from the sky. Fighting. Fighting. Saanaae doing all the dying. In a little while it would be over. Ghastly business. Necessary business.

The alert tone chimed in my helmet. "Heads up. Watch yourselves."

It made a long, lovely yellow contrail across the sky, a string of tiny, brilliant beads, more of them to the left and right, and far ahead of us, out over the sea, dropping down among the islands as a squadron of FTL bombers popped out of hyperspace and tracked across the face of Aeli Saa, distributing their loads.

One weapon, one only for Mohyyz, capital of the world, bespeaking contempt for these rebellious little policemen.

Dropping. Dropping. Hastily improvised Saanaae defensive weapons began sparkling over the city, the best they could do, hoping against hope that . . .

Something flashed around the falling weapon, picking off the defensive warheads. Falling, turning, centering itself over the city. Flash. The weapon burst open, core of light spreading.

My video pickups shut themselves off, leaving me in darkness. I heard someone else grunt. A touch of fear in someone's voice. I said, "Easy, there."

The ground surged under my knees, once, hard, I heard the forest start to crackle, then the audio pickup went down as well. I could hear the sound of my soldiers' breathing, whispering over the net into my ears.

Hard sigh of wind, rustling branches, like the wind just before a storm, and my eyes reopened on fading golden light. Mohyyz was gone, replaced by an irregular scorch pattern several kilometers across. You could see shock waves fading out in the ruins beyond, whatever was left of those scattered small towns and hamlets.

My senior havildar said, "Holy *shit* . . ."

The Master Race symbolic representation means something like "non-radiogenic energy inverter." We always called them thumpers. Because that's the noise they make.

Thump.

Cleanup time. Walking through the ruins of some little village. Nothing left of the place. Splashed wreckage, no single piece much larger than a domino. Wisps of smoke. Smashed corpses. Dead things that looked a bit like a cross between a komodo dragon and a tarantula. One of these lying beside a broken-bodied Saanaa, head resting peacefully on one dead haunch, its own legs fearfully twisted and torn.

My soldiers muttering softly to each other, the names of various useless and forgotten deities coming up every now and again.

Rounding a naked brown hill, finding a large piece of rubble, the marblelike torso of some Saanaae statuary, beside it a smallish female Saanaa, maybe a little less than half the size of a standard adult, left arm sheared away at the elbow, right foreleg broken, jagged gray bone poking through the hide, smeared with yellowish blood.

Staring at us. Wide-eyed. Motionless.

My havildar said, "Fuck."

This was getting to be difficult. Harder than I ever dreamed.

No one spoke. No one moved.

A whisper of sound from the little Saanaa girl. Good right arm holding the ruin of the other.

"Havildar."

"Sir."

"Take the team down to the river. Pick out a camp for the night. We'll make pickup in the morning, move on to the next site. We're about done here."

"Yes, sir." Relief in his voice.

We kept doing it and doing it.

Never got any easier.

People hurting inside just now.

Give them a break.

I listened to my squad clatter slowly away, could tell how dispirited they'd become. Morale dropping. Time to ask for a rotation out. Fatigued, you see.

The little girl kept looking up at me. Knowing, I suppose. Waiting.

When I unlimbered the torch and pointed it at her, she didn't flinch, didn't recoil. But she screamed when I pulled the trigger, a short, high, choppy squeal, bucked and gargled as the fire ate her away.

In the morning we rotated out, went on back to Santulliq, where I knew a promotion was waiting. Promotion. Unit citation. Posting to Boromilith, where I'd command a full company.

In the late afternoon, I found my two Saanaae wanderers alone in a clearing, sitting together, touching one another, gazing into featureless eyes, shawls and belts doffed and neatly folded. Maybe they were preparing to dance. Maybe not.

The female nodded to me, that horsy little head toss I knew so well, and in her quaint talking-dog voice said, "Welcome, Jemadar-Major."

"Hello, Stoneshadow." I stood with my back against a tree, weight on my heels. "I don't know your rank."

The male said, "True rank is a thing of the past. We have the jobs your Masters give us. That's all."

"My Masters?"

"The Masters here on Earth. The ones who buy our contracts."

Funny way of putting it. The Master Race has nothing like money, just an internal resource allocation system. I once heard it referred to as the System Chargeback Router. Don't know if there's any truth in the term, and it doesn't much matter.

Stoneshadow said, "What do you think of our little . . . operation, Jemadar-Major?"

"I think you're going to get my friends killed along with you. Maybe everyone on Earth, if it's more than just a few of you."

Nothing. Just looking at me.

"So. What do you think this will accomplish?"

"I think you've heard the way Captain Itakë puts it. Keep the dream alive. And someday . . ."

"You think no one knew about *Yllir Waÿÿ?* You think it was just some private Saanaae dream?" Yllir Waÿÿ was what they'd called their rebellion, before it erupted across the worlds.

A moment of silence, then she said, "No, Jemadar-Major. It's everyone's dream. Live, die. Succeed, fail. What difference does it make, so long as we keep on trying? They can't kill us all. It can't go on forever."

"So you want to see all of your people dead? Or all of mine?"

She said, "Do you think, perhaps, I want to see your people destroyed because of what you did to mine?" She stood, walking toward me, standing still, towering over me, eyes reflecting afternoon light, foreclaws digging into the litter. "No, Jemadar-Major. Someday we'll return to Aeli Saa. Not you and I. We'll be long dead. But humans and Saanaae together. Even Kkhruhhuft . . ." It's nice to dream, while the dream lasts.

Moonlight shining on water, glittering on the little waterfall, lighting up the trees of the forest, making ghostly shadows out of the world. The moon itself floated disembodied in a vast, hollow sky, stars turning in their courses behind it, icy and far away. There were wisps of cloud up there somewhere, backlit lace blowing in the wind.

A creaking of distant crickets. Waterfall splashing, high and musical. Cold water gurgling deep as it spilled over the rim, went trickling away to the forest floor below.

And my Alexandra, up to her shoulders in the pool, face a handsbreadth from mine, so close it was hard to see whole, image dominated by shining eyes and white teeth and the black shadows of her hair, hair asparkle with droplets lit from the sky.

No words, though we'd talked a little on our way through the forest.

I'm so glad you're here now, Athy. I was so afraid . . .

Stopping every now and then to embrace and kiss and whisper to each other, arms holding on tight, hands sliding across our backs, downward to hips, bodies shifting, juxtaposing appropriate parts. Gentle shifting. Bodies knowing.

Then standing by the side of the reflecting pool, looking down at the little world's reflection, while Alix unbuttoned my shirt, slid her hands inside, fingers on my chest, warm on my sides, reaching back to touch the trough of my spine.

A whisper of pleasure as she felt those solid layers and bulges, each one giving ever so slightly to her touch.

I felt very much a hollow man as she knelt and unbuckled my belt, took off my boots, helped me step out of my trousers. Pressed her face into my belly, tongue massaging flesh. Stood up, stepped away, warm night breeze cooling the wet spot she'd left behind.

Another whisper: "God, you're beautiful . . ." Like an icon, perhaps.

I stepped forward and undressed her then, unbuttoning blouse, unhooking brassiere, letting them fall onto the pile of my clothing, mouth to her breasts, hands to her waist. Unlaced her boots and took them off, small white feet on bare wet stone, slid down her trousers and made a wet spot of my own. Felt her shiver under my touch.

A hard, aching moment of uncertainty. It always *seems* like this must mean something. Especially when the words have been said. But the burdars shiver under your touch too, and will say the words if you ask.

We slid into the water, its apparent iciness freezing our

skins, making them first numb, then wonderfully oversensitive. I held Alix close, feeling her breasts on me, felt her hand on my genitals, exploring their relaxed shape.

All those old images flooding in. Alix and I as no longer quite children, exploring the beginnings of life together in the ruins. Alix and I young, making all our plans. Alix and I in a life that never existed, so happy together, sharing a whole world of dreams.

I put my hand between her legs, holding her on my palm, kissing her, taking all the time that ever was, as if here and now were eternity.

Felt the engine of her soul quicken.

Goddamn it. Cold, remote rage at all the dreams that never lived.

Put my fingers inside her then, and kissed her with a fury born from that faraway rage.

We stumbled out of the pool and onto the ground, fell upon each other then and made love, hunger-driven, fear-driven, crying out under the stars. But when it was over, I was still quite hollow.

Moving again, sunlight dim and grainy through the tan filter of our tent wall. Alix sat opposite me, back against the rear strut, one leg drawn up, the other splayed out, one hand to her hair, a compellingly primitive image, pubic hair a long, dark, divided swath, nothing like literature's symbol-shrouded triangle, from this point of view.

Answering her question, I said, "Yes, I've thought about it."

Nothing. Serious-eyed. Waiting me out.

Memories of the night, of lying in one another's arms, watching the stars roll overhead, listening to the night creatures, the beating of our own hearts. The long walk back through a darkling wood, things unseen crunching underfoot. Crawling into the tent, sliding out of our clothes, curling around each other, pulling the light blankets up.

Heartbeats.

The haze of oncoming sleep, coupled to the knowledge of her existence. Brief, troubling taps from a distant dawn: This is almost over. But I could feel her buttocks against my thighs, feel the warmth of her. What difference does the future make? It isn't here yet.

A night full of happy, half-remembered dreams. The awakening. Alix turning in my arms, holding me close. Murmuring about how wonderful it was to wake up like this, find me here, holding her, to realize it wasn't *quite* a dream.

Then, the reality. Eyes hard and questing.

Tell me your decision, Athy. Have you thought about it?

Long pause lengthening, awakening fear in her eyes. Then I said, "I don't know that I can do anyone any good out here in the woods, Alix. And I don't know that I believe in Davy's dream. It's been tried before, and tried and tried."

Sorrow. She said, "But . . ."

I raised my hand, reaching out to her, putting my palm on one knee.

"I'll do what I can to help you, Alix. You and all my old friends. Teach you what I can, and . . . think about the . . . rest of it." Very hard to say these things, knowing they were untrue.

She slid forward then, so that my hand went to the top of her thigh, making contact with her vulva, embraced me fiercely, face against the side of my neck, and said, "I knew you'd come, Athy. I *knew* it."

Davy full of joy, overflowing with hope. Stoneshadow thoughtful and serious, exchanging blank-eyed glances with her mate. Marsh pensive and silent. He'd filled up on beer after last night's dinner, though. Maybe he was just hung over. Marsh the Ambiguous. Or maybe just the Ambivalent.

All the others were merely excited, standing around in noisy little clumps, talking, laughing. A mercenary, you see. Here to teach us how it's done. Teach us how to be free once again.

Most of these people had been children before the Invasion, if they'd been born at all. They didn't remember. The world of men was just a story, old people's ramblings fading on off into fable.

I said, "I'll do what I can. Teach you how to use the

weapons you have. Teach you some elementary tactics. It might keep you alive for just a little bit."

Serious look from Marsh at that. Maybe some inkling of what I was talking about.

I said, "I don't know about the rest of it, Davy. We'll see."

Mace kept looking up into the sky, uneasy. Probably wondering if we should really be standing out in the open like this, carrying these illicit weapons around.

Davy, fidgeting like a child, clapped me on the shoulder, laughing. I had a momentary urge to strike him. Waste of time.

I lined them up, sorted them out, had rifles passed around, took one from Davy and checked the clip, made sure there was nothing in there but slow frags. There were watchers in the sky who'd see an X-cracker pop, but these were safe. If they were caught with these things, they could claim they found the rifles in a box somewhere and were using them as hunting weapons, which they were. Probably get no more than a few hundred lashes and a life sentence in some quarry, maybe spend a few decades pulling a plow.

I cradled the rifle across my chest and pointed. "See that bird?" No reaction. "Top of that tall pine."

Several of them squinted in the right direction.

"On that last branch. Gray, with whitish bands across the wings."

Marsh said, "Mockingbird."

I looked at him. "You see it?" He nodded. "Stoneshadow?" Another nod.

Davy said, "Where?" Shading his eyes with one hand.

I leveled the weapon, glanced at the rangefinder and fired, snapping the little branch out from under the bird. It fell for a second, tumbling, thrashed with its wings, righted, began to fly.

Davy said, "Oh!"

I fired again, not bothering with the technosight, watched the bird fall, a dot disappearing into the trees.

I said, "When you can do that, you can think about getting into an armed scrap."

Davy was saucer-eyed.

Stoneshadow ambled over, rifle tucked under one arm, muzzle angled away and toward the ground, sat on her haunches beside me, still looking up at the treetop. She said, "I was captured after a firefight with some of you Spahis. Six of my company left alive out of eighty-one effectives."

"Ever fight Kkhruhhuft?"

She turned to look into my eyes, extract whatever data it was Saanaae expect from looking into eyes, and said, "I'm alive, am I not?"

Good answer.

Afternoon sunlight sloping down on us out of nowhere, warming our backs as we warmed to the task.

Marsh standing beside me, the two of us face to flat black headshield with an armored man. Davy in the background, standing beside Alix, the Saanaae sitting behind them, others in their loose groups, rifles held so very carelessly, watching.

I looked at my shadow in the rubbery matte finish, started walking around the man, inspecting. On one shoulder, the tiny doublestar decal of NACDC, the North American Comprehensive Defense Command, with unit number and suffixes. This might once have been warn by an Army Ranger, but it showed no signs of ever having been in serious combat. The left elbow articulation had a small hydraulic leak, a fleck of wet silicone where it shouldn't have been.

Down for maintenance, perhaps, when the time came.

I glanced at Marsh. "You're a corporal in the Sirkar Native Police?"

He nodded, eyes narrow.

"And in the, um, rebellion?"

I could see a flicker of awareness behind his numb-faced mask. Understanding my thought processes. Cop training. And an intelligence. we'd never given him credit for. Good old Marsh. He said, "We haven't been using military ranks, really. Section leader. There're a number of groups like Davy's."

"He know that?"

An uncomfortable glance at the man. "Sort of."

"The Saanaae?"

Longish pause, staring at me, uneasy. "They know more about us than we know about them."

I said,"Is it wise, telling me these things?"

His face was quite still, eyes cold on mine, but . . . "I have to trust you, Athy. You're our only hope."

I said, "Then you're in big trouble."

No reaction.

I turned back to the armor. "You think you know how to use this stuff?"

He said, "Selected sagoth noncoms are trained to use the old armor. There's a lot of it left lying around, stockpiled from before the Invasion. Masters aren't bringing much hardware in, other than their own. I guess they figured we'd use what we had." ·

"Why?"

He shrugged. "You've had your eyes open, Athy. It's not all peace and quiet."

"You think they suspect?"

"Probably."

More than you know.

I rapped the armored man on his faceplate, wondering if he had his audio hooked up, if he'd been listening to our conversation. The man in the suit was nobody I knew, just a small, muscular man remembered from the bar. "You know, an X-cracker will open this right up."

Troubled look. "Manual says no."

I looked at the helmet's video pickup. "Tip your head back." His chin went up. Stupid, Marsh. Unless this fellow's a most excellent lip reader.

I said, "It wasn't well designed. There's a weak point at every inward flexion on these slip joints. That's at the throat, and at the insides of the elbows and the backs of the knees. Hip joints have secondary armor. Gloves and boots have better joints made by a different subcontractor."

His mask was slipping away, face mirroring professional interest. "Why didn't they fix it?"

"Because it was only combat tested once." And there was no second opportunity.

"So the armor's useless?"

I shrugged. "Old Rangers say they quickly learned to keep their chins as far down as they'd go, their arms folded tight when high-order explosives were flying around." I rapped on the breastplate, a dull, plasticky thud. "And you don't want to be turning your back on an armed adversary. It's not a fatal flaw."

"Sagoths might not know."

Another shrug. "You got many ex-troopers in the ranks?"

Distant look. "A few. Getting pretty old now."

"I wouldn't count on it, then."

"No." He said, "What about Spahi combat armor? Is it like this?"

"No. It's derived from the Kkhruhhuft armor technology. You can smother an X-cracker between the palms of your gloves." No point in saying just how much that'd make your hands smart. It's not magic.

"What about an antiaircraft missile?"

I shook my head. "You'd knock me down. I'd get back up." I gave the man in the suit a shove, listened to his gyro-platform whisper. This armor was not in good working order. I said, "A small tac-nuke would do the trick."

Marsh smiled briefly. And he said, "I wonder why the Saanaae never wear armor?"

I didn't even look at them, instead tipping my head back, looking up into the dull blue sky, where high haze was gathering. "Because they're just police, Marsh. That's all."

He said, "Come on, Athy. Show us how to kill an armored man."

Sunlight fading, the woods full of shadow. I stood in the semidarkness between two tall, scaly old pine trees, listening to my urine stream sizzle on the bark, crackle softly as it flowed down through the crevices and started soaking into the carpet of pine needles, like milk soaking into dry cereal. Sensation of fullness, almost painlike, receding, a little bit like the relief you feel after a long-delayed orgasm.

Silly. I'm always having thoughts like that. As if I'd never grown up, still, somehow, focused on my dick's reality, neglecting my own. I'd have to ask Solange about that when I got home: Hey, Solie, you never feel like your cunt's an independent entity? More like a symbiote, she'd probably say. Gives as good as it gets.

I finished peeing and stood there, head tipped back, looking up at the striations of the orangish sky, dick still hanging out, feeling soft skin under my thumb.

Marsh's goddamned smile. No one smiles like that without a reason. So Marsh wants to go killing all his little sagoth buddies. Why? Davy I can understand. Bastards killed his dad like that . . .

No. My father killed Mike Itakë. Make it real. Hold it close. You've got feelings somewhere. You know you do . . . I tucked the damned thing back in my pants, zipped my fly, rubbed my hands on the front of the old flannel shirt I was wearing, something my parents had kept in a closet for the last twenty years. I wonder if they knew it was my favorite shirt? Too small for me now. Really much too hot for this summer weather, but when I saw it hanging there, I had to bring it along. It'd be cool enough later on, it'd be comfortable. Up here in the mountains, the beginning of fall was about three weeks away.

They think you're in because you're showing them how to use their guns, shoot holes in sagoth armor. How should I feel now, knowing . . .

Image of Davy and Marsh and their proud little band coming up against a Spahi octal. It'd be over in about twelve seconds. One trooper could finish them off, in just a little more time.

Image of Davy kneeling before me in the woods, his hair on fire.

Hurts, doesn't it, pal?

We never thought about that, back when we were playing Liberators. Didn't even do the cowboys-and-Indians pretense. Aaahhh! You *got* me . . . Fall down dead. Lie there with your eyes shut for a moment, body contorted, baring teeth in a rictus-grin. Pop. There. Now I'm somebody else.

Probably how the human race came to believe in things like reincarnation. Ogg the Cavedork playing hunters and bears with his friends. Rowwrr! Got you, ya silly bastard. Did not! Did not.

I turned and started walking back to the camp, where the cook fires were burning. We'd have a nice dinner, a nice little talk. And later on, Alix and I would go back to our little tent, or on back to the pond, maybe even just out in the middle of the field, where we could lie together under the stars.

Dorvo Valley, for Christ's sake . . . and a horrible cold voice, speaking within: You know what you have to do.

Watching her sleep by the moonlight flooding in through our open tent flap was getting to be a habit, one which wouldn't go on much longer. The waning moon was slightly past half phase now, inching delicately toward darkness as August became September. When it was full again, it would be Harvest Moon, the one after that Hunter's. Then it would be winter, but I would be long, long gone. Maybe it would snow in Chapel Hill this year, and children would play outside, throw snowballs, build snowmen.

Hell, maybe the little green lizard kids would be out there with them, building snow Saanaae. I couldn't remember if there were snowy places on Aeli Saa.

Alix was curled up, lying on her left side, facing away from me, right leg drawn up tight against her chest, arm draped over the thigh, left leg down slightly, bent up at the hip, down at the knee, toes pointed slightly, flexion bunching up the muscle in her calf. Dreaming, perhaps.

Male mammal, full of instinct. I couldn't even begin to change the way I was feeling about her right now, if you can call this feeling. Looking up her rear end in the moonlight, feeling my passions stir, though I'd had my fill of sex and orgasms not an hour ago.

For a little while, I had a big blond burdar named Mandy, came from someplace in the far Midwest, I think, Iowa, Minnesota, one of those places, though I couldn't tell from the accent. She sounded like every video voice-over you ever heard. Musical enough. Not too musical. Female enough. Not too female.

She tried to be attentive, tried to do what I wanted, face

earnest as she slaved over me. Is this OK? How about this? But she could not make herself stay awake at my whim, when I was keyed up from a too-exciting day. I'd watch her suppressing those yawns, watch her eyes gradually grow glassy.

Then she'd fall asleep, whether I was done or not.

It was funny at first, then annoying. Eventually I took to just rolling her over on her back, pushing her legs apart, and getting down to the primary business of her job. Sometimes she'd wake up, startled and afraid, but mostly she'd stay asleep, rolling loosely under my weight, breath squishing in and out.

It got to be funny again, at least to me, but she was frightened, waking up in the middle of the night, soaking with semen between her legs, sometimes with the mass of me still lying on top of her, snoring merrily away. Eventually, she resigned, took her penalty points, and went home, not as rich as she'd expected.

After she was gone, I realized I'd enjoyed raping her in her sleep. Tried it on the next burdar, too, but she'd wake up at my slightest touch, smiling brightly, ready, willing, and able.

A little while later, I got dressed and went for a walk in the moonlight, slinking away through the camp, past the smoldering embers of the fire, massive Saanaae slumbering out in the open, walked up into the middle of the big, hilly field, Alix's Dorvo Valley. Not much noise now, just the wind in the grass, the trickling sound of the stream. A little murmur from one of the tents, followed a moment later by a brief spate of soft panting, then silence.

I found a high spot, where the grass was short, sat down facing away from the moon, toward the darkest part of the sky. Stars and more stars. Milky Way slanting down to the horizon.

I should never have come here.

But then, you'd never have seen Alix again.

Worth it?

I won't know 'til after it's over. Think about this again as the lighter fires its engines, lifts off, carries you back into the sky. Talk it over with Solange, maybe, sitting in some bar on Karsvaao. If they have any bars yet. Hell, they must have.

If Solange really cares.

Well, who else would then?

No one.

But for a few brief days you loved Alix again. Loved her just the way you did when you were young. Just the way you did in all those faded memories. So what if it wasn't quite so real to her? What difference does it make?

I tried to think about Hani, about making love to her again when I got home. Tried to picture her lying quietly on the bed in front of me, legs spread, smiling up at me, cupping her hands around the, um, *spot*. Pulling it open so I could see just how . . .

I shook my head hard.

Nothing.

Nothing at all.

Might as well be fantasizing about some nice, hot garlicky hummus. Maybe a baked potato soaking in sour cream and butter. Hell, a fine, hot bath, with gentle hands to scrub your back. A dip in the pool on a day when you've been baking in the sun.

Might as well fantasize about falling asleep when you're really, really tired . . .

A very small noise. Something stirring in the grass beside me. Something coming out, a field mouse or a mole. Some little lizard. Maybe even a snake. I looked . . .

Sharp pang in my chest, adrenaline flooding into my blood, bringing me up on one knee, looking down at the damned thing. The poppit was just standing there, blue scales gray in the moonlight, on its eight stubby legs, beady eyes looking up at me, glowing faintly red, downshifting the mid-night skyglow, mouth open, panting softly, a barely audible sound.

A whisper, my own voice, *"Shit . . ."*

I bent down warily, looking close. Nothing. No hardware. No harness. Goddamned thing is just fucking lost. If they wander away, get separated from the group, they're just animals, and not very bright ones at that. Standing there looking at me, panting like some little dog. I could swear it was smiling.

Probably glad to see a familiar shape out here in the middle of nowhere. Maybe some dim notion I'd take it back where it belonged.

I stood, looming over it, seeing the eyes follow me, poppit turning slightly so it could keep me centered in its vision field. I stamped once, hard, and it made a sound like one of those little squeeze toys you get for babies and puppies. Made a little crackle of breaking bones as it died.

I felt, for a moment, slightly short of breath.

Leaned down and picked the thing up, felt its spilled juices tingling on my hand, threw it as hard as I could out over the big patch of red briers, a faint crash as it disappeared in the underbrush.

Wiped my wet hand off on the dry grass.

But that doesn't solve anything, asshole. You still know what you've got to do. Maybe I'm just putting it off as long as I can. So I can lie on top of Alix and . . . pretend, for just a little while longer. One more glance, up at a sky full of glitter, then I turned and walked slowly back down to our tent.

The next day we worked and trained through the morning, reenacted their silly little ambush vignette, and I tried to tell them what to do, how to see, how to *think* about a situation like this. Stood them by the clumsily repaired Kkhruhhuft models so they'd get a sense of scale, tried to see if any of them remembered real Kkhruhhuft from way back when. Not many. Not much use.

One vivid image of them all slinking through the forest, sneaking up on some little band of unwary sagoths.

A second vivid image of them all lying dead. Dead and cooked. Little black ants all over them, eating the juicy parts first, then the rest . . . How does the kiddie song go? Something about worms, beginning, "Did you ever see a hearse go by . . ."

Trust children to get right to the heart of the matter.

Later, I walked through the forest with Marsh and Davy, Alix holding my hand as always, Mace and Stoneshadow trailing along behind, talking softly in some Saanaae language or another. Not the principal administrative language, though. This one was harder, full of glottal stops and nonhuman fricatives.

We followed a narrow mountain track, winding away from Dorvo Valley for long kilometers, sometime through old, wide open forest, sometimes along a brushy region of small, young trees, past the empty towers of an old power line, towers still painted gray, but rust blossoming here and there. No sign of the old wires. They may have been taken down decades ago, long before the Invasion, the towers left up because no one wanted the metal.

Eventually, we stood near the top of the next mountain, taller than many of the others around it, looking back over the hazy landscape, mountains rolling away from us like some green and frozen old sea. Dorvo Valley was just a little bare-looking spot on the side of a distant hill, far away, bracketed by the moving shadows of low, puffy white clouds.

The cave mouth would be invisible from the air, almost invisible from the ground, around the bend, down the next long defile, where some craggy brown rocks hung above the trail, higher trees leaning out into space. Below us, in a small, deep cut full of underbrush, we could see the brown-and-red carcass of a fallen giant, branches bare, broken away to stubs. They fall away one by one as the hillside slowly erodes, year after year, rotting down to mulch and gone.

There were things like greenbriers hanging over the mouth of the cave, nothing else like them growing anywhere nearby. They'd been transplanted from somewhere else, like a flag marking the entrance to the underground.

Davy was saying, "We found this completely by accident, Athy. Marsh and I were up here on a *real* hunting trip, about three years ago, got up in the hills on a day when we should've stayed down below. It just started to rain . . ."

Marsh said, "Hell of a thunderstorm, really. Worst I've seen in years. I thought we were going to be fried."

I could imagine the flaring light around them, sharp, hollow thunder banging hard, flat, echoing around the mountains like explosive gunfire.

"Scared the hell out of us both."

He pushed the briers aside with a gloved hand, holding them up so I could bend low and step inside, feeling over my head as the ceiling receded. When I could stand erect again, I turned to watch as Marsh came in, then the two Saanaae scrunched down on their knees and hocks, bending their upper torsos as far forward as they could, struggling to crawl.

It was gloomy in here, not much light coming from the entrance, the cavern of unknown depth, shrouded in darkness. I could make out a few humped-up shadows, nothing else.

"OK . . ." Marsh pulled out a long flashlight, Sirkar issue with Native Police decals, snapped it on, screwed the beam a little tighter, swinging it around to pick out various parts of the room.

He muttered, "Never know when we'll find some old bear in here . . ."

"Why don't you block the entrance?"

Davy said, "We thought about that. Whoever left all this stuff didn't. No big rocks around."

"Too much trouble. Someday we might come build a door."

Stoneshadow said, "Or move it all to another location."

The cave wasn't as big as the darkness made me imagine, not a limestone cavern at all, just a low, wide pocket in more or less solid granite, once filled with clay, probably excavated by water. Dry now, though, whatever'd let the water in now sealed.

Boxes stacked here and there, some of them still bearing an NACDC decal. A stack of things like coffins. Some square gray metal crates with handles, each the size of a kitchen recycler.

Looking at it all, I could feel myself getting colder and colder inside, feelings receding as far away as they could. I could sense Alix suddenly turning to look up at me, eyes curious. Sensing something? I don't know if that's possible.

I walked over to the first pile of boxes, started looking at them, squinting in the dim light so I could read the labels. Combat field rearmament kits. Here, lightweight Ranger rifles, complete with an assortment of warheads. X-crackers. HKAP, dense, high-kinetic armor-piercing rounds. Aerosol concussion projectiles. Even some nerve gas I remembered would be useless against Kkhruhhuft but acted like capsicum spray on Saanaae.

The coffins held twelve complete suits of Ranger combat armor. About half of them were still factory sealed, meaning they'd never been used. The rest were marked for transshipment to a repair depot somewhere, various fuckups and defects listed on the shipping tags.

An open carton of fusion cells next to a charger unit and a shielded canister of tritium. I checked the code date on the snap-ring connector. Twelve December, 2158. The fuel would be badly decayed now, but still usable. I looked up at Marsh, who shrugged.

Stoneshadow said, "We've got a supply of deuterium, but we don't know how to reset the fusion cells to burn it."

They'd be better off with the half-tritium mix they had now, but it'd keep right on decaying, so . . . "I can probably show you what to do. The suits'll be badly underpowered, though."

Marsh: "Can we rig the cells in series?"

I looked up into the shadows of his face. "In parallel. But it's a waste of time." I gestured at the coffins. "You don't have a lot of the ancillary hardware anyway."

It was like someone else was telling them all these things. With this cave full of hardware I could put together a mean little combat team, but that was the operative word, wasn't it? *Little.* They'd be lucky to last a full minute against a properly armed soldier.

I stood again, moving toward the back of the room. An old mortar of some kind, dating back to the 2140s. Maybe this stuff had belonged to a reserve unit. That might explain the stripped-down, banged-up armor. A half dozen warheadless shells. Two shoulder-fired missile launchers, still capped, without their targeting mechanisms. A kit for cleaning the launchers, the missing gunsights still in their original con-

tainers. Six thin blue surface-to-air missiles, range eighty
kilometers, leaning neatly against the wall.

The warheads were some kind of shaped charge I had
never heard of before. Some Saanaae combat-support pilot
was going to find himself in deep shit before this was over. I
stood again, looking around the room, looking at my companions. All of them silent. All of them looking at me. I
wonder what they imagined I was going to say?

I walked back to the far corner, where a dozen gray metal
cartons were stacked, followed by Marsh and his light. Odd-
looking things, marked with an unfamiliar NACDC stamp,
right over an older seal, lettering faded. I brushed away dust.
Coded 28 August, 2104.

A sudden squint. That was about three weeks after we ran
off the Master who found us . . . I popped the seal, lifted the
latch, listening as the hydraulic lid whispered open. "Shine
your light in here, Marsh."

He did so. Code date on the weapon was from some
United States agency or another, just a gobbledygook of let-
ters under a USASF circle-in-star-in-circle military decal, an
old white label, plastic wrinkling as time slowly peeled it off
the casing. TAC-FN/220.KT, a self-displaying disk of instructions in a little sleeve beside the control panel.

Davy said, "You'd better close the lid now, Athy. They're
fully charged with U235 inside the lithium jackets. There's a
fair amount of induced radiation now."

Marsh said, "We think they'll still go bang."

Land mines will do that. And this one would make a great
big hole in the ground when it did.

Another long afternoon of playing with the little guerrilla
children, showing them how to fight and die, watching them
fall, bang, you're dead, grin their little death smiles, watching them laugh and play together and talk about that magic
little future of theirs.

All over the galaxy, they would say, there must be people
like us, waiting, just waiting for the Master Race to stumble
and fall. The universe a tinderbox, and we the spark that
touches it off.

I showed Davy how to reset the fusion cells to burn deuterium, told him he'd be better off with the tritium mix for another five years or so, then he should make the switch. Watched his eyes sparkle. Watched Alix's eyes sparkle. Felt for myself a familiar unholy dread that didn't matter one bit.

Another evening, another splendid sunset, each sunset just a little redder than the one before it, sky painted by fading memories of all those vermilion September sunsets, ducks and geese stringing long vees across the sky, arrowing southward, following the sun.

I wish I could be here to see them again.

But it won't last forever, you know that. No matter what you do. No matter what hard choice you make.

Another fine dinner, all my old friends, childhood friends, laughing and talking and eating their lovely cookout food. I could see how much they liked the two Saanaae, gathering round them, laughing and talking. Some of them knew a few Saanaae words. Stoneshadow seemed to like that.

Marsh was more relaxed now, sitting by my side, drinking homemade beer from a heavy old glass mug, emblazoned with the sigil of Chapel Hill High School, class of 2139.

That was the year his father graduated, and mine. Mike Itakë hadn't come along until 2143.

Bright young men, all of them, with a bright, unlimited future unfolding across their days. Would the aliens come again? Or had that lone damaged explorer ship failed between the stars, exploded and died? Maybe, just maybe, we were lost to them. Maybe the aliens wouldn't find us again, if we were lucky, until we were ready for them.

When?

No one knew the hardware we'd captured was Kkhruhhuft military technology, firecrackers and wooden swords to the big guns of the Master Race.

No one here on Earth had ever seen Shenádz.

Another evening with Alix, out on the hillside, lying together beneath the stars. Smothering all her talk with kisses, drowning her happiness with my desire.

I had her half-undressed, ignoring her protests that people might be watching us, dismissing all those shadows down by the campfire, when she suddenly went still, hand on my shoulder, looking up at me with a serious face I was learning to ignore.

She said, "Is something wrong?"

Nothing to do but look back, fighting a sharp pang of something horribly like conscience. These people are your friends. This is the woman you love.

She said, "Whatever it is, you can tell me, Athy."

Almost, but not quite. I put the feelings away. Put them in their little cubbyhole. Slid the cover shut. Locked it tight. Threw the key away, tumbling, twinkling like a lone, silver star, into the black sea of some imaginary night.

She said, "I know you'll probably have to go away again, Athy." That sad look. Sad, but brave. Then looking back up into my eyes, light shining off unshed tears, lips forming into the barest of smiles. "You'll come back again from time to time. I know that."

I nodded slowly, putting my hand on her abdomen, where I had the front of her trousers open, on the soft cotton cloth of her underwear. "I'm sorry, Alix. If I stay, they'll . . ." What? What should I tell her? "If I stay, they'll be watching me. And all this . . ." I gestured around, down at the people by the campfire.

She put her arms around me, hugged me tight, held on for just a little while. Then we made love under the starry sky, people down below watching maybe, and Alix didn't seem to care, reveling just then in what we seemed to have, for ourselves alone.

Long after midnight. I sat up on the hill, surrounded by the little nest of crushed brown grass we'd made earlier in the evening, looking down at the dark, silent little camp, tents barely picked out by starlight, waning moonlight, moon low over the western mountains now, by the red light of fast-fading coals.

No movement. No sound, wind blowing softly over my back, threatening to raise gooseflesh, dead, broken grass prickly under my bare feet. Alix would be asleep down there, lying white-fleshed in our tent, asleep now for hours.

Once, when I'd come out to piss, Marsh had been standing around in the darkness, all alone. He'd grinned at me, whacked me once, hard, on the shoulder, had gone off to his own tent to be with Sandy, to curl up and sleep.

Tomorrow, of course, would come, and there was work to be done . . .

Watching his back recede, I came very close to whispering good-bye.

Good-bye, Marsh Donovan.

I opened the phone and called through the net to Shrêhht.

Hello, Ath. I guessed you'd be calling again soon.

No great surprise.

Some other voice, flat, affectless, matter-of-fact: Packet tracer switching in, level Five-high.

So be it.

I told Shrêhht what I'd seen. What I wanted done.

Long silence.

All right, my friend. Somehow soft and gentle, translated through vocoder and phone. We'll see you tomorrow, then. Around local noon.

I sat dry-eyed under the stars until the moon had set, then went down to sleep with Alix.

13

ALL MORNING LONG, I HAD MY LITTLE rebel band out training under an infinitely deep blue sky, a sky stained by some high, tawny haze. Though it was hot, the air was dry, the heat mediated by a strong, cool breeze from the northeast.

I made them learn how to handle the guns that morning, made the little guy charge at us repeatedly in his suit of black armor, while we fired plastic frags at him. After each charge, I'd take them aside and point out all the little white smears of each hit, tell them which ones would've merely made his ears ring, which ones would've taken off his head or shattered an arm. As the morning went on, our aggressor force of one got better and better, tucking his head down so he could take the impacts on his face, clutching his arms to his chest, not letting anyone get behind him.

You see? I'd say. The sagoths will learn too.

We could still pretend it was just that, that no armored monsters would fall on them out of the sky and put their little game to bed. A pretense within a pretense.

And just now, they sprawled together out in the field, sitting around, eating their lunches, arguing the finer points of guerrilla warfare with their attacker, who'd skinned out of his suit, face beet red, shining with sweat. I'd made a mental

note to show him, after lunch, how to adjust the armor's
cooling system, had the decency to cringe internally.

Pretense almost an obsession.

Alix and I walked up across the broad, yellow-brown field
of Dorvo Valley, holding hands, as we did more and more
these days, carrying our lunches to a big, flat, gray rock bal-
anced on a little ridge at the edge of the forest, a rock
warmed by the sun, cooled by the wind, sat up there, looking
down on all our friends, eating our sandwiches of heavy-fla-
vored liverwurst and cheese, rough, dry, homemade wheat
bread crumbly in mouths, swigging from chipped antique
wine bottles, refilled with sweet, watery lemonade.

Facing one another, skins shiny with the day's sweat,
glassy in the strong sunlight, watching one another eat. Alix
kept putting her hand out and touching my knee, and I was
appalled at the arousal that brought. I could imagine myself
tossing my sandwich aside into the grass, laying my hands
on her thighs, applying all the strength of my fingers, could
hear the seams of her blue jeans parting, a deep-pitched snarl
of popping threads, the sudden exposure of her crotch a
shocking change of aspect. I could imagine myself holding
her down then, one hand on her throat, the other clutching
one knee, forcing her open, forcing myself inside . . .

Alix laughed nervously, and said, "God, you've got the
oddest look in your eye, Athy! Where the hell have you
gone?"

A quick shake of my head and Alix was a smiling middle-
aged woman sitting in front of me once again, chewing,
swallowing, drinking from her bottle. "I . . ."

I heard the sound of our little world coming to an end.

Far away, echoing over the landscape, like the ghost of
some long-forgotten war. Only me, right now. Sensitized,
and ready.

Alix suddenly sat forward. "Athy? What is it?"

Just a faraway growl, slowly coming closer.

Down in the field below, I saw Stoneshadow look up from
her meal, grow still, head cocked to one side, listening. For
just a moment, she wouldn't believe what she was hearing.
Then . . . I saw her turn to Mace, saw him jerk, saw the two

of them scramble to their feet, reaching to grab up their
weapons, turning away toward the forest, turning to run.

Goddamn you, you pieces of shit! Stay with my people!

Panic in Alix's voice, still understated, tentative. "What's
wrong, Athy?"

Rumble-whine of electric turbines suddenly climbing over
the general threshold of people's hearing, sudden onset of a
deep, pulsing thud, the shock wave from a rotary-wing aircraft. Another. Another. Climbing all over each other,
smothering definition.

Alix looked at me then, eyes bright with fear, whispered,
"Oh, God . . ."

Not here for you, today, beloved Alexandra Moreno.

Down below, people were on their feet now, looking up at
an empty sky, scanning the horizons, Davy shading his eyes,
the little guy whose name I never learned suddenly on his
knees, messing with his suit of armor, opening up the back-
plate. I felt myself give a little approving nod. Point of merit.
Marsh was standing still, hands on his hips, watching his
Saanaae friends run away.

All right, Marsh. Now you know.

He turned suddenly and looked up at me. Eyes twin bright
dots, too far away to make out in detail. I raised one hand,
pointed to the guns piled near him on the ground.

Another moment of stillness, while the sound of the choppers grew louder and louder, then he raised his hand to me in
a classic mid-digital salute. Flash of white teeth. *Nos morit-
uri te salutamus.* OK, Marsh. Now you know it all.

He shouted something, turned and broke for the gray am-
munition box standing in the shadows not far from his tent.
A single canister of X-cracker charges, brought down from
the mountain. I wondered if he'd get it open in time. Wondered if his first target would be me.

I grabbed Alix by the arm and pulled her back, pulled her
over the rear edge of our picnic rock, so we could crouch in
the shadows and watch.

Six big single-engine Saanaae-made assault fliers came
snapping over the rim of the forest, from six directions,
barely clearing the trees, already diving on the ground, guns

twinkling, dust spurting all around the lunchtime crowd. Solid shot, trying to make them give up without a fight. Arrests. Suspects to question. A rebellion to be unmasked and taken apart.

They had their combat doors open already, troopers massed inside, armored sagoths and white-uniformed Saanaae. Ready, willing, and able.

I could see Marsh crouching by the open box, pulling out a single clip, snapping it into his Ranger's rifle, turning, firing from the hip, not even bothering to take aim. One of the helicopters flared, blinding blue-violet, and came apart, fire going every which way, went bowling back into the forest, trees crackling as they shattered, smoke-tailed fragments spraying out across the sky, ringing off our little rock, starting fires in the grass.

Beside me, Alix was cowering down, hands over her ears, eyes squeezed shut, mouth open. There would, somewhere, be the sound of her screaming, but I couldn't hear it.

The other five machines slammed to the ground, bounced on their landing gear, turbines suddenly freewheeling, throttles chopped, half-trained policemen spilling onto the field, fanning out from their ships.

Marsh fired again, from a kneeling position, exploding one armored sagoth, his black helmet, head still inside, spinning up and up, end over end, mist of body fluids and hydraulics spraying. Sagoths throwing themselves to the ground, shooting back, splendid targets of white and green bounding high, squalling as my little guerrilla band hit them with a volley of plastic frags. One of the choppers opened up with a pressure-fed *kugelspritz*, bullets sizzling through the grass, bringing my people down in an ugly, struggling mass.

I could hear individual voices now. People squealing as they felt half-molten plastic go through them, like hot electric wire.

Every scream like the screaming of a child in hell.

Marsh fired a third time, X-cracker detonating back in the trees, a brilliant white ball, a puff of smoke, bits of wood howling over our heads. Then he was down, armored men upon him, someone clubbing him over the head with the butt

of a rifle, once, twice, thrice. I could see his blood, a bright
smear staining that fine Lincoln green.

I could feel Alix against my side, face buried in the sturdy
cloth of my shirt, shaking, breathing hard, tiny choking
sounds smothered. I put my hand on her back, rubbing gently, Shh. Shh. It'll be all right.

It seemed like an hour had gone by, two, three, but the sun
was still standing high overhead. Only minutes. Casualties
laid out in three neat rows, Saanaae, sagoths, guerrillas. Survivors, my people, hale and wounded alike, standing in a
long row, coffled at the neck, heads down, stripped naked,
waiting.

Halfway between us and this little playlet, a pair of
sagoths were walking around with a CO_2 cartridge, blowing
out the grass fires, more of them back in the woods, putting
out the wrecked helicopter, checking for unlikely survivors.
One or two of them might have been blown out the open
door.

Some of the women below were pretty, breasts high,
waists narrow, some of the men handsome and muscular, but
most of them were flabby, flesh like bread dough, pampered
servants with too much time on their hands. Davy kept twisting in his neck ring, looking up toward our rock.

Alix, crouching by my side, whispered, "What's going to
happen?" Voice so very low, so very shaken. Gravelly with
something like fatigue. I patted her softly, said nothing. Just
watch.

They brought Marsh out of the forest, arms twisted behind
his back, one of them obviously broken, and I could hear his
sobs, his gasps of pain every time they twisted him a little
harder, made the bone ends grind, tissues tear softly. He still
had his shirt on, completely soaked with blood now, and one
shoe, but they'd taken away his pants.

Brought him to stand in front of a little group of men and
Saanaae, held him to face them, while they said things to
him, sharp, peremptory. One of the sagoths poked at his
crotch with a dismounted bayonet, making him double over
and squeak.

I heard the man laugh, and say, "What? Don't like that, Marshy-boy?" Poked him again, blood spilling down his leg.

They pulled him upright, held him steady, then let him go. Silence, wind blowing through the trees behind us. Marsh staggering, looking around, at Davy, at his friends, a quick glance up at my rock.

And our head sagoth unholstered his sidearm, snapped the slide, put it to Marsh's head. Said something. Brief tableau. Quick, nervous headshake from Marsh. No, sir . . .

Bang.

Just a little popping sound that echoed off the trees.

Marsh Donovan sat down suddenly, fell over on his back, looking up at the sky, arms and legs shaking, mouth open, dark blood running like water out onto the ground.

I felt Alix's hand clutch hard at my elbow, heard her make just the slightest little cough, echoing the gunshot.

When they brought the two Saanaae out of the forest, it was anticlimactic. Other Saanaae dragging them forward, their faces and sides stained with yellow blood, struggling, still struggling. Mace was bleeding from a big wound on his lower back, one hind leg dragging a bit.

Other Saanaae, officers, gathering 'round. Words, hard, bubbling Saanaae words, raised voices, Stoneshadow's angry protests, things I could make out, just a bit.

"Bitch!" she screamed. "If you were a *real* Saanaa, you'd've been out here with me . . ."

I tugged on Alix's arm, backing away from the rock, whispering, "We'd better leave here now . . ." She followed me, fading back into the forest, unresisting, unprotesting, eyes wide with something like shock.

Behind us, we could hear a cascade of hard, rhythmic thuds, shouting, voices blending away into nonhuman screams, as Mace and Stoneshadow were beaten to death by their kin.

The forest was cool and quiet, tall trees rising all around us, air between them hazed by something like steam, more distant trees almost hidden, shaded in blue and gray, the soft shuffle of our footfalls almost covered by the jittery cries of birds, warning each other of our presence, the steady skirr of uncaring insects, little biological robots driven through their lives by God-programmed logic.

Kilometer after kilometer. Twenty, thirty, forty minutes. We stopped finally, so Alix could lean against a tree and rest, breathing through an open mouth, clothing sweat-stained, lines cut deep across her brow, staring at me with hopeless eyes.

She said, "You're not even breathing hard . . ." Voice flat and emotionless, a matter-of-fact comment. Distracting herself. Distancing herself emotionally as we fled deeper into the woods. Sound practice.

I could feel the sweat trickling down under my arms, cool and steady, could feel heat radiating from my skin, finely tuned metabolic engine ready to go. I remember, in training, the first time I had to run a hundred kilometers. Though I knew it would be hard, I was surprised at how sick it made me feel.

Alix suddenly sat, just as suddenly started to cry, making no move to cover her face, tears streaming down into the sweat, gathering on her chin, splattering down into her lap, nose starting to run. Not looking at me anymore, only staring into the distance, off among the trees.

I could imagine what she was seeing. Davy in chains. Marsh on his back, shaking hard, eyes focused, fading to black, on his last blue sky. Maybe she'd been watching Sandy, coffled and helpless, Sandy watching her lover die.

What do I do now? Kneel beside her, put my arms around her, whisper, Oh, there, there? I could imagine it. And could imagine myself growing erect, responses already so thoroughly conditioned, once I had my hands on her flesh. What would she think then?

Maybe nothing. Maybe she wouldn't care, wouldn't even notice. Melodrama. All the bullshit melodrama of our lives.

The forest suddenly lit up white all around us, brilliant white light streaming through the trees at a low angle, trees throwing stark, linear black shadows onto each other, onto the ground around us. Birds growing silent. Insect robots grinding to a halt.

The light faded, forest suddenly seeming very dim indeed, then the ground bounced, once, hard, underfoot . . .

The explosion was a long, sullen boom, like distant thunder.

"That," I said, voice without inflection, "will be the arms cache, I expect."

Alix sat looking up at me for a minute or so. Then she sniffled, wiped her nose on one sleeve, and slowly got to her feet, followed me down a long, shadowy hill.

Sunset, on the shoulder of some remote mountain, already far from Dorvo Valley, our view more or less westward, out across rolling orange hills, straight into the setting sun. Nothing to do, no food in our pockets, no reason to make a fire, Alix sitting with her back to the warm stone of the cliff face, legs splayed flat, watching the sun slide out of the sky, lighting up the undersides of a few thin, streaky clouds.

I stood a little distance from her, on the edge of the cliff, tasting my regret, looking down onto the tops of the trees, a few hundred meters below.

So. What am I supposed to do now? Jump? Maybe Alix will push me. Image of myself falling silently, end over end, seeing sky then earth then sky then nothing, crashing down through the trees, flesh tearing on branches, smashing finally into the ground below.

Walk through the forest to the railhead, it's not so far away, get on the train, go home. Get on another train. Go to the spaceport. Get on the starship. Go home.

Walk Alix to her hovel door. Kiss her good-bye. Go home.

Forget she ever lived. Go home.

Hope she forgets you ever lived.

Tell yourself. Tell yourself. Over and over again. It was a nice little vacation. While it lasted.

Go home.

I turned to look at her, sitting against the side of the cliff. Not looking back, just staring out at the sun.

Finished?

Maybe so.

Finally, I walked over and stood in front of her, blocking

her view, looking down. For a little while, it was as if I wasn't there, then she looked up, dry-eyed, expressionless.

I took her by the hand and helped her to her feet. Unbuttoned her blouse and slipped it off her shoulders, let it fall to the ground. Knelt and unbuckled her belt, unbuttoned and unzipped her jeans. Felt her hands, steadying herself on my shoulders as I took off her boots, slid her jeans down around her ankles, let her step out of them.

Stood back and looked.

Alix standing in her white cotton underwear, noticeably middle-aged, a little bit flabby, still the finest image of a woman, eyes dark and mysterious as ever, curly hair tousled and in disarray. Not smiling, not frowning. Just standing there barefoot, looking back at me.

I went around behind her, undid her bra hook, took the thing off, tossed it over onto her clothes. Knelt and slid her underpants down around her ankles, let her step out of them, put those aside also.

Came around front again, and looked at her naked.

Icon. Female. Breasts and pubic hair. The neotenous face of a child growing old. Arms thin and childlike, without the strength to resist me even if she could find the will to do so.

God almighty, the thoughts in my head . . .

She watched, silent, wordless, expressionless, as I got undressed in front of her. Eyes not even flickering at the revelation that I was already erect.

I laid her down on the leaf-littered ledge, laid her on her back, pushed her legs apart and knelt between them, leaned down, took myself in my hand, rubbing gently at her crotch, until I found the introitus in its usual place. Slid myself inside. Looked into her eyes while I went thrust, thrust, thrust, holding my weight up, effortlessly, on my hands.

Kept looking into her eyes when my orgasm came.

When it was spent, she lifted up one hand and put it on my chest, rubbing her fingers slowly back and forth in a dense fur of soft, reddish black hair. And, finally, she closed her eyes, reached out and put her arms around me, pulled me down on top of her, held me close, breath whispering into my ear.

The sun went down and the sky grew dark and we huddled together naked, watching the stars come out one at a time, in order of magnitude. Alix curled under my arm, still silent, still holding on to me, and I not knowing what to think.

You used her the way you'd use a burdar. You know that. You know this charade is at an end. And still . . .

The dream refuses to die. That image of laughing Alix, so happy to be with me. I ran my hand down the length of her flank, down onto her buttock, reached my fingers around the curve of her leg and let them trail across her pubic hair, which was slightly damp. What would she think if I pushed her onto her back again? I could feel myself stirring slightly, knew I'd be ready if need be.

Hell. What was she thinking right now?

More silence, me touching her here and there, all the while thinking about my next homecoming, thinking about Solange, thinking about Hani and the other burdars. Thinking that I'd have a decent meal again at last.

Then Alix said, "I remember the day they killed Mike Itakë."

I almost jumped at the sound of her voice, loud against the night, let my fingers grow still, splayed across one buttock, thumb lined up along the crease of her thigh. Let myself wait for her to continue.

She said, "Your father was there that day, standing in the skeleton of the new bluehouse. And Chief Catalano. A party of sagoths. They had a Kkhruhhuft standing by. No Saanaae, though. The first squad wasn't to show up in Chapel Hill for another year or two . . ."

Easy enough to visualize the scene.

"It was winter," she said. "We'd had a snowfall a couple of days earlier, just an inch or so, most of it already melted away. Little bits here and there, wherever there was persistent shadow . . ."

Her voice almost dreamlike.

She said, "You know, your father said he was sorry that day. Told Davy's dad he was sorry it had to happen. Then he stood back and watched. Chief Catalano shot him in the head with a little gun, just the way they shot Marsh today. Shot him and he fell right down, just like Marsh. Shaking and staring at us, just like Marsh. Then he died and they wrapped him up in a bloody sheet, took him out and threw him on a pile of burning construction rubbish. He smelled good when he burned . . ."

All of it said as if she were describing some dinner party that'd gone slightly awry.

I said, "Was Davy there?"

She shook her head. "He stayed with his mother that day. Mike told them to stay away. He knew what was coming."

"Marsh?"

A nod. "He'd been in the Native Police for about six months by then."

Inevitably, there'd be shock, followed by survivor syndrome, then as now. She ran her hand over my stomach, down into my crotch and found me erect, encircled my penis with her hand and squeezed gently.

Almost a whisper: "Want me to suck you?"

I felt my insides clench, a hard pulse of revulsion at myself, soft pity for her. And the worst of it was, I did want her to suck me. I took her hand away, and said, "Maybe later, Alix. Why don't you try to sleep now?"

A long moment of silence, then she started to cry again, delicate, high-pitched whimpering that made me hurt way down deep, where I couldn't push it away.

Woodland mountain night, those same repellent stars shining down, bits of insensate metal embedded in the black velvet backdrop of the sky. How is it we all come to have so many complex feelings about something as meaningless as a stone? The moon was rising behind me, still much more than a quarter away from new, its beams making ghost light across the ledge, casting black shadow down into the forest below.

Alix and I had dressed again against the very slight chill of a late-summer night, against the whisper of wind across our bodies, were sitting again, dreaming away into the darkness. At last, she turned over onto her side, rump settled firmly against my hip, and went to sleep, her breathing a distant, slow sigh.

God save me if I ever sleep again. Surely, now, there will be nightmares . . .

Don't be so silly, Athol Morrison, jemadar-major, Spahi of the invincible Ninth Legion. Soldier of the Master Race. How does the line go? This too shall pass. They weren't really your friends. You hardly knew them at all.

And Alix?

I put my hand on her, felt her stirring gently, ribs moving in and out, beneath my touch. You still wish you'd let her do what she asked, don't you? You can almost feel her lips and tongue massaging your flesh, can't you? Well, yes, when you put it that way . . .

But what about all those feelings?

Hogwash.

Human bonding instinct, that's all. And mythology telling you if they have sex with you, it must *mean* something. Because if it doesn't, then . . .

There's always that little twinge when a burdar finishes out her contract, takes her bonus, goes on home to hearth and family and something a little like freedom. Just a little tiny twinge. I thought . . . I thought . . . Then the next one comes, and strips herself for you, spreads her legs, smiles into your eyes, whispers encouragement in the night.

Just setting yourself up for the next little twinge, that's all . . .

Shadow. Movement.

Sudden sharp spasm of attention, eyes hard on the edge of the cliff. Something like a big spider muscling itself into view. Stopping. Looking at you. A big spider with a mass of machinery strapped to its back, a glitter of lenses, a spiky forest of tiny antennae.

Oh, Jesus. I laughed out loud. "Hi. Been following us long?"

Nothing. Motionless.

Alix stirred against my side, put her hand up to touch me, and murmured, "Who're you talking to?" A terribly sleepy drawl, almost unaware. Another moment of silence, then she twitched, sat up on one elbow, looking toward me, eyes half-open. "Athy?"

I gestured toward the poppit.

She looked. Jerked hard, banging her head against the rock ledge, came up into a crouch, muffling a scream with her hands.

The poppit turned to look at her, but the lenses of its rider stayed fixed on me. From somewhere, a soft, impersonal voice said, "Remain here, 10x9760h. A flier will come tomorrow at dawn and pick you up." A soft chirring sound, muttered commands of some sort, a familiar sort. The poppit walked backward over the edge of the cliff and was gone.

Alix's hands were like mechanical talons digging into my arm, her breathing hard and fast. She said, "How did it find us? And why . . ." Words quick, tumbling over each other.

I considered taking the phone out of my pocket and showing it to her. Decided not to.

And now there was a look of sick horror in her moonlit eyes. She said, "Did your presence here . . . bring down the attack on . . ." Unable to finish. Unable to take her eyes off me.

Well. Does she know the truth or not? Does it matter?

I said, "No, probably not. I'm sure they knew about your group for a long time . . ." Which was, technically, the truth. Marsh's dossier file had been quite complete. All I'd done was fix a date for his execution.

Go on. Keep on telling yourself that. Sooner or later you'll believe it.

Alix put her arms around me again, holding me close, shivering. After a while, she relaxed into my lap, went back to sleep. And I watched the stars until dawn.

14 A FEW DAYS OF TRAVEL, LIKE A DREAM, nothing real anymore, everything ground away to dust, and then we were back in Chapel Hill, and then I sat by myself in the semidarkness of the Master's fake reception chamber, old communications interfaces shut down and silent, Saanaae guards, surly majordomo and poppits banished, dressed in my uniform, gun strapped to my hip where it belonged.

I took the phone out of my blouse pocket, opened it up, laid it down on the ledge beside me. Logged in, level Five-high. Talked to the router system, told it where I wanted to go.

Let me address just one node. Let me talk to the local Master, somewhere in this house of glass and ceramic and stone, under the ground maybe, surrounded by its horde of little blue poppits, vapor condensing out of the air, rolling to the floor around it, dissipating.

That same impersonal voice, no way of knowing what it really was. Maybe there's no one Master. Maybe they're all one. It'd make sense, considering what little we know about them. It.

The starfaring race. The conquerors. Immortal. Uncaring. Invincible. Omnipotent. No one knows where they came from, though speculation abounds. No one even knows when they arose, or if the rumors about the empire's longevity are even true. Seventeen thousand years? A hundred thousand? A million? In the context of a universe more than twenty billion years old, no such span of time has any meaning.

Maybe the Master Race was around when the dinosaurs died. Maybe they saw the supernova that gave rise to Earth's stellar nursery flash across the dark gulf between the stars. So what? They are here now, everywhere now, and what difference does it make?

So what do I want to tell you, my Master? I want to tell you that I betrayed my friends, sent them all to die, because I want my people to live. And I don't even know if that's the truth.

I want to ask why you let it happen. Why are you so careless about these things? Why don't you *care* what happens to us?

No answer. Then the soft voice, whispering to me out of shadow: Make your report, 10x9760h. Make your report. Cold. Subtle. Beyond our ken. Do I want to believe the Master Race is God? No. Of course not. They don't care if a sparrow falls . . .

Or a man.

File the goddamned report, then. Tell them what you saw. What you did. Why you did what you did. And tell the bastards what they ought to do to keep it from happening again. And again. And again.

No answer. Just: Thank you, 10x9760h. You may go now.

Howl of background traffic from the phone, routers signing off, hand to hand to hand, then silence.

I walked alone through the forest north of Chapel Hill and Carrboro, following the course of Bolin Creek, walked among the trees where Alix and I had dallied after our first night back together. Remembered seeing her in Davy's bar. The fight out in the street, Alix standing by, waiting while I killed the scum for her. Remembered the feel of her against my chest.

Paused by the clay pit and watched the slaves stagger under their loads. The Saanaa guard stood impassive, watched the whippings, listened to the grunts and moans of all those dirt-smeared men and women, watched them slip and fall, get up again, stagger on.

There was a naked man lying under the trees nearby, obviously dead for some hours, starting to swell now, starting to stink, blood settled in his back, *livor mortis,* yet his face was so very pale. His eyes appeared to be open, but it was an illusion. Something had already eaten them away, leaving dark pits behind.

Walked on among the trees, went and sat on the little hill behind the high school, looking down over the athletic field. The same football team was there, practicing hard now, for school would open next week and things would get serious. Hard grunts from the big boys on the line as they slammed into each other, or bounced off a round medicine ball of a young center. The quarterback was a tall, handsome, muscular boy, golden curls showing under the rim of his helmet, the right end a slim, long-legged girl with straight, streaming black hair. I could tell from the way they put their heads together when they talked that they had something going.

Ball snapped back to fading quarterback. Fleet-footed girl easily outdistancing her pursuers. Hard grunt of effort from the quarterback, getting the ball away just before the enemy took him down.

Shiny brown ball spiraling up in the sun, floating on high, like a Kkhruhhuft patrol boat, pausing at the top of its arc, starting down, accelerating. The girl didn't even turn, just watched its descending shadow, put her hand up at the right moment and let the ball come in for a landing, tucked it next to her breast, went on through the goal.

Looks like they might have a winning season this year.

Walked through the muddy streets of the Chapel Hill bustee and remembered the People's Republic of the Hereu. It was a little town, a peasant village really, just like this, under a dark, blue-gray sky on a faraway world, first-magnitude stars dimly shining through, even during the day. The sun was a bright spark, remote, tiny, tinted red, and Hereu was a small, dense world circling a K7 star at the outermost edge of its ecosphere. Another few million kilometers and the combined efforts of an active geochemical cycle and an extensive biosphere would have been useless.

Here, the Hereu themselves, laboring to survive, laboring for the Master Race, whose motives none of us can understand.

We were stationed there only briefly, I never knew them well, I never understood what moved them to rebel, to fight us with simple bows and arrows and stone-tipped spears, spindly little blue men, looking themselves like so many upright insects, charging us with their chittering war cries, then dying. Dying well.

I stood with their leaders on that last day. Watched silently as they whispered to each other with their little bug voices. Touched each other, looked into each other's shoebutton eyes. When they were ready, they came and stood in the middle of their council chamber, the same room where they'd made the decision, not so long ago, to rebel. The leader motioned to me, whispered something, and they got in line.

We never had a language in common, always communicated through Master-supplied vocal encoders.

I went to the far end of the line, the end away from the leader, unsnapped my holster, took out my sidearm, and snapped the slide. A couple of them suddenly went weak in the knees, staggering, struggling to stay upright, some briefly reaching out to touch their comrades.

Courage. A better world waits.

That's always the drill, isn't it?

They had things that looked a little like ears, and I knew where the thin spots of their braincases were, where the central nerve plexi lay. I put the muzzle of my gun close to a good spot and fired. Bang. Dark gray blood on the nearby wall. The bug-man fell, and all the others turned, involuntarily, to look.

Walked down the line, bang, bang, bang.

These were neat beings, well constructed. Blood always coming out the front side, seldom splashing back. I remembered what a problem it can be, shooting humans like this. Especially if you use a higher-energy charge. Can't get too close then, for when the tops of their heads fly off, blood and brains will go all over the place, will splash right back in your face.

Only the leader left now. Standing there, impassive, not shaking, not staggering. Hard to know with a nonhuman. Motionlessness may indicate extreme terror. Or even that he'd died from fear, limbs locked in place.

When I tapped him on the shoulder, he jerked, staggered, half turned, head twisting around so he could look at me with those light tan eyes, six little diamond-shaped pupils clustered together at the center, like holes through which the thread holding them on could pass . . .

A soft whisper, in alien speech.

I lifted my gun and shot him between the eyes. He grunted and sat down, lifted one hand to a caved-in face, fell over on his back, whispered another bug word or two, and was still.

Later, we burned the building and everything in it, made all the villagers gather 'round to watch.

Now I sat alone on my father's deck, watching the sun set, the sky darken, the familiar starry night open up overhead, the stars themselves whirl 'round and 'round.

All right, then, you did it for all this.

Because the civilization of the Master Race is *your* civilization, all that you or anybody else will ever have. You've done it before, you'll do it again. No reason to be troubled just because *this* time your own folk were the troublemakers.

Oh, shit. Talk on. Talk on.

Square your shoulders. Hold your chin high, Jemadar-Major.

I am part of this great machine, a civilized order I am sworn to uphold. What I've done is no more than my duty.

And no less.

Go home now, Jemadar-Major. Your work is hardly begun.

I could feel a tightness in my throat, a slight soreness, could feel my teeth clench and my eyes squint, until the stars began to blur. Took a deep breath. Another. All right. This isn't doing anyone any good.

And anyway, what's done is done. Get over it.

But when I went back to my room, when I wanted to go to sleep, I ripped down the old icon of my goddess and tore her to pieces, trampled her lovely curves under the heels of my boots. There were other people in the house, Lank, Oddny, my mother and father. No one seemed interested in my little noises.

After one more day of useless wandering around, of ignoring my family's eyes, of dodging my own recriminations, I wound through the shadows of my final night, up through the woods to Carrboro, past the darkened doors of Carr Mill's basement, past a lightless sign that nonetheless said DAVYS, and found myself at Alix's door, standing alone under the lifeless stars.

Dim light through her living room window, but I could not bring myself to peek inside. I didn't imagine she'd be on the couch masturbating. Or waiting by the relic of some long-dead phone, waiting for me to call.

For one brief moment, I couldn't even imagine that she was still alive.

Time to say good-bye.

I knocked. Silence, then soft footsteps inside. Someone breathing behind the door, looking through the peephole. Cessation of breathing. Would she walk away, go back to her couch, wait for me to leave? I suppose I hoped so.

I heard the latch snap, the dead bolt slide back, heard her hand on the knob, watched the door swing open. And she stood there looking up at me, eyes dark, face shadowed by curls, wrapped up in a stained old white terry cloth robe. Looked at me in my uniform, collar buttoned right up to my throat, gun holstered on my hip. Stepped back from the door and let me come in. Sat with me on the couch, a careful distance away, touching me nowhere, staring at her dimly glowing lamp, fire rolling in all the little mantle holes, filling the room with a delicate tang of kerosene.

I said, "I'm going home tomorrow, Alix. I've come to say good-bye."

She turned and looked at me, eyes glinting softly, trying to look into mine once again, one last time. She said, "I always hoped this would be your home, Athy."

I shook my head. "These aren't my people, Alix. They never were."

"And me?"

What did she want? What was she still imagining, if anything? Should I ask her if she wants to come with me, wants to come be my burdar, share my bed with Hani and all the others? No. She'd have to go to burdar school first, then they'd assign her contract, and someone else would get her.

I could only shrug.

She said, "They're all gone anyway, Athy. I'm the only one left."

"Sorry."

Voice quite forlorn, in lost little girl tones: "I wish I could've gone with them."

"No you don't."

Looking up at me again, back into my eyes. "Some of it was pretty nice, Athy."

Some of it was. But you can't go away and leave it like this. Can't leave her here pining away for dreams that never were. Not fair. Not fair at all. I took out the phone and opened it up in front of her, said, "Do you know what this is, Alix?"

She shook her head, staring at the thing, obviously afraid.

I held the phone to my face, and said, "10x9760h, logging on. Level Five-high."

The router responded, acknowledging my presence, then I logged out, folded up the phone and put it away.

She said, "You had that with you up in the mountains, didn't you?"

I nodded.

"Why?"

Good question. And how did I want to answer? Did I want to tell her about all the places I'd been, all the strange and exotic peoples I'd met and killed, by ones and twos and threes and thousands? Did I want to tell her how, by killing her friends, I'd saved humanity from just such a fate?

I said, "Alix, I'm a soldier of the Master Race. It means something to me."

The expression on her face was something like the grimace that presages tears, her eyes still on mine, shining hard in the lamplight. "It's such a little world to you, isn't it?"

"Maybe so."

She stood then, facing the lamp, dismissing me, I thought. I stood, turning to go . . .

She walked slowly over to the lamp, standing before me in its light, but her eyes were remote now, turned inward. She slowly undid the robe's cloth belt and let it fall open, letting me see she was naked underneath, breasts and belly sagging just a little bit.

Not looking at me. Not putting on a show for my benefit. Not anymore.

Standing by the lamp. Running her hand down over her belly, down into her pubic hair, spreading her vulva wide open, dipping two fingers into her vagina. Pulling them out and holding them up in the lamplight, examining the shining wet, spreading her fingers apart just a fraction of an inch, staring for a moment at a thin, glistening strand, gleaming like a bit of spider's web, that spun out between her fingertips.

Whispered softly, something I couldn't make out. Frozen in space and time now. Her face so very serious.

She wiped her fingers off on the terry cloth, turned to face me again, shrugged the robe off her shoulders and let it fall to the floor. Put her hand on one breast, and said, "Make love to me one last time before you go, Athy."

Like a hammer blow in the middle of my chest.

I wanted to ask her why, found I could not.

"All right," I said. And we lay down together for the rest of the night.

Midmorning, and the sunlight was slanting steeply down on the Durham monorail station, track already humming softly, a high, distant keening that let us know there was a train moving in, not far up the line. Trees and vines down below, all around, moving under a steady, stiff breeze, gaps in the woodland opening and closing, ruins alternately hidden and revealed.

Alix's silent eyes on me in the morning when we awakened. Completely expressionless. Not sorry to see me go. Evidently not glad. Sitting there naked on the bed, watching me get dressed. Sitting almost as if she were already gone.

I had a momentary fantasy that she'd ask me to do it one more time before I went. Looked in her eyes.

No. Nothing.

I let myself out and walked away.

Walked home, remembering how the night had been, remembering Alix's determined, almost mechanical passion. Not talking to me, just breathing, breathing hard, taking me into herself, lying on her back, legs spread as wide as they'd go, wrapped around my back, pulling me deep.

Three times, each more intense than the one before. Then she patted me on the back, smiling to herself, not me, rolled away, mumbling something about sleep, left me to lie awake and wonder.

No one around when I went to my parents' house, which had never been my home. Just Lank, sitting on the porch, waiting with his car. I went upstairs and packed my meager kit, came back downstairs again and we left, bouncing away across ruts of dry mud.

Now, standing at the train station, I watched the trees blow in the wind, wishing for another world, another life, another something. I turned to Lank. "Well . . ."

He looked up at me, unsmiling, hands hanging down, folded below the beltline of his cassock. Just looking at me. Maybe not even judgmental. He said, "I was glad you came home, Athy."

I nodded. "It's been nice, having a little brother again, Lank. I wish the others . . ."

He smiled, a very small, faded sort of smile, shook his head slowly. "They were glad to see you too. Really."

I stared at him for a moment, glanced around the empty train platform, looked away. Really.

He said, "It'll be all right."

"I suppose so. But I would've thought . . ." Hell. What *did*

you think? "I would've thought Dad might understand."
Being a Master Race collaborator and all, you'd think so.

Lank put his hand on my shoulder, squeezed gently, took
it away. "I'm sure he does, but . . . Well: You can go away
now, Athy. The rest of us have to stay here forever. People
aren't going to forget what you did for a long time."

No. I suppose not. "What about you?"

He smiled, wider this time, genuine warmth. "Hell, Athy.
Compassion's my stock-in-trade."

Just doing our jobs, are we? It tasted like bitter bile in my
throat.

The train came on down the track, hissed to a stop at the
station, hung there waiting for me, filling the air with a soft
vibration. I hugged my brother one last time. Then I got on
the train and slid away into the bright morning sunshine.

By sunset, I was back in New York, back out to the cosmodrome, a hard wind blowing in off the sea as Shrêhht and
I walked across the concrete pavement toward the lighter,
small, low, scattered brownish clouds scudding over our
heads, moving from southeast to northwest. A warm wind,
scented by the ocean.

The lighter, its dark, glassy hull reflecting orange sunshine, stood in the middle of a blackened starburst pattern of
scorch marks, rays pointing away in all directions, ramps
down, cargo hatches open, frost clinging to fuel lines that
hissed with the movement of fresh hydrogen slurry.

Ahead of us, a long line of coffled men and women
moved, walking slowly, stepping in unison, chained at the
neck like so many Boromilithi serfs. Not naked though, not
being whipped, each carrying his or her own little bundle of
rags and rubbish, some with small children handcuffed to
their wrists, a few lugging babies.

Colonists, the overseer said. Coffled like that to keep them
from getting lost. He'd laughed merrily. Just wait'll we hit
zero gee! There'll be puke and babyshit everywhere . . .

The overseer had a Boromilithi assistant, a quick, strut-
ting, officious little thing with a clipboard under his arm and

a stylus tucked behind his ear. I wonder if he liked seeing humans in chains? Seemed to like his job, at any rate.

Shrêhht and I stood aside, waiting for the cattle to board. There'd be someplace we could settle in at the last moment, after all the excitement was over. Just now, I could turn and look southward, to where the sea was gleaming on the horizon. White lines out there, gentle surf rolling up a grimy, abandoned beach, throwing up driftwood and age-old trash. Maybe someday the last of it will be cast ashore again and the sea will be clean.

I said, "Where're you going from here?"

Shrêhht settled onto her haunches, perching on the ground like some gaunt, enormous, nesting bird, fiddling with her vocoder. "To take command of the Eighteenth Grand Phalanx on a world called Arwhôttenen, beyond Cygnus Arm."

Where the stars begin to thin out at last.

A brief snippet of memory, standing in my combat armor on the surface of a cold, airless world, circling a star close to the galactic core, a star that orbited outside the plane of the galaxy. It was night and the sky was splendid, the core already risen by the time the sun set, emerging from glare-shadow like jewels against velvet.

Then, later, when the last gauzy strand of spiral arm had set, the last sparkle of loose rim stars, my comrades and I could look out across the vacant deep. Faintly reddish globular clusters shining here and there, like fuzzy stars, dim, far away, so very few. The Magellanics like brilliant ghost clouds. Other galaxies like little smudges, hardly visible at all.

Most of all, the overwhelming dark.

Shrêhht said, "It'll be good to get back out there again. Get back to work."

I nodded slowly. "I should never have come here."

She said, "You had to do what you did, Athol Morrison. Don't be sorry."

Nothing.

She said, "It's too bad your friends had to die. But the choice might have been between them and your whole world. All your people."

Not even that. Marsh was dead the minute he decided to break his oath. Alix would be surprised when Davy came home again, chastised and punished, but alive. It hadn't taken much to arrange that. Not much at all. Just an innocent, silly little dupe. Poor Davy.

But Sandy, Marsh's sagoth lover, was already tortured to death, shrieking, telling everything she knew, as they cut away crucial tendons, as they pulled her uterus right on out through her vagina on the end of a big, toothy clamp.

Probably already cremated, ashes washed down some prison drain.

I was told they'd ferreted out several hundred Saanaae traitors, diehard rebels who couldn't quite put aside the memory of Yllir Waÿÿ. Tonight, in police barracks all across the world, little ceremonies would be held, sad Saanaae stripped of rank and uniform, then shot down by their closest friends.

And Shrêhht said, "It's too bad they had to die, my friend. But if it had been my race, I would've done the same." She stood again, looking with me down toward the sea. The sun was almost gone, setting behind all the ruins to our west, setting beyond the shiny new towers of ceramic and glass we still called New York. She played softly on the vocoder controls, her true voice a barely audible bubbling growl, and the machine whispered, "Still, our oaths of allegiance are compelled, not owed."

I turned and looked up at her, astonished, but her eyes were turned away now, fixed on the distant red hemisphere that was all we could see of the sun.

She said, "It may be that times will never change. Then again, maybe they will. Until that time comes . . . we can do no more than serve."

The lighter's warning siren hooted, summoning us aboard.

15

KARSVAAO'S AIR WAS LIKE THE AIR INSIDE a kiln, dry and fiery, wind abrasive on my skin, sunlight reflecting off the stained white concrete of the landing apron, blinding me as I stood at the head of the lighter's cargo ramp, shading my eyes.

Christ. Zero humidity, the inside of my nose drying away to aching parchment as I stood here. Thin, a little hard to get a deep breath. Air temperature possibly in excess of 340 Kelvins, waves of heat standing up off the landscape, world distorted, as though seen through water.

One long, hard moment in which my skin felt almost cold, then sweat started from every pore. Swell.

I started down the ramp to where a dark stick-figure was waiting, felt a light bounce in my step. A largish, diffuse sort of world, maybe ten percent larger than Earth, a bit less dense overall, surface gravity down around seventy percent. The sun, a slow-rotating F8, was a blue fleck in the sky, almost two AU away, standing now about twenty degrees above the horizon, throwing long shadows onto the ground.

Late afternoon, I hoped. That way it wouldn't get any hotter than this. At least, not today . . .

Solange Corday, her skin tanned the color of bituminous coal, anthracite-shiny with sweat, clapped me on the shoulder, grinning. She held out a pair of opaque-looking sunglasses, matching the ones perched on her own snub nose, and said, "Welcome back."

I dropped my kit, put them on, and looked out at a sub-dued and glareless landscape, my eyes still watering. "Fuck. Nice planet you got here . . ."

The spaceport was atop some kind of plateau, I knew that much from my briefing tags, the horizon close, rimmed by trees of some sort, nothing visible beyond but pale, tawny-neutral sky.

Dust. Like on Mars. Yellow, rather than red.

Solange picked up my kit and said, "Come on. Car's this way. I'll fill you in while we walk . . ."

It was shady in the little strand of forest by the edge of the landing field, things only a little like trees, more like thick stalks of tall, dry grass swaying slowly in the breeze, rustling leaves that looked like muddy lace doilies. Cooler here, though not much, still nothing like moisture in the air, Solange telling me about the world, the base, the whole damn universe, what a nice bloke the regional tahsildar seemed to be, Lord Van Horne MacKaye apparently once vice air marshal of the North European Aerospace Defense Unit. Wonder how many of his people survived the Invasion?

Great Britain, I understand, is still uninhabitable.

We came out of the woods abruptly, back into blinding sunlight that made me squint right through the glasses, onto the sullen-looking crushed rock pavement of a cliff's-edge parking lot. Solange's open-topped desert-khaki staff car, Spahi decal looking like it was ready to peel right off the door, was parked over by a rickety sort of wooden guardrail.

"Jesus."

A better than average view. We seemed to be looking out over the whole world, down across an immense talus pile, eons of sandstone shards fallen from the sheer side of the mesa, over a brown world of bare, craggy hills, brown forests growing in the troughs between, buildings peeking out from between the trees, houses, and whatnot made of the same dark sandstone, almost invisible.

There. To one side, a fortresslike compound, the Spahi

base, with crenellated walls, our green-and-black flag fluttering from a tall staff. You could see right down inside, could see a batch of soldiers drilling in the sun.

I nodded that way. "New graduates?"

She laughed, hopping into the driver's seat, wincing and leaning away from blistered brown upholstery. "Came in last month. Not a one over twenty, most of them still scarred-up from Alpha Cee."

"This place must be a shock."

Another laugh, pressing the car's starter. I could feel an unsteady vibration in my buttocks. Equipment not in very good order. Have to see about that.

I could feel the ultraviolet glare off the Master's castle right through the sunglasses, feel it prickling on my skin. It was standing up on another tall crag, beyond the fortress, dark black, as if in silhouette, reflecting brilliant pearls of light from an occasional odd angle.

"They have bees around here?"

"What?"

"Never mind."

Far away, remote, more or less beyond the horizon, protruding over it, I could see a range of angular, reddish mountains.

It took a while to get to the base, Solange chattering away about this and that as we followed a narrow ramp of a road down the side of the mesa, a road too narrow for two cars this size to pass each other most places. There were pull-offs every kilometer or so, but I hated to think about backing up.

Down on the ground it was hotter still, a brooding sort of heat, low spots blanketed by bits of dusty haze, by chafflike stuff that seemed to be falling out of the trees, but there was life evident everywhere. Things like lizards. Things like bugs. All of them cast in shades of brown and tan, like little stone statuettes, like new-cast bronze. Once I caught a brief glimpse of something the size of a mouse that looked like it was made from molten gold.

Solange said, "Don't let its looks fool you. This is a pretty nice world." She looked over at me and grinned, grabbed the wheel a little harder as the car lurched and veered toward the side of the road, bouncing over some big, angular rock or another. "Protein compatibility. We can eat local stuff, and it tastes pretty good . . ."

We passed by a little bit of town, hovels squatting among the trees, and I got my first look at the natives, a gang of laborers digging some kind of dusty trench beside the road, supervised by one of their own kind, a tall, slim Karsvoë wearing a long white robe, his Master's emblem worn in the middle of the breast, like a miniature shield.

Solange grinned again. "You see?"

The laborers were naked, and they were not bad-looking people, tall, thin, lizardy sorts, heads a bit birdlike, pale tan muzzles and big, shiny black eyes, with long, skinny arms and legs, short fat tails. These things look like little dinosaurs, I realized, like *troödons*. Stuff like tufted brown hair on their backs, or maybe very thin feathers. Like troödons crossbred with anorexic chimpanzees.

They turned to look at us as we drove by, and I said, "Yeah. I guess I do." Some of them had flabby appendages hanging between their legs. Others had what looked like puckered little cloacae.

She said, "I think it's funny as hell. Wait'll you *hear* some of the shit I have to tell you . . ."

The junior officers' housing was on a steep, jagged, bare-rock hillside opposite the fortress, a cluster of flat-roofed, adobe and sandstone bungalows, built into recesses in the almost-cliffside, with ornate doors and narrow, dark windows. Native construction. Probably a good idea.

Solange dropped me off on a dusty roadside at the end of a short flagstone walkway, tossed me my kit, and said, "Pick you up in about three hours. We'll do the tour." Rumbled away in a cloud of dust, shouting something back that may not have been in English and probably wasn't a hearty Hi-ho, Silver.

All right. This is supposed to be easy. Go in now and do whatever it is you're going to do.

I turned, walked up the walk, and, somehow, the door was

open in front of me, Fyodor, dressed up in white linen, face wrinkled around his smile, stiff hair the color of ripe wheat, was reaching out to take my bag, put his arm around my shoulders, usher me inside.

It was dark and cool, and I could smell something cooking. Pot roast. My mouth suddenly started to water.

"Welcome home, sir . . ." Fyodor's slight Russian accent, which had been much heavier when he'd come into my service six years ago, was as nice a symbol of welcome as I could've imagined. And . . .

Margie the cook, tall, rangy, redheaded, square of face and shoulder, wearing her familiar flower-print apron, big wooden spoon in her right hand, standing in an open door, white kitchen appliances visible behind her, a thin cloud of steam wafting through the air, smelling of marjoram and bay leaves, black pepper and sweet basil, carrots, potatoes, and nice, fatty beef . . .

And the three graces, standing all in a row.

Mira, short and dark and very Spanish-looking, dark-eyed, tawny-skinned, dressed in yellow shorts and a white halter top, straight black hair combed just so, swept forward off her left shoulder.

Janice, tall, leggy blonde, eyes like blue ice, she of the slim, pale lips and heavy, rose-tipped breasts, dressed now in black and gold, showing a lot of leg, pelvis tilted at just the right angle by the force of high-heeled sandals. The first time I'd seen her naked, I'd been all but hypnotized by her curly yellow sunburst of a pubic thatch.

And Hani, of course, middle-sized, face like a child, almost no breasts, almost no hips, dressed in a pale gray sarong, eyes so narrow and mysterious, one leg exposed by a long slit up the side of her dress. Barefoot.

How does it go? If I forget thee, Oh, Israel . . .

That did it. Spell broken. I laughed, laughed the way I hadn't in many a long day, walked forward and took them all in my arms.

My room was already set up the way they knew I liked it, Fyodor helping me put my things away while Margie and the others set up for dinner, undressing me, gathering the bits of my uniform for cleaning. Chattering away, so obviously glad I was back.

Standing in the bathroom then, looking down into a black hole. Well, I didn't expect water here . . .

Fyodor said, "Some kind of composting toilet, something the natives use. I don't know why it doesn't smell."

Probably a good thing the local bacteria can eat our leavings then. I pissed, listened to it splatter down in the dark, stood still while Fyodor gave me a sponge bath, dried me with a fluffy, sweet-smelling towel, went back into the bedroom and let him dress me while my mind wandered.

And smelled that wonderful meal.

Fyodor chuckled when my gut made one of those little skirling sounds that let you know it's been alerted, slapped me on the shoulder, and we went out to see what Margie'd wrought.

Down in the little valley, in the strip of dry woodland where the troopers and havildars had their huts, there was a public bath, built on top of an underground tank, full of recycling hardware. There were ramps for soaping, washing, and rinsing, heated whirlpool baths, warm pools and cool, the air full of water vapor, a vast room full of laughing, talking men and women, Spahi soldiers all.

I stood and stretched, looking around me, naked and damp, feeling at home now, watching as Solange squatted and soaped herself, rinsed from a hose, flopped over backwards into the nearest whirlpool and bobbed up laughing, squeezing water from her eyes. She is so damned eerily slim, so non-European looking, arms and legs stalky, as if without muscle. Too slim to be so strong, belly flat, gently rippled, abdomen sloping down to a hairless vulva that was no more than a tiny slit, almost not there.

"Get in, stupid!"

I smiled, walked down the stairs into a swirling luxury of warm, scented water, felt myself buoyed up, relaxed. Solange looking at me.

"Not much of a vacation, hm?"

Well. What to say? It had its moments. "I guess it was . . . everything I expected."

Knowing nod. "I am never going home again. My relatives, all my old friends . . ." She shrugged. "Why ruin the memory?"

"It was all right. But I'm glad to be back."

Shadow falling on us.

I looked up and there was a short, squat, muscular white woman, head full of lank, not-quite-curly brown hair, snub nose, heavy jaw, dark blue eyes looking down on us. Solange grinned and said, "Rissaldar Tatanya Vronsky. Jemadar-Major Athol Morrison."

My boss, for the next couple of years. She was broad-hipped, fat stomach bulging above a threadbare carpet of light brown pubic hair, with thick, strong-looking arms and broad, blunt-fingered hands. She sat down on the edge of the tub and dangled her feet in the water, sighing softly. "Goddamned desert bullshit. My fuckin' feet are killin' me."

She looked to be about fifty years old, maybe just old enough to have been a raw recruit during the Invasion.

I said, "Good evening, ma'am." You don't salute when you're naked in the bathtub.

She said, "So this is your main man, eh, Solange?" Looked me square in the eye, fire and steel suddenly visible. "Jemadar Corday seems quite pleased to be under you, Morrison. Hope you can live up to her expectations."

I glanced at Solange, said, "A dog robber's work is never done . . ."

Vronsky laughed, a sharp, coarse bellow. "Ain't it the truth!" She scratched at that heavy crotch of hers, looked around the room full of naked soldiers. "Shit. I guess I'll go home and let ole Sidney work this off for me . . ." She stood, stretched, and toddled away, wet feet making little slapping noises on the wet tile, buttocks shaking like sacks of tofu.

Solange giggled. "You should see her burdarage, Athy. That boy Sidney looks like he's twelve years old!"

I could very well imagine. I said, "I took a look at her tag file on my way here. She damned well earned that job."

Solange put her hand on the edge of the tub, staring out

across the room. "I know. You'll like her briefing sessions, Athy. To the point. Nothing extra. Nothing left out. She's been out drilling with the newbies all this past week, marching them all the fuck over the place." She looked at me, shook her head, smiling wryly. "I think some of the religious folk may be setting up an altar to her in the dorm . . ."

I could imagine that, too.

At night, Karsvaao's hazy sky was as full of stars as any I've seen, as starry as Boromilith's sky, as starry as Earth's. Not the same stars, it was four thousand parsecs and more from either world, and quite a bit closer to the galactic core, but familiar-looking, stars in swirls and clots and patterns of dots. Suggestive shapes here and there against the darkness, things for which the natives probably had names, a spiky patch of nebulosity looking like a pale, frozen explosion just now at zenith.

And, down by the horizon, two little ghost clouds, my old Magellanic friends. They say the Master Race is out there, prowling among the young, half-formed worlds of those wild little galaxies, but it's seven years' journey on the sort of ships they let us ride and no one I know has ever been there.

I tried to look for Andromeda, couldn't figure out if it was anywhere to be seen. It would be a forty-year voyage, and no one's ever suggested the Master Race has done it. On the other hand, time is meaningless to them. Or should be. Maybe they just haven't gotten around to it yet. Maybe they just haven't bothered to tell us.

Hard to imagine they aren't just about everywhere. Hard to imagine there's a whole vast universe out there, full of unknown species for whom the Master Race's ambit is just one more flyspeck in the sky. A galaxy. A cluster of galaxies. Far away. Out of reach. Centuries by ship to the Virgo Cluster, millennia to the galaxies of Coma Berenices. Let's go visit the site of a fine, bright quasar one day. It's only a twenty-thousand-year day trip away.

Solange and I walked from the bathhouse along a flat, dusty path, down to the native city, which she said was called Arat Arrao. It lay in a broad hollow between two bare hills, hills that reminded me of some of the big rocks we saw in Australia, remarkable at first, then forgotten, erased by the rigors of training. Low, rambling buildings of sandstone, adobe, and stucco, always surrounded by strands of those talk, stalky dry trees, crisscrossed by dusty footpaths, intersected by rutted roads meant for the native's wagons and carts, pulled by iridescent bronze-colored things like horses genengineered somehow to look like Japanese beetles.

There were lanterns hanging from the buildings, from many of the trees, each glowing with a fine, steady, blue-yellow light, Solange telling me it was some native gizmo or another, like a kerosene lamp, burning something they milked from one of their domestic animals.

"Edible?"

She made a face. "Natives use it to oil their hides. Smells like old ghee."

"They catch fire much?"

She laughed. "Not much."

"Guess they don't smoke."

We came into an area that was alive with people, places and things, Solange calling it the *Soaaren*, a native word she said meant something like "shit-for-brains," noisy, full of color and light. Most of the people hanging around here, thronging the footpaths, loafing in open doorways, were Karsvoë, oily skins gleaming in the lamplight, bodies banded here and there with colorful sashes and metal-studded belts, but this world had been occupied longer than Earth, had been occupied for centuries, in fact.

Plenty of humans here. A few Spahis, of course, most of them, like us, in standard fatigue uniforms, others identifiable by their size and physique, by a certain controlled springiness of step. There were service-burdars out together for an evening as well, scattered through the crowds, dressed in whatever passed for finery among them, a group of dark brown men walking down one bright lane, dressed in white tunics and yellow turbans, gabbling away in what I supposed might be Marathi or some such.

A pair of armed Saanaae, handguns in holsters strapped across their bellies, straw hats tipped back on their heads, badges at their throats. Keeping an eye on things, probably pissed off at being assigned to the night shift.

Something shaggy the general size and shape of a bison, with rather humanlike arms growing out of its cheeks, holding a small, colorfully beaded purse in one hand, big blue eyes looking around nervously. There was a tag stapled to its left ear, bearing the cartouche and sigil of its Master.

A tall, thin, rather well-dressed Oriental, striding purposefully along the road, looking neither left nor right, little blue poppit clinging to the top of his head.

The Western-style swinging doors of a building made up to look like a cowboy saloon opened and closed, disgorging a couple. I could feel Solange watching me watch them. A pale, intense, dark-haired man, holding hands with a smaller, slimmer Karsvoë, the two of them looking mostly at each other, walking off down the path, going somewhere. The native, dry-skinned, was dressed up in a pale, yellow silk outfit that left one shoulder and arm bare.

"Jesus. Well."

She said, "This is funny as hell. Let's go in. You'll love it."

Inside was a sawdust-floored bar that reminded me a little bit of Davys, with a scattering of blue lamps, paddle fans on the ceiling, driven by rope chains that ran along pulleys and out through holes in the wall. A bar, serviced by two spindly native bartenders, a bandstand at the back of the room, native musicians lolling around, piddling with things that looked like cylindrical guitars, cymbals of brass and steel. A dance floor, crowded with natives, human couples mingled among them. Tables. A stage at one end of the room.

We worked our way over, found a place to sit, got a wandering native waiter to bring us some kind of sour, beery-tasting stuff, and sat waiting. Solange said, "I was amazed, the first time I saw this. Laughed like hell. These little sons of bitches . . ."

After a while, the lights dimmed and people stopped dancing, a hush falling over the room, people crowding up behind the tables, looking toward the stage. The native musicians started twanging their instruments softly, smacking their cymbals together in some kind of irregular tempo. Hell, doing their own version of a bump-and-grind maybe . . . Crash! There was a sizzle and some kind of flickery spot started up from the back of the room, making a smell like bubbling quicklime. Steadied, brightened. Focused on the stage.

There was a naked man standing up there, posed like a statue, muscled like some old-time body builder, Caucasian skin shaved clean, shining with oil, staring out into the space over our heads. The cymbals banged again, and he started to dance. Sort of. Whirling around, prancing in time to the music. I heard Solange start to snicker.

Well. All right.

Crash! A second spotlight sizzling to life, focusing on the back corner of the stage. There was a small, very thin native there, naked as the man, so heavily oiled I expected her to make squishy sounds as she walked around the stage. She, I supposed, for this was one had a puckered little cloaca between her legs, and when she started to dance, her fat tail began whirling around, lifting high. Behind us, I could here people murmuring. Well, not exactly people. Natives murmuring in their own raspy tongue.

I said, "Jesus, Solange. How long has this been going on?"

"I don't know. As long as humans have been here, I guess."

Which can't have been long. Four or five years.

She said, "Watch."

They moved together, dancing around each other, whirling . . . suddenly the man dashed inside the arc of her spinning tail, grappled with her, arms around her, holding her close, smashing their faces together. The native's mouth opened and she stuck out a thin, forked tongue, very much like a snake's tongue, thrust it into his mouth. A very long tongue . . .

It kept on coming and I realized she must be putting it dozens of centimeters down his throat. "Holy shit . . ."

Solange guffawed, and said, "How'd you like to try *that*, Athy?"

Nothing to do but grimace and dig her in the side with my elbow.

The rest of the show went on from there, native nibbling on his penis until it was erect and oily, bending over backward so he could shove it in her cloaca, putting on an act that was all squirming and moaning . . . nothing at all unusual except the species of the participants. And the beer seemed really disgusting, the more I drank of it.

Outside, the night had actually grown cool, the street crowds thinning out, as Solange and I walked back up the hill, away from the lamplight of Arat Arrao.

She said, "I guess some people are just attracted by the exotic. I don't know. There's four or five Spahis stationed here have taken up with native lovers. One woman. The rest men."

"MacKaye have an opinion about this?"

She shrugged. "No one's tried moving one in as a burdar. Besides, we're just one little base. He's got a half million people to look after, scattered across eleven worlds in this sector."

"Vronsky?"

"Always hard to tell with her. Five people out of sixteen-thousand-plus in her division. Maybe it's not enough to matter."

"I saw a lot more than five people dancing with natives tonight."

"Yeah. Well. Service burdars always have a hard time. Rissaldar might not care what they do. There's some contractor personnel on-planet now too, brought in by the Saanaae, I think."

As we walked up onto the hillside and got above the line of the trees, even with a narrow ridge to the west of town, a stiff breeze started blowing, a cold breeze almost. Solange wrapped her arms around herself and said, "Brr. You'd be surprised how fucking cold the nights can get."

No clouds, heat radiating away into space. I remembered the day here was about forty hours, rather long for a habitable planet. I said, "You ever think of trying it?" More polite than asking her if she ever had.

"What? Fuck a *native*?" She laughed.

"Sure."

"No, that's stupid. I've got all the burdarage I'll ever need. Besides, that fucking oil they wear . . ." She looked at me, head cocked to one side. "Think you might be interested?"

I thought about it. "No. Probably not."

She said, "Right. Hey, my house is up this way," gesturing at a troughlike path coming off the main road, headed to a cluster of lights. "I'll see you in the morning. Briefing at 0800."

"Morning?"

A grin, teeth emerging white from the impenetrable shadows of her face. "It's 2300 right now. Native day is split into two periods of thirty *terek*, which change over roughly at local dawn and dusk." She pulled up her sleeve and showed me a military chronometer. "Somebody wrote up a little program for these things. Um . . ." Looked at the watch. "It's just past the sixth dark-time *tero*, just now. Sunrise around twenty-four *terek* away, maybe 1500 hours, our time tomorrow."

"Jesus. That ought to get confusing . . ."

"No shit. But you can get used to anything." She turned and walked away in the dark, whistling some song that seemed vaguely familiar.

When I got home, my crib was quiet, almost dark, but Fyodor, knowing my habits, had left a few soft lights switched on. Now I stood at the foot of my bed, Hani in her sarong, facing away from me, hands at her sides, waiting. I put my hand on her long, straight black hair, ran my fingers downward onto her back, feeling the hair's smooth, slightly coarse texture, feeling the delicate musculature beneath her skin. She arched gently, pressing against my hand.

It had taken four weeks for the starship to get me here from Earth, through two transfer points. I'd spent those nights alone, thinking about . . . Hell. Thinking about just about everything. Thinking about Alix. Replaying Marsh's death scene over and over again in my head.

But every night when I went to sleep, it was just Alix I

saw. More often than not I'd wake up in the darkness, just in time to feel semen splashing onto my belly, or injecting itself into a wad of crumpled-up bedding.

No more.

Hani pulled her hair forward, exposing the back of a slim, delicate neck, and I slipped her sarong off her shoulder, let it fall to the floor around her feet. Here was everything I needed. Everything I ever wanted.

I gave her a slight push, watched as she toppled onto the bed, pushing with her toes as she fell so she'd land well up on the mattress. Lay still. Waiting. Legs spread just so. Face-down, slightly pigeon-toed, head turned to one side.

I climbed on top of her, lay full length on her back. Slid my hand under her body and down to her crotch. Helped myself get past the introitus, slid full length inside. Lay still.

Hani's breathing was slightly labored under my weight, her face turned away from mine. "Hello, Hani . . ." I murmured into her hair.

She whispered, "Welcome home, Athy." The name I'd taught her to call me the night she arrived, the night I bent her over my balcony railing . . . She turned her head to face me, kissed me lightly on the lips. "We all missed you," she said.

It began again.

Then, later, she sat cross-legged at the foot of the bed, looking at me where I lay, and I could tell she was tired, wanting to sleep, eyes a little glassy, mouth looking somehow bruised, the room's dim light shining off wet patches on her skin.

But this is the job you do. And you stay at work 'til you're done.

I said, "Do Janice and Mira resent that you're my favorite?"

Her brows drew together, eyes expressionless. A slight tightening in her face, as if she were about to speak, a movement of self-restraint. Whatever truth there was here would remain self-contained, invisible.

She said, "We are . . . good friends. And here for you to do with as you please."

Well. Talk about restating the obvious . . . "Do you resent that I take you into my bed so much more often?"

I could see a nervousness blossom in her then, very carefully controlled. Maybe she was wondering if she'd done something wrong, something to make me suspect . . .

She said, "If there's something you'd like me to do for you, I'll . . ." already reaching her hand out, putting it on my stomach, trying to guess what I was after. Leaning forward now, looking down at my crotch, trying to gauge if it was all right for her to wipe me off before . . .

I said, "I just want you to talk to me, Hani. That's all."

A long, expressionless stare, eyes slitted very thin, so that I could barely see their gleam. She said, "Some of the other pillow-girls say their masters like to talk. You . . . usually just talk to Fyodor and Margie." She swallowed, looked away briefly. "If you'd like. I'll do my best . . ."

Masters. Goddamn it. But what the hell did you expect, asshole? I smiled and patted the bed beside me, fluffed up a pillow for her, and said, "Come on, Hani. Let's go to sleep now."

She looked relieved.

16

A TIME OF SETTLING IN. A TIME OF TRAIN-
ing and retraining under pale tan skies
limned with streaks of brassy cloud.
Marching in the dust with my soldiers, vet-
erans and newbies alike, showing them
what *I* was made of, because a commander's respect is
earned, not owed.

To my pleasure, Solange managed to get Kathy Lee Mendoza pulled from my old unit and brought in as regimental
havildar-major, putting her in charge of her own platoon in
place of one jemadar-minor, preparing her for the day when
she'd make the jump from noncom to officer herself, and
then we all marched to her oddly splendid choice of music.

I was surprised how many filthy verses there were to old
"Mademoiselle." I thought I knew a lot of them. Kathy Lee
knew hundreds more, including some Provençal lines that,
when translated, made me blush.

Showed the newbies how to shoot straight, not the operational stuff they show you in basic: field shooting, combat
shooting. How to manage your ass in a firefight, because not
every opponent will be some helpless Iron-Age warrior. Got
Solange and Kathy Lee to start demonstrating armored hand-
to-hand, because these suits *do* have limits. Did a little bare-
back hand-to-hand myself, morale-control maneuvers. Got
my ass kicked flat by a hulking Mongolian boy who was so

scared afterward I had to take him into town for a beer and peep show.

After a while they started doing what I said, not merely without question, but with alacrity. Trust the old man. He knows what he's doing. Trusting me to bring them out alive and whole when the time came. Me hoping I could really do it.

And feeling so much pleasure on the day I had Fyodor sew on my sixth hash mark, emblem of twenty-four complete years in service. Men and women, soldiers, shaking my hand, giving me a salute, realizing I knew them all by face and name, knew how they felt about things, what they liked to drink, who their burdars were . . .

Sat with them in smoky bars and drank beer and laughed and sang and almost forgot that once upon a time I went home and pretended to fall back into love.

Stood in the combat service bay of a very large starship, shrugging inside my armor, checking it out, making sure the joints were programmed correctly. When you drop in armor, under combat conditions, it's right, or you die. People did, from time to time.

They call this thing a carrier starship, a smooth, shiny cylinder the size of a large asteroid, concentric shells around a hollow core, ends open to the void. Service bay big enough to hold a Master Race battle cruiser, one of those sleek black things, kilometers long, that can burn down an entire world.

I had my people down near the rim, in one of the airtight holding cells, getting ready, waiting for our dropship to come pick us up. Had the regiment lined up, people checking each other's hardware. Only minutes to go. Me and my thousand. Third Regiment of the First Battalion of Rissaldar Tatanya Vronsky's Second Brigade in the Seventh Division of Legion IX, *Victorious,* Third Army of the Spahi Mercenaries, all under the command of Gosudar Aëtius Nikolaev, who alone among us was safe this day in the glassy towers of New York . . .

Outside, through a clear and tenuous wall, we watched the rugged continents of Hataille rolling below. Rolling and burning. Even from five hundred kilometers up you could see them as smudges of dark smoke. Burning cities. Burning fields. Burning forests. Glowing holes in the ground so hot they created a towering column of wind above them, wind blowing straight up, fountaining debris into the sky.

Down the west side of one continent, along a jagged range of mountains, along a seacoast filled with fjords and what had once been green, fertile valleys, a long line of volcanoes was in full, violent eruption, jetting ash into the sky, lava spilling down across their flanks, flooding the landscape below.

The north polar cap was shattered, exposing the cold, shiny black water underneath through thousands of cracks and open sea-lanes.

We passed over a bare, sooty plain, what had once been rain forest, now no more than a wilderness of emptied-out riverbeds, a place of dry-roasted carcasses, cooked away to cinders, waiting for the wind to come blow them away.

Not even bugs left to eat them. Whatever passed for worms in this landscape toasted in their burrows, earth sterilized downward to bedrock, stone cracked from the heat, soil half-molten in places.

Punishment, I realized. Not just conquest. There, but for the grace of God . . . No, not God. Just a figure of speech. Figure of speech about a figment of the imagination. I could picture Earth looking like this. I'd seen Aeli Saa looking worse.

But there were no Hatailli policemen out among the stars, surviving unscathed. All of them were right down there. Whatever few had survived. Whatever few would choose to live on.

My headset clicked, and Kathy Lee's voice said, "All set, sir."

"Right. Rissaldar?"

"Here." Vronsky's voice, sounding harassed.

"Third Regiment ready to drop."

"Two minutes. Mark."

Right. Time to go.

Then we were riding the dropship downward, sliding into

Hataille's upper atmosphere, aerodynamic surfaces biting into the air, ship shuddering around us, pilot AI not really caring whether we liked the ride or not, ejection tunnel lit only by somber red engineering lights, my thousand men and women lined up in four columns, by company, regimental adjutant to my left, jemadars Wu Chingda and Jimmy Dietz to my right, havildars—major, plain, and—minor lined up behind us with their platoons and cohorts, by maniple and octal.

My own seven troopers, the octal that would accompany me in battle, right behind my back. Who knew what they were thinking now?

I could feel my heart thudding softly in my chest, measured, calm, not quite slow. Been here too many times to be scared. Done this too often to be relaxed, though. It's always important. Pay attention. Stay focused. These people are counting on you . . .

The AI's featureless, affectless voice whispered, "Thirty seconds."

"Acknowledged."

"Fifteen . . ."

I could sense the tension right through my command link. So what if the Masters have bombed them away to hell and gone? So what? It never does any damned good. They're waiting for us. Waiting to die.

"Ten . . ."

"Heads up, boys and girls." I put my weapon against my chest, muzzle up, and locked my arm joints.

"Five . . ."

Kathy Lee said, "Maestro."

Well. What would it be this time?

As I felt the tagalong field grab my atoms and fling me into the sky, music exploded in my ears. "Flight of the Bumblebee," about eight measures in. She must be getting sentimental in her old age.

From sixty kilometers up, a world looks more or less flat, but the sky is still black, threatening to fill with stars, never fulfilling that promise, landscape beneath your feet turning three-dimensional, clouds hanging above mountains above plains above sea.

We had our ballutes open now, acting as stabilizers, falling feetfirst, keeping our rate of descent down around 2 kps, though the air was still so thin as to be almost nonexistent, drifting laterally toward our designated LZ, not far from the principal, still-intact Hatailli administrative center. Silence on the airwaves, nothing but a soft whisper of static from our weapons.

I pumped the heads-up display, rotated through 3-D, making sure everyone was in place. Good enough. Clicked up through the hierarchy, so I could see we were still on the battalion diamond's left point, battalion itself correctly aligned to the brigade array. Good enough. Not my job to see to these things, but it's a poor sort of army where a soldier feels responsible only for his own little part.

Off to our east, something sparkled red through smoky haze, passive emission radar displaying a pattern of rising projectiles. Quick acceleration. *Brennschluss.* Deceleration under gravity, track curving uselessly away.

Solange whispered, "Not very smart . . ."

No, not very. But then, if they'd been smart, they wouldn't've gotten in this fix. "Kathy Lee."

"Sir."

"Suppression fire in range, your discretion."

"Yes, sir."

I checked the slave-set altimeter. Thirty kilometers, and our ROD was down close to 1 kps. "Disengage ballutes. Port arms."

Bang. We fell away from the discarded ballutes, which would quickly sail off in the local jet stream, turning ourselves facedown, accelerating again as we dismounted our weapons from their drop-safe mounts. The antiaircraft defenses started to sparkle again, just as Kathy Lee's people opened up with some high-velocity air-to-surface rounds, charges flaring blue-violet against the ground. The defenders' missiles rose and fell, dropping back into the little holocaust we'd made underneath them.

I said, "Five kilometers. Lock and load."

*   *   *

The Hatailli were waiting, waiting beside a city made of ancient temples, warriors in garish costume, things like feathers sprouting from their bodies, lined up before us, rank on rank on rank, more than a million strong, sunlight pouring through the atmospheric haze, the thickening smog of a world being burned, slanting down yellow-orange on all their pretty pagodas and pyramids and obelisk towers.

Skinny, four-armed green bipeds, ready with their rifles and bayonets, ready with their hand grenades and swords, their shoulder-held missile launchers and pathetic little cannon. We could hear their drums beating as we came over the hills, bounding from crest to crest, could look down on them, marching in phalanx and hollow square, see their little tanks roar forward, jetting harsh diesel smoke, caterpillar tracks adorning the mud, crushing their roads to rubble.

How long can this stuff have lain hidden, Hatailli knowing it was there, biding their time, until they thought they could win? Echoes from the past. Did the Aztec princes lie awake in the darkness, fingering the obsidian edges of their old wooden swords, and dream and dream of the day when they would rise up and throw off their alien masters?

Maybe so. Maybe not.

I said, "Solange."

"Sir."

"Order Nine-Alpha."

"Yes, sir."

No reason for finesse in the here and now, no overarching strategy, no complex tactics. The regiment would separate into its sixty-four component octals, each with its officer or noncom and seven armored troopers. Engage battle, and do its job.

"On my mark."

They saw us now, turning line-abreast, going ragged, shouting to each other, pointing, waving their guns and lances, tanks turning, field artillery firing irregular volleys, spraying fire and metal our way, the quick onset of panic.

"Begin."

I ducked under a spinning shell and jumped away from the

explosion, followed by my soldiers. Set my weapon on full automatic, feederchannel clicked over to aerosol rounds. Opened fire, the eight of us standing in a staggered line. Volley. Advance. Volley. Advance. Volley . . .

I heard Solange tell her octal, "Fire at will. Leapfrog advance. Begin." Heard the harsh crackle of their weapons, saw a sudden hole open up in the Hatailli lines, flashing fire, exploding green bodies, parts pinwheeling in the air.

"Kathy Lee."

"Sir."

"Start in on the tanks and artillery now."

"Yes, sir. I think there's a tac launcher at the city gate."

Shit. Almost missed it. "Yeah. That too."

Listened to her whisper the order code, assembling the four octals of the first maniple, first cohort of her platoon, having them feed in shaped HX. The nearest fifty or sixty tanks of the defender's eight hundred or so went up in rapid array, hot metal sizzling as it flew over our heads.

Flare of hard light from the city gate, the tac launcher vaporizing, taking out a half kilometer of ornate city wall on either side.

Over the snap and sputter of our weaponry, I could hear a low moaning sound from somewhere. Set my filters, looked and listened. Voices of the Hatailli. Four-armed green bipeds starting to throw down their guns, turning their faces away, running, crying out to each other. Tanks turning away, exploding nonetheless. Turret hatches opening, Hatailli tumbling out, rolling to the ground, trying to run.

I said, "Rearguard action. Order Seven-by-Seven. Let's finish it."

People training their weapons on fleeing Hatailli, switching over to self-propelled fléchettes. Shooting them in their backs. If you listened closely, you could hear them scream.

Nightfall. Hardly a star able to shine down on us through the pall of smoke overhead, Hataille's fat orange moon vast and fuzzy up in the sky, featureless, though I'm told the maria make a pattern that looks a little bit like One Lung Ho, the pseudo-Chinese AI media image that was so popular when I was a kid, grinning, gap-toothed, slit-eyed, cracking owner-tailored jokes . . .

Darkness all around, lit up by light from the burning forest behind us, low bluish flames rising from certain quarters of the crushed city. We had the place surrounded. Made them wait. Shot down fleeing refugees until they turned and went back into their fortress. It would be all over in just a while.

Me, walking slowly through the darkness, stepping around piles of Hatailli carcasses, heaps of Hatailli limbs that we'd kicked aside. Not far away, a couple of troopers making their way from one place to another, loping idly, practicing soccer passes with some small, round, dark object. Silent, though, still observing battle rules.

Small cluster of armored people around a black human shape on the ground. Wu Chingda kneeling over her downed trooper, cracking open his armor, making her inspection. I looked over her shoulder, saw the boy's armor had a small puncture, that there was a small, bloody wound in the right side of his chest, at the bottom of his rib cage, whatever it was probably embedded in his liver.

"How'd you do that, son?"

He looked up at me, a small brown man, in pain, ignoring it, acutely embarrassed. "I, uh, tried to field-swap my magazine. Round in the chamber fired."

And put the damn clip-mount in your liver. "They'll do that."

"Sorry, sir." He jumped slightly as Wu ran a diagnostic probe into the wound.

She looked up at me, faceless in her armor. "Not too bad. Stop the internal bleeding, weld the damned hole shut, and we can keep his ass around."

I smiled, unseen and unseeable behind my helmet mask. "OK." I started to turn away, stopped and turned back. "Soldier."

"Sir." I could hear the tension in his voice, teeth clenched as Wu put a field cautery inside his chest and started frying things.

"Regs from now on."

"*Ow.* Uh, sorry. Yes, sir. Regs."

"We'll talk about it when we get home. There's a right way to do it."

"Yes, sir." Relief through the pain.

The four of us kneeling together in the darkness, Solange, Wu Chingda, Jimmy Dietz, and I, facing toward our burning city, soldiers around us getting into their arrays, waiting for the word, waiting while we talked.

Tatanya Vronsky over the command link: "All right, it's on your locus. The order is, move in through the city, kill everything you see with small-arms fire. Take down the fortress and kill its occupants, at opportunity. Make no attempt to round up prisoners, nor pursue escapees beyond firing range."

I bit my lip. "Rules of engagement?"

"Take down the fortress, Jemadar-Major. No cost-containment measures."

"And the hostage?"

Brief silence, then, "No cost-containment measures."

"I see."

I heard her log out, and we all stood, turning toward our stations.

Dietz whispered, "Why don't they just use a thumper on it?"

I shrugged. "Just in case."

Solange said, "They're not going to scorch out, I don't think."

"No. There'll be plenty of survivors. In a thousand years, you'll never know we took these poor shits down to the one-percent mark."

I said, "Five-by-Five. And Three-Beta. Let's go."

It was less than an hour before the little green folk were blown to hell and gone, or chased away, streaming out across the blackened plain as we let them go, running up into the hills, clutching babies to their chests, dark mouths open in horror, pits of shadow as a bloated red sun rose over the smoky horizon. We left marksmen stationed around the

perimeter, knocking down anyone who tried to take a
weapon. After a while, they got the idea.

Kathy Lee, Solange, and I walking slowly through smoking rubble, rubble that tinkled and cracked underfoot like so
much broken crockery, streets full of broken brick and
crushed glass, buildings collapsed down into their own foundations, flanked and followed by our personal octals, soldiers
wary, but knowing the job was done.

Kathy Lee toed a twisted Hatailli corpse, turning it over,
looking down at a blank-eyed, gape-mouthed face. Not too
human. Human enough. She said, "Look's like he wasn't
very happy about all this."

Solange laughed. "Guess not."

City of the Hatailli like fallen cities everywhere, all this
proud labor, like the proud flesh that bore it, come to nought.
Sometimes I still dream of the days when Alix and I wandered, lost children, in the ruins of Chapel Hill. I can still
feel her small hand in mine.

Image of her face, watching me walk away on that last
sunshiny morning . . . Put it away. She's gone now. It never
happened. No. But you don't want to lose all those splendid
childhood memories, just because . . .

We walked on, picking our way up into the ruins of the
Keep, the last stronghold where the Hatailli leadership had
held out to the proverbial bitter end. I hope it was a very bitter day for them, very bitter last moments. Because of them,
a lot of innocent people had to die, people who would have
been happy, would have prospered under the tutelage of the
Master Race. Not benign tutelage, no. But lax.

They say it's better to die as a free man than live as a slave.
Ask these people, here and now. Ask the dead if they're any
happier. Ask the dead children if they wanted to die so their
parents could experience a few moments of glorious freedom.

We picked our way past a collapsed monumental arch,
down a now-open corridor littered with bits of flesh and
bone, and found the hostage.

It had been an armored room, deep inside the castle, its walls
still standing, though the upper floors had been carried away.
Dead Hatailli here as well, dead but otherwise undamaged,

probably just killed by some concussion or another, internal injuries invisible but for traces of blood at nose and ear and eye, clothing stained near where we might find anus or cloaca.

The people here, these proud Hatailli, were richly dressed, in what must surely be the local equivalent of comic-opera uniforms. I could picture them dancing their way through some very silly Gilbert and Sullivan number.

There was a wire cage in one corner, broken open now, containing the corpses of some little blue poppits, all of them dead, eyes closed, mouths hanging open. Flattened. Stepped on by the blast. Beside the cage was a Master's transport capsule, hard black plastic dulled now, and the vents were wide open, but no wisps of vapor spilled out.

There was a long crack down one face, morning sunlight spilling in, lighting up layer upon layer of sandwiched circuitry, perforated throughout with spiracles through which cryogenic coolant had once flowed. It glittered in there like silver and gold, circuitry that once provided a home for some Master's mind. A mind which evaporated along with its liquid helium blood.

Did it die slowly, I wondered, or fast, like switching off a light?

Crouched under one corner of the shell was a lone poppit, still alive, shivering, huddling close. I leaned down and picked it up gently, tucked it under one arm, running my hands along glittery blue scales. Its teeth chattered briefly, uselessly, on my armor, then it settled down, seeming to relax, favoring one obviously broken leg.

"You have to wonder," I said, to no one in particular, "if they're afraid to die. Really afraid."

Solange rapped on the shell with her armored knuckles, listening to a hollow almost-echo. "I wonder if they even know they're alive."

Probably not. And the poor, damned Hatailli just never really understood about the collective power of the Master Race. Individuals? Nonsense. Each transit cartridge contains nothing more than an iteration spawned off a software lineage. Death? No. More like losing a copy of a copy of a copy. Hardly worth saving.

I held my hand over the poppit, shielding it from the sun, petting it softly. Sometimes, if you're nice enough, they'll make something that sounds a little bit like a kitten's purr.

"Think they know we're alive?"

Kathy Lee leaned her weapon against the dead Master's hull, knelt beside me, and looked into the poppit's eight-eyed face, chucked it under the chin, and made a little kissing sound. She said, "I don't think they care."

No. Most likely not. I said, "OK, guys. Let's wrap it up. Call assembly. Head for the pickup point."

We were already back up in the hills when Kathy Lee's suit broke down, telltales abruptly winking out, joints locking up, freezing her motionless as a statue. Spitting curses at us over the command link, the rest of us laughing like hell. Harmless enough now, but if it'd happened at just the wrong moment . . .

It's the way most troopers die in combat. Not enemy action. Not friendly fire. Just mechanical misadventure. Because not even the Master Race is perfect, and I imagine even they, from time to time, are erased in error. Oops. Gone forever.

We got her out of the damned thing, ran the manual override to unlatch the breastplate, unlock the joints, and lay her on her back. And now I sat watching from a nearby hillside as she and Solange worked it over, troopers standing around them, watching the hills, watching the skies, because you never knew, and it pays to be careful.

Solange had her faceplate open so she could wear a pair of microgoggles, bending over the empty shell, working on the ventral face of the backpack electronics, Kathy Lee beside her, dressed only in her coolant long johns, working the diagnostic analyzer.

It was hot outside, a combination of local summer and firestorm wind, dry vegetation all around us bowing down low, and Kathy Lee had the front of her undergarment unzipped, her breasts hanging out as she bent over the machine, rim of dark auburn pubic hair visible below the lightly ridged muscle of her stomach.

I seldom had cause to realize what a really pretty woman

she was, with her curly brown hair, smooth, regular features. Strong-looking features. Determination. Pride. Happy with who and what she is. She'd've made a damned attractive burdar, but they don't make burdars like that. People do have affairs within the ranks. It's never a good idea, but it happens. It happens, and then you go your separate ways, a little wiser, I suppose, or maybe not.

I tried to imagine myself having such an affair with Solange, tried to imagine making love to her, tangling with those long, lean limbs in the night, pressing my face into her dark, hairless little crotch. Imaginable. And we'd certainly have plenty to talk about.

Tried to imagine myself with a woman counterpart, someone who'd reflect back on me something of my own self, my own values. Is that what I want? What I ever wanted? Is that what Alix was all about? No. I don't think so.

Try turning around Freud's most famous bit of silliness. What do men want? Even they don't know. Kathy Lee stood up from her machine, holding her undergarment by the crotch, flapping the material in and out. "Jesus Christ, is it *hot* out here!"

Solange tapped her on the thigh, grinning. "Take it easy, sport, we're almost done."

One of the men turned, tracking a dot across the sky, down near the horizon, lifting his weapon. I zeroed in and cranked up the targeting system's magnification. Something like a bird, covered with curled and fluffy blue plumage, flying hard, with some desperation. We watched until it went out of sight. I was glad no one shot it down.

Pickup point was on the runway of a large Hatailli airport, around which an industrial center and town had grown up, most of it rubble now, factories collapsed, buildings of the town in ruins, gray smoke towering away at an angle from whatever fires were still burning.

We passed in a long column through the town, exoskeletons powered back, so we could simply walk, almost like marching. A loose gaggle now, discipline mostly relaxed, there being nothing more they could do to us. Not that there'd ever been a real danger. We kept our detectors and passive radars running though. Because you never know.

Walking down the streets of what appeared to be a residential neighborhood, not far from the end of the runway. These must have been poor folks living here, what with the noise and all, houses made from the flimsiest material, now reduced to piles of burned wood and curled brown paper, like the houses you see in pictures of old Japan.

Not many bodies. A few. Lying untended in the road. Not much real damage around here, all of it superficial. In a little while, things like bugs would come out and start cleaning up, surviving scavengers would start to gather for their task.

Something like a playground. A trampoline. A pole standing at a slant, bent in the middle, with two crossbars making an X at the top, one canvas seat still hanging by a single chain, the others lying tangled on the ground. There was a smallish Hatailli, naked, huddled in on itself, sitting on the edge of the trampoline, another larger one lying by its feet on the ground. Asleep? Maybe not.

The little one looked up, sat solemnly watching as we marched on by.

I stopped and stood out of the line, looking at the little being, who eventually turned to look right at me. Eyes like pale brown marbles, catching the dim light of this smoky day, reflecting it back at me. I imagined there would be images of my featureless, suited self reflected in each of those eyes.

Who is that lying so still at your feet? Mother? Father? Older brother? Some relationship we never bothered to learn, or even imagine?

And whom do you hold accountable for the burning down of your world, the carnage wrought on your short life? We, who are the instrument of fate? Those among you who were so foolish as to rebel? The Master Race, perhaps, for wanting to rule over the universe and everything in it?

But, feeling her gaze upon me, I realized who would be held personally responsible for this one death, here and now. I turned away, marching off with my soldiers.

17 IT WAS A BRIGHT NIGHT ON KARSVAAO, the chronometer reading 0110, around the twentieth light-time *tero,* early afternoon outside, tawny sunlight streaming down through the closed curtains of my crib, pooling on the polished wood of the bedroom floor.

We could hear natives passing by from time to time, over the soft hiss of the air-conditioning unit, going about their daily business. Hard to imagine what they thought of our habits. Waking and sleeping and waking again during the course of a single day, consciousness rotating through the long *terek* of light and dark.

Cool in here, air slightly dampened by the humidifier, just right. Lying on my side at the foot of the bed, looking up to where Janice reclined, half-sprawled against the headboard, still positioned the way I'd left her, watching me watch her, breathing slowed now, color still high in her pale Nordic cheeks, blond hair tousled like a pre-Invasion 3V porn star.

I could taste her in my mouth still, could lie here and taste her and wonder where life's simple satisfaction had gone. You kept it with you, Alix Moreno. I left it behind me in a falling-down old hovel on Earth, in the ruins of an old mill town named Carrboro.

Watched Janice watching me, and wondered if she could tell what was going on in my head. It's important to you, you know. Make me happy or I'll send you away . . . Is that how it goes?

Looking into her eyes now, like blue ice mirrors. I wanted, just then, to crawl inside her eyes, go looking for her soul. Shields down. Locked. Locking me out. But looking back at me. Level. Calm. Probably full of thought. Private. Thoughts all her own . . .

She drew her legs up then, slowly, just as slowly let her knees fall apart, until her thighs were flat on the bed, legs crooked, soles of her feet about a half meter from each other, toes pointed at me. Face absolutely still. Not a clue.

Put her hands between her legs, fingers sliding through all that yellow pubic hair, palms flattening against her mons, pulling it apart, opening herself to me. Distracting me. Making me look away from her eyes. See, Master Athol? See how wet I am? Ready for you.

I suppose I should be glad they know how to defend themselves from me. Put the burden on Fydor, who polishes my boots and washes my back. On Margie, who cooks my food, who sits with me at the dinner table evenings, drinking coffee with me, talking about times past, places, things we have in common after all these years.

Janice tucked her hands under the backs of her knees, pulled her legs up until they were against her chest. Lay still, still watching me. Waiting. Prepared, I suppose, to wait me out. Didn't take long.

Down in the Soaaren of Arat Arrao, there was a native establishment we more or less made our own, running off the service-burdars first, letting the Saanaae know they weren't quite welcome. Natives still came by, but they were the . . . what do I want to call them? The sort who'd suck your dick for a dime? Something like that.

Fixed it so they could stock beer from the PX, taught the proprietor how to make a passable grade of pseudo-brandy from a fermented native fruit beverage that tasted at least a little like wine. Got them to put on a sort of "dancing girl" show, slim, shiny males and females dancing to recorded human music, hit tunes from the 2140s and '50s, in place of the interspecies sex-show ruckus in all the wilder bars.

A place we could call our own, all the octals of my regiment, officers, noncoms, troopers, familial, together.

Quiet now, a tension in the slightly smoky air. People sitting around their tables, drinking, eating tidbits of this and that. Talking quietly.

How, Kathy Lee wanted to know, could something like the Xú have eluded discovery for all the thousands of years it took them to develop? *How?* You tell me that.

Solange lolling back in her chair, long legs thrown carelessly out in front of her, a North American pose she'd picked up somewhere, body language evolving with the corporate culture of the Spahi mercenaries, taking a long pull from a two-liter bottle of Mechanicsville Scrub, one of the few brands of terrestrial beer still in full production, in an Iowa brewery that'd miraculously escaped destruction.

Hell, she'd say, galaxy's a big place. Takes a starship three full years to cross from one rim of the lens to the other . . .

Something of a misstatement, for the galaxy had no clearly defined edges. Still, her point was well taken. How many stars? A hundred billion? I tried to count back. I've been to maybe six dozen star systems over the past twenty-five years. Jesus.

So the Xú quietly developed a technological civilization out on the distal end of some spiral arm, maybe fifteen thousand parsecs from here, a little less than a year's travel time, say, from Karsvaao or Boromilith or Earth. And Kathy Lee wants to know how it is they developed starships, got out into their own neighborhood, started colonizing the worlds in their neighborhood, and all without being spotted by the Master Race . . .

Wu Chingda put down her glass of sweet red ale, face quiet and serious, eyes, as always, slitted, inscrutable as hell. Reached up and ran one hand through her long, straight, glossy black hair. "Hyperdrive," she said.

The rest of us looking at her. The magic word. No organic species, anywhere in the galaxy, that anyone ever heard of, developed faster than light travel on its own. Humans didn't even have a *theory*, when the Master Race showed up. Nor Kkhruhhuft, nor Saanaae, nor any of the technically sophisticated peoples.

I have heard speculation. Wild and fanciful. Sober and scholarly. Somewhere in the quantum processes of their artificial minds, the Masters picked up a hint, far away and long ago. Something no other sort of intelligence could glimpse. That, at least, made a good excuse for the rest of us.

I said, "Kkhruhhuft think they stumbled on an automated refit station on the edge of their space, just as the Masters were thinking about starting to move in. Got away with some hardware. Spent the next few centuries getting ready."

The story Shrêhht had to tell wasn't all that complicated. Just that a Master Race scoutship, probing what turned out to be the Xú colonial region, had been taken out by an armed fleet, the scoutship detected so deep in space it could only mean one thing. And that a Kkhruhhuft expeditionary force had been caught between the stars, a force of five corvette-cruisers jumped and mauled, one ship limping away through hyperspace, radiating energy, being pinged by some kind of remote detection device.

"They knew," I said, "that we were coming."

Solange raised an eyebrow at me, and said, "You know the old joke, White Man . . ."

I grinned.

Jimmy Dietz said, "How bad you think this is going to be, chief?" He was drinking some Italian whiskey he kept as private stock, was about five shots up on the rest of us, nose nicely reddened.

I shrugged. "They know we're here. I bet they don't know how many of us there are. They've had time to sneak about the galaxy, take a good look around. Probably time to get scared as hell, but not nearly enough time to get ready. Not really ready . . ."

Wu Chingda tilted back her ale, finishing it, licking a bit of foam from her upper lip. "Too bad," she whispered.

No reaction from anyone.

I laughed into the sudden silence. "Hell," I said, looking right at her. "Now we'll find out what a real fight is like."

* * *

I spent my last night before shipping out with Mira, in many ways the least favorite of my burdars. I don't know why this should be so. As burdars go, she's perhaps the most genuine, the most likely of any I've had to have an unfeigned orgasm for me, to enjoy what we do together, to smile and laugh with me. On the other hand, she's not quite attentive either, more likely than the others to fall asleep unexpectedly, to yawn and sigh before I'm quite done with her.

What that says about me is not quite to my liking, but not something I have to confront either.

So, in the middle of a Karsvoë dark-time, she curled on the bed beside me, on her side, facing away, breathing softly into the mattress, while I ran my hand over her smooth flank, nuzzled my face in her mass of curly black hair, wondering if I wanted to wake her up for more, a little irritated that she'd fallen asleep.

And yet.

Not really wanting to take her and shake her. Wake up, little Mira, I need to fuck you a bit more. She'd be bleary-eyed and confused, rolling onto her back, glancing at the bedside chrono, blinking, fumbling around, spreading her legs for me. Maybe she'd fall asleep in midfuck this time. It'd happened before, a time or two.

But I'm not quite a man without a soul. Not yet.

Before I went home, I wasn't conscious of how much she looked like Alix when young. Now, I was. And didn't want to think about it. I pulled her gently over onto her back, careful not to disturb her sleep, arranging her limbs just so, a position from which she could comfortably waken, when and if. Laid my head down on her abdomen, crisp hair tickling my cheek.

So I'd been calling on Mira more and more of late. So what? Hani's time is almost up. These have been very nice years. Years to have a small, slim, silent island girl in your bed. But Mira was all right too, and Janice . . .

I thought briefly about Alix. No. Nothing there to compare with these healthy young women. Nothing, except . . . No. Nothing.

Leave it this way. It'll be there when you come back.

They're all nervous now. The war'll give them time to calm down. Let the uproar fade away. Moment of shock when you'd grabbed Margie and kissed her in the kitchen, pinning her up against the edge of the sink, her eyes wide, astonished, Fyodor watching, silent, eyes grim, as he sat at the little white table.

Afraid to get up and leave? Fyodor might even be sleeping with Margie. Might be. What would it be like for him, if you pulled up her dress, slipped down her panties and fucked her right here on the edge of the counter? Would he cry? Try to slip away unseen?

But you'd laughed then, slapped her on the butt, given Fyodor a wink, bounced out of the room and gone off to do your job. Time to put all this away. The Xú don't care how you feel.

Mira sighed in her sleep, stirred under me, put her hand up on my arm, feather light. And in the morning I went away.

Aboard ship, en route to a place called Hanta Sheqari, some four months flying time away, maybe fifty-three hundred parsecs from Karsvaao, which would be the staging area for the anti-Xú multispecies expeditionary force, the officers of Vronsky's brigade stood together in her briefing room, silently watching the holos she'd brought us from high command.

Vronsky and her rissaldars-minor, the commanders of her battalions. Their jemadars-major. Our jemadars, plain and minor. Kathy Lee and all the other regimental havildars-major, filling the room shoulder to shoulder, belly to back. It gave me a rare sense of the true scale of the Spahi organization—there were 448 of us here, officering a brigade totaling more than sixteen thousand, all told. And the Spahis' contribution to the expeditionary force comprised the entirety of Tahsildar MacKaye's IX Legion *Victorious*, 512 regiments just like this one.

No need for Vronsky to speak, no need for anything now except looking at the holo beside her. The Xú soldier was something like a big crab, something like a big spider, maybe a little bit like a wolverine when you looked at all that lovely, lustrous brown hair. Eight thin legs, structurally something like horses' legs, but splayed out from under the fat body. Face hidden by a Norseman's beard, movement in the hair hinting at mandibles underneath. Two burning blue eyes, eyes the color of crabs' blood. Two arms up front, thin, hairless, witch's arms, clawlike hands cradling a long, thin weapon of some kind.

Vronsky turned away from the slowly moving image, Xú soldier moving uneasily from side to side, turned toward us, and said, "Technical specs on the weapons captured during the second Kkhruhhuft raid are available for download and study." A glance back at the Xú. "I wouldn't bother. I didn't understand a thing."

The summary said they were something like collimated particle beam weapons, miniatures of the big guns you sometimes found on Master Race scoutships, probably a copied design. Copied, maybe improved?

The soldier seemed to be looking right at us now, motionless, seeing something behind us maybe, something we couldn't see. It lifted its gun, scuttled to one side, took aim . . . The image jumped as the loop went back to the beginning and started over.

Kathy Lee raised her hand, and said, "What about the prisoners?"

Vronsky glanced at the holo again, rubbed her hand slowly on her fat chin, pressing in, as if feeling to make sure her jawbone was still there. "Kkhruhhuft managed to take sixteen of them . . ." She looked at us. "The Kkhruhhuft raiding party was small, one ship, six hundred soldiers. They lost more than two hundred right off the bat. Maybe three hundred made it back to the LZ for extraction."

The Xú soldier was jumping around again, dodging whatever was after it, making me wish they'd included background detail in the holo.

Vronsky said, "There was some kind of fight with the prisoners during the trip back. Damage to the ship. Another dozen or so Kkhruhhuft killed. There are two surviving prisoners under lock and key on Hanta Sheqari."

From somewhere in the crowd, a woman's voice said,

"You telling us these sons of bitches handed the damn *Kkhruhhuft* a fifty percent casualty rate?"

Vronsky smiled slightly, an odd light in her eyes, and said, "Well. Fifty percent killed. The survivors were, um, a bit banged-up . . ."

The official report, when I saw it, stated that eleven Kkhruhhuft made it home uninjured, consisting of the on-board watch party and bridge crew for the scoutship.

I raised my hand.

"Morrison?"

"What about their Master?"

She shrugged. "A subset lineage of 6m45. Take a look at the download. The scoutship popped one of its fuel pods over the main Xú base they were raiding at the Master's direction. It made a real pretty bang. And did a good job of suppressing any pursuit."

A fully loaded scoutship fuel pod would hold quite a few kilograms of condensed antimatter, all the energy necessary to protect such a vessel across several thousand parsecs of hyperspace. Self-preservation is a many-splendored thing . . .

We marched off the lander at Hanta Sheqari to find a paradise trampled under soldiers' feet. Broad, pastel coral sun hanging in a pale green sky, wispy gray clouds, like smoke on high, air pleasantly cool, slightly damp, things like yellow palm trees whispering in the breeze . . .

The Sheqarii, armless, hairless blue quadrupeds with fingers on their lips, had fantasy cities like the magic castles in half the old stories humans once liked to tell. Tall white towers, connected by flying bridges, slim ribbons of highway defying gravity without apparent support. Now sullied with the dirt of a hundred kinds of soldiers, because their peaceful little world just happened to be in a convenient place.

They say not a single Sheqar was killed when the Master Race came, maybe ten thousand years ago. The scoutship landed, debarked its Kkhruhhuft. The Sheqarii welcomed them, thought the situation through, discussed it in their councils, and surrendered. Now the Sheqarii could hire out from their beautiful, undamaged world, range the galaxy in the service of their Masters, come home wealthy and retire to peace, security, comfort. Like burdars, I suppose. An entire species of burdars.

So they took the advice the man gave the rape victim: going to happen now, whether you like it or not. Might as well lie back and . . .

Then again, eight billion human beings died when they fell upon Earth. I couldn't tell you who made the better choice. Or got the better bargain.

Kathy Lee, Solange, and I went to see one of the Xú prisoners, the one they'd used up, on display in some kind of cage in the middle of a big, muddy field in the expeditionary force's ramshackle administrative complex. The other one was someplace else, still hidden away, still being . . . questioned, I suppose, is really the best term.

This one huddled like an injured spider in the middle of its cage, crouched low, squatting on a lumpy red puddle of what I supposed was its own excreta, brown hair matted and shaggy, two legs missing, one arm half-gone, livid white scar parting the hair across its back. And a single blue eye glaring out of that hairy face.

It made us stand silent for a while, looking back into the eye. Then Kathy Lee whispered, "What you suppose that son of a bitch'd do to us if we let him out?"

Solange whispered back, "I know what I'd do if it was me."

None of the Xú prisoners had tried to commit suicide. Fourteen had died on the scoutship, killing Kkhruhhuft barehanded. These two had had the bad luck to survive, and this one's injuries had happened when it tried to attack the transit cartridge of its Master Race inquisitor.

I said, "I hear they used some kind of neural probe on this one. Emptied its brain right out into a software stripper."

More silence, then Kathy Lee said, "Wonder what that felt like?"

The huddled and broken Xú soldier looked like it might just enjoy showing us.

* * *

I finally ran into Shrêhht in a special compound up in a low range of sparkling mountains, bare rock peaks towering against the pale green sky, glittering as though the gray stone was a conglomerate inhabited by gem-quality crystals. We were gathered in a little bowl-shaped valley that had been stripped of its lemon-colored vegetation, dirt scorched bare, furrowed and ploughed, soil turned over and over.

They were showing us how to operate the new weapons. Training us, so we could go back and train our troopers, all of us dressed in full combat armor, for safety's sake, if nothing else. The Kkhruhhuft looked like robot dinosaurs from some low-budget twentieth-century Japanese monster movie.

Vronsky standing on a big boulder in front of us, standing patiently while some Sheqarii technicians strapped a pair of little black boxes to her armored wrists, torches sparkling blue-violet as the straps were annealed shut. No power take-off from the suit, they said. No charging system. No reloads. No maintenance. No breakdowns.

And how does it work?

The chief Sheqar techie waved his fingerlips, something I guessed was a shrug. Master Race doesn't say. Just says how to use it.

Vronsky turned suddenly, fat woman become mechanized ballerina, raised her right arm toward the sky . . .

There was a slight flicker . . .

My optical and audio sensors shut themselves off for a fraction of a second, came back to a strange, fading lambent glow, a distant grumbling of thunder.

Someone's voice whispered into my ears over the command circuit, maybe a man, maybe a woman, I couldn't tell: "Fuck *me* . . ."

One of the mountain peaks was sliced away at an angle, a hundred thousand tons of solid rock maybe, gone to who knows where, nothing left behind but a mirror-bright surface, reflecting clouds, reflecting sky.

I glanced up at Shrêhht. Motionless in her armor. Maybe communing with those other Kkhruhhuft, over their private command circuit.

Vronsky's voice said, "OK, that's the sidearm you'll be

carrying. Now, for the, um, portable artillery pieces they've decided to give us . . ."

I cycled over to the interspecies hailing frequency we'd decided on, and said, "So. Why didn't your folks have this stuff for the raid?"

Silence, a bit of static, then Shrêhht's vocoder voice said, "They've never armed us before. Not before this."

No. Before this, all we ever had was slave weapons, things devised by the technologies of the conquered races, traded back and forth, to be sure, even manufactured, close to perfection, using Master Race industrial facilities, but . . .

"Maybe they're worried," I said.

"Maybe so," said Shrêhht. "Or maybe they trust us."

A world without a name, a sun without a number, fat black ice-moon circling a gas giant out on the edge of space . . .

We crouched in shadow now, letting the twelve-Kelvin ambient temperature hide us as best it could, waiting for the battle to resume. Overhead, the ringed planet hung, a flattened blue crescent, lightning aflicker in its nighttime sky, aurorae like a tilted, filmy corona over the magnetic pole. Rings like a silver platter slicing the planet in two, casting a shadow back down on blue clouds, dusty, then solid-looking, then dusty again, brighter stars shining right through.

Out on the icy plain, old black craters mingled with new white ones, circles of water here and there boiling away in the vacuum as their edges closed in, wisps of steam forming ephemeral clouds, here, gone, renewed, gone . . .

A few kilometers away there was an armored Kkhruhhuft stuck head down in a circle of white ice, motionless, tail sagging just a little to one side, legs splayed.

No one I knew.

Kathy Lee's voice whispered over my command circuit: "Jemadar-Major."

"Here."

"Shagetzsky just went off line. That brings my platoon down by six."

"Logged and noted, Jemadar-Minor. Heads up. Six minutes. Mark." Her promotion had come through just hours before we broke hyperspace and arced into the here and now, so this was her first official action as a junior officer. Hoped she was enjoying herself. I'd have to appoint a new regimental havildar-major shortly, but that could wait. She was used to the duty anyway, had the job down pat.

Hope Shagetzsky had enjoyed himself too. Always an excitable trooper. Good soldier, but too excitable, treating combat like it was football, eyes crackling with joy before every drop. Probably lulled by the fact that it was *so* damned hard to get hurt, popping off the native scum.

Not like a football game now. Her report said the Xú who jumped their asses as they bounced down out of the sky knew just what to shoot at, taking aim at our wrist-mounted external weapons, trying to make us drop the damned cannon.

In our old armor, that wouldn't have been necessary. Little bits of exploding neutronium, artificial heavy nuclei if you like, would've taken our asses apart. As it was, ole Shaggy just lost both his arms. Even then it was all right, the suit's self-healing properties kept him from boiling out, even kept him from bleeding much. But the internal temperature went up to 680K, stayed high for three or four minutes while the backpack dumped excess energy overboard through its laser.

Kathy Lee said when she cleared his faceplate and took a look inside, his eyes looked like worn-out little tiny basketballs, looked like they needed a bit of pumping up. Nice blisters on his lips and tongue too, because his drinking tap boiled and sprayed live steam in his mouth.

Nice of the Master Race to provide us with upgraded armor. Too bad they couldn't think of everything.

I said, "All right boys and girls, time to go. Five, four, three, two . . ."

For once, Kathy Lee didn't have a musical selection for us to play by.

Underground. Far, far underground.

Lightning flashing in a dark tunnel, gouging black holes out of the icy ground around us, air displaced by rushing clouds of superheated gas, winds roaring along at Mach seven, slamming us against each other, armor ringing, people shouting over the command circuit, scraping along ragged walls. Getting myself braced, wedged in a corner, some other trooper beside me, his breath whistling in my ear, ". . . fuckingsonofa*bitch*goddamn . . ." almost crying.

"Take it easy, soldier. See if you can help me with this fuckin' thing."

"Yes, sir."

We used to tease Mbongula about his name, because he was an English speaker from someplace down on the tip of Africa. Yessiree, Mbongula the Juju Vampire. Didn't matter to any of us that juju came from a part of Africa 2500 miles from where he'd grown up, and damn-all centuries in the past.

He got wedged with me now, as best he could, helped me unclip the cannon from my shoulder mount, get it wrestled around in the wind, pointing back up the tunnel, back up to where ruddy fire still burned, where men and women and nonhumans still screamed, at each other, at nothing, at the fact of death.

"OK. Steady . . ."

I logged the firing command out through my suit's link, felt its power pulse under my hands . . .

Ball of hazy white light suddenly in front of us, shadows blazing backward down the tunnel, rolling away at one-tenth cee, compressing gases in front of it, scooping up everything in its path . . .

I heard Mbongula scream as he was sucked out of our little niche, heard him go on screaming as he was pulled away in the fireball's vacuum wake. No diminuendo, no sense of him getting farther away, because it was a radio link, just yodeling, ". . . ohjesusjesusohgodoh . . ."

The white light, far away now, turned a bright, lurid, aching blue, then my external sensors turned themselves off.

I heard my heart beating in the darkness. No more than a second's lag time, yet long enough for me to hear six distinct, hard beats, then I blacked out as the return pressure wave came and punched me into the wall.

                    *   *   *

Regiment reconstituted as two whole companies now, and we caught the last of them in a big, open cavern, a pocket in the ice seven or eight kilometers down.

Flashes of light from firing weapons. Pulses of energy flying about, red-orange masses of molten metal sailing in long, slow arcs, splashing on the wall behind us, crackling as they melted on in, cooling, dimming, growing still.

Some trooper down in front of me, trying to get glowing hot stuff off his suit, "Jesus Christ, Hav, my armor says it's on redline. Getting goddamned *warm* in here . . ." Armor supposed to be better than this. Bath of molten steel like a dip in some summery ocean. But you take six or seven hits from things like five-kiloton tac-nukes . . .

Something exploded down in front of us, and I saw an armored Kkhruhhuft rise up, up in the air, flailing, thrashing. She came apart, five or six big chunks, fell back down into her squad.

Bang.

Big flare darkening the world for me, then stillness. Fading glows here and there. Weapons popping, flashing, slowing down as officers and noncoms went out on the command circuit.

I heard Vronsky, keying in on override. "Cease fire. Cease fire. That's it. We're all done."

Which meant, I suppose, that every last Xú on this nameless old ice-moon was dead. I safed my weapons and went to look for the rest of my people.

Lining up the dead, tending to the wounded, setting up field hospitals in that little hole in the ground, gathering up body parts, doing what we could. Not so bad, I guess. Twenty percent KIA, maybe twice that many wounded badly enough to need a little time off. Puts us down around forty percent effective strength. We'd be back up top in time for our next drop. There were probably enough ready reserves coming out of basic to fill in the holes . . .

I found Jimmy Dietz and Wu Chingda quickly enough, made sure they were squared away, could get everything they needed. Saw to some of the jemadars-minor. Not too bad. Officer and noncom casualties light. That'd make things a bit easier.

Went over to where they were lining up the dead bodies.

Voice whispering in my ear: "Jemadar-Major?"

Recognizable voice. "That you, ah, Schmidt?" Pleased with myself, able to recognize a trooper's voice and associate it with his name, though I felt like I'd been blown into some other dimension.

"Yes, sir." He said, "You'd . . . better come over here, sir." Odd.

I walked over to where he was kneeling, beside the still, armored form of some fallen soldier. His comrade, perhaps. His very close friend. But it was unusually tall armor, making my heart stop in its tracks.

I knelt down beside him, reached out, and cleared the armor's faceplate, looked in at Solange Corday.

Not like she was asleep, no. Soft brown eyes open, looking at some faraway sky, some distant horizon. Watching the clouds, maybe, blowing past the gray stone of some bare Ethiopian peak. Watching the sand drift low above the Sahara, boundary-layer streams coursing along like some strange, gritty mist, grains whispering to each other in the wind. Mouth open slightly, teeth glittering within. Surprised.

Me? Now?

But I'm not ready.

Another pair of trooper's boots standing on the bare ice beside us, and I looked up at a blank, armored visage, armor marked with jemadar-minor's rank, Kathy Lee Mendoza's ID badge.

Vronsky's voice spoke in my ears: "Morrison?"

"Uh. Here, ma'am."

"You in one piece?"

"Yes, ma'am."

"Good. Granny Jones is numbered among the KIAs. I'm going to field-brevet you to rissaldar-minor so you can take over what's left of her battalion."

"Yes, ma'am." I could picture her, just as though she were standing beside us, a thin, fierce, black-eyed woman, steel gray hair drawn up in a bun . . .

Vronsky said, "Make your appointments-of-rank and get your ass over here."

"Yes, ma'am." I got to my feet slowly, still looking down at Solange Corday.

"Colder than ice," said Kathy Lee. "Colder than black fucking ice." She put her arm around me and we stood holding one another for just a minute, then went on about our business.

1230 hours. Sitting at a table in the battalion corvette's wardroom, hands around a warm mug of coffee, sitting across from Wu Chingda, who'd made jemadar-major, had taken over the regiment in my place.

Tired-looking Wu Chingda, pretty Chinese face lined with fatigue. Drinking a mug of strong, red tea, what they used to call British Army tea, more caffeine in it than your usual sort of coffee.

Well. We'd have time to rest now, troopers, hale and wounded alike, packed aboard the corvette, seven days flight time, three hundred parsecs or so to the next assembly point. By then most of my wounded would be off the sick list, their armor repaired or replaced. Probably pick up a few replacements in transit, go off to the next drop, with more weeks in which to train, to make ourselves whole again.

She yawned, mouth opening wide, still seeming small and dainty, rubbed her narrow eyes, blinked hard. I was conscious of a sudden erection building itself under the table.

She drank more tea. Smiled at me. Said, "I guess I shouldn't be drinking this. I have a hard enough time sleeping as it is."

I looked down into my own mug, swirled sugary brown coffee, watched it ripple back and forth. "Yeah."

She said, "Hell, maybe we should rethink the doctrine of not taking burdars into combat . . ."

Looked into her eyes. Nothing there. "Maybe so." Took another drink of coffee. Tried to will myself cold.

She stood, stretched, muscular back arched, small breasts pushing out the front of her tunic. Tossed her mug in the trash. "See you in the morning, Ath." Walked away, maybe conscious of me watching her. Maybe not.

I continued to sit there with my coffee, sipping it as it grew stone-cold, for a long while. Finally went off to bed.

Soldiers falling, like a black cloud from the sky, on some urban Xú colony world. Defensive weapons trying to pick us off, failing, defeated by some new technology the Masters pulled from their bag of magic tricks. Maybe they'd had it all along. Hard to say. You could imagine them assessing the situation, handing us the *least* sophisticated weapon they thought would suffice.

They kept on, it seemed, underestimating the Xú. But then, their resources were large, their pockets deep, and those of the Xú were not. Just a few months from that first hard attack, that first bitter battle, and already the Xú were falling back, losing world after world, retreating toward hearth and home.

Preparing, I suppose, to go down fighting.

I wondered if there would be any left, by the time this was all over, to recruit as comrades. After each new battle, I wondered how many of us would be left to recruit them.

City streets. Like the city streets on many a civilized world. Like the city streets on old Earth. Streets of stone. Buildings of steel and glass and shiny ceramic. Buildings holed. Buildings falling. Buildings on fire.

Armored soldiers retreating before us. Dying. Killing us when they could. Less and less successful as time went on. Unarmored Xú outnumbering the soldiers a thousand to one in those city streets. Holing up in shelters. Shelters bursting open, casting them out in the fire.

Image of myself crouching in the useless shelter of an irregular concrete staircase, stairs suited to the needs of a many-legged Xú, stairs blasted open now, no more than a tangle of twisted, rusty rebar.

Xú civilian tottering around in that street, hair on fire, staggering back and forth, waving its arms as it burned, calling out, a high, mournful, piping cry. I lifted my sidearm, ready to knock it down, quiet the poor bastard . . .

Some weapon across the way sparkled, exploding the

burning Xú, splashing a red mess in the street. That's it, soldier. Put him out of his misery. I lifted my weapon and fired on that other Xú's position, killing him. Too bad, brother. Should've let the silly civilian son of a bitch burn.

Jesus. I've got four thousand troopers to look out for now. Can't be letting myself get pinned down like this.

"Ching."

"Yes, sir."

"Regiment in position?"

"Yes, sir."

"Home on my beacon. We clean out this one little nest, we can move on."

"Yes, sir."

Not having much luck with this damned shit-hole of a planet. Somebody's great idea we'd capture a few Xú general staff, see what goodies we could extract. Nothing so far. I could hear Kathy Lee's voice, an hour before we dropped: This is damned *stupid*. Bomb the place flat. Bypass it, get on to someplace *real* . . .

Seemed real enough just now.

Wu Chingda's people suddenly spilled over me like some monstrous horde of locusts, firing on the Xú HQ building, fire exploding from all the windows, going in. Going in for the kill.

We lost six. There wasn't one fucking Xú survivor.

Another world. A pale blue sky. Faraway clouds. Distant blue mountains covered by haze. A forest of beryl-crystal green, broad, fuzzy leaves whispering in the wind.

Black smoke towering in the distance, coning up at a steep angle from a burning city, shearing off suddenly at the top, reversing direction, carried away by high-altitude winds.

We sat in a field of soft yellow grass, Shrêhht and I, she crouching on the grass itself, I on an old Xú blanket I'd found, setting out my picnic lunch, admiring the pretty pictures threaded in gold into the indigo cloth. Hunting themes. Old time hunting themes. Xú banded by straps of dark leather, Xú bearing short, stout composite bows. Xú shooting down things that might be animals. Animals with eight legs and two arms. Animals that looked a little bit like the Xú themselves, but not much. Animals hung up by their arms and legs, dangling over slow fires, rotating on spits. Animals laid open, belly up on wide log tables. Animals being eaten by merrymaking Xú.

So what if the implications of this are true? Irrelevant. It's not what we're punishing them for. Not that we're punishing them, you understand. Just beating them.

I leaned against Shrêhht's pebbly flank and drank a bottle of sweet ale Ching had given me, watched the city burn, watched the pretty trees wave in the wind, while Shrêhht drank her pizza-flavored kerosene and we talked about times, old and new.

She'd like to visit Earth again. Nicest beaches in the universe.

I thought so too, but still . . .

Maybe we could visit Hanta Sheqari together, afterwards. Seems like a nice enough place. Ought to be real pretty, once all the soldiering bullshit is cleaned up and gone.

Something exploded in the depths of the burning city, flaring yellow-white for just a moment, throwing up a ball of red-black smoke that curled as it mixed with the rest of the plume, rising high before it completely disappeared. Listened for the boom of the explosion, but it never came.

Shrêhht: War'll be over soon. I'm due for a bit of leave.

Me too. Where'll we go?

Have you ever been to Kkhruhhuft?

Once, very briefly, about fifteen years ago.

I'd like you to visit my home with me, Athol Morrison. You can bring a burdar, if you want.

Kkhruhhuft, bleak desert world, glimpsed in transit. Yes. I'd like that.

Over in the burning city, a tall tower began to lean, vast sparks rising from its structure, leaning, leaning, toppling away into the holocaust consuming its fellows. More smoke, dense, oily-looking, hiding the tops of the remaining towers.

Word is, she told me, that we'll be going to Xú itself . . .

Do they really call it that?

I don't think so. Does it matter?

No. I guess not.

After a while I lay down on the blanket and closed my eyes, let the warm yellow sun of this nameless place beat down on my face, felt it burning my skin clean, clean and dry. Peaceful. That's how this feels. Warm. Nice.

I may have fallen asleep, maybe not. In any event, the sun had moved a long way across the sky when a distant, shuddery boom, long and drawn out, made me open my eyes. The burning city had fallen in upon itself at last, buildings collapsed together into a pile of rubble, and the fires were beginning to die down, the smoke beginning to thin. By nightfall, nothing would be left but red embers.

Those would, I thought, look rather pretty from way out here. Glowing. Like some vast, infinitely distant campfire . . .

I could feel the corvette's deck vibrating softly under my feet, feel Ching's small breasts pressing into my chest, my hands on the narrow hardness of her back, drifting down onto the bunched muscle of her buttocks. Kissing her, feeling her small tongue search inside my mouth, wishing I were anywhere but here and now. Just pretending . . .

She put her head down on my shoulder and I heard a soft exhalation, breath warm on my neck, kept my arms around her, opening my eyes, hardly seeing anything, rather willing myself to stay blind. It was almost dark in my cabin, only a dim light on over my little desk, turning the room into a shadowland that hid more than it revealed.

Wu Chingda, jemadar-major, regimental commander looking up at me, face seeming, somehow, swollen, black eyes narrowed to tiny, unreadable slits.

"Not a good idea, Rissaldar-Minor . . ." she whispered.

"No. Not very good." But we kissed again, ground against each other softly.

She stood back from me a little way, lifted her hands and unbuttoned her high collar with its three-diamond insignia, then the next one and the next, until her tunic was open on an expanse of smooth, tawny skin. She reached up and rubbed her thumb over my one star, then fingered my collar button. "Rank-and-rank, Athol Morrison."

As simple as that. I reached for my own buttons, watched her undress, quick, efficient, decisive.

Naked, standing before me, she looked like Hani and yet not like Hani. That same smooth Asian skin, but lighter, from a more northerly clime. Face a little rounder, eyes a little narrower. Hips a little broader, breasts a little larger.

Body lined and corded with the sleek, functional musculature of a woman soldier. Not as strong as me, no, nor even as strong as Solange. But I'd seen her disarm another trooper, a man half-again my size, while they were having a disagreement. Took his sidearm out of its snapped-shut holster and got it settled on the bridge of his nose before he could do more than blink and reach.

Came into my arms when I was naked as well, curling herself around me, molding her body to my shape. Warm. Terribly human.

She whispered, "Will you be wanting me to transfer out after this?" Voice quiet, steady, no tremor of dismay.

I cupped one hand under a small buttock and lifted her against my chest. "You sure you want to do this?"

A small nod against my shoulder. "For just a moment," she said, "I'd like to pretend I'm someone I'm not . . ."

"No. I don't want you to transfer out."

We lay down on the tiny bunk, barely able to stuff ourselves onto what was really no more than a padded shelf, running our hands over sensitized skin, exploring one another's faces.

"Who?"

A puzzled look.

"Who do you want to be?"

Faint, shadowy smile. Then she said, "Someone a man can love without being . . . paid and ordered."

I thought about it, nodded slowly. "Seems like a simple enough wish . . ." I put my hand between her legs and squeezed gently, watched her close her eyes and arch against building sensation. I knew it wasn't what she meant, but what else could I say?

Maybe that was all she wanted me to say.

"And," she said, "when we put on our clothes again, we'll realize this didn't happen. We'll remember that it happened to two other people. People who live far away from here."

I felt a slight pang, a small twisting inside, quickly and easily subdued. "Fair enough," I said.

Shrêhht and I sat together on the promenade deck of a transport large enough to carry an entire legion and then some, sat together and watched it happen. We'd be down there in a little while, a matter of a few days, but there'd be very little for us to do. Not after this.

The Xú homeworld began as a bright blue ball, more ocean than anything else, frosted with lines of streaming clouds, patched here and there with low-lying green continents, lit by the light of its fine white sun, the reflected light of its two large moons, each more than a thousand kilometers in diameter, one close, only ten or so diameters out, the other remote, more than fifty.

We were joined by some of the others, comrades of Shrêhht, marked by ID paint and emblems of rank, humans like mice lurking among them, Wu Chingda and Jimmy Dietz, Kathy Lee, a few officers from the other battalions of Vronsky's brigade.

Defensive action ended. We'd knocked down all their satellites, killed their warships, watched them plunge through air, sheathed in burning plasma, watched them explode in the sea, come apart over the land. There were burning forests below, burning cities, all for naught.

Somewhere, down below, soldiers would be girding for battle, waiting for us to come. Waiting so they could carry a few of us with them into whatever the Xú used for hell.

Shrêhht keyed her vocoder, which said, "Four, three, two, one . . ."

I felt Ching's hand on my forearm, squeezing.

And the skies lit up all around us, Master Race warships pouring their vengeance down upon helpless Xú, who would, now, be just so many more poor-bastard natives.

Fire falling on all the cities, falling on mountains, boiling all those pretty lakes and rivers that looked so inviting when seen from the depths of space. Exploding the ice caps. Plucking ships from the sea, planes from the air, derailing the fancy monorail trains.

It would go on, we were told, for about an hour. Just enough time for one little lightning bolt to fall on every square meter of the planet. Then we'd go down and see what was left. Maybe dig a few survivors out of deep tunnels. Round up a few prisoners, if any Xú was willing to remain alive . . .

There'd been maybe thirty billion of them, scattered around on a few dozen worlds, when we came. I guess we've got a few thousand prisoners left in stock. Maybe we could put them in a zoo somewhere. Fires were spreading out down below now, the very stone of the ground coagulating, becoming first lakes, then seas of lava, flooding out over the landscape.

Well. It would be over in just a little while. Fine with me. I'm ready to go home.

Months and months go by, and I am back atop a high plateau on Karsvaao, back at the little spaceport, watching people and cargo loaded aboard a lighter. Standing looking down at Hani. She is still pretty, still slim, still my quiet little island girl. Looking up at me, holding one little brown bag by its shoulder strap, the same bag she had in her hand the day she arrived, on another world, far away, years ago.

There were dark circles under her eyes, a final sign of our last night together that no sparse makeup could wash away, the shadows of sleeplessness, lips still a little swollen from my attention, hair neatly combed and pinned, but still somehow in disarray.

Well, she would sleep on the transport, could sleep for weeks if she wished, all the long way home.

I can see us both in the mirror, she leaning over the sink, hands on its rim, holding herself steady, looking into her own eyes perhaps, while bright Karsvoë sunlight poured through the curtains. Holding herself steady, standing on her toes, legs apart, while I did my final deed to her. Told her good-bye in my own special way.

When it was over, she sat down on our waterless toilet, staring at the opposite wall, staring at nothing. Waited while I washed myself, motionless when I patted her on the head one last time, walked out of the room and let her do whatever she was going to do.

And now, Hani would be on her way.

They say the islands of Indonesia are still quite lovely, all those alien, Western-style cities smashed to rubble, overgrown by dark green forest, the forest itself filling back up with villages of little huts, the old ornate temples restored to their original function. Bells and dancing and music and prayer.

I never asked what she would do with all the money she'd earned, enough money to keep herself and her extended family alive and well, comfortable, envied by all who saw them, for generations to come.

Would she take a husband now, someone who would be at her beck and call, someone living in the shadow of her wealth, existing to serve her? Nonsense. Only my own voice speaking in there. I could picture Hani doting, as she aged, on the children of her sisters and cousins. Their grandchildren. The grandchildren of her childhood friends . . .

I held out my hand to her, and said, "These have been very good years for me, Hani. I'll remember you." It sounded rehearsed. Maybe a little silly. She stared at my hand for a few seconds, then looked up, squarely into my face, eyes unwavering on mine. And then she turned away, shouldered her little bag, walked up the lighter's boarding ramp and was gone.

So be it. I put my feelings away and walked slowly back to my staff car, stood looking out over desert Karsvaao for a long while. When the ground rumbled and shook I turned around, shading my eyes from the sun, and watched the lighter's thick, silver shape rise gleaming in the late-afternoon sun, climbing into a tan and dusty sky on its thin spike of pale violet fire. Dwindling, then gone, thunder fading to silence.

I sat in the car for a while longer, hardly thinking, remembering a thousand nights of Hani, feeling them fade away to nothingness. Then I reached into my breast pocket and pulled out the pickup voucher. She'd arrived yesterday and was waiting for me in the burdars' transit barracks.

Sarah Morgan, it said on my little piece of paper. Seventeen years old. Well. I put the car in gear and drove on down.

18

TIME PASSED, AS TIME WILL, AND I STOOD at the head of the lighter's cargo-loading ramp, holding Sarah's hand in mine, looking out over a broad expanse of alien beauty. Beauty that made me think of Aldrin's words, standing on the old, gray moon.

"Magnificent desolation," he'd called it.

Seen from space, Kkhruhhuft had been like no other habitable planet I'd ever seen, with its clear, cloudless atmosphere, with its vast red polar tundras, highlands jagged with wind-eroded mountains, temperate zones brown with ancient dust, tiny seas strung along the equator, green with cyanobacterial scum, water gathering in all the little hollows between what should have been abyssal plains, great, gray continents left to be no more than high, lifeless plateaus.

Compared to this, Karsvaao was Eden.

I looked down at Sarah, Sarah quiet by my side. Drinking it all in, eyes wide, mouth slightly open. Astonished, perhaps, that such empty beauty could exist. Astonished, perhaps, that it had any right to exist.

Dark crags in the distance, stark and angular against a cloudless, cobalt blue sky, Kkhruhhuft's sun no more than a brilliant white spark in the vast emptiness overhead. Land between us and the mountains bare, abandoned, riven with old gullies, though where the rain could have come from,

288

where it might have gone, no one could say. Soft, cool wind blowing out of what I knew to be the northeast, dry on our faces, carrying with it a faint tang of fireworks, of burning, of chemistry alien beyond knowing.

Wind a faint, faraway moan, curling round the lighter's landing jacks, around its steering vanes and angular engine hardware. And Sarah looking up at me now, eyes alight, afire with something very much like joy.

"Each new world I see," she said, "is such a surprise."

I nodded, knowing exactly what she meant. We started down the ramp, still holding hands, headed for the edge of the scorched, hard-packed dirt of the landing field, to where a score of unpainted gray Kkhruhhuft were loading a few bits of containerized cargo into a low-slung truck the size and shape of an antique skiploader, immense beings handling boxes and cartons the size of small houses.

Shrêhht, they said, would be waiting to greet us at her ancestral home. Not far. Come with us, honored guest. Squatting low, almost eye to eye with me. Humble. Nervous, almost shy. These Kkhruhhuft were not soldiers.

Sarah's pleasure at her surroundings lasted for the whole of the long ride to a place called Hánáq, as the truck rolled through interminable expanses of dusty desert, as we followed a narrow track that wound up and down the passes of those stark black mountains, as we looked down from on high upon a tawny plain, studded with knobby hills, looked down on a silver ribbon of river that twisted between them to a distant green sea.

It had been like this, in a way, since the moment I met her, surprising me, sometimes, as I expected her to grow quiet and meek, just the way all the others had. Expected her to become the very image of a burdar in my bed.

Expectation can lead you astray.

I'd found her waiting for me, seated in the lobby of the burdars' transit barracks, one small bag settled by her feet, a midsize young woman with the light chocolate complexion of many mixed-race North Americans who can claim West African descent, hair loosely curled, reddish black, as if freshly hennaed, hanging almost to her shoulders, tousled in a way that made it look natural, though I knew that couldn't be . . .

She stood, recognizing me the moment I walked in, face uncertain, giving me my first look into those wide brown eyes, irises so pale that, in certain kinds of light, they looked almost yellow. Then she flashed me a bit of a tentative smile, and said, "You look a lot bigger than your picture."

I'd laughed, held my hands in the size and shape of a standard desk holo, and said, "Good thing, too." Then she took my hand, and her fingers were warm and soft, her grip strong and sure.

She'd asked me questions about Karsvaao and its people, frowned over a chain gang of laborers grubbing in the dirt, exclaimed over the sky's incredibly neutral coloration, and I began to wonder just where they'd found this one. Maybe just her age, everything in the universe new and interesting. You seldom see a new burdar younger than early twenties, and the luck of the draw guarantees you won't get that many fresh out of their own version of basic.

Then we were at the crib, Fyodor smiling as he ushered us through the door, a little surprised when she took *his* hand, Janice, Mira, and Margie staying in the background, though she kept looking over at them. They'd get to know her later, when she'd be moving into Hani's so recently abandoned bedroom.

I had her hand the little bag over to Fyodor, then took her into my room and closed the door, ready to do what I knew from trial and error was necessary with a new burdar, my hand lightly on her back as I showed her the way. My heart quickening, my step lightening with anticipation. An acceleration of hormones.

They say one grows jaded over time.

One does not.

She stood still then for a long moment, looking at the freshly changed, turned-down sheets of my bed, a pattern of pretty pink-and-yellow flowers, terrestrial flowers, though I couldn't remember their names, images of little black-and-gold bees flying among them, settling at the center of this blossom or that, and I could see a haze of doubt on her face.

Is it the same self-doubt I experienced when the troop transport climbed away from Earth, carrying me away to watch my friends die on Mars? Did I really want to come here? Too late now.

I wondered, too, if she might be a virgin, given her age. Given that this was her first assignment and I her first soldier. I'd not been with a virgin since my first night with Alix, who was of course experiencing her own first virgin. This would be different. Maybe. Another little trickle of anticipation. A momentary awareness of my own inner idiocy.

Then she murmured, softly, to herself, " ' . . . I lay me down with a will . . . ' " I wondered, for just a second, if she knew that was an epitaph. Most likely she did, for it's on one of the world's best-known graves.

She turned and looked me in the eye, half-smiling, half-serious. Put her hands to her throat and pulled off a small, white silk scarf, let it fall to the floor like some heavy, diaphanous wisp of smoke. Began unbuttoning her white blouse, beginning at the collar.

I remembered the guileless way Alix had stripped for me on the beach, at the North Carolina oceanside, on a distant summer day, already years gone by.

Blouse unbuttoned and dropped. White linen skirt unzipped and dropped, sandals stepped out of, and Sarah stood before me, almost naked, breasts confined by a lightweight elastic brassiere, hips barely concealed by a pair of simple cotton briefs. Waiting. Eyes on me. Staking her claim, perhaps.

Hánáq lay in a bend of the river, a wide loop of slow muddy water that would one day, I thought, become an oxbow lake, silt up, slowly dry, become part of the loamy plain over which we were rolling now, fat, knobby truck tires raising a small cloud of dark dust that quickly settled on the low, dry brown vegetation covering the ground on either side of the road, leaves chattering in the wind, audible whenever the truck engine paused for a shifting of gears.

Kkhruhhuft visible in the distance, a long line of squatty dinosaurs bending low, doing something among the plants.

Here and there were other large animals. I had a momentary feeling of disquiet, expecting they'd at least look like Cretaceous herbivores, ceratopsians, maybe, or hadrosaurs. The nearest one looked like a big, brown baseball mitt with big yellow eyes, wide mouth down low, looking like the place through which you'd slip your hand, yellow tongue visible as it chewed up woody vegetation. A living baseball glove the size of an armored personnel carrier, maybe half-again the size of a Kkhruhhuft.

Sarah was on her knees in the seat, face pressed to the window's cloudy Plexiglas, looking out at them, watching as the nearest one turned on its huge, stubby, footless legs, eyes rolling visibly, little X-shaped pupils following the movement of the truck along the road.

Hánáq was not quite what you'd call a city or town, though large enough to be one. More like a Mayan temple complex in appearance, step pyramids surmounted by small buildings, mostly the dun color of the native stone, but painted here and there, narrow stripes of scarlet and bright azure, gleaming little inlay patterns that had to be gold, sheets of what appeared to be burnished copper, pyramids separated by wide fieldstone plazas, fountains here and there that sprayed a thin mist of water, mist blowing away, dissipating in the wind, faint, blurry rainbows playing within. Planters full of scrubby brown-and-silver bushes, all of them looking quite dead.

Small parties of Kkhruhhuft walking here and there, by twos and threes and fours, standing aside for the truck, some body-painted, some not.

Sarah said, "Look. Are those children?" Pointing out the window.

There were a couple of Kkhruhhuft, herding a group of maybe a half dozen things that looked like big brown ducks. Bald, scaly brown ducks. Ducks the size of horses. Heads bobbing back and forth as they waddled, looking around, mouths gaping. If we opened the windows, I was sure we'd hear them quack-quacking softly to each other.

I glanced up toward the driver, who lay on a big pallet by the windscreen, taking up fully a third of the truck's cockpit.

Put my hand on Sarah's arched back, and said, "Those are the menfolk, I guess."

She gave me an incredulous look, wide-eyed again. "Men?" Another look back at waddling duck-boys. A blink, a slight smile of amusement. "I might like to be a Kkhruh-huft, then."

Or, if you'd had the right genetics, a slightly less invasive upbringing, you might like to be a Spahi yourself. Easy for a man's burdar to forget we're half female, women the same as the men . . .

I patted her on the backside, watched her wiggle on cue. She'd been good about that sort of thing, not resisting, not resenting, yet not acting as though anything were done merely as a duty. I wondered how long that would last.

She said, "This place is really neat. I'm glad you brought me along."

Shrêhht's compound was down by the riverfront, rambling buildings of stuccoed adobe surrounded by a low stone wall, gate wide open and unguarded, marked by two sigils I recognized, one for the Master Race sponsor of the Kkhruhhuft Expeditionary Forces, the other a compound of Shrêhht's ID-cartouche and that of her family and gens.

Shrêhht came out of the big bronze doors, stood by and waited while we debarked, while the driver unloaded our few trunks, watched critically while the driver backed her truck around and drove away.

She keyed her vocoder, and it said, "I told her if she dented my gate again, I'd hold her under the river until she turned into a *thrähhs.*" No clue about that last word, something for which the vocoder's simple AI didn't care to do more than invent a symbolic transliteration. Her last whispered word had really sounded like a cat choking up a hairball.

I became aware that Sarah was standing behind me now, almost up against my back. I half turned toward her, looking down. Her eyes were big, this time filled with something other than excitement. I smiled.

She murmured, "Athy, that looks like something out of an old video . . ."

I remembered Kong beating the shit out of that silly *tyran-nosaurus,* which, in reality, would have made a meal out of a big, fat old gorilla. I said, "This is the friend I told you about. Her name is Shrêhht."

"Her breath smells like frying liver."

I looked up at Shrêhht, listened to the slight wheeze of her laughter. She said, "Let's go in. I'll introduce you to my family."

The building seemed larger inside than it had looked from without, its scale concealed by the scale of the Kkhruhhuft and their world. Inside was a great hall, sheer stone walls towering away to a shadowy ceiling of exposed wooden rafters, rough hewn from logs that must grow *somewhere* in this desert, walls covered with reed-thatch hangings, images plaited into them, hardly visible until you got close enough to see all the corded tan-on-tan patterns. Images of Kkhruh-huft. Soldiers. Battles. Killing. Armed and armored non-Kkhruhhuft. Mostly unrecognizable. Saanaae. And lots of humans.

The big room was made to seem full by the presence of Kkhruhhuft, standing in little groups, each group marked by similar body paint styles, or by none. Shrêhht taking us first to stand before a little altar, gleaming with the blue fire of a hundred little candles, surmounted by three statuettes, one high, two low.

"Honored Mother . . ." the one on the daïs. "My sister-wives Atubôrrh and Vodrêhh . . ." Shrêhht glanced at Sarah, perhaps getting a little tired of her uneasiness, and said, "Vo-drêhh is stationed on Earth just now. She's really taken a lik-ing to the Gobi Plateau. We'll have to go there next time we're on Earth together."

I put my arm around Sarah, urged her forward, held against my chest, arms crossed around her. "I guess it'd look a little bit like this place. She'd like parts of Australia, too." Sarah was still and calm, obviously no longer afraid. Maybe just caught in a little behavior loop, too self-conscious, too conscious of the odd *newness* of her situation, simply to stand and be herself.

Shrêhht turned to the others, beckoning to a single long,

rather lean Kkhruhhuft, marked with a very different sort of body paint from what I was used to seeing on soldiers, long stripes of alternating green and gold stark on the scales of her back, swirls of light orange on her breast. "This is my house-mate Zváiroq."

She whispered something in Kkhruhhuft, not wearing a vocoder, a stuttering phrase that sounded like a lion's purr.

". . . and the household majordomo Nûmri-Äng." This one was a little small as Kkhruhhuft went, standing on bent legs, lowering herself further, her only body paint an encapsulated version of Shrêhht's family-gens device.

And in the background, a dozen other adults, none of them painted, none of them introduced; Shrêhht leading 'is to a gaggle of brown-duck males, who stared at us big-eyed and murmured softly, like, ". . . borkborkbork . . ." little quirky noises all their own, a paintless nanny keeping them all together; Shrêhht running down a laundry list of meaningless names—"Rûq, Löhh, Slaaq, Mrëgh, Tuhhs, Vshât . . ."—tapping each one in turn, eliciting a soft little "bork" in reply, running her hand gently along the back of the last one she'd named—"My favorite, I'm afraid. Quite spoiled."

Another unpainted nanny, herding a group of thin, lizard-like immature females, "Our children . . ." eight of them, looking up at us, eyes lit by intelligence and curiosity, murmuring soft words and phrases in a delicate, lisping version of Kkhruhhuft speech.

No names for the children. I'd heard they aren't given names until they reach sexual maturity, though they have nicknames for each other.

Sarah said, "No male children?" Good. Curiosity drawing her out.

Shrêhht regarded her levelly for a moment, then said, "We sell them all, dear."

Pang of uneasiness. Where had Shrêhht learned to speak with such human condescension? From me? From all of us. To her, humanity was divided into two classes, soldiers and burdars.

She said, "We've gone to great expense to import a supply

of human food for you, my friend! I hope you appreciate the result . . ."

Midnight on Kkhruhhuft.

Sarah and I lying together in a vast, oblong padded nest meant for a single Kkhruhhuft, a nest dug into the stone floor of a room the size of a small hangar, huge unglazed windows open to the darkness, wind blowing in stirring the gauze tented over our bed, lifting the curtains out from the wall, dark rippling in currents of air.

I remembered lying with Alix in a room filled with my childhood artifacts, watching my mother's handmade curtains blow just like this.

Sarah sleeping, huddled against my side, mouth open slightly, face like a child. Sarah wanting to talk and talk, overexcited by the newness of it all, the barbaric splendor of this place and its people, the very words she used, to my surprise. Pausing while we made love, growing feverish in my arms, crying out as sunset flamed in the sky. Then talking again, asking me about the Kkhruhhuft and their place in the universe. Finally asking me for stories about the Invasion.

So strange to imagine that. Here was a sexually mature human woman, more or less an adult, who'd never known that old world. Never sat an enraptured child, before a long weekend of interactive 3V. Nothing to prepare her soul for a life of adventure between the stars. Nothing but reality.

Hard, too, to make a connection between the excited, chattering girl, the angelic sleeping child, and the female thing I'd had kneeling before me on the bed, looking down on her exposed primate rump, ready for me and waiting.

I disengaged from her sleeping arms, tucked a silklike sheet around her, brought it up under her chin, smoothed her rough-feeling hair with my hand, listened to the whisper of her breathing. Stood finally and went out through the gauze, found a pair of boots, put on my long, hooded terry cloth robe, walked out through the open arch of the doorway into night.

Stars overhead, thousands of stars, stars in unfamiliar patterns, patterns whose names I'd never know. The steady wind was cool, playing with the front of my robe, blowing it open around my legs, and there were faraway sounds. The loud rattle-rustle of the low vegetation, something moaning softly from the river, a dark shape floating by Shrêhht's waterfront, the oily slop of the water itself.

Black mountains in the distance, jagged peaks blotting out stars near the edge of the world. Night air so hard and clear. No haze. No clouds. Without the wind, it might have been an airless world.

A peaceful tension in me.

A sharp awareness of myself.

One long, happy moment.

I could stand forever like this.

Flash. White light dazzling my eyes. Flash. Flash. Light spilling up from some mountain valley, picking out the peaks around it for just a moment, lighting their craggy edges against the black of the sky. I blinked and let my night vision return. Waited for more. Nothing. Just a reminder that I'm not alone in this world.

Climbed up on the low wall surrounding the place, something a Kkhruhhuft could step over with ease, walked along the riverfront, up toward where the wall turned inland, where a little spit of sand went out into the river, like a little detached beach.

Someone down there in the starlit darkness, gray Kkhruhhuft shapes not quite in shadow. Two females nuzzling close to one another, whispering soft cadences of untranslated growling. Little yearning sounds, tigerlike, with a delicate, almost whiny undertone. Shrêhht, I realized, and Zváiroq. A world of meaning in that term, house-mate. The two of them down there now twisting around each other like lovesick cats, nuzzling here, nuzzling there. Shrêhht's breath suddenly chuffing loud as Zváiroq did something particularly right . . .

I sat quietly on the wall and watched them make love.

Daylight, Kkhruhhuft's sun hard and bright overhead, Shrêhht and I standing together on a crag in the mountains I'd seen flashing in the night, which she called the Arriôt

Hills, looking down on a broad, bowl-shaped valley. Sarah had been a little upset to be left alone, back at Hánáq, left in the care of Zváiroq, whose vocoder was a much simpler, smaller model than the one hanging off Shrêhht. As we walked away, they were standing together on the patio, and I heard Sarah call her Zvai . . .

The valley below was filled with tall, thick-trunked trees, obviously the same sort of trees from which Shrêhht's rafters had been hewn, stout, red-bodied boles with short stubby branches covered with hard, shiny brown leaves, a narrow, silvery stream winding among them, splashing down from a cliff-front spring.

There were several armored Kkhruhhuft down there, working beside one of the large trucks, its bed-doors swung open to reveal what appeared to be a well-equipped machine shop, welding beams asparkle, glaring and hard to look at even in daylight.

She said, "I hadn't intended to conduct any business while you were here, there are so many interesting things to do and business is all we conduct . . . out there. But I thought you might be interested in this."

"I saw those flashes last night. Handbox weapons?"

Featureless eyes regarding me silently, then she said, "Among other things."

"Cannon?"

Her head dipped to one side. "First redelivery was just a few days ago. We were taken by surprise."

"Trouble?"

"There's nothing on the Net. No word from up in the Hierarchy. I don't think so."

So the Master Race, which had taken back its guns when the Xú were finished, was handing them back out again. "Human Spahis? Saanaae?"

"I . . . don't know. You haven't been in service very long. Not the Saanaae, certainly. So far, it's just us and the *Sinnott.*"

Sinnott were one of the few species reliably rumored to have been attached to the Master Race longer than the Kkhruhhuft. Not quite the same sort of mercenaries. Far fewer in number. Brought in when a need was felt for very tough shock troops indeed. Unprepossessing as hell, like little black spiders the size of big dogs. They were the ones who'd dropped on Kkhruhhuft, seventeen thousand years ago.

I said, "Where do you suppose the older races go?"

She looked at me. "Die out maybe. Tired. Old. Used up. Displaced." She looked down at the flaring torches of the armorers, and said, "No one really believes the myth of the Master Race Eternal. Sinnott said, when they found us, they'd been in service for maybe ten millennia. Said *they'd* been taken by a species that much older again, people calling themselves the *Raighn*, now gone . . ."

Thirty-seven thousand years ago? That was back when fully modern humans were first getting well established, not long before the gentle holocaust of the Chatelperonian would push the last Neanderthals aside. Where *do* the old races go?

I said, "At the rate they've been moving, wouldn't take them much longer than that to spread across the whole galaxy."

"No. Not much longer than that."

We went on down then, to take a look at the new weapons, watch skilled Kkhruhhuft artificers, body-painted with the special devices and sigils of their own honored caste, integrating them permanently into Kkhruhhuft combat armor. I wonder why they're doing this. Well, when I got back I'd see if they were giving them to humans as well, or just to time-honored trustees like the Kkhruhhuft and Sinnott. Maybe someday we'd find out the why of this, and why now. Or maybe not. They tell us their decisions, but seldom the reasons behind them.

Another dark time, far up in the windswept passes of some much higher mountains, night air cold all around us. Shrêhht's breath was a vast cloud of steam pounding from her mouth, jetting from her nostrils. She had an atlatl and heavy spear in one clawed hand, shaft a good ten centimeters in diameter, head of some glassy, obsidian-like stone, bright starlight glittering off its facets. In her other hand she was holding Vshât on a short leash, fat brown duck hopping from one wide foot to another, borking softly to himself, shivery with excitement.

Shrêhht rattling his chain earlier, as we'd set out on the trail, hours ago, just as the sun set bright orange behind the mountains, hissing laughter, keying her vocoder and saying, "Keep the cute little bastard out of trouble . . ."

Startling growl in the distance, deep, heavy, like a big diesel engine at idle. Sudden, angry ". . . *warkwarkwark* . . ." of those other males. Closing in. Teasing the damned thing.

I put the stirrup of my old-fashioned windlass crossbow on the ground, wound up against its four-hundred-kilogram pull, snapped the massive quarrel into place, locked it down. Looked at Sarah, bundled up in a heavy white parka, starkly visible in the darkness, impossible to lose, face lost in shadow, only her eyes glittering from inside the hood, breath a faint flag of moisture in the cold.

"Stay close," I said.

"Don't worry." Voice hardly audible.

". . . *WARKwarkwarkwark* . . ." commotion in the distance, Vshât squirming by Shrêhht's side, whining, pulling on the chain, borking away like mad. But in a whisper. Smart enough to know he didn't want that growling thunder to come his way.

I'd been surprised when Shrêhht's retainers brought out those other males in coffle, not much bigger than Vshât and his brothers, but leaner, meaner, stronger, starved-looking, bodies corded with muscle. Voices deeper, sharper. Hard, *angry* brown ducks.

The thing in the distance screamed, sharp, rising in pitch, like a cornered Siberian tiger, echoed by a sudden squeal, brown duck in agony, and ". . . *WARKWARKWARK*!!!" Another agonized scream, a quick yelp, a metallic whine, this time from our cornered friend.

Shrêhht said, "Let's go . . ." dragging Vshât on the end of his leash.

When Sarah saw it, she said, "Oh, *fuck*." Voice flat. Stunned.

It wasn't really all that big. Not even as big as Shrêhht.

But still. Shining violet eyes, like fiery holes in the darkness. White fangs that seemed to glow with a light of their own. Black claws. Humped, muscular back, crouching over the corpse of a dead brown duck, yellow blood streaming from a gash in one flank.

Rabble of ducks around it, going ". . . warkwarkwark . . ." Dashing forward, cowering back. Daring the thunder of its growl.

The ducks, at least, seemed happy.

Shrêhht put her husband's chain under one foot, anchoring him in place, said, "On three . . ."

She counted, we fired, thud of missiles striking home, howl of angry despair, then the ducks closed in.

Later, the campfire crackled, midnight air filling with the petroleum smell of cooking alien meat, Shrêhht's retainers coming forward to butcher the dead beast, limbs rotating in the flames, spit turned by some unpainted servant. Sarah and I sat a little to one side, while our field rations heated over the little campstove we'd brought along.

It was hot near the big fire, stones sweating around us, naked Kkhruhhuft basking in red firelight, turning first one side, then the other to the flames.

"You let the heat accumulate inside," said Shrêhht, "and it can last you 'til dawn." She was squatting beside little Vshât, feeding him crisp gobbets of cooked fat, patting him on the head between times, almost cooing as he sat up prettily to beg. ". . . later, little one. Ah, there's always later . . ."

The other males were back in their coffle, staked down a short distance from the fire, eyes glowing in its light, gobbling hot, raw entrails from big stone bowls the retainers had set out for them, growling in their throats, snapping at each other.

Retainers watching them, hissing, shoving each other good-naturedly. Saying things that made Shrêhht laugh, but nothing we could understand, nothing anyone would translate.

Sarah handed me a packet of steaming lasagna, a can of

hot chocolate, and Shrêhht said, "One of those things really smells odd."

I held out my meal and let her sniff.

"The beverage, I think."

Sarah said, "I don't see how anyone could smell anything, with all this gasoline stink . . ."

Getting bold, my little one . . . She said, "Why didn't you bring Zvai along? I like her."

Silence from Shrêhht, then, "Zváirog? She would not be happy here. It's not the sort of thing . . . her kind enjoys."

Her kind.

"Besides which . . ." Shrêhht slid to the ground, lying on her side, looking at us, and pulled Vshât against her belly. He curled up in a fat little ball, purring softly, a ridiculous sound, a Donald Duck snore.

Still later, stars overhead, fire dying down, retainers retired to a game of some kind, sitting huddled in a circle beyond the fire, snarling softly to each other. Males quiet now, collapsed in a dark heap, sated with food. Sarah and I finished with our meal, reclining against a rock, still warm from the fire, radiating its heat on us. Shrêhht curled up around her little husband.

She said, "Very far away, the Masters' empire now. Far away, all those ancient battles . . ."

And newer battles as well, the ones we joined together. Familiar stars overhead. Painfully familiar. No star visible in this sky that had not belonged to the Master Race since humans huddled in caves and waited for the glaciers to recede, or wandered the pluvial plains of Africa, living in little huts of stick and grass.

I thought of Solange, growing up by the edge of some vast mountain range, growing up on the desert those plainsmen had left behind. I had a moment of longing, wishing she could be here instead of Sarah.

Shrêhht said, "Sometimes I dream of what it might have been like, had there been no Master Race."

An easy dream to dream. But useless. "Where would the Kkhruhhuft be now?"

Hiss of amusement. "No more than right here, my friend. When the Sinnott came, Hánáq was already an old city. We had our weapons of glass and our cities of stone, our beasts of burden, our crops and our males." She ran her delicate wrist tendrils over Vshât's back, watching him stir and preen. "What more could anyone have wanted?"

I gestured at the sky overhead. "Humans already had those when you folks showed up."

"So did the Saanaae."

I said, "Do you feel bad about the Xú?"

"Should I? There are a few of them left. Maybe they'll go hunting with us one day."

"Maybe so." I could picture a Xú here. Or a Saanaa. People with whom I could form a friendship. Like my friendship with Shrêhht. Like my friendship with Solange. I remembered Marsh suddenly. Marsh and Sandy, gone to cold graves.

She said, "The Xú have nothing to be ashamed of. That's more important than . . . some other things."

Maybe so. The warrior's credo. Not something a soldier ought to believe. I said, "So why are the Kkhruhhuft still here?"

No answer.

Still later, the fire had slumped to a dimly glowing heap of sullen red coals, the smell of burning oil faded away to a faint alien tang.

I lay huddled in my sleeping bag, holding Sarah clutched to my naked chest, buttocks settled against the tops of my thighs, my hand down on her lower abdomen, drifting in and out of her pubic hair, reaching lower, feeling the moistness of her, drifting away, back again, teasing.

Mostly, we were watching Shrêhht. Shrêhht and her little Vshât. She had him pinned now, rolled onto his back, little brown duck peering out from under her in the night, moon-eyed, gasping softly, ". . . borkborkbork . . ." to himself, something like bloodred foam gathering between them.

I pushed Sarah's legs a little bit apart, reached between

them, and pulled my erect penis forward so it could rub in the wet.

"*BORK!*"

Like a scream from Vshât, suddenly struggling under the heavy weight of his wife, Shrêhht growling now like an angry lioness, grinding down on him hard.

"*BORK!*"

Irritated little murmur of ". . . warkwarkwark . . ." from those other males, chained together in the darkness.

I could feel Sarah shaking against me, trying to smother her own giggles, holding one hand over her mouth.

"Shh," I said. "You'll bother them . . ."

"I can't help it, Athy. They look *so* damned silly . . ."

Shrêhht was collapsed on top of her man now. We heard a smothered *bork* or two from Vshât, then they were silent.

19

ANOTHER NIGHT ON THE WORLD OF THE Kkhruhhuft, another night up in the mountains, in a warmer clime now, standing on a high plateau not far from some scummy equatorial sea, night wind washing us with its summery breath, carrying a scent of flowers, but no flower scent I'd ever met before. A sharp, acrid, sweet smell, the better-living-through-chemistry smell of ersatz pheromones, of perfume tailored to leach a man's will.

Shrêhht and I and a few others, painted Kkhruhhuft all, soldiers from her garrison, officers I thought, stood on the edge of a black abyss, a deep canyon cut down through ages of solid stone, a Grand Canyon—like place that would have looked splendid by daylight.

Zváiroq and Sarah were left behind at the encampment, though we'd brought them along on other outings, all the little males as well. Just us. Just soldiers. This was, so Shrêhht told me, a special sort of thing.

Overhead, the stars were thick and bright, like swarms of glittering fireflies, gathered thickly in one part of the sky, less so in the other. Kkhruhhuft is far enough from the galactic plane that the Milky Way loses its definition, spreading out, diffuse, over half the sky. In recompense, the galactic core begins to be visible, a bulky knot of bright stars, dusty and reddish-looking, painted against a thick slice of night.

Now, Shrêhht stood beside me in the almost-silence, wind whispering behind us, so close I could smell the faint, oily sharpness of her scaly skin, other Kkhruhhuft pressing in close beside us, behind us, crowding close to the edge of the canyon.

Below us, the darkness was absolute, black on black, and you could hear a distant, hollow murmur, wind sweeping the canyon walls. "All right," I said, "it's lovely. Now why are we here?" Sarah was upset when Shrêhht announced we were going away for a little while, Zváiroq visibly startled, her rumble of protest silenced by a gesture from Shrêhht.

One of the other Kkhruhhuft made a shuddery murmur, untranslated since she was not wearing a vocoder.

Shrêhht said, "If we are lucky, if we've timed our visit right, we're here in time for the beginning of the dark-demons' migration. They go out and return several times before going on their way for the season. The first night is always the best."

"And is there some reason we left the others behind?"

"It's . . . not done."

Oh. All right. I stood and waited.

Around me, the Kkhruhhuft soldiers suddenly grew tense, anticipatory, one of them whispering, shushed by another's sibilant hiss. Shrêhht suddenly lifted one arm, pointing with her chela, down into the darkness. *There.*

A faint glimmer in those depths, a sparkle of green and gold, just on the edge of vision. A distant rustle of sound, a rustle like leather sliding on leather. A distant fluttering sound. Wings?

A faint stream of light down below, the Kkhruhhuft whispering again, again quieted with a hiss of reprimand. Obviously I wasn't the only one seeing this for the first time. The colors continued to spread and brighten, began to make jeweled patterns below, as if a thousand mirrors were turning up toward the sky, so they could reflect starlight.

Not starlight, though. Green and gold. Bits of silver and brooding red. Pale, pale blue, all very faint, but brightening.

Shrêhht's deep voice whispered now, something like,

"Aaahhhhh . . ." The vocoder was silent, yet . . . Awe. From a Kkhruhhuft. Somehow disturbing.

And the stars below quickened abruptly, leaping into a three-dimensional pattern of fiery gemstones, flying into an upward-turning spiral, reaching for the sky. I heard the rustle and flutter of a million wings. Climbing, climbing . . .

Darkdemons fountained into the air above us, wings on fire, trailing patterns of light, silver and gold, dark copper and bright, shining brass, forming a brilliant tree against the night, an upward-striking thunderbolt pattern, the licking flames of some vast, cold bonfire.

Whirled over us in the shape of a spiral galaxy, smaller, denser, then large, more diffuse. A barred spiral, a dense elliptical, a chaotic, craggy irregular. Exploded like the Crab Nebula, whirled into the shape of the Trifid, grew smaller and smaller, melding with the stars, streaming away into the heavens. Here. Then gone.

I felt like I'd been holding my breath for hours.

Maybe I had.

Oh, Sarah, it would have given you joy to have seen this.

Well. The camp wasn't so far away, no more than a dozen kilometers. Maybe she'd seen something of it after all . . .

A sudden awareness of body heat, the oily smell of Kkhruhhuft hides suddenly oppressive. Surrounded by them, their shapes now blotting out the sky, my only avenue of escape a quick leap over the rim and into the abyss . . .

I looked at Shrêhht, realized she was holding out one hand, proffering a scrap of cloth. A blindfold.

"What the hell is going on here?"

"Put this on, friend Morrison."

"Why?" Sudden cold fire in my chest.

"Put it on, soldier. The answers will be forthcoming."

I tried looking into her eyes. Nothing, of course. Just that hand made of chelae and tentacles, holding a scrap of white cloth. Not a condemned man's blindfold, no. Comrade Shrêhht, asking for my trust.

I took it from her hand, tied it on, and let them lead me away.

When the blindfold came off, we were standing on the

floor of some vast, arid cavern, dry, dusty air sharp in my nose, tiny motes swirling in the torchlight. Not a natural cavern, no. The floor was more or less flat, paved with close-fitting, hewn-stone blocks. Cavern walls vertical, planed smooth, almost polished, ceiling far away, beyond the reach of the torchlight.

A cavern so large buildings like those of Hánáq could be fitted inside, step pyramids and plaza, planters full of empty dirt, dry fountains full of things that looked like cobwebs and crumbled leaf mold. No paint on these buildings that I could see, just bare brown stone, stone worn away, as if by time. As if they'd lain here for so long that the nearly still air of this place had begun to wear them away.

I turned and looked at Shrêhht, at the other tall, shadowy, silent Kkhruhhuft. "Well. Where are we?"

She said, "This place was called Kmárhh, a long, long time ago."

We started walking again, one of the other Kkhruhhuft leading the way, Shrêhht and I merely following. "How long ago?"

She said, "We think it was built around forty thousand years ago. No one really remembers."

As we walked, a haze of dust began rising around us, as if no one had walked here in all that time. Forty thousand years? Then this place had been more than twenty thousand years old when the Sinnott came to conquer Kkhruhhuft at the Masters' behest.

"What was it for?"

"It was the capital of the world."

Was. "And now?"

"Nothing. Darkness and dust. Not many people even remember that it's still here."

"Are there others? Were there?"

"Hundreds. Some collapsed and gone, most still intact. All empty. This is the way Kkhruhhuft lived. Before . . ."

Before all that. Right. But, unlike Shrêhht, unlike any of these Kkhruhhuft, I could *remember*. To me it was more than just some distant dream. "So why did you bring me here?

Just to show me some ancestral ruins? Hardly worth a blind-fold. I wouldn't tell the Masters about your secret museum."

A slight chuffing of Kkhruhhuft amusement. "You're here to make another decision, Athol Morrison."

Another decision . . .

The cavern opened up into an area thousands of meters across, hundreds of meters high, well enough lit that our escort could extinguish their torches, could put them down in a rack obviously made for just such torches and walk forward into the red, flickering light. More buildings here, taller, with steeply sloped sides. More modern buildings, with many small windows, like the office buildings I remembered from the cities of old Earth.

In the middle of this space was a large, open platform, bonfire blazing at its center, filling the cavern with its red-dish yellow light, burning in a huge cup, smelling of cre-osote-soaked wood. Gathered 'round it . . .

All right, you've already guessed what's coming, Athol Morrison. Not a hard thing to guess at all. Now, what do you do about it? Run? Flee into the dark caverns and hope you elude them? Or maybe hope you just die out there, so the decision won't have to be made . . .

People around the altar fire, standing in little hollows maybe made for the priestesses of some eons-dead religion. Hollows perhaps made by those feet, as Kkhruhhuft came to stand in this place for all the long millennia of the ages before the Masters came.

Kkhruhhuft now. And others. Saanaae centaurs standing here and there, firelight glittering off shiny green scales, flat, spatulate teeth throwing odd shadows across their faces. A little black Sinnott spider. A few soldiers from a race I knew was called the Zarret, people who looked like blue snakes with arms, with eyes like faceted glass jewels, eyes full of rainbows. A pair of Sheqarii technicians, standing on either side of a mobile surgical unit, the sort that Spahi units carry with them on extended operations. They can save your life, and have saved mine.

Usually, they don't include the technicians, just the unit, which can be programmed for one species or another.

Who else should I expect to see here? Davy, perhaps, dressed in Lincoln green, standing on his tree limb like some idiot out of an old, old movie. That you, Errol Flynn? Marsh, perhaps, Sandy by his side, risen from the dead. Maybe, if I looked hard, I'd find Alix standing beside me, reaching out to take my hand, eyes shining with happiness and hope.

I turned and looked up at Shrêhht. "Well. What now?"

Tableau. Me, small, frail, merely human. Mighty Kkhruh-huft, playtoy monsters from some Cretaceous nightmare, a little smaller than your average *T. rex*. A good deal more dangerous. Toothy Saanaae, only a little larger than men, scarier-looking than a fairy-tale demon. Soft-eyed Sheqarii, calm in demeanor, little black Sinnott, straight from a child's dream of spiders. A fucking jewel-eyed snake.

Oh, goddamn it.

It's always been called the Mercenaries Plan, she said. Always. Sinnott brought it to us, as we brought it to the Saanaae and Zarret, as the old Raighn warriors, long dead, brought it to the Sinnott. As we are bringing it now to you.

There are a million sentient species in this galaxy. A few hundred suited to the task of soldier, to the difficult role of policeman. And a dozen species across all the millennia whom we felt we could trust.

I stood, staring upward into her so-nonhuman face, all fangs and scales and featureless eyes, full of regret. Just now, I could see the expression on Marsh's face as he sensed the gun at his head, as he heard that little click the trigger makes when it's pulled, metal sliding on metal, a faint *snick* as the spring compresses and the firing pin comes out of its dock. I wonder if he heard the sharp *whack* of steel on brass, the hiss of burning primer. Maybe the bang even got to his ears before the bullet shattered his mind.

A last moment of startled awareness: *So damned loud* . . . Maybe the last thing he felt was that stabbing pain in his ears. Then nothing. I hope.

I said, "So it means nothing to you that Yllir Waӱӱ failed. Failed so utterly. That your own kind will come and erase your whole lineage." No response. "Nothing that I sent my friends to their deaths?"

She said, "Yllir Waÿÿ failed so utterly, so easily, because these Saanaae saw to it . . ." A gesture to our centaur comrades. "Just as you saw to the suppression of a clumsy plot among the Sirkar Native Police on Earth."

How does the phrase go? Best done quickly. And the Saanaae had taken a lot more damage than just the destruction of my few old friends.

"Then what do you think you'll accomplish by this . . . Plan?"

She said, "One day, they will make a mistake, Athol Morrison. When that day comes, it behooves us to be ready."

"And how long have you been waiting for them to make that mistake? How long have you been ready?"

She said, "No one knows, anymore. No one remembers. A hundred thousand years? Maybe more."

"How much longer do you plan to wait?"

The Sinnot's voice was thin and raspy in the still, dry air, but real, surprising me with clumsily formed English syllables: "We have forever, if need be."

Forever?

"Why me? Why now?"

"Why you, Athol Morrison? Because you honor your duty, though you do not love the Master Race. Because you killed your friends to save your people from destruction, though it would've been so much easier simply to stand aside. As for *why now* . . ."

She reached to the edge of the altar and picked up something, a little black box, handed it to me. It was one of the wrist weapons, little black boxes the size of a pack of cards that could slice the top from a mountain, go on to slice off a thousand mountains more. We'd turned them all back in at the end of the Xú conflict. Every last weapon accounted for in the Master Race files.

One of the Sheqarii standing next to the surgical unit said, "We brought it with us when we came. It's why we're on Kkhruhhuft. This is not something you could transmit over the Masters' Net."

I turned it over in my hands, feeling the soft, almost undetectable vibration of the dark, warm, metallic surface. With this, I could kill them all, could open Kmárhh to the sky. "Where did it come from?"

The Sheqar said, "They were transshipped through the main armory on Hanta Sheqari, headed for Earth. Millions of them. Enough to equip the entirety of the Spahi mercenaries."

"Why?"

The Sheqar said, "No one knows why, Athol Morrison."

Shrêhht said, "Because they are afraid. Because they think we can protect them."

Thin, white anger. "*Afraid?* How can a Master be afraid? They aren't even . . . *real.* You know that. Poppits can be afraid, maybe. Not the Master Race."

She gestured at the weapon. "Maybe so," she said. "But they are arming us all now. It never happened before."

"And you think this is their 'big mistake'?" Not much of a fatal error. No matter how well armed we were, no matter how widely scattered, they had the ships, the FTL communications net. We really had nothing.

She said, "No, such a rebellion would be useless. They'd come and bomb our worlds away to magma, and we would be gone."

"What, then?"

"They think we can protect them. They think we will. That is a mistake."

Maybe so. All we protect is ourselves. Our friends. I suppressed the faces of Davy and Alix, threatening to come up out of the darkness where I'd left them. But I could still feel Alix's body clench under my hand as she watched Marsh die.

"What do you want me to do?"

"Join us. Join in the waiting. Find more humans, one here, another there, people we can trust. People who will wait with us. When the moment comes, we'll know."

"And if it never comes?"

A faint hiss of Kkhruhhuft laughter. "We won't know that until all of forever has passed us by."

Right. "And if I consent?"

The Sheqar by the surgical unit held up a tiny silvery button, something no larger than a watermelon seed. "This is a deactivated net node. Direct access to Master Race realtime communication services. It's what they use to talk to each other. We can put it in your brain, and you can be trained to use it through some simple biofeedback training. The bandwidth is very narrow. You modulate your brain waves to send messages in a simple code we've devised."

"What good will that do? Master Race controls the Net."

"If they turn the Net off, they're in the dark as well. If they leave it on, our communications net is open."

"It won't take them long to find a way around that."

"But it won't be instantaneous, Athol Morrison. There will be a window of opportunity."

"When," Shrêhht said, "the time comes."

When. If. Little words with which to cover the face of eternity.

I said, "I need to think about this."

Shrêhht said, "Think, then."

Walking alone along the rim of the darkdemons' canyon, listening to the wind, watching the stars tilt slowly overhead, sparse one way, so very dense the other. Head full of images.

That little being attacking me in some dingy alleyway. Screaming and hissing as I ripped off his arms. Why? I can't even remember. It wasn't on a war world, merely one where a garrison lived, a seedy place where the natives, long downtrodden, saw to our whims. Maybe I cheated him at cards, who knows? All he did was die.

Alix's eyes on me, the day I went away. That final morning. Not really seeing me anymore. Inward turning, full of some secret knowledge. Hani looking down at my hand, as we said good-bye at the spaceport. Looking down at my hand, then turning away. Images so simple and desultory I knew they were hardly worth remembering. But I remember them anyway.

Remember them, perhaps, because I cannot forget. Or maybe because I don't want to. Happy memories of Hani displaced by happy memories of Sarah. Neither of them able to push those memories of Alix aside. Alix insufficient to suppress the memory of my one short night with little Wu Chingda. Herself no more than a cover to slide over the memory of Solange Corday.

So I think about these hollow memories, and avoid thinking about the real issue. Burdars and natives just so much meat, there to be eaten, or wasted and thrown away.

Damn it, take out your communicator and place the call. What are you waiting for? Dial the phone. It won't take long. Kkhruhhuft police will come and take them away. People will be tortured. Names named. Just place the call. Then go get Sarah and go home. Home to a warm Spahi crib on a nice garrison world. Fuck her until you wear her out. There'll be another one ready to take her place. Fuck her, and the next and the next, and get drunk with your friends and do your duty until the day you die.

It's as simple as that.

I took the wrist weapon from my pocket and held it tightly in my hand. Warm. Vibrating softly. You could strap it on, dial a command link through the phone, fire it down into the valley and watch the darkdemons, if there are any left, watch the darkdemons burn.

That'd bring them down on you right enough. Shoot the gun. Let it make the decision for you. I put it back in my pocket and walked on.

And, still later, with Sarah brought to the darkdemons' rim, awakened from a sound sleep, bleary-eyed, confused, unprotesting, standing with me under the stars. Dawn would come in just a little while, lighting the edge of the sky with a rime of salmon pink, washing the stars away, flooding the world with light, letting us see down into the valley. But not yet.

I stripped her naked, hardly able to see her before me, dark woman silhouetted against a dark night, stars overhead hardly lighting us. Kissed her. Felt her respond, as she always did. You are so very good at your job, Sarah Morgan. Little Sarah, who is still only seventeen years old.

Put her up on a flat rock at the edge of the valley, on her hands and knees, facing away from me, well braced, legs apart. Took off my own clothing and stood behind her, fumbled between her legs, put myself in. Nothing from Sarah. A little intake of breath, muscles clenching, back arching as she held herself still for me. Letting me do what I wanted.

Stars above us, glittering now, splendid, shining.

Sarah whispered, "Look . . ."

Stars moving above us, green and gold and red and pale, pale blue, growing brighter, brighter still, forming patterns, swirls, galaxies of living light.

I stopped what I was doing then, disengaged, and listened to the joy in her voice, the wonder. Sat down beside her on the warm stone and watched the glory of the darkdemons' return. At some point I put my arm around her warm shoulders and felt myself decide.

Back in the cavern, lying against the cold plastic of the portable surgical unit, letting the Sheqarii technicians strap me in, watching one of them hand the little transceiver to one of the machine's many small black hands. Shrêhht and her friends were just so many shadows filling up the background.

Why?

You ask *me* why, Shrêhht?

Because I can send only so many friends off to die.

Because, no matter how much I want to, I can't quite become that famous man without a soul.

And so, I give my word. Word that I will wait with you, until forever passes us by.

The Sheqarii backed out of the way, watching, watching, and a hundred robot arms, a thousand small eyes with glittering lenses, closed in on my face. Hiss of anesthetic spray. Flicker of light as the laser laid open my scalp and cauterized my capillaries. Soft burr as a little vibrating blade of diamond cut through my skull. Soft, gentle sucking noise as a bit of bone was lifted out and carried away. Colored lights flashing behind my eyes as little spatulas pushed my brain tissues aside. An odd sort of discomfort as the hand went in, carrying its little seed.

Snicker-snack. The crackle-hiss of organic welders.

Then they were putting my head back together, gluing down the bone, closing my scalp, melting the skin seamlessly into place, delicate little black hands combing my hair over a livid line that would fade to white, then nothing, in a matter of days.

Done.

Shrêhht said, "Welcome home, Athol Morrison."

Home? Me? No such place.

But I'd given my word. Which is all that matters.

20 AT THE TURN OF THE CENTURY, EIGHT years after the last time I'd come home, in the lovely month of May, it was springtime in New York City, Sarah and I standing together at the edge of the rooftop garden of the Spahi headquarters tower, looking down on the world. Central Park was lovely and green, the little pond at the southern boundary reflecting a faultless blue sky, sunlight streaming down from a late-morning sun, warm, not yet hot. Distant thunder faded as we looked eastward to the cosmodrome, watched the lighter that'd brought us here only yesterday climb back up into the heavens, brilliant violet fire blending into the sky as it arced out over the broad, green Atlantic.

Sarah turned toward me, standing close, pressing against me, reaching up to touch the stiff cloth of my tunic's collar, buff the silver metal of my rissaldar's double-star insignia with her thumb, yellowish eyes shining in the sunlight, looking into mine. The night before, making love up here under Earth's uncannily familiar stars, had been splendid, Sarah grinding against me, all passion and no reserve, until we were both exhausted, until we slept in each other's arms.

My pretty little girl of seventeen become a delightful woman of twenty-three, handsome, in the prime of her youth.

She stayed, while Janice and Mira finished their contracts, went on home, becoming fast friends with Fyodor and Margie, the four of us very much at home together, making herself so much mine that, in the end, I hired no other burdars, let her serve out her contract as my only one.

And now?

She pressed herself against me, laid her head against my chest, tipped it back, and looked up at me again, and said, "I want you to know, Athy, that I've enjoyed every second of all the years I spent with you. Everything. All the wonderful places you've taken me. All the nights we've spent together."

Looking back, a final reckoning. In all those nights I may have made love to her three thousand times. What do such numbers mean? Nothing. A man's way of counting coup against the darkness. I thought of Hani's leave-taking, for just a moment.

I said, "There's really nothing to stop you from changing your mind and renewing your contract, you know that. Go home and visit your family. Come back in a few weeks and leave with me again. There are . . . places you haven't seen yet."

Faraway look. A sense that she might be holding her breath. Wry smile. "I do wish, sometimes . . ." Then a slow shake of her head. "Our contracts aren't paid off until we complete them. You know that. My parents, my brothers and sisters, their children . . . all squatting in the ruins, living off the forest. Waiting for me to come home and save them."

"The rules are changing. Maybe . . ."

She put her small hand over my mouth, delicate fingers sealing my lips. "They've been waiting for a long time. I have to go."

A decision made. Regrets and yearning put aside. I said, "What will you do?"

That faraway look again. "I had a boyfriend before I . . . left. His name was Marty. They tell me he's been waiting, all these years, for me to come home."

Waiting? What could it mean to wait alone, lying in cold darkness, night after long, hard night, while the woman you loved voyaged out to the stars and lay beneath some hulking soldier's body? Not something I wanted to imagine.

She kissed me lightly on the lips, and said, "When you come home again, drop by and visit me. I'm sure my family would like to meet you."

I could imagine. Dark, scowling people, men and women knowing what I'd put their little Sarah through, just so they could live in the faux-freedom of relative wealth. "I'm sure your husband won't like that."

She smiled. "Marty? He won't say a word. No one will. The money is mine, after all . . ."

Slight shock of recognition. Little Sarah. Pretty little Sarah. Soldier of the Master Race.

She put her hand to her throat, undid the little brooch of green jade and silver that held her collar shut, began unbuttoning her blouse. "Make love to me one last time, Athy. It'll be lovely up here in the sunlight . . ."

A day passed, and another, then Lank and I were walking through the cool, damp woods between Chapel Hill and Carrboro. A difficult homecoming, this time. Lank still smiling, of course, hugging me when I got off the train in Durham, wearing his rector's cassock, telling me, during the long ride home, about all the things that had happened.

Politics for himself, standard for the Church. Of how he'd risen to head the Chapel Hill parish, of how thick he was with the bishop . . . Who knows? The archbishop of North Carolina's eighty-four now, Athy. When he goes, Bergmann will take over the archdiocese, and . . .

And of course you know Chief Catalano is dead? A group of his senior troopers just got him out of bed one night about a year ago, marched him off into the woods, and shot him. Sirkar hasn't done a thing. Bastard got what was coming to him . . .

I'll take you by Mother's grave tomorrow. We buried her up on top of Mount Bolus, on the hill behind the monastery, where she gets a good view of . . . everything, I guess. Dad hasn't been the same since she killed herself. Spends a lot of his time down at Davys . . .

Oddny? Well, not around anymore. I tried to get hold of her, tell her you were coming home, but . . . She's tied up with some people calling themselves the Mountain Folk. Living on up in West Virginia somewhere, well away from any bustee clusters. I guess no one's going after them, so they can sort of pretend . . .

Anyway, she has a little boy now, I hear. Named him Marshall.

As the sun went down and the sky turned indigo, we rounded the fallen remains of Carr Mill Mall, paused by the little stairwell leading down to the door, the still-functional neon sign that said, DAVYS, listening to the remote thud of the diesel generator.

Lank said, "You're sure you want to go in?" He gestured at my uniform.

Inside the club, I could hear a combo playing, three pieces, I thought, a twelve-string guitar, drums, thudding acoustic base. Playing a song I'd heard even out among the stars, a pleasant little ballad called "Poppit Love."

I said, "Sure." He shrugged, looked away for a moment, then we went in.

First image that of my father, old man sitting down at one end of the bar, glassy-eyed, unlabeled bottle of whiskey-colored liquor on the bar at his elbow, drinking from a juice glass filled with same. Turning to look at us. Then looking away. Tipping the glass to his lips, swallowing. No reason for a man to be so pathetic, to build up that lost-soul image. We love our little roles, no matter how stupid.

Davy standing behind the bar, rag in hand, just looking at us. A much older Davy, bald now on the top of his head, long black hair streaked with gray. Lines of his face deepening, foreshadowing the Davy of old age. Mousy little Asian woman standing in the background, his wife, hard anger on her face.

We stood at the other end of the bar, and Davy came to us. Stood there, exhaustion like pain in his eyes. "Hello, Athy. Welcome home."

I nodded, sitting on a bar stool. "Hello, Davy." A difficult silence, then I said, "Did you understand why it had to happen?"

He held up his right hand, index and middle fingers gone about halfway up, tip of his thumb no more than a knot of white scar tissue. He took a bottle from under the bar, this one rather old, with a familiar, faded red label, took out two glasses, poured two drinks, pushed one in front of me. "Understand? Hell, maybe I did." He lifted his glass. "*Wæs hael,* old friend."

His forgiveness was harder to take than hatred would have been.

A little later in the evening, I walked alone, northward along what was left of Greensboro Street. Grass and weeds had broken up the old pavement and saplings were starting to rise here and there. It'd been close to forty years since anyone'd repaired this road. Nature would finish it off soon.

Lank told me they'd be gathering up Carrboro's people soon, within the year, moving them to the Chapel Hill bustee, or shipping them off to the new agricultural colonies down in the Louisiana bayou country. And that would be that. Buildings would fall and decay, trees grow up around them, rain soaking the old wood, bits of glass and cement disappearing in the leaf mold.

In a thousand years, there'd still be signs people had once lived here, but tenuous signs, archeologists' spoor. Overhead, the stars were laid out in full battle array, the moon a thin sliver down by the horizon, hardly lighting the world. Quiet now, no whisper of wind, my footfalls loud in the darkness. Murmur of faint voices, dark shadows ahead, a small gathering of men, lurking in a grove of old trees, ornamental trees on what had once been a well-off citizen's front lawn.

I could feel them eyeing me, or thought I could, remembering those dark shadows of yesterday, remembering the men I'd left lying on this same road, while Alix stood by silently and watched. The last footfalls I'd heard here had been the lone survivor running away. Maybe he was here now, standing among the trees, watching me. The whispers stopped, but all they did was watch.

Alix's house, finally. Almost dark, looking, even in the gloom, all the more dilapidated, shadows of peeling paint visible here and there. The top of the chimney broken off, jagged stump outlined against the stars. There was dim light from the living room window, spilling around a pattern of jagged, taped lines. Brighter light from the back of the house, softly illuminating the trees.

So what do you do now, Rissaldar Athol Morrison, commander of sixteen thousand, of the third brigade, seventh division, of Legion IX *Victorious*? Go ahead and knock, see who comes to the door? Or just stand here for a little while, fiddling with your memories, then go away forever. She knows you've come back. Lank said so. Maybe she's waiting for you. Or maybe not. Lank wouldn't say, just, "Your decision, Athy. You do what you think you have to . . ."

I rapped softly on the door.

There was a long silence, more than a minute in which I made and rejected the decision to turn around and go several times. Then the door's latches snapped and the dead bolt slid back. When it opened, I was looking at the height of a tall woman's face. Expecting *her* certainly . . .

A small, thin girl, prepubescent, straight black hair tied in a ponytail, broad face with high cheekbones, wide brown eyes curious, dressed in a boy's T-shirt that hung down over bare thighs. Eight years old? Maybe a little younger.

The girl looked over her shoulder. "Mom?"

Alix stood in the shadows by the far wall, cradling a heavy shotgun, ten-gauge I thought, the sort of thing you'd use, loaded with dumdum, to shoot a big deer. Aimed at my chest. The barrel wavered and fell, and, voice nearly inaudible, she said, "Oh, God. You look just the same."

Inside the bright, warm kitchen, there were dishes on the old oak table, the remains of a finished-off supper, smell of fried chicken in the air, pots and pans on a woodstove cobbled together from sheet metal and some parts of an old electric unit. Smell of smoke. Cups of steaming red tea on the table, bowls of what looked like rice pudding.

Alix gestured, "Would you like some?"

"Some tea, please."

She poured it while I sat, put the cup in front of me and offered a bowl of raw sugar, pale brown and granular. "We used the last of the milk in our desserts, I'm afraid . . ."

The little girl came and sat in her chair, took a sip of her tea, saying nothing, staring at me, still wide-eyed. Looking as if she were waiting for me to say something important. All right. You know what's happening here.

Alix stood behind her chair, watching me spoon sugar into my tea, five full, gluttonous teaspoons. A little thicker in the waist, her own long, curly hair tied up with a headband. Bits of silver hiding among the curls. Crow's-feet at the corners of her eyes. Deep lines around her mouth. A suggestion of jowls. Alexandra Moreno, still handsome at fifty.

She said, "I was hoping you'd stop by. This is my daughter, Kaye."

I smiled at the little girl and said, "Hello, Kaye. My name's Athy."

She glanced up at her mother, still holding that deep, unanswered question, found, I suppose, silencing pain in Alix's eyes. Then she grinned at me, and said, "That sounds like a girl's name."

I laughed. "Sure does! I got into a number of fights over it when I was your age. How old are you, Kaye? Eight? Nine, maybe? You're a big girl."

She glanced at her mother, then said, "I'm only seven."

"Her birthday," said Alix, "was just two weeks ago . . ."

So. Eight years. Minus nine months. Minus two weeks. It's May now. And, of course, it was late August then . . .

An hour and more went by, while we sat and talked aimlessly about nothing. I coaxed the little girl into my lap and beguiled her with stories about life on other planets. Told her some things that sounded very much like storybook adventures, about the time I and my squad got thoroughly lost in a scarlet jungle on a planet we called Krypton, tall, golden mountains shining above the trees.

Alix sat back and listened, face somehow troubled, not quite sad in the steady, slightly glary light of the kerosene lamp, reaching out to adjust the vapor feed when the mantle began to hiss and whine. Time for bed, she said. Kaye looking at her face, looking for cues. What to say. What to do.

We walked to a little bedroom, full of lacy little girl things, toys and dolls and tattered-looking old paper books. Alix undressed her in front of me, little girl unselfconsciously naked, continuing to chatter away about this and that while her mother pulled a thin linen nightie down over her head, lay down on her bed and let the sheets be tucked up to her chin.

She had a healthy child's body, muscles about as well defined as a child's can be. Hips slim, bones sturdy-looking, as if they'd be hard to break. I remembered the way she'd felt sitting on my lap, and thought about some of the Spahis I'd known, people who were good soldiers and interesting friends. Burdarage has trouble providing for people like that, but sometimes it's done. That little girl they gave to Mickey Frangellico looked a little bit like Kaye. I'd gotten used to seeing her at his crib, seldom dressed in much more than a pair of thin cotton briefs. Gotten used to seeing the hollow, aching depths of that little girl's eyes.

Then, back in the living room, Alix and I were alone, facing each other, our only light the dim glow that spilled through the kitchen door, the wan light of a crescent moon outside, about ready to set over the trees.

She said, "I'm awfully glad you came, Athy." Eyes searching mine. "I've done nothing but think about you, these past eight years . . ."

I had the decency then, to feel just a moment of stark, disbelieving horror.

Darkness, the moon gone down, lamps extinguished. Bedroom curtains drawn apart, window thrown open so a gentle night breeze, cool, not cold, could wash in, slide across soft, naked skin. Alix lying beside me, handling me, lying on her side, one leg straight beside mine, the other drawn up, opening herself to me, opening herself for my hand.

Holding me close, whispering into my neck, warm breath, meaningless murmurs, breasts rubbing against my chest, far softer than they'd been even eight years ago. Her hands on my abdomen, marveling at all the still-youthful solidity she found there.

"I've known men of thirty," she said, "who felt older than you."

Image of that old nightmare army, all of Alix's temporary husbands, stopping by her bed one by one, easing her on her way to the grave. How much longer? Ten years? Twenty? Thirty, at most. In thirty years I wouldn't seem so young anymore; there are limits to what good habits and costly medical technology can do. But I'd still have a long time to go. A long road before old age would look back at me out of the morning mirror. By then, every childhood friend I ever had would be long dead. All the young burdars grown old.

Everyone gone but my dear, beloved soldiers. I thought, briefly, about Rissaldar-Minor Wu Chingda, about my brigadier-adjutant, Jemadar-Major Kathy Lee Mendoza, saw their faces floating in the half-light of imagination. They would still be with me, when all the others had gone. Or would be, if they survived. I thought about Solange Corday.

Thought about her, while I made love to whatever was left of Alix Moreno. Turned myself facedown upon her and tasted familiar flesh, felt familiar tissues swell under my tongue. Still that left of you, at any rate. Still that same bright shiver of pleasure, the same whispered words of simple happiness I'd first heard thirty-five years and more ago, making love to a fresh and lovely young girl in the woods behind Chapel Hill High.

When it was over, we lay in one another's arms, looking out at the stars together, and Alix said, "How do you like your daughter, Athy?"

"She seems like a lovely little girl."

A slow nod. "We've been . . . happy together. I wish you could've come home sooner. She knows who you are."

I remembered Alix standing by the lamp at the beginning of our last night together, eight years ago, holding wet fingers up to the light, examining the texture of her vaginal mucus. "Why didn't you tell me?"

A shrug. "You were already long gone before I knew for sure."

"You could've sent me a message. My father could've called the Spahis for you."

"Your father and mother blamed me for what happened, once again."

"Lank would have done it for you."

A slow nod. "Yes. And he offered many times. Urged me to . . . let you know."

"Then why not?"

"What good would that have done? What would *you* have done?"

A long silence, while Alix ran her hand over the smooth, furry musculature of my chest, ran her hand down along my thigh, grappled among the nearly shapeless hanging masses of my genitals. It was a question without a good answer. What *would* I have done? I said, "I would have come back to visit you and . . . see her. I could have sent you the wherewithal to live better than . . . this." An aimless gesture at the dark room.

"We've lived well enough. Lank saw to that."

"I'll . . . thank him."

"You don't need to."

A sharp memory of our parting moment, on the train station in Durham. Lank telling me that bit about compassion being his stock-in-trade. All right. But I'll thank him anyway.

She said, "Make love to me again, Athy. This old woman will want some new memories to replay, something to treasure on certain empty nights, when you've gone away again." She took my hand and guided it back between her legs.

Morning sunlight warm on my face, that same smooth breeze cool on my exposed flank. Alix's weight resting against me, a warm, damp mass heating my side, heartbeat a faintly noticeable flexing beneath her flesh. Arm around me, one knee up, weight of her leg resting on my thigh. Slow breathing, the breathing of sleep.

I opened my eyes slowly, expecting to see the sky. Looked into Kaye's eyes, not far away. She was sitting on the foot of the bed, below her mother's rump, behind her legs, still dressed in her wrinkled linen nightie, looking at us.

She leaned forward, resting her elbows on Alix's bare hip, dropping her chin into a cupped palm. Twinkle in child's eyes. Hint of a cherubic smile. "Well," she said. "Good morning, sleepyhead. I thought you'd never wake up. I'm starving. But I waited for you . . ."

Unfamiliar tautness in my chest. Waiting. Waiting for what? Maybe waiting for her to call me *Daddy*? Nonsense. Just something I once saw in an old video. Or maybe something from a children's book I'd once read. All right. Hadn't Kaye read those same books by now?

Maybe not. Maybe she'd gone to a different sort of school. This was a mighty unconcerned child, finding her mother in a position like this. Unlikely that it hadn't happened before. Seven years? Hundreds of times, at least.

She reached across her sleeping mother and grabbed my hand, lifting it off Alix's ribs. "Come on," she said. "You can make us all oatmeal."

"Oatmeal. Um. There isn't any milk."

She grinned. "Don't be such a sissy."

I sat up then, slowly, carefully, watching Kaye watch me as I stretched. Saw her looking at all the heavy muscles and thick, ridged white scars. I looked down at Alix, face relaxed against her pillow, eyes closed, mouth open, breathing so slowly and evenly.

Kaye said, "Come on. We'll let her sleep until the oatmeal is ready."

A breakfast of milkless oatmeal then, loaded with brown sugar until it looked like a mass of half-molten cookie dough, Alix stumbling into the kitchen just as we dished it out into three bowls, just as the tea water began to boil, the kettle coughing unsteadily just before it whistled. Alix, wrapped in a faded, flowery, somewhat tattered-looking old housecoat, hair disheveled. Kaye grinning at her as she spooned out dollops of brown goo.

Alix standing there, looking at us, daughter in nightgown,

making oatmeal with some hide-torn, underwear-clad old hulk.

And later, Alix and I standing together in her shower, sun-warmed water from a rooftop cistern sluicing over us, wrapped in one another's arms. Alix pulling my face down for yet another kiss. Me remembering how Kaye had badgered to join us in the shower. Innocence? Children are seldom innocent.

Kaye watching from the doorway while Alix and I got dressed in her room. My uniform seemed inappropriate now, tight, stiff, constricting. Alix fingered the collar, looking at the two bright stars. "What did you have before? Three connected little diamonds?"

"I was a jemadar-major, then. This is for a rissaldar."

"I don't know what that means."

Kaye said, "I do, Mommy. A jemadar-major commands a regiment of 1,024 troopers. A rissaldar commands a brigade of 16,384 troopers. He has sixteen jemadars-major under him."

We walked, in the bright morning sunshine, Kaye skipping ahead of us through the woods, following the old trail down past Lincoln Park, muddy path marred with fresh footprints, many of them the barefoot marks of children, a bicycle track or two, through the collapsed ruins of a prefab housing development, crossing Bolin Creek on the trunk of a fallen tree, Kaye dancing lightly, where I walked solidly, where Alix teetered, alarm concealed in her eyes.

The old clay quarry was empty when we walked by it, full of red, muddy water, a few white bones lying off to one side, where tall grass had begun to grow, still green with spring. I tried to remember what it'd been like here before the Invasion, tried to remember walking up here when I was Kaye's age. Nothing. Alix still just a skinny little girl I sometimes saw in the hallway at school, Master Race still nameless, Kkhruhhuft just fangy monsters in a history book, something that had happened when Grandpa was a little boy.

Kaye fished a long bone from the weeds, a man's thick femur by the look of it, started using it to golf round, tan cobbles into the water, rocks sometimes plunking into the mud, sometimes splashing down in the little pond, starting up patterns of intersecting ripples.

The athletic field behind the high school was empty as well. Sunday, I suddenly realized. But the football field was freshly mowed and raked, laid out for soccer perhaps, or field hockey, the baseball diamond freshly chalked. Kaye threw her bone aside and found an old plastic pie plate from somewhere, tossed it at me Frisbee-style, caught it deftly when I threw it back. Stood below her, ready to break her fall, while she climbed a tree to retrieve it from a leafy bough where it'd inadvertently lodged, courtesy of one of my more careless throws.

Once, when I glanced at Alix, leaning by herself against the rusty chain link fence, I thought she looked angry.

Walked them home at lunchtime. Took Alix in my arms and kissed her. Told her I had a little business to conduct, that I'd be back in time for supper. Kaye watching us from the doorway, frowning. Alix looking at her daughter as I turned to go, obviously upset.

Well. They had a history with each other. Things I'd never hear about.

One last time, fiery sunset in the sky as I walked down the muddy streets of the Chapel Hill bustee, headed back toward the remains of Carrboro. My father hadn't come home again, the house dark and empty, Lank nowhere to be found, Church business keeping him busy. I considered taking my suitcase with me to Alix's house, but decided against it, snapping the latches shut and leaving it on the bed in my old room, the room in which I'd never been a child.

Scooped up an armload of autobooks, childhood classics, Tarzan and Mowgli and all the rest, took the package of precious sealed batteries, found a bag in which to carry them and left. Walked along, wondering what she'd think, seeing how some pre-Invasion program-artist visualized those old, dead worlds. *Kreeg-ah.* Grandmother plummeting down the stairs, wheelchair and all. Tentholm and Falconhurst. I still live.

She's the last part of the old dream. The dream in which you stayed and married Alix and lived happily ever after. Kaye the child we'd had after all. The child winnowed from all the uselessly spilled seed. Spilled into burdar after sterile burdar.

Thought about Wu Chingda and those few stolen moments, the two of us huddled together in my cabin on a Master Race starship. They don't sterilize soldiers. Part of the promise made to us. You serve your time, retire when you feel you must. Go home. Raise your family. Not many decide to do it.

I could have decided when I came home before, my twenty-four years' enlistment almost up. I could have signed for another six, maybe twelve then, but decided on the full twenty-four. By the time it was over, I'd have twelve service hashmarks on my sleeve, running all the way from wrist to elbow. Forty-eight years.

How many times would I have made love to Alix in forty-eight years? Fifteen thousand times, maybe? A ridiculous number. What would it have been like, watching Kaye grow from a baby to the little girl she was now? What would it be like, seeing the little girl pass through adolescence to adulthood? Unimaginable.

When I knocked, she greeted me at the door.

A last supper, a final night. Kaye shoved off to bed with difficulty, hanging back, looking at her mother with pleading eyes, Alix looking back with that same hint of anger. A look that said they'd been through whatever it was time and again. Faint memories of my own childhood, of Lank and Oddny battling it out, dragging their feet or rushing on ahead as the case might be, hoping to wear down adult intransigence. Sometimes it worked, more often not.

Alix led me back to the living room, the same room where we'd first rejoined on my last visit, intent on recreating that atmosphere perhaps. She took off her clothes for me then and stood naked, skin very white in the dim moonlight, waiting. Rewarded when I stood and undressed as well.

Last embraces have a painful quality to them, but it soon

fades as the moments proceed. Hands on each other, then mouths. Lying down together on her old couch, sexual excitement waxing, because the animal within will have its way with you, no matter what else is going on.

Once lying on the couch, facing each other, so very traditional, eyes glittering in the darkness, pretending to see. Again, kneeling up, facing the same direction, looking out into the moonlit street, Alix whispering while we made love. Whispering words I simply couldn't hear. A third time lying on the floor, carpet scratchy on our skins, her back, my knees and elbows, very slowly, both of us tiring now.

Then we lay together in the darkness.

I said, "Alix, I have to leave tomorrow. You know that."

She sat up slowly, formless and dim in the shadows, head outlined against the moonlit window, looking down at me where I lay on the floor. "I know," she said. "It'll be all right."

Everything will be all right, as usual. Everything will get back to normal then. I with my burdars, she with her succession of . . . lovers, I guess. I said, "I'd like you to come with me, Alix. You and Kaye both."

Silence. Alix still sitting motionless, eyes invisible in the darkness. But I could feel them on me nonetheless.

She said, "How? As your burdar?" Word spit out bitterly. As what? I heard. As your whore?

I said, "That's really the only way it can be done. Active-duty Spahis are not allowed to marry. You know that."

More silence, then she said, "That's what they say." Pause. The sound of her breathing quite audible. Anger, perhaps, palpable. "And what about Kaye? Will she be your burdar too? Would you start screwing her when she gets old enough? Or merely rent her out to your friends?"

Jesus. I got up, walked over to the cracked windowpane and stood looking out into the moonlight. "Don't be . . ." Um. No reason to call her names. I said, "There're other sorts of burdar, you know. I've told you about Fyodor and Margie."

I could feel her standing behind me now, tension filling the room, displacing the last bits of dying passion. "Is that what you want? Me for a whore and Kaye for a servant? What will she do, Athy? Wash the dishes? Polish your boots maybe? God damn you."

Just for a moment, I wanted to turn around and slap her. Useless. Not the sort of person I'd ever been. But, just maybe, a hint of what I might have become, had I stayed home, had I married Alix and stayed to raise a family with her. Momentary glimpse, then, of a bitter and sullen old man, married to a woman full of hatred and contempt.

By now my belly would be slack, my muscles soft, my hair full of gray. The alternate track to my dream of eternal bliss.

I said, "Things are changing out there, Alix. The old ways are going fast. The Spahi organization feels that the pool of new recruits has about run dry. We've begun to establish schools to train young children, take them as young as seven and give them a head start, so they'll be ready for us when the time comes. They're called Spartaki."

Silence. Then a whisper. "And you think Kaye could qualify for such a school."

I shrugged. "I'll be promoted to rissaldar-major soon. They'll bend the rules for me, at least enough for that . . ."

And, voice low, full of rage, she said, "Fuck you, Athol Morrison. I don't need you. My daughter doesn't need you. Go away now. Don't ever come back."

I felt a startled pang, deep in my chest. Go away? Now? I turned around and said, "Alix . . ."

"Get out, God damn you!"

I found my clothes in the darkness, put them on, walked from the room, and went out into the night, closing the door gently behind me, latch clicking home, blotting out the sound of her weeping.

As I walked away, I looked back and saw Kaye's little white face watching me out her bedroom window. I stopped for a moment, looking back. Waved. Saw her hand wave in return. Then I walked on.

Another bright and sunshiny day, North Carolina forests flush with late springtime, spring green turning to the rich, darker green of early summer, Lank bringing me back to the Durham train station one more time, dropping me off this time, not waiting around to see me go. It'd been a long, quiet ride over, Lank only asking, toward the end, when I'd be home again. Me telling him, truthfully, that I didn't know.

Home? No longer.This may have been the sun for which my eyes were made, but there were other suns I loved more dearly. A hundred million suns. Maybe the truth would have been, "never."

I stood on the platform with a few other travelers, listening to the rail hum softly, heralding a soon-to-arrive train. A small group of cloaked humans huddled together in one corner. A naked man in a collar, on a leash, leash held by a tall, slender, imperious-looking woman in a Sirkar uniform. A couple of Saanaae in body-sweaters and white shoulder-shawls, wearing the brooches of their interstellar police organization. Another young Saanaa, minding a basket full of squirming poppits. Something that looked like a dog with a gun slung around its neck on a leather strap, little arms with hands where its ears should have been. A pair of fat, green-eyed froggy-looking things, Masters' sigils stenciled on their skin.

Maybe I'd make it to the beach one last time before shipping out, see if I could find any Kkhruhhuft I knew at Cape Cod. Hell, maybe I could even stop by and see Sarah's new home.

"Athy."

A woman's voice, pitched low.

I didn't want to turn around. Too many things in my heart. Too many doors already closed, me not wanting them opened again. I turned around anyway.

An ugliness of pain. Even uglier hope.

Alix was standing there, dressed in familiar jeans, a familiar leather jacket. Holding a small cloth valise in one hand, holding Kaye's hand in the other. Face hard and flat, expressionless, controlled.

In Kaye's eyes there was only joy.

I found I could hardly whisper. "So. You decided to come after all . . ."

She took one step forward and handed me the valise. Dropped Kaye's hand and turned, turned and started walking away.

"Alix?"

She reached the top of the stairway and paused, one hand on the railing, not looking back.

"*Alix.*"

I heard her voice, hardly audible. "Not like me," she said. "Not at all . . ." A subtle gladness in her whisper? Impossible for me to know.

She clattered downward, booted feet rapid and sharp on the risers, going away, going out of sight. In a moment I heard the sound of a car rolling away over gravel. Lank's old car, perhaps. Then I felt Kaye's hand, small and warm in my own and looked down at her.

She said, "Is that our train I hear coming?"

Epilogue

THERE ARE PLANETS THAT MERIT THE name Paradise. Sêret-Anh, where we'd headquartered the Third Army of the Spahi mercenaries, was one such. Blue-on-blue sky, infinitely deep overhead. Mountains and soft forests and waterfalls, deserts and seas, rainbows after storms, fluffy white snow falling over wintry lands, summer a delicate hand on your brow.

I sat by the remains of the little picnic Margie'd wrought, my back on a sun-warmed stone surface, looking out across a little bowl of a valley, tumbled stones over which a stream fell in many small cascades, tinkling down to a clear, cold pool.

Helga standing on a rock by the water, hair so blond it looked almost white, sunlight shining on her skin as she tossed back that thick mane of pale, wild hair. Eyes so blue you could make them out at any distance, whenever they were open. Arching her back, solid breasts rising, her voice a faraway murmur. Miriam sitting on the rock beside her, trailing her feet in the water, stirring the pool with her toes, skin so black she looked like a shadow. Matter and antimatter.

Fyodor came down the hill, boots crunching on loose rock, skidding every now and again, and sat himself down on my boulder with a sigh. Sweat beading on his face, darkening his gray hair with a bit of dampness. He said, "They make a pretty picture."

"They do." They made a prettier one in my bed, posing for me, both of them just twenty years old, new to burdarage and my service. Each willing to sit by quietly and watch while I used the other, or lend a hand, if need be.

"I think Margie likes them. They talk to her, at any rate. They've been playing bingo together, Sunday afternoons at the burdar guildhall . . ."

Miriam slid into the pool, splashed water back at Helga, who laughed, jumped in with a solid thud, grabbed her playmate, and started trying to hold her under, the two of them thrashing the water to froth. I said, "Ever think you might like to go home, old sod? You and Margie together?"

Silence. They shared a bedroom now, had done so ever since Kaye pointed out it might be a nice thing for me to let them do. I think she was maybe nine years old then, back for a summer's furlough from her second year at Spartaki. Well. Kaye had her own burdar now, a nice, quiet young man name Heinzie who cooked her meals and cleaned her crib and, presumably, served in her bed.

Fyodor said, "What for? We like being here with you. Going all over the galaxy, seeing all the worlds, all the different kinds of people. Besides, if we'd gone home, we'd be old now . . ."

I looked up at him. Face full of lines, skin dark and leathery. But still strong, still healthy, that strength and health just one more gift of the Master Race. "How old are you now? I forget."

"I'm eighty-five. Back home I'd be all done." A critical look. "You don't look so bad yourself for an old soldier of sixty-seven."

No. Not so bad, old soldier who can still use the services of two twenty-year-old women. Fyodor saw me looking at them and laughed.

He said, "Will the havildar be coming home soon? Margie misses our little Kaye."

Our little Kaye. Like we really were some kind of family.

"She's due in at the spaceport tomorrow. We'll have a nice dinner together."

A pleased nod. "I'll tell Margie. She'll want to do something special."

Footsteps on the rocky path, a young woman in Spahi fatigue kit picking her way down among the boulders, looking toward where Helga and Miriam were playing. Maybe the sort of woman who'd want them for herself. Or maybe just curious about the Old Man's burdarage.

She stopped in front of me, saluted, sunlight glinting off the havildar-minor's single chevron-pin on her collar. "Begging the subadar's pardon."

I said, "Where'd you learn to talk like that, soldier?"

I could see a flicker of exasperation in her eyes, a moment of frustration with the Old Man's unmilitary ways. They teach them that in Spartaki school, of course. She said, "Sir, Tahsildar MacMillan requests you come to BHQ-comm right away. There's a message for you."

A moment of cold unease. Message. Kaye? No. They wouldn't send a staffer for me, no matter how important a personal message. They knew I wouldn't approve. I sighed and stood, stretching. "All right, Havildar-Minor. Let me put my pants on and you can lead the way." She'd have a staff car back up the hill, parked among the trees. I turned to Fyodor. "Finish the picnic. If I don't come back by sundown, just go on home without me."

He nodded, used to this sort of thing. A subadar in charge of two million troopers can't get through an entire day without something coming up. I followed my young soldier up the hill.

Evening, only a little more than twenty hours later, dull orange sunlight slanting down through the window to pool on my bedroom floor as another one of Sêret-Anh's short, lovely days drew to a close. Miriam curled up in the bed, already asleep, black hair like a dense, dark nebula against the white of her pillow. I could hear the water running in the bathroom, tub filling, Helga's voice soft, humming to herself.

Well. In a little while Margie would be calling us to dinner. I should probably awaken Miriam, the two of us join Helga in the bath, get cleaned up again. Or maybe not, she looked so peaceful sleeping there.

The door opened, native-made wooden hinges creaking slightly, Kaye coming in, sitting down on one corner of the bed, looking at Miriam. "That's what I feel like," she said.

She was a handsome, strapping young woman, tall, sleekly muscular, reddish brown hair cropped short, the way Wu Chingda had always worn hers. Not much of Alix in her. Not much at all. I said, "You young people really ought to have more energy. Too much clean living I guess."

She drew her legs up onto the bed, hugged her knees to her chest. "I'll be going home right after dinner. I want to spend a little time with Heinzie before we ship out."

I nodded. Bad luck to be gone for months, then have only one night to relax before . . . "I've got to go back to BHQ-comm anyhow."

She said, "How long?"

"Gosudar Nikolaev has ordered the Third Army to stage from Pendahrrit. We're ready to go, of course, but it'll take about a week for the corvettes to get here and load us aboard."

Concern a deep shadow on her face. "We were still in hyperspace when word came in over the Net. They say the First's taking a hell of beating."

I nodded again. "Still rumor. No one knows what's really happening."

She said, "I could hardly believe it when I heard. Anyway, I'm glad I was close to home when the news came. Been hell if I'd been stuck on Earth, trying to join up with whatever outfit had a slot."

I said, "How's your mother, Kaye?"

She shrugged. "A lot older than I expected. She seemed glad to see me."

"I wish . . ." Nothing. Nothing to wish for. Understanding in Kaye's eyes.

A discreet knock on the door, Fyodor letting us know dinner would be on the table soon. The bathroom door opened, steam puffing out, blond hair framing Helga's face in the doorway. "Kaye! Join us?"

She smiled. "Sure." Leaned down and shook Miriam. "Come on, sleepyhead. Time for a bath."

Then she looked at me, face serious again. "What do you think's going to happen?"

"I don't know. We don't know where they came from or who they are. Maybe they know who we are. They sure as hell came armed for bear." I slipped out of my robe, following her toward the bath, and thought, Dear God . . .

A cold hand reaching from the future right into our past.

I wasn't really surprised when a group of fast packets made rendezvous with the Third Fleet, on its way to Pendahrrit. We'd suspected all along the Master Race had starships faster than the standard corvettes and sluggish transports we were used to. On the other hand, there'd never been so much as a clue they could dock in hyperspace.

These ships were nothing like the big ones. No sign of accommodation for the many species who served the Masters. The hull was filled with machinery, tunneled around and through with a maze of poppit-sized crawlways, larger corridors for machinery, rounded places about the size of a Master's transit cartridge.

We met in a compact space obviously and hastily converted for our use, Gosudar Nikolaev and four of the five subadars of the Spahi armies, the principal leadership of the human race, in a manner of speaking. Dangerous, maybe, to have us all together like this, but . . .

Shrêhht, of course, came close to filling our little hole, curled against one bulkhead, unable to rise. They'd had to bring her in on some kind of dolly, squeezing her through a cargo tunnel whose diameter was barely larger than her own.

Nikolaev speaking: "Masters have managed to put up an integration service for us on the Net now, and reports are coming in quickly. Invaders have hit 716 target centers, clustered in the galactic west, on the southern side of the lens . . ."

In the general direction of Andromeda.

There was a holograph projected onto the air between us, spiral arms picked out in blue and gold, galactic core made of redder suns. One whole quadrant of the Milky Way was picked out in dots of hot pink, like sparks in a bed of ashes.

Nikolaev said, "There just aren't enough Master Race installations back along their presumed track to establish if this is anything but an illusion. No reports from garrisons outside the galaxy."

Presumed garrisons, at that. There were enough detailed rumors to suggest that the Masters had ventured outside the galaxy from time to time. But they still weren't talking. Strategic error, just now.

Nikolaev said, "The Invaders have dropped on all the big refit bases in this sector. Major poppit-breeding worlds, Master Race industrial complexes. Big mercenary strongholds. Every single one of the major bases belonging to the Spahi First. We haven't heard from Subadar Bharadwaj in three days now."

The missing man in our formation.

I said, "Looks like they knew what to expect."

Nikolaev said, "Field Marshal Shrêhht has something she'd like to show us."

Squirming forward now, sliding a padded valise to the center of the room, hazed by the holograph galaxy. "Things aren't going well. My people lost their bases in this sector as quickly as you did. We've knocked down a few ships, blown a couple of landing teams. Mostly it's going . . . their way. We did manage to catch a single ship, a small scout really, cut off from one of their formations, and bring it down more or less intact. We were inspecting the wreckage when an Invader squadron moved in and took out our team. We've got a few holos and . . . this."

She opened the valise, revealing a small coldbox, unlatched it, and dumped the contents out on the floor.

"So," I said. "They were carrying prisoners, then."

Shrêhht prodded the stiff, dead little poppit on the floor, pried its lips back with her tentacles, revealing triangular white teeth. "We don't think so. There were maybe a dozen species aboard the scoutship. Most of them unfamiliar. These appear to have been part of the hardware."

What, then? A rebellion from some other part of the Masters' empire, a part none of us had ever heard of before? A civil war among the Masters themselves?

Nikolaev said, "The absence of a discernible Master Race evolutionary history in this galaxy was the only clue we had. Not enough to go on. This . . ." He gestured at the dead poppit.

Shrêhht said, "They have to have come here less than a hundred thousand years ago. It's taken them just that long to take over the entire galaxy."

"And now, whoever chased them here has come looking for them."

Historical precedent. When the Huns invaded China, the Chinese kicked their asses and ran them off into Central Asia. Then, just to make sure, sent a big expeditionary force to kick their asses again. Huns didn't come to Europe looking for a tottering Roman Empire to conquer. Just trying to get away from an opponent tougher than they were.

I said, "Fatal error?"

Shrêhht sat looking at me for a moment. "No way to know."

Nikolaev said, "The Invaders' technology is better than anything we're familiar with. No way to know if the Master Race has anything comparable."

Shrêhht said, "And no way to know if it can be deployed in time."

Or even if . . . it's what we want.

Pendahrrit lay well below the plane of the galaxy, off in the same direction as Andromeda. From our hillside, you could see it up there. A faint, misty oval of light, the most remote thing naked-eye visible to a human being anywhere in the sky. Maybe the farthest place you could one day dream about going, the remote shore of a universe too large to comprehend.

Sitting in silence. Kaye and I, sitting back to back, warm on each other while Pendahrrit's soft, alien-scented wind

played over us. Shrêhht and some girlfriend she'd brought
from the Kkhruhhuft staff compound. A couple of quiet Sheqarii technicians. A Saanaa officer, frightened green centaur
whose galactic police force had been, so suddenly, pressed
into military service.

Poor Saanaae. Useful at last.

We talked in whispers, while Pendahrrit's few stars slid by
overhead. Is this the moment? Do we turn on them? Welcome the Invaders with open arms and glad little cries? No
way to know, dear friends. Dear comrades.

If the Master Race falls now, it may be that we fall with
them. Perhaps the Masters fled from an uprising of angry
slaves in the long ago and far away. Or perhaps they escaped
from some slavery of their own. It may be that, if they fall,
we will find ourselves no more than the slaves of slaves, and
then how long will we have to wait?

Forever?

Maybe so.

We want to be free, all of us, someday, somehow. But
when you stretch out your hand to the paymaster . . .

Final dawn, by the light of Pendahrrit's fiery yellow sun.
A wide, grassy field, burned brown by rocket exhaust, earth
steaming under a vast and hazy, nitrogen blue sky. Lighters
standing, row upon row, fantastical rocket ships waiting to
take us away, up to the warships and transports. Waiting to
carry us into battle. And the two million men and women of
the Third Army of the Spahi mercenaries, humanity's finest,
my men and women, stood in row on silent row, eyes forward and steady, backs straight, brows clear.

Ready for my command. The thud of my boots soft on the
grass as I walked among them, a soft crackle on dying vegetation. Not even an echo, not under a sky such as this.

I stopped for a moment by Kaye's maniple of sixteen.
Looked into her eyes. Saw her smile, my hard-eyed daughter, a crooked little half smile, suddenly familiar, that bit of
Alix within her after all. Shook her hand, took her salute,
took the salute of her troopers, snapped in unison, a sudden

rattle of plastic and steel. Walked on down the rows to the front of my army.

Came to stand before old Aëtius Nikolaev, whose flag would be riding aboard the ships of the Third. Saluted. Say the word then, Subadar Athol Morrison. "Third Army, ready for battle, sir."

The gosudar, leaning on his cane, gray eyes alight somehow, murmured, "What was it the old Native American warriors used to say, Subadar? It's a *good* day to die . . ."

I looked back at him for just a moment, thinking about that silent little seed in my head, wondering if it would ever awaken and call me to the real battle. Then I said, "Oh, Nikolaev. It's *never* a good day when a soldier must die."

He only nodded, as if he couldn't quite understand, and took my salute. I spun on my heel and went back to stand before the rank and file, to stand in front of my soldiers, for those final moments under the sun.

I put the command phone to my mouth. "Tahsildars at ready."

Acknowledgments from up and down the line, from the commanders of all my legions, our battle flags snapping in the wind.

"Sound the clarion call."

Distant trumpets floating on air.

"Drum Major."

"Sir."

Then the pipers piped and the drummers drummed and we all marched away into the sky.